THE GIRL IN THE GREEN DRESS

CATH STAINCLIFFE

Constable • London

CONSTABLE

First published in 2017 by Constable

1 3 5 7 9 10 8 6 4 2

A CIP catalogue record for this book is available from the British Library.

ISBN: 978-1-4721-2537-8 (hardback)
ISBN: 978-1-4721-2538-5 (trade paperback)

Typeset in Times New Roman by TW Type, Cornwall
Printed and bound in Great Britain by Clays Ltd, St Ives plc

Papers used by Constable are from well-managed forests and other responsible sources.

Constable
An imprint of
Little, Brown Book Group
Carmelite House
50 Victoria Embankment
London EC4Y 0DZ

An Hachette UK Company
www.hachette.co.uk

www.littlebrown.co.uk

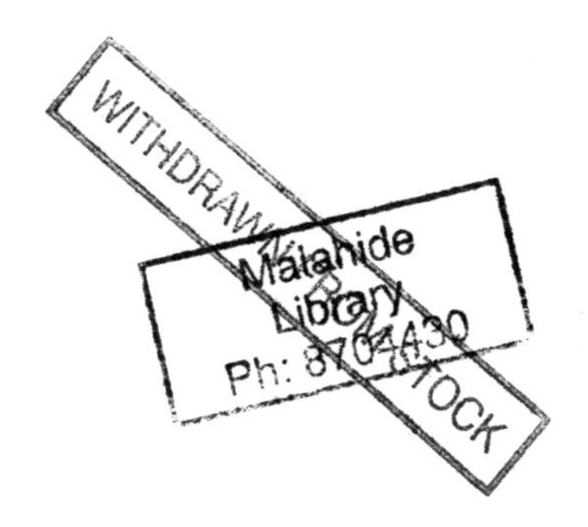
Malahide
Library
Ph: 8704430

Also by Cath Staincliffe

The Sal Kilkenny Mysteries
Looking for Trouble
Go Not Gently
Dead Wrong
Stone Cold Red Hot
Towers of Silence

The Kindest Thing
Witness
Split Second
Blink of an Eye
Letters to My Daughter's Killer
Half the World Away
The Silence Between Breaths

To my wonderful Kit, who inspired this book.
With love always, Mum.

CHAPTER ONE

Steve

'Time to go,' Steve yelled up the stairs, though whether the girls would be able to hear him above the racket they were making and the loud pulse of the dance music was debatable. 'Teagan, give them a knock.'

'OK.' His younger daughter stretched out the remote and paused the film, *Kick-Ass*. It was rated 15 but Teagan, only twelve, had always defied categories.

'An old soul,' Sarah used to say.

Steve saw nothing wrong with Teagan being exposed to stylized violence and profanity. Not when a small girl was calling the shots, and they were served up with a strong dose of black comedy.

Teagan thundered up the stairs and Dix raised his head, eyes bleary, drool strung from his muzzle.

'Go back to sleep.' Steve reached out a foot and nudged the Labrador. 'You'd be useless, wouldn't you, eh, if someone had just broken in?'

The dog slumped down again, eyes flickering shut.

Whoops and screams came from above. Then the music cut out and he heard them all coming down, felt his chair shake with the vibrations. 'Let's see you, then,' he called.

Teagan ran in followed by the three others: Allie and her friends Bets and Helena, all glammed up, giddy and powdered and perfumed, eyes outlined in black. Chattering and teasing, everything at high volume.

The dog got slowly to his feet and limped over to the French windows. Arthritis in his back legs. Still able to go for walks. Just.

'Photo!' Teagan said.

Another chorus of shrieks and exclamations.

'Here.' Steve got up and held out his hands for their phones.

'Get my selfie stick, Teagan,' Allie said. 'I want to take it with me. It's on my bed.'

'Get it yourself.'

Allie hiccuped, which set her off giggling.

Steve blamed the frontloading. He knew they'd been downing something, probably rum and Coke or vodka and lemonade. Old enough to drink legally but still mixing the hard stuff with pop. 'How much have you had?' he asked Allie, who was still doubled over, flapping one hand in front of her face.

'I'm crying,' she gasped. 'My make-up.'

Bets grabbed Allie's face, turned it left and right. 'You're fine. The mascara's waterproof anyway.'

'And the liner?'

'It's good. Chill.'

Allie patted her chest and straightened her back.

'Rum, vodka?' Steve said.

'Malibu,' Allie said. 'And just enough, in answer to your question.'

'They'll be serving punch,' Helena said, 'with, like, nought point one per cent alcohol in it.'

'And low-alcohol beer,' Bets added.

'Like, what is the point?' Allie said. 'You'd explode before you could get drunk. Or drown.' A cackle of laughter. Then another hiccup. 'I'm not drunk, I'm . . . What's the word?'

'Pissed?' Steve suggested. They all laughed.

'Merry.' She beamed at him. 'Look, straight line.' Arms out like a tightrope walker, she picked her way across the room.

'Perfect. Now, photo?' Steve said.

'Teagan, please!' Allie begged, and Teagan rolled her eyes but ran off to fetch the stick.

Steve used Allie's phone first. He lined up the trio and got three good shots.

She looked beautiful. They all did. But of course it was her his eyes lingered on. If only Sarah could see her now. She wore an emerald-coloured prom gown that they'd bought online from a company in China at a fraction of the price the shops here charged. It had a high neckline, edged with beads and a flared skirt. Black heels made her five foot nine. Her dark blonde hair, which she usually wore tousled, like she'd just come off the beach after a day's surfing, had been subjected to some sort of treatment and was now tamed with a slight wave. Steve had been party to some of the discussions in the months before about whether she should grow it longer (it was shoulder-length) so she could pin it up. Her arms and legs were bare and tanned.

'What's that stink?' Teagan had said last week, when they sat down to eat.

'Fake tan,' Allie said.

'Smells like homebrew,' Steve said.

'Well, it's safer than a real tan or sunbeds,' Allie said.

'Skin cancer.' Teagan had nodded wisely.

It never tripped them up, the C-word. Sarah and he must have done something right. Or maybe it was just so common a part of everyday life nowadays – quoted for fun runs and charity shops, the latest studies and news items – that memories of their own mother's death from ovarian cancer wasn't the first thing they thought of when they heard the word.

'Swap places,' Allie said now, and scooted round to the left of Bets, stumbled and righted herself.

Steve groaned.

'The shoes, Dad.' She pointed. 'Chill.'

He opened his mouth to explain that he just wanted to make sure she was OK, not too drunk to function, when she cried, 'Cheese!' Steve reverted to photographer, swapping Allie's phone for Bets's.

He thought it was daft holding the sixth-form prom at the start of June when most of them hadn't even finished their exams but the college argued that students drifted away if they waited until all the papers had been completed. An earlier date had proved most successful.

Teagan returned with the selfie stick and, once Steve had done a final batch with Helena in the middle, they set about taking selfies, pulling faces and larking about.

Teagan perched on the arm of the sofa, dark blue eyes taking it all in, face intent but she laughed with the other girls.

She and Allie were both like Sarah, with oval faces, high cheekbones, full lips, and a slim build. They'd been lucky, Steve reckoned. His family were all thickset like him, square-faced, podgy even, with high-coloured complexions. Allie had the same blonde hair as Steve, while her little sister had inherited Sarah's unruly dark brown.

Bets's phone trilled and she glanced at the display. 'My mum!'

'You all look gorgeous,' Steve said, as they moved towards the front door. 'Coat?' he said to Allie.

'Seriously?' Allie turned, eyebrows arched.

'It's forecast to rain.'

'Dad, we're getting a lift to college now. Then we'll be in the coach going to the prom in town and coming back.'

'And my mum is meeting us at college after and dropping us all home,' Helena said.

He held up his hands. 'Key?'

'Check,' said Allie.

'C'mere,' he said. He pulled her close and hugged her. 'Have fun.' In the heels, she was the same height as him. He smelt her perfume and caught the fruity scent from the booze.

Yeah, and what were you up to that age? he asked himself, waving them off. Or Sarah, for that matter, who had told hair-raising tales of teenage life in semi-rural Wales. 'Nothing to do in the valleys but get totally munted,' she'd explained, not long after they'd met. 'No shortage of places to meet up if you didn't care about the rain and cold – and if you drank enough cheap cider, or smoked enough weed, you soon didn't care about anything. The hardest thing was getting the booze because everyone knew everyone else in town and precisely how old we were. Usually older brothers or sisters did it, for a consideration. That's all there was, really, drink, drugs and sex. That and school.'

Same in the city but maybe more of it done indoors, those homes with unsuspecting or liberal parents, kids who had the luxury of a cellar den or a converted shed to hang out in. People didn't like teenagers mooching about on street corners, and the police were quick to move them on. There was nowhere else to go. Not until you were old enough for the pub. And then you needed money.

Now Allie was that age, eighteen, an adult. And before Steve knew it she'd be flying the nest, moving to Loughborough to study Communications and Media, if she got her grades, which Steve had no doubt she would. Out in the big, wide world. Finding her feet, relishing her independence. She'd be brilliant, he was sure, whatever field she ended up in. She loved film and graphic art. Maybe she'd end up leading poster campaigns or directing movies. He was excited for her, proud of her, but there was an ache of sadness, too, at the prospect of letting her go.

'Dad?' Teagan called. 'Are you going to watch this?'

'Five minutes,' he said. 'Popcorn?'

'Yeah.'

Steve was listening to the popcorn erupt in the microwave when Teagan wandered in. 'Science,' he told her, nodding to the appliance, 'is a truly awesome thing.'

'I know.'

'And not just biology.' His specialist area. He worked as a patent adviser for new inventions in thc field.

'Did Mum do biology too?'

'No, nursing.'

The microwave pinged. Steve opened the door and lifted out the carton.

'I think I'll do biology,' Teagan said.

'Yeah?'

'Maybe. It's cool – cells and animals and plants. Life, really.'

Steve smiled. 'You've plenty of time to decide. Two years till your options for GCSEs.'

Teagan grabbed a handful of popcorn and, munching, went to the fridge and poured herself some juice.

'There any lager in there?' He didn't think Allie's lot would have bothered with cans but you never could tell.

'Four.'

'Great.'

Back on the sofa, Dix at their feet, the popcorn between them, Steve cracked open his beer.

It was still light outside, though the cloud was thickening. If it rained much he'd have to leave cutting the grass yet again. It was an ongoing battle, the garden trying to revert to scrub and Steve barely stemming the tide.

'Ready?' Teagan said.

He nodded. 'Cheers.'

She tapped her glass on his can.

Steve took a swallow and settled back. 'Living the dream, kid.'

And Teagan hit the remote.

Sonia

Before Sonia had even got her coat off, her lad Oliver was in her face. 'The bank says my account's overdrawn but I need some money for tonight.'

'Maybe you should have thought about that sooner,' she said.

'I didn't know it was all gone, did I?'

'Well, you're the only one spending it, Oliver, so you can hardly blame anyone else.'

'Mum,' he moaned. His face was flushed, mouth pinched. She could sense him reining in his temper, knowing if he stormed off in a strop he'd not get the cash he wanted for his night out.

'I'm not made of money,' Sonia said, 'you know that. Maybe you'll have to miss it.'

'No way!' His voice rose. 'It's Seggie's birthday. I'm not missing that. No way. And I promised.'

Seggie was one of the lads she'd not met, though she'd heard Oliver talk about him often enough.

'I'll pay you back,' he said.

'How, exactly?'

At that, he had the grace to look shamefaced. He was on an apprenticeship. He earned ninety-nine pounds for a thirty-hour week, and at least half of that went on his travel and his lunches. The prospect existed of money in the future – a small, misshapen carrot at the end of a very long stick. *If* he completed his training, *if* he passed the tests, *if* he found a vacancy, *if* he got an interview, *if* he was offered a job. If he, Oliver Poole, aged eighteen, of Firswood, beat dozens of others, all after the same few chances, to the punch.

'Oliver, I haven't budgeted for this. The debits go out next week.'

'Use my birthday money, then,' he said pitifully.

'What birthday money?' As if she had it sitting there already, didn't have to save up over the next few months to give him something.

She took off her coat and picked up the shopping bags. Christ, she wanted him to have fun, enjoy himself, but he'd no sense of the cost of things, of how hard it was to manage.

The supermarket had introduced the so-called Living Wage (which was a barefaced lie) and Sonia was now getting seven pounds twenty an hour. Fifty pence more. To compensate for the change her employers had docked her hours. So she was actually worse off on the Living Wage. Luckily she was still doing the same hours in her second job, at the laundry, and Cynthia, who owned the business, had increased the rates but had had to let Govinda go, which wasn't fair but wasn't as bad as it might have been, because Govinda was a bit slow on the ironing side of things. With only two staff on at a time, instead of three, they all had to work even harder and it wasn't as if things had been slack beforehand. She tried not to dwell on it because it only made her miserable.

'Mum, please?' Oliver trailed behind her as she went into the kitchen, watching as she lifted the bags onto the counter. Her hands ached from the plastic handles, red weals on the skin. She brought home reduced items, or those close to their sell-by or use-by dates, and special offers of things they liked.

She scratched her head, tired, resentful. She found her cigarettes and opened the back door. 'How much?' She lit up.

'We're having a meal.'

'Twenty, then – thirty? What sort of place?'

'I don't know,' he said.

'You don't know where you're going?' She felt hot, her skin greasy, and her neck ached from reaching over all the time on the checkouts. There was never any chance to swap from one till to another and face a different way.

'It's a place on Peter Street. I haven't checked the prices.'

'I'll give you thirty.'

'And we might go on to a club after. We probably will.'

'Fuck's sake, Oliver. You might just have to skip that part.'

His face tightened. She turned away, and blew smoke out into the yard. She guessed he'd want to buy his friend a drink for his birthday.

'Forty and your bus fare,' she said.

'The buses will have stopped by then.'

'They run till eleven at least,' she said.

'I'm not coming home that early.'

She stared at him. 'You asking for the cab fare?'

'Unless you expect me to walk.'

I walked, she wanted to tell him, countless times. Had no option. But she'd never let on to her parents that she was tramping about at all hours, and they'd never asked. Then again, kids like Oliver, young, hot-headed, out on the town on Friday and Saturday night, it only took one drink too many or looking at someone the wrong way for stuff to kick off. There was no way she wanted to put him at any greater risk by leaving him to walk back on his own in the dark.

Ten for the cab. Fifty altogether. *Shit.* Cancelling her hair appointment would save half of it.

'Right. Get fifty. You'll have to go up the petrol station,' she said. She knew she had only small change in her purse.

'Thanks, Mum.' He grinned, the tension melting off him. He rubbed his hand over his head. The hair was cut so short he looked like he'd joined up.

She gave a shake of her head, took another drag. 'You won't be wanting any tea, then?'

He shrugged. 'Not meeting till half eight.' Always hungry.

It was just after six. 'Pizza or pie?'

'What sort of pie?'

'Steak and ale.'

'Pie,' he said. 'No – pizza.'

'My purse is in there.' She nodded at her handbag.

He helped himself to her card while she finished her cigarette.

She heard the slam of the front door. He always banged it too hard, rattling the glass in the windows and the pots on the kitchen shelves.

She could hear next-door-but-one – him shouting again, on and on. And one of the kids crying. They'd not been moved in long but had soon made their presence felt. There were times she wanted to go round, knock on the door and ask if they were all OK. Maybe it was just verbal but that counted as abuse, these days. Still, interfering would probably only make things worse. At the end of the day people had to help themselves, didn't they?

She'd bought a lottery ticket, £16 million rollover. She knew the odds were like a trillion to one but somebody had to win. And she liked to dream it would be her, fantasize about how she would spend the money. That was what she thought about going to sleep at night, instead of fretting over the debts or worrying about Oliver. The only thing worry brought was an early grave.

Top of her wish-list was a house, a beautiful house in a nice area. She'd buy a business as well, something Oliver could make a go of. She wouldn't be idle. Well, not after a good holiday or three. She'd volunteer for charities and make a really big donation, for Alzheimer's Research and the RSPCA, maybe even set up her own foundation, hospices or animal rescue. Not sure which yet. If she ever hit the jackpot she'd have to settle on one thing and stick to it. Mind you, if she won enough, she could maybe have a few good causes, spread the love.

She put away the groceries and tucked the washing powder under the sink behind the old box, which was nearly empty. She used half the recommended dose and the clothes still came out perfectly clean, though she had learnt to soak anything very mucky, like the stuff Oliver wore for kick-about at the park, before running it through the machine.

She made a cup of tea, and when the oven had heated she put in the pizza and checked the time.

She'd have a soak, she decided, after Oliver had showered and finished in the bathroom. A soak and some telly, an early night, although she never slept properly till she heard the door go and knew he was home safe. She was on at eight in the morning. She could make a few more cards tonight. Aseef took them at the corner shop, sold them for one fifty apiece and split the takings with her. She was low on bits and bobs to fancy up the fronts but had enough to rustle up half a dozen or so. *Congratulations* would be good and *Good Luck*, what with exams and results in the offing. She had some silver *Congratulations* stickers somewhere, she was pretty sure.

She heard Oliver's key in the lock. 'Don't slam it,' she yelled, but if he did hear it was too late. 'You'll have the house down,' she said, as he came in. 'If I've told you once, I've told you a thousand times.'

He handed her back her card. 'I got sixty,' he said. *Another ten!* 'They only had twenties in the machine.'

She believed him – well, ninety per cent. 'You can bring me a tenner home, then.'

'I knew you'd say that.'

'Well, it's that or no more cereal when those boxes are done. Your call,' she said.

Another shrug. His phone rang, some jangle of music that always set her nerves on edge: too brash, too loud.

'Foz!' he said in greeting, wheeling away. No doubt plans for the night ahead.

'Fifty quid,' Sonia muttered, fetching plates, then the Coke bottle from the fridge. *I must be mad. I hope it's bloody worth it.*

Still, she daydreamed, when my numbers come up, there'll be no more begging and scraping. I'll set him up with all he needs, clothes and games and the latest phone, and he'll soon be making his own money. The details of what the business might be were a little hazy but you could get advice on that. They'd need an accountant and everything. She'd tear up the tax credit forms.

She emptied the bag of ready salad into the colander, rinsed it and tipped it into a bowl – it needed eating today. She cut up the pizza, poured the Coke.

'Oliver, it's ready.'

He'd be there in a minute. Never knowingly missed an opportunity to eat.

He came in and loaded his plate, lifted the Coke, headed up to his room. She'd half hoped he'd eat with her, play nice, given he'd talked her out of fifty, sixty quid, whichever. Suck up, you mean? Why bother when he'd achieved his objective?

'And bring your plate down,' she shouted after him.

'Right.'

'*Before* you go out.'

'Got it,' he said.

He didn't. She was in the bath when he left. 'I'm off now.' Then the thump of the door.

Once she was dressed, she checked in his room, and there were his plate and glass, as well as several bowls and three mugs. She itched to pick them up but then he'd never learn, would he? 'You can clear that little lot up tomorrow, lazy sod,' she said.

It was nearly time. She fetched her ticket, thumped the sofa cushions to plump them up and got comfy.

A spark of anticipation inside her as the music started.

After all, somebody had to win.

Donna

Donna had turned off the light, had literally just turned it off and fallen back onto her pillow, hearing Matt's hamster, Morris, giving his wheel some welly through the wall. She was wondering whether to move the cage downstairs – *But he'll be lonely, Mum, and there's nowhere to put him downstairs* – when her phone rang.

Beside her Jim grunted once and turned over.

Donna answered, 'DI Bell.' Her desire for sleep had been undermined by the adrenalin prickling in her veins, kick-starting a faster pulse.

'City Central Division here, ma'am. A suspicious death, location Swing Gate Fold, off New Mill Street, close to Deansgate.'

'Exterior?'

'Yes, ma'am.'

'Message me the coordinates. I'm on my way.'

In ten minutes she was dressed, suit, shoes, raincoat. Smart enough to portray the authority of rank, the gravity of her role, but practical enough to attend a crime scene in the rain, in the dark. Queasy with anticipation.

She left a note on the kitchen table, *Gone to work xxx Matt, clean out Morris*, aware of all the adjustments the family would have to make to their day ahead. The recalibrating of plans, the managing of expectations. She and Jim were past masters at it. The cinema trip would go ahead without her, no refund available. When she next touched base, the kids would vie with each other to tell her what she'd missed and what the best bits were. Maybe not Bryony: at fifteen she was getting chippy, wanting to differentiate herself from the younger ones. Still, she'd agreed to go.

So Jim would cook the chicken, chivvy people about homework and uniforms, act as taxi service to the twins, if they were still going round to their friend's house for an evening on the Xbox. She wouldn't swap places with him for the world. She loved her kids but she loved her work too. And his job as a driving instructor, self-employed, meant he could tailor his hours to fit round the family.

They'd most likely be tucked up in bed before she got home again. The first few days of a murder were completely full on. Notions of shifts or eight-hour days went out the window. The weeks that followed weren't much better, not at her level, heading an inquiry, hand on the tiller.

She left the house and hurried to her car through the rain, a steady, fine, soaking drizzle, the sort that could go on for hours, days. She checked the GPS location on her phone, and set the satnav to direct the route.

'Turn left onto Upper Chorlton Road,' it said.

'I know that part,' Donna muttered, clicking on headlights and windscreen wipers, her mind leaping ahead, wondering what she would find when she reached her destination. A knifing victim or someone on the wrong end of a broken bottle? A hit and run?

Manchester on any Friday or Saturday night was heaving. All the tribes: tourists, locals, students, footie fans and hen parties, people flooding in from the satellite towns that ring the city, drawn to the bright lights. A carnival every weekend. Party Central.

Donna drove carefully, knowing some of the more drunken revellers might spill into the road, try to cross it, convinced that enough Jägerbombs made them invincible.

A large group of middle-aged men was standing outside a bar to her left. They were mainly smokers, cupping their fags to keep them dry but otherwise oblivious to the rain. Further along she glimpsed a couple kissing under an umbrella, the woman's dress, short and shiny gold, glinting in the streetlight.

People were on the move, some heading home, perhaps, others exchanging bar or restaurant for club.

As she turned off the main road under the railway bridge a man bent forward and vomited in the street. A cheer went up from his pals, who burst into song, 'Chuck it up, chuck it up, chuck it up, up, up.'

Opposite she saw some beat officers keeping the peace. In this case that consisted of them restraining a young woman, who was screaming and spitting at another. The target was clearly not helping matters by giving the first woman the finger savagely and repeatedly.

Life's rich tapestry.

Halfway along Deansgate, Donna took another left onto New Mill Street, between two of the tall warehouse buildings that dominated this part of town. The road curved, and as Donna rounded the bend she saw the cordon on her right, fifty feet ahead, blocking a smaller side street, Swing Gate Fold.

The satnav announced, 'You have reached your destination.'

A few figures stood outside the tape, some in police uniform. And the others? Perhaps friends of the victim, otherwise witnesses or gawkers.

When she drew level she could see the white tent down the small road glowing in the gloom. Her stomach tightened. She pulled in beyond a row of police cars and forensic vans.

At the cordon she introduced herself to the officer keeping the scene log and asked who the first responder had been.

'PC Collins, in the middle.' He gestured to the three uniformed officers huddled in a wide doorway. Donna could hear music coming from somewhere nearby, a disco beat, a snatch of voices raucous in chorus.

'You got the call?' Donna asked PC Collins, who was tall, narrow-faced and looked like she'd been crying. Her first dead body, perhaps.

'Yes.' The constable pulled out her daybook. Donna noticed the shake in her hands, the blood smeared on her fingers, as she opened it. At least she'd had the wherewithal to get some notes down in spite of the shock she must have had.

'Eleven forty, I was on Deansgate. Told there was a possible incident here. She was—' The officer swallowed. 'She was unresponsive.'

A woman, then. 'You checked for signs of life?'

A nod. 'Nothing . . . The state of her . . . A lot of blood. Just a girl, you know? The ambulance was right behind me. They confirmed it.' She shook her head quickly. 'She hadn't even got a coat on.'

The officers beside her shifted, as if they shared her distress and outrage.

'I got back to Control, reported a suspicious death. Asked for Major Crimes and Forensics. I secured the scene.'

'Well done,' Donna said.

The officer dismissed the praise with a twitch of her head.

'You touch anything else?' Donna said.

'No.'

'See anyone?' Donna said.

'No.'

So whoever had called 999 hadn't waited for the police. Or had it been the victim herself?

'Did you remove anything from the scene?'

'No.'

'You've been swabbed?' As well as the blood on her hands, Donna could see another dab on her chin.

'Yes. I need to leave my uniform – I'm just waiting for spares.'

'Any trouble earlier tonight?' Donna said.

'Usual public-order stuff, a few cautions, no arrests.' An arrest would have taken her back to the station, and she'd have spent most of her shift processing it. She'd not have caught this job.

'Thank you,' Donna said. 'Good work.'

The constable dipped her head, tears springing to her eyes, and Donna felt a wave of pity. The murder sounded vicious, *the state of her . . . a lot of blood.* People didn't always understand how traumatic it could be, facing something like that. Donna had learnt to deal with it – no use as a detective otherwise. A trick of distancing, of focusing on the task at hand.

She returned to her car and changed into her protective clothing before entering the scene. A lamppost on the main road cast some light into the mouth of the alley. The narrow street smelt of wet stone and rotting rubbish. The buildings either side, four or five storeys high, were dark. One place was boarded up but the others had obviously been renovated – offices, she assumed, given there were no signs of life at this time. She could see a rubbish skip further down the street, past the illuminated tent.

There was a sense of isolation in spite of the steady activity as the crime scene investigators went about their work. A set of lights had been rigged up now to illuminate the area that the photographers were recording inch by inch. A fingertip search would follow. It was imperative to recover everything as quickly as possible, with the scene exposed to the rain.

Yellow numbered markers were in place indicating items of interest. Donna saw a single shoe next to one, a black high-heel. *Oh, God.* She took a breath, then followed the series of stepping plates along the road to the tent and slipped inside.

Sweet Jesus.

The girl lay on her left side against the kerb, her cheek touching the kerb stone. Her left arm was trapped beneath her, the hand visible, torn and bloodied, close to the base of the spine. She wore a green dress, an evening dress, ripped and mottled with dark bloodstains. Blood caked her hair and face, marked her bare arms and legs. Donna could see bruises too. A teenager at a guess, though the cuts and swellings on her face made it hard to be sure.

'Donna Bell, SIO,' Donna said, to those already present.

'Anthea Cartwright, crime-scene manager,' said one of the suited figures.

'Beaten?' Donna said, gesturing to the victim.

'Looks like it. We have a bank card from the clutch bag, here.' Anthea pointed to a small black bag on the floor, beside a yellow marker. One of the CSIs held out an evidence bag with the debit card inside it and Donna took a photograph of it on her phone. Noted the name A. Kennaway.

'Phone too,' Anthea said.

'Hers?'

'We're pretty sure. Look at the screen.'

'Excellent.' Phones were a treasure trove of information. It was in another plastic evidence bag and it took Donna a couple of swipes with her gloves on to activate it. On the home-screen was a photo, a picture of the girl, same colour hair, same slender build, wearing the green dress, posing between two friends. So young, the three of them. Seventeen? Eighteen? Donna copied the image and opened the contact list on the phone. She found an entry for *Dad* and one for *Home*. Perhaps Dad didn't live with them any more. She copied the numbers into her own phone.

After calling the coroner to report a suspicious death and getting permission to hold a forensic post-mortem, she phoned the Home Office duty pathologist, who would attend the scene to confirm death. Then she rang Jade Bradshaw, her new DC, who answered on the second ring. 'Boss? What's up?'

'We've a suspected murder. A young woman beaten up in an alleyway near Deansgate. I'm waiting for the pathologist. Once they've been, I'll be contacting family.'

'I'll come with,' Jade said, sounding for all the world as if this had made her night. 'Where shall I meet you?'

Jade

Jade couldn't believe her luck. She'd been in CID only a fortnight – half of that'd been training, paperwork and induction – and already she was partnering with the DI, in at the start of a major inquiry. Twenty-five and playing with the big boys. She must be doing something right.

She pulled on her trousers and her black sweater, feeling a swooping sensation in her belly. What if it wasn't a sign of confidence? What if it was the opposite? A way for the DI to keep Jade close because she wasn't to be trusted. A newbie. Unknown quantity. Her colleagues might suspect she'd been given the opportunity to work with the boss on the murder-investigation team because she ticked the black and ethnic-minorities box. Selected because she was mixed race – half Pakistani, half Irish – rather than because she was the best candidate for the job. Fuck 'em. She just had to prove them wrong and show herself more than capable.

She raked her fingers through her fringe. She still wasn't used to the sensation of air on the back of her neck but the pixie cut was practical, it looked OK, and there was no longer any chance of someone grabbing her ponytail if things got physical.

She laced up her Docs and got her leather jacket from the chair by the door that served as a coat rack. She should probably tart the place up a bit, get some proper furniture – she wouldn't need to spend a fortune if she went somewhere like IKEA, like normal people did. Three years here and she'd still not got a bed frame. With the mattress off the floor she could store some stuff underneath. Not that she had much.

Or was now a good time to move? New job, new place. Find

somewhere furnished. She'd pay more, though. And here was as good as anywhere else. There had been rumours from a couple of the neighbours that the flats might be sold, knocked down to make way for some development connected to the hospital nearby. They were past their best, three storeys high, a rectangular block, three flats at the front, three at the back of each level. Eighteen in all. None had double-glazing and, as the tenants paid the bills, the landlord, who was a miserly fucker, showed no interest in installing any.

Jade checked her bag: warrant card, phone, charger, purse, tissues, pepper spray and wet wipes, spare nitrile gloves and sterile evidence bag. Extremely unlikely she'd be picking up any evidence doing the death call but a good cop, a good detective, was always prepared. Like Scouts, but with powers of arrest. And she had to be good. She had to be excellent. A roll of anxiety made her shiver. *Tablets*. She shook two out and dry-swallowed them, then put the bottle back into her bag.

When she opened the door onto the corridor, the place was quiet. Most of the residents were middle-aged or elderly, had moved in years back, and were tucked up tight by now. Jade kept herself to herself but had got to know Mina next door, who needed help getting her shopping up and down the stairs. Mina had pounced on Jade the first week she was in, wanting to know whether she was married and why not, where her family was. A sally of questions in a thick Polish accent.

'Got none,' Jade had said. 'An orphan.' Not exactly true but she thought it might be easier that way. Wrong move. Mina going all mother-hen babushka style, baking her biscuits and plying her with vodka that left Jade with the worst fucking hangover of her life.

'Don't babushka me,' Jade had said one day. 'I'm a grown woman.'

Mina made a tutting noise. 'Babushka? Babushka is Russian.'

'Nanny, then. Don't nanny me.'

'*Babcia*,' Mina said.

'That, then – don't do it.'

'Who else am I gonna look after, eh?' She patted Jade's cheek.

Jade had jerked away. 'Whoa. No.'

‘You need a coddle,’ Mina said, eyes sharp.

‘I’m fine. I’m not a kid.’

‘Good coddle.’ Mina had wrapped her arms around herself and rocked from side to side in her armchair.

‘No, ta. And it’s “cuddle”, not “coddle”.’

‘What’s “coddle”, then?’

Jade shrugged. ‘Dunno. Eggs, I think.’

After that, Jade had made sure not to get too close to Mina when she went in. Just in case.

Mina had burst into tears when she saw Jade’s new hairstyle. ‘Your beautiful hair, your beautiful, beautiful hair,’ she sobbed.

‘Gets in the way,’ Jade told her. ‘Takes hours to dry, gives me headaches,’ *in more ways than one*. ‘I like it.’

‘You’ll be sorry,’ Mina muttered darkly, and blew her nose.

Wrong there.

Then there was Bert opposite. No sign of life from him tonight. Bert was old and thin as a twig, covered with knobbly bits. He kept falling over but refused any help. He repeatedly told staff at the hospital, or the district nurses, that he had a good neighbour, a saint, who helped him every which way. That was a gross exaggeration, verging on slander, if you asked Jade.

‘What about a home?’ Jade had said, last time they were waiting for the paramedics.

‘I’ve got a home. This is my home. I’d rather jump out the window,’ Bert said. ‘In fact if they ever threaten that, I give you permission to chuck me out the window or kick me down the stairs. Bit of police brutality, that’d suit me fine.’

‘Deal,’ Jade had said, thinking the best of all possible ends would be for him to drop dead during *University Challenge*, his favourite programme.

Now she went down the stairs, the security light on the middle flight flickering on and off.

Her first official murder investigation. If it was murder. Had to be, didn’t it? She’d found a dead body once that had turned out to be a murder when she was on the beat. She’d been called to a hotel where one of the guests had not checked out (well, not in the usual sense of the word). Anticipating a suicide, Jade hadn't taken long to change her mind when she'd seen the body on the floor had a pattern of bruises around the neck.

As soon as it was classed as a suspicious death, the cavalry arrived in the shape of a DI Harris. A big bloke built like a rugby player but pleasant with it, a sense of drive and energy as he'd walked into Room 302. Jade, in her uniform, was yanked out of the picture at that point and dropped back on her beat.

Later Jade had looked him up on the computer. He'd won two awards for bravery.

But this time she was *with* the cavalry, leading the charge.

Unlocking her car, she glanced up at the flats: hers was the only one with the lights still burning.

She always left the lights on.

No matter how long she might be.

It was a small price to pay.

Donna

Donna had agreed with the crime-scene manager that they disturb the body as little as possible to minimize the risk of losing any trace evidence. A body-bag would be used to transfer the victim to the mortuary for examination.

Donna looked unflinchingly at the girl, noting the bloodstains, like dark poppies, on her dress, the pulped face, the clotted hair, swollen arms and, here and there, glimpses of the person she actually was: silver nail polish, strands of soft hair the colour of Demerara sugar, a silver chain on her neck. Someone's daughter, someone's friend. A girl who had come into town for a night out, all dressed up, no doubt smelling sweet. A girl like any of the others who thronged the clubs and bars and pavements this Saturday night.

Not many years older than Donna's daughter, Bryony, she guessed. Guesses were a stop-gap, a crutch for her, until they could assemble the facts: the girl's full name, her date of birth, whom she'd been out with, her movements during the evening and in the days before, any recent problems, anyone who might wish her harm. And ultimately, crucially, the most important fact – who had taken her life.

Donna was clammy inside the protective clothes, could feel a sheen of sweat on her back and under her breasts. The temperature in the small space steadily increased under the blaze of the lights, with the combined body heat of those present. The rain, heavier now, tipped and tapped on the roof of the tent.

The Home Office pathologist arrived, gloved, masked and suited, like the rest of them. She said very little as she crouched beside the body, checking for respiration and circulation. Then, 'Death confirmed. She's still warm. No rigor. Do you want a body temp?'

The internal body temperature would be a useful guide in estimating time of death and was almost always carried out at the scene. 'Yes,' said Donna. Although, given their victim was still warm, there wasn't going to be a huge margin to consider.

The pathologist nodded, opened her case and retrieved a rectal thermometer. 'If we can raise the skirt here?' she asked.

One of the CSIs helped ease the fabric up over the victim's thigh.

'Underwear intact,' the doctor said.

That was something, Donna thought sadly. Unlikely to have been raped during the attack. A small mercy. Poor love.

'Ah . . . OK . . . right . . .' The pathologist sounded disconcerted.

'What is it?' Donna said.

'She's a he, biologically speaking. Male genitalia.'

A boy! 'Oh, Christ,' said Donna, her thoughts crashing and ricocheting back. For a moment her composure and confidence deserted her. She'd never handled a case where someone was – what? Transvestite? Transgender? There'd been training some time back and the force had policies in place but Donna couldn't remember much of what they'd said. What if she messed up? Got it wrong? She quelled the rasp of panic.

No one spoke. Anthea caught Donna's eye, gave a shake of her head, sharing the sorrow. *Oh, you poor child. You poor, poor child.* And the rain spat on the tent, wind snapping at the fabric, again and again.

CHAPTER TWO

Steve

Steve yawned and stretched. He ought to turn in but he'd started watching *Monty Python and the Holy Grail* after Teagan had gone to bed and there was only another half-hour left.

He was startled by the phone ringing. The landline. Felt a tightening in his guts.

'Hello?'

'Steve, it's Bets. Has Allie come home?'

'No,' he said slowly. 'Why?'

'It's just . . . we're not sure where she's gone.' Bets sounded tearful, slightly panicked.

'What do you mean *gone*? Are you still at the prom?'

'Yes, it's just finishing.'

Steve glanced at the clock, half past midnight.

'We thought maybe she got a taxi back or something.'

'Why? She was getting the coach with you.' Thick, dull, as though he was missing something. 'When did she go? Did something happen?' *Why would she leave early?* 'Was she sick?' He thought of the hiccups and Allie doubled over, giggling, walking the line.

'No, she was fine. She went outside looking for me,' Bets said, 'but she never came back.'

The doorbell rang and relief flooded through him. 'Bets, I think she's back now. Someone's at the door.'

'Oh, good.'

'Bye.'

Steve went to the door, words building on his tongue: *You gave us a scare, Allie. You should have told your mates you were leaving. What's going on? Didn't you enjoy it?*

He opened the door to see two women, strangers. An older one, maybe his age, lines around her eyes and her mouth, chalky complexion.

'Yes?' Steve said, looking from one to the other. The younger woman, a girl really, skinny with big eyes, brown skin, met his gaze, then glanced away.

'Mr Kennaway,' the older one said. 'I'm DI Bell and this is DC Bradshaw. Can we come in a moment?'

'What's happened?' Dizzy, he put a hand against the wall to steady himself. 'Is it Allie? Is she all right?'

'Let's talk inside,' she said softly, but moving forward, forcing Steve to step back.

'Is Mrs Kennaway here?'

'No. She died three years ago,' Steve said. A flush bloomed on the woman's cheek. Why were they asking about Sarah? 'Allie, she's all right?' he said.

The woman was steering him. 'Is there somewhere we can sit down?' The girl shutting the front door.

The television was still on, the sound muted. Steve tried to turn it off, pressing the remote again and again but nothing happened.

'I'll get it,' the girl said. He couldn't remember her name. She looked spiky. Like an urchin. Her hair. She picked up the other remote, the one for the TV, and switched it off.

'Please, Mr Kennaway, have a seat.'

Steve sat heavily, almost kicking Dix beside the sofa.

DI Bell sat next to him, the constable on the armchair.

'What's going on?' he said. 'Where's Allie? She went to the prom. She should be—'

'Is this Allie?' DI Bell was showing him a photo on her phone, the one he'd taken earlier, Allie all dressed up.

'Yes.'

'And could you please tell me her phone number?'

'Erm . . . I don't know it.'

The younger one spoke: 'It's probably on your phone.'

Steve reached for his mobile. His fingers were clumsy and he had to swipe several times to get her details. He read out the number.

'Thank you,' DI Bell said.

'Please?' Steve said.

'I have some very bad news,' DI Bell said. 'A person has been found in Manchester, in the city centre this evening, with fatal injuries. We have reason to believe that person is Allie. I'm so sorry to tell you that she is dead.'

'Allie?' There was a thundering in his head.

'Mr Kennaway, do you understand what I've told you?'

He shook his head. 'It must be a mistake.'

'I'm afraid not. I am sorry.'

'Where is she?' He was cold as stone.

'She's on her way to the mortuary. When someone dies like this we have to carry out a post-mortem.'

He shuddered, exhaled, the air making a rushing noise.

'I'm so sorry. It's dreadful news and there's a lot take in. We will ask you to make a formal identification of the body, probably tomorrow, if you feel able,' DI Bell said.

'You said it was Allie.' They could be wrong – they weren't sure. *Oh, thank God!*

'It is Allie,' DI Bell said. 'The formal identification is part of the procedure we have to follow. Can you tell me what Allie was wearing this evening?'

'Her prom dress. The green one in the photo.' He cleared his throat. 'Black heels.'

'And when did you last see her?'

'Half past seven. They were getting a lift to college with Bets's mum. The coach was picking them up there and— You said injuries?'

The younger woman shifted in the chair. She'd been writing. Now she was watching him, eyes peering up from under a jagged fringe.

DI Bell said, 'We're treating Allie's death as suspicious. We believe the injuries were caused by someone else.'

Steve raised a hand. He couldn't find any words. Inside, something buckled, broke.

'I'm so sorry,' DI Bell said. 'Please can you tell me, was Allie transgender?'

Steve tried to rise, to get up and away, anywhere, but his legs wouldn't support him. 'Yes,' he said.

'Dad?' Teagan was in the doorway.

Steve sat rigid, no sense in his head, no comprehension. His eyes filled with tears.

'Dad?' Teagan said again and flew to him, stumbling over Dix – he yelped – then climbing onto the sofa, her arms around his neck, burying her head in his chest.

Jade

Jade went to make tea. The boss had told her that, if it was possible, they'd take initial statements from the family on this visit. 'All depends,' she'd said, sitting next to Jade in Jade's car on the road outside the house. Jade had got there first and waited for the DI, who had driven up and parked behind her five minutes later. Then she'd come and got into Jade's car for a confab about how to handle the death call. Now it looked like no one was going to get any sleep and they might as well recover any information they could. Though it was anybody's guess whether the dad would be up for it. Obviously knocked into the middle of next week by the news.

Jade looked round the kitchen, a big one, with a table in the bay window to eat at, a whiff of dog and tinned meat from the bowl near the back door, pots on the side waiting to go in the dishwasher. She studied the photographs and notices on the board on the wall, most of them old with corners curling. She identified some with the mum, some in which Allie was much younger, long-haired but dressed like a boy. New-born baby pictures too, with the mum and dad grinning. Jade couldn't tell which baby was which. They all looked the same, babies, bald and lumpy with big heads and potato faces.

She wondered if Allie had always wanted to be a girl. Must have taken some bottle going to the prom in a frock. Kids could be cruel. Fucking brutal. She knew that as well as anyone. The thought of it made her stomach turn. She put the milk back and slammed the fridge door – slammed the memories in there with it.

A phone started ringing. Jade took the tray of drinks through and heard the boss answer it. 'Steve's phone. Who is this? Ah, from the college? You were at the prom, Mrs Fallon? Right, my name's DI

Bell.' She moved into the hall out of earshot, no doubt breaking the news, asking that the teacher keep it confidential until the rest of the immediate family had been notified and the formal identification made.

'My arm's gone to sleep,' the kid said, twisting out of her father's embrace. He looked catatonic, eyes fixed somewhere a thousand miles away, face slack.

'Got you some tea.' Jade put a mug on the table at his side

'What do we do now?' the kid said, her face set, a scowl bending her eyebrows. Eyes red-rimmed.

'There's one for you too.' Jade put another cup down at the far side, along with one for the DI. 'Do you drink tea?'

The kid ignored the question just as Jade had ignored hers. 'What do we do now?' she repeated.

Her dad put a hand on her knee, as if he'd settle her. The kid squeezed it then let go, staring still at Jade. What did she want to know? The practical stuff? Or was this more a 'How do we cope?' sort of question, 'How do we carry on?' which Jade had no way of answering. And what was she to do with the kid, anyway? About twelve, she was, and a minor. Never to be dealt with unless a parent, carer or appropriate adult was present. Her father was there but only in body. The kid gave an impatient shake of her shoulders, a little flick of outstretched palms, that fierce look still on her face.

'The rest of the family need to be told so no one gets a shock by hearing it on the news,' Jade said.

'Nanny and Granddad,' the kid said. 'And Auntie Emma.'

'Your dad's parents or your mum's?'

'Dad's. And his sister.' She looked at her dad but he didn't respond.

Jade thought they might need a doctor. Give him something to knock him out for real so he could sleep, check out for a while, switch off from the horror.

'What about your mum's side?' Jade said.

'They died before I was born. Nanny and Granddad will be in bed,' she said.

'Probably best to ring in the morning, then. We'll see what your dad wants to do.' Jade went out into the hall and, as the boss finished talking to the teacher, Jade updated her on the close relatives. 'I think we're losing him,' Jade said.

'Let's see.'

'Tea's there,' Jade told her, as they entered the room.

'Mr Kennaway? Steve?' said the boss.

His eyes refocused. He ran a hand over his face a few times, as if he could kick-start his brain with a bit of massage.

'Would you like us to call your GP?'

'No,' he said.

The boss sat down beside him again. 'If you change your mind at any time please let us know. There's a family liaison officer on the way. They will stay with you and help out. They will also keep you up to date with the inquiry.'

He nodded. Jade wasn't sure it had gone in.

'They can help you inform your family,' the boss said.

'Yes,' he said.

'In the morning,' the kid added.

'What would really help now,' the boss said, 'is if you could answer a few more questions about Allie. If you feel up to that.'

He nodded. He lifted the cup and drank from it. It must have been scalding but he seemed oblivious.

'Teagan, if you want to wait with DC Bradshaw, you can call her Jade,' the boss said. 'And I'm Donna—'

'No.' The kid folded her arms.

'Is that all right, Steve?' said the boss. 'For Teagan to stay? It might be better if she—'

'No,' the kid said.

'It's OK,' Steve Kennaway said.

The kid shuffled on the sofa, sat up straighter, as if she was about to enter some quiz or something, keen to score the highest points. Why wasn't she in bits?

Jade took more notes as the boss began, asking what time Allie had left the house, whom she'd travelled with, getting their contact details. She broadened it out to questions about sixth-form college and friendships, social media activity, asking about any problems or difficult relationships, digging for any hint of animosity or aggression that might have led to tonight's savagery.

Nothing. Yes, Allie had been for counselling sometimes, unhappy in her own skin, as her dad put it, his voice faltering every so often, and then after the death of the mother there had been a difficult couple of years but the last eighteen months had been much more positive.

'She socially transitioned for sixth form,' the kid said, the jargon rolling off her tongue, 'and she'll be starting hormone treatment soon. She's happier now.'

Was happier.

'Socially transitioned?' the boss said. 'That means living as a girl, as a woman?'

'You have to do that before you can have surgery,' the kid said. 'It's important. You have to be sure, and you mustn't do it too quickly.'

The dad blew air out, and shuddered.

Someone walking over his grave, over and over. Stamping on it, Jade reckoned, with massive fuck-off hobnailed boots on.

Martin

Martin was at the social club when he was called in. He'd watched the match live that evening, a charity game at Old Trafford, then gone on for drinks. He had a season ticket. He took Dale with him sometimes when Dale wasn't busy.

It had been a beauty of a game, the home team playing a blinder in the first ten minutes, and by half-time the opposition might as well have hung up their boots and knocked off early. He could still feel the warm glow of victory. Well, that and the pleasant flush from a few pints. Not strictly supposed to drink, given he was on call, but by the time things got moving, he'd have pissed away the alcohol and be up to speed.

'Sue,' he called to the barmaid. 'Can you do us a coffee, take out, please?'

'Coming up. You leaving us?'

'Duty calls.'

Sue's eyes widened but she said no more, knew better than to ask because her bloke had been a copper till he retired on long-term sick. A nasty situation: a break-in that turned out to be an armed robbery. Machetes and baseball bats. Chaos by all accounts. Tasered one of the scumbags and got beaten halfway to Blackpool. The bruises faded but the flashbacks never did. Poor sod. Retired at thirty-six.

Martin had two years left before he got the carriage clock, and he needed to make plans. There were the usual options – security, close protection, but he knew how ball-achingly tedious that line of work was. On high alert for eight or ten hours at a time with absolutely fuck-all happening. Some people took up a hobby, sailing or climbing. Gardening, for Chrissake. Rather slit his own throat.

Training was an option, work as a consultant for the force. Competitive, though.

He liked doing what he did, appreciated the respect he was shown, not just because of his rank as sergeant but because he had earned it. He enjoyed the camaraderie of the team, the power they had as an institution, the biggest gang on the planet.

'Here you go.' Sue passed him his coffee. 'On the house,' she said. 'You take care.'

At the station, Martin parked, then signed in. He took the stairs up to the fourth floor, pausing on each landing to catch his breath. As he opened up the offices, the motion-sensitive lighting flickered into life. He was the only one there as yet, tasked with setting up the incident room ready for the inquiry.

All over the city, detectives and support staff were being woken or summoned to the phone to be notified of their next major investigation.

He pulled the whiteboards into place, faint dabs and smears of black and green, indicating the ghostly notes from a previous inquiry. The room was kitted out with computer stations and desks for all the staff who would be logging in and creating the hundreds of reports that a major incident generated. More and more of the work was computerized or involved digital technology.

Twenty-eight years Martin had been serving. Two-thirds of that he'd worked in the Major Incident Team but he'd done stints in uniform throughout. Periods when he got tired of the slow shuffle, the pen-pushing and double-checking that made up most detective work. Nothing came close to the rush of being a front-line copper. The blues and twos, the chases and collars. All officers started in uniform, learning the basics, and after that the majority put their chips down on one side of the table or the other. There was little love lost between the beat bobbies, risking life and limb, and those in plain clothes with their paperclips, driving desks not Panda cars. Fran worried herself sick he'd be on the receiving end of some scrote with a shooter or a nutter with a knife (not an entirely misplaced fear, given what he had encountered and his two commendations for bravery) so he'd had a pendulum career, bouncing between the two wings of the force.

This last stretch on the fourth floor had been eight years. But once he was off the streets, and wearing civvies, Fran had started in again. Mithering now about his sedentary lifestyle. Frightening herself with stories in the paper about men's health. She'd forced him to see the GP, who had confirmed that Martin was overweight, with high blood pressure and high cholesterol. He was prescribed medication and advised on dietary changes and an exercise regime. That jag must have lasted all of a month, he thought, as he powered up a computer and began a request for information to the emergency call-handling centre. Rabbit food was not his notion of a decent diet.

'I like my food,' he had told Fran, 'and I like a drink now and then. It helps me relax. And if I relax my blood pressure comes down.'

'But they say drinking—'

'That's the end of it, Fran,' he said. 'The medicine can do its stuff but I'd rather drop down dead a few years sooner than live like a fucking saint.'

'Your funeral.' She shrugged.

'As I said.' He spread his hands.

Eight years as a desk jockey and he'd be hard pressed now to run fast enough to catch the clap. He could hold his own in a fight, always big and strong, but fit? Well, fit was stretching it.

Martin looked at their Dale sometimes on the pitch, moving like lightning, dodging through the defence to line one up, and he pined for those years, that grace and skill, the physical prowess.

The trials should be any time. Dale was training hard. It still felt like a knife in his gut when he thought of the boy's injury. A tendon torn to shreds just as some of the major clubs were showing an interest. It had put the lad out of the running and in with the physios for months on end. Touch and go for a while whether he would ever recover full strength and flexibility and so be eligible for consideration again. But he was getting there, working his way up now, playing in the local league and about to make his bid for a chance at the next level. Martin's pride in him was a physical thing, a fist in his chest opening wide. He knew Dale could make it. He was professional standard and he deserved to make it. And Martin would be with him every step of the way.

He heard steps in the corridor outside and the door swung open. Support staff there, arms full of boxes – stationery and office supplies.

'Sarge,' one said, and they moved into the room.

Outside there was the peal of a siren from a car leaving the station. Martin went to the windows, looked at the city skyline. He could see the Hilton Tower dominating the vista and the distinctive sloping wedge that was the Great Northern Tower, all the lights smeared by the veil of rain. Somewhere down there was the victim, the crime scene, the centre of his universe for the foreseeable future.

Steve

The two detectives had gone and there was another policeman at the house, the family liaison officer. A Chinese guy. He was staying with them.

'Sleeping here?' Teagan had said.

'No, I'll be awake. I go home for breaks but I'll be here all day today and for as long as I'm needed. When I do go home I'm at the end of the phone, day or night, for anything you need.'

Steve had come upstairs for a piss and now stood in the doorway to Allie's room. When he switched the light on he saw the clutter of the earlier preparations, hairdryer, brush and a jumble of clothes on the bed, the long table littered with glasses, make-up and a pile of college books and papers. On top of the chest of drawers, her screen, console and laptop among a tangle of wires. The smell of Malibu in the air, coconut and alcohol, along with perfume and the bite of nail varnish. He spotted a bottle upturned on the table, a small pool of bright silver, congealing. All as it should be. Which didn't make sense. Nothing made sense. His throat ached. He wanted Sarah, with a sudden vicious craving. He needed her to be here now, to help him, to guide him. His wife. Allie's mother. She should be here – she should fucking be here. He couldn't do this. None of it. Not on his own. He felt sick.

Allie's booklet, her final project for media studies, lay open on the computer chair. He picked it up and sat down on the edge of the bed.

The pages were thick, a high-quality paper with a subtle sheen that took the printing ink well and was satisfying to touch. He remembered Allie debating the merits of different weights and finishes, talking about various options for the binding. The objective had been to create a product that could be accessed cross-platform, as an app or game or website as well as a physical item, book, poster, DVD and the like. Allie had created the booklet, published it as an e-book, too, and made a series of podcasts available to download as an MP3. *An A–Z of being T.*

'It ought to be A to Zee,' Teagan had said. 'Then it would rhyme.'

'Zee is so lame,' Allie said. 'Too American. I could do A to B.'

'Too short, though,' Teagan said.

Allie began to laugh. 'Not literally, you muppet.'

'But you'd never buy an A to B of Manchester, would you?' Teagan said.

Both versions of the book included simple illustrations, cartoons, graphics and some photographs, when Allie had been able to find images that were copyright free.

Steve read, *Gender Recognition Act – became law in the UK in 2005. It allows people to legally change their gender and to obtain a new birth-certificate showing the acquired sex. To apply you must have socially transitioned for two years. You DO NOT have to have gender reassignment surgery to apply.*

He stroked the page, flicked ahead and stopped at a drawing of two figures wearing brightly coloured saris. *Hijra – in India, Pakistan and Bangladesh, a third gender of people recognized by law. Hijras have existed in South Asia since ancient times. Two-spirit is the term used by some Native American tribes to describe people who have more than one gender identity.*

Steve thumbed through a few more pages. *Pronouns – he, she and they. Pronouns are very important in how we think of ourselves and how we want other people to refer to us. Some transgender people use the pronoun of their acquired gender, others may use 'they' and 'them' (even though they are just one person). Respect what people say. If you're not sure, ask. Terminology is changing all the time.*

He turned towards the back of the booklet, an entry decorated with hearts and cupids. *Sexual Orientation – who do you fancy? That's all it is. Nothing to do with gender identity. Transgender people can be straight, gay, bi, fluid or any other sexual identity. Just like cisgender people can be.*

And overleaf. *Trannie – shorthand for transvestite. We'd rather you didn't call us this. (Also can mean a transistor radio, if you're an old-age pensioner.) See Cross-dresser.*

Steve smiled. He remembered Sarah coming down from putting Aled to bed. Aled, he was then. Sarah's choice. 'He won't speak Welsh, will he? He won't even have a Welsh accent living here. He'll have your surname, so the least I can do is give my babies Welsh names.' So it had been Aled, and when they had a girl, Teagan.

'He's had my knickers on.' Sarah had laughed.

Aled had been seven or eight. 'Bit big, aren't they?' Steve had said.

'Huge, but he'd got his shorts on top.' They'd not realized then. Why would they? Kids were eccentric, unique. Kids liked dressing up. Kids had phases.

'Steve?' The police officer, the family liaison officer, was there, Yun Li. 'We need to leave everything in here undisturbed. For the inquiry. We don't know yet if there's anything in Allie's room that might be significant. I realize it must feel very intrusive but it's likely that the team will want to examine her room.'

Steve got to his feet.

'The book?' the officer said.

'Yes?' Oh, he was so tired. He felt a great pressure, as though everything, his bones and muscles and skin, had doubled in weight, an overbearing strain on his heart.

'It was in the room?'

'I just—' Steve closed his eyes, folded his arms around the booklet. He didn't know what he wanted to say. When he looked at the man again he saw a flicker of indecision in his eyes.

'OK,' Yun Li said. 'As long as we know where it was. Do you want to try and get some rest?'

'No,' Steve said. 'Where's Teagan?'

'She's almost asleep, on the sofa. Is there a blanket or something to put over her?'

'Her duvet.' Steve nodded towards her bedroom.

Through the circular window on the landing he could see it was getting light. The pale grey of a new dawn. Which didn't seem possible.

CHAPTER THREE

Jade

They had gone from the victim's house to interview the two friends who had been with Allie at the prom and Mrs Fallon, the teacher whom the boss had spoken to earlier. All of them gathered at one of the girls' houses.

The families were ranged around a large oval dining-table, one with a high sheen and straight-backed matching chairs. The sort you'd not dare sneeze anywhere near for fear of making a mark. Did the family actually eat their tea there or was it just for dinner parties and that sort of thing? There were empty mugs on coasters and several mobile phones on it now. One of the mothers held a packet of cigarettes and was turning it end to end, over and over again. Jade could smell the stale smoke coming off her.

The girl whose house it was, Helena Jones, blurted out, 'It's not true. Tell me it's not true.' Close to hysteria. Her parents on either side, hushing and shushing her. She was still in her party clothes, a tight black sheath with lace panels, but her eye make-up was smudged, and her nose swollen with crying. Her friend Betsy Millington was so pale she looked like she'd keel over or float away at any moment.

'I'm so sorry,' the boss said. 'What has happened to Allie is a terrible thing. And it's crucial that we find out exactly what did happen. You can help us.' She looked from one girl to the other and Helena made an effort to quieten her crying, taking the tissue her mother offered her.

'It's been an awful night for all of you and we'll try not to keep you too long. As I explained to Mrs Fallon, we would ask you to keep Allie's death and our inquiry completely confidential at the moment. No postings on social media, no texting, no messages left on Allie's Facebook page or anywhere else.'

Fat chance, thought Jade. Word would be out already. There'd've been – what? – fifty or so kids at the prom, maybe more, and only forty-nine on the coach back, the air thick with panic and speculation. The news, the rumours would be bouncing from phone to tablet, bedroom to bedroom, website to Twitter feed, spreading like flu. One could only hope the family would be too poleaxed to try googling Allie's name before the official announcement tomorrow.

The boss suggested they talk to the girls one at a time, and Jade saw a flicker of anxiety pass between them. No one liked talking to the police. But did they have something to hide?

'If we could use the other room, perhaps?' the boss said.

There was a bustle of activity as people rearranged themselves. Jade and the boss ended up on one huge squashy sofa opposite Helena and her parents on another, Jade ready to take notes.

'Tell me about the evening, in your own words,' the boss said.

'We got ready at Allie's and Bets's mum took us to college for the coach.' Helena paused and looked across as if she needed reassurance.

The boss nodded. 'Yes, go on.'

'At the prom there was a buffet and disco, and a band from school played a set and then—' Her voice shrank to a squeak. The mum put an arm around her, kissed her head.

Helena blew her nose. 'We'd been dancing and Allie had been to the loo. When she came back, she wanted to know where Bets was. I told her she'd gone out for a smoke.'

Jade saw the dad roll his eyes and the mum's lips tighten.

'So, Allie went after her but Bets had come back in. She was checking her make-up and I didn't know, or I'd never have said.' Jade could hear the girl's sense of guilt, hear it in her voice. Daft. How was she to know?

'Of course,' the boss said. 'What happened then?'

'When Allie didn't come back, we rang her phone and there was no answer. Bets texted too, then we went out to see if she was there. But she wasn't.'

'Where did you look?'

'On the steps and then along each side of the building. Just there. We couldn't think where she was. And we looked back inside and asked people. And then we rang her dad.' She began to weep, a horrible sound, and Jade clenched her teeth. She checked her notes. The room was too warm, airless.

The boss spoke over the noise, soothing words, not saying much at all, until it was possible to carry on. 'I just have a few more general questions and then we're done for now. Was Allie involved with anyone, in a relationship?'

'No.'

'Had she been in a relationship recently?'

'No. She didn't . . . she . . . She'd got a lot going on, with her identity, you know? I don't think she was ready for that yet,' Helena said.

'OK. Had she had any problems with people at school, or on social media, any bullying?'

'No. Well . . .'

Jade watched her remember something.

'There was a bit of trouble, back in year nine. High school. People knew Allie was trans, but some of them, they called her names, homophobic stuff. We went to the head of year and they sorted it out.'

'Are those people still around?' the boss said.

'No.'

'What about online? Did Allie have any trouble?'

'She was really careful – she had the most private settings and everything.' She wiped her nose.

'Good,' the boss said. 'Thank you, Helena. We may need to talk to you again. OK?'

Helena nodded. The three got to their feet. The dad waited. He was grey-haired, grey stubble on his face, complexion almost the same colour. He looked across at the boss. 'It's just—' He had to stop, cheeks sucked in and mouth all bunched up.

'Is there anything we can do? For Steve and Teagan?' Helena's mum said.

Raise the dead?

'I'm sure they'll be very grateful for your support,' the boss said. 'They'll be informing the rest of the family now so perhaps leave it a day or so. And, of course, Helena will need you now.'

Slick, Jade thought, wondering if she'd be able to remember that sort of answer in case she got asked a question like that in future.

Bets, short for Betsy, still white as milk, confirmed the account Helena had given. 'I'd gone out for a smoke, and when I came in, I went to wash my hands and brush my hair. We must have just missed each other.'

'This was about twenty past eleven?'

'Yes. Then when we realized she'd gone out, I texted her.' Bets lifted her phone.

'Before or after you'd been outside to look?'

'Before. Helena had already tried ringing, but she didn't answer.' She covered her mouth with a hand.

Jade prayed she wasn't going to throw up. But the moment passed.

'Any bad feelings at the prom? Any fallings-out?' the boss said.

'No. One of the boys had to be sent home because he was so drunk.'

'A friend?'

'Not especially,' Bets said.

'And how was Allie?' the boss said.

'Fine.'

'Was she drinking a lot?'

Bets hesitated. 'Not really.'

'How much did she have to drink?'

'Four or five cups of punch. It wasn't strong,' Bets said.

'Was she drunk?'

'No, just . . . not like you'd worry about it.'

'And had she taken anything else?' the boss said.

'What like?'

Buying time, Jade could smell it.

'Pills, weed, powder, legal highs, anything?' the boss said.

A pause. 'Bets?' A note of surprise from the mum.

'Some green,' Bets said. She ran a hand over the back of her short blonde hair.

Her father groaned.

'Sorry,' Bets said. 'It was only a bit.'

'That's what you were smoking outside?' Jade said. The boss glanced across. Was Jade meant to just sit there and keep her mouth shut?

'Yes,' Bets said.

'And Allie had some as well?' the boss said.

'Earlier,' Bets said.

'At the prom?'

'Yes, outside.'

The boss wound it up, and everyone regrouped around the table, Bets's mother tapping her cigarette carton against the wood, probably desperate to get outside and fire one up.

Once Bets and her family had left, the teacher, Mrs Fallon, echoed what Allie's friends had told them about the evening. No trouble. No cause for concern beyond a boy who'd had to go home.

'She was such a lovely girl,' she added, shaking her head. 'Ask anyone. She never deserved anything like this. How could it happen? How could someone do that? Who would do such a thing?'

'We don't know,' the boss said. 'Not yet. But that's why we're here.'

Outside, even with the rain still falling and it barely light, the birds were making a right racket. Jade felt her stomach rumble. There wasn't a canteen at work any more due to cuts, but she knew an all-night café near Piccadilly station. 'Fancy some breakfast, boss?'

The boss paused. 'You obviously do.'

Jade told her where the greasy spoon was – they'd have time before the briefing, wouldn't they? For a moment it looked like she'd argue but she didn't and Jade's mouth was watering already at the thought of a full English, no mushrooms, and a pot of coffee.

Steve

His thoughts kept breaking, brittle stalks, crumbling and snapping. Losing the thread.

He held the phone, Teagan, awake now, beside him and Yun Li perched on the side of the armchair.

'If you need me to talk to them, that's fine,' Yun said. He'd told them to call him Yun. Steve didn't know if that was his first name or not. They did it the other way round in China, didn't they?

'Dad?'

'Yes, yes,' he said quickly, scrabbling to remember what she wanted or what she'd asked, what he was supposed to be doing.

'Nanny will be up now.'

'She will.'

She was up at seven every morning, earlier sometimes, while his dad stayed in bed until nine or so since retiring. She'd be in the kitchen, in her dressing-gown, eating eggs on toast or Weetabix, a book propped open. Always reading. The clock on the wall ticking away, a vase of flowers from the garden on the windowsill.

He couldn't bear to tell her.

'From thread to needle': one of her sayings – 'I got the whole story from thread to needle.' All the plants that make thread, and string, and rope. Cotton, hemp, jute. Spider's silk was an incredible material, stronger than steel.

'Dad.'

'OK,' he said. He pressed her number. In the hiatus before it began to ring, he prayed that she'd be out, that the line would be busy.

'Hello?'

'Mum?'

'Hello?' The slightest edge of uncertainty in her voice.

His throat was full, thick. Teagan sat with her legs straight, knees and feet pressed together, fists making a heart shape in her lap.

'Mum, I've got bad news.'

'Oh.' An intake of breath. He heard a chink, as if she'd set down a cup or a knife.

'I'm sorry. It's Allie. She's . . . erm . . .' The word was foul in his mouth. He had to be clear, Yun had explained, clear and direct. 'Mum, she's dead.'

'Oh, my God. What? She can't be.'

He sniffed hard, wiped at the sudden tears that made his face itch. 'She was attacked.'

'Oh, Steve.'

'In town last night and the police are here.'

'Oh, God,' his mother said. She kept repeating it.

'Will you tell Dad? And Emma?'

'Yes, of course. Oh, Steve, I don't know what to say. I really don't—' Her voice was cracking.

'I know.'

There was just the sound of her breathing and clearing her throat.

'Do you want to talk to the police?' he said.

'I don't think so. Do they know who—'

'No. And they don't want us to tell anyone else yet – just family – not until later today. After I . . . I've got to . . . When things are confirmed.'

'Oh, Steve, oh, my boy. We're coming over.'

'Yes. I'll go now.'

'I'm so sorry,' she said. 'Oh, my poor love. Oh, Allie.'

He hung up, and covered his face. Teagan put her arm round his shoulders and he pulled her close. He felt the vibration of the floor and sensed the displacement of air as Yun left the room, giving them some privacy to grieve.

Donna

An air of anticipation, of expectation, like a buzz of electricity charging the air, greeted Donna when she entered the briefing room. An answering sting in her fingers and she flexed her hands as she took her place at the top table. All eyes on her. She began by introducing Jade Bradshaw to the newly assembled team. Donna knew most of those present but not all, and she let them go round the room introducing themselves, announcing rank and name or, for specialist and support staff, name and role.

Donna did know Detective Sergeant Martin Harris. They'd worked together twice before. Martin was highly experienced and hard-working. He was one of the lads but not to the exclusion of anyone else. Yes, he was a little old-school at times, didn't suffer fools gladly, and he could be brusque – she'd witnessed him losing his temper once or twice – but all in all he was a safe pair of hands.

Donna summarized the facts: 'Allie Kennaway, date of birth twenty-fourth of April 1998, an eighteen-year-old transgender woman, was found dead in Swing Gate Fold, off New Mill Street last night.'

She heard murmurs travel round the room. 'The gender identity of our victim may be significant. In any case I'd like you all to review our policies and guidelines on dealing with the transgender community. It's one thing doing a training session but now we need to make sure we're operating as responsibly and effectively as we can.' Donna had skimmed as much as she could of the guidance before the meeting, anxious to set an example for the team and avoid any crass mistakes.

'Eighteen?' Martin said. He sat beside Jade, looming over the new DC.

‘Eighteen,’ Donna confirmed.

‘Very young,’ he said, ‘for that sort of thing.’

Donna saw one or two heads nodding ‘Young, yes, but the family were aware of and fully supportive of Allie’s gender identity, as were her friends and the college community. Although legally male, we will, through the course of the inquiry, be referring to the deceased as a transgender woman. As “she” and “her”. OK.’

She took them back to the sequence of events. ‘A nine-nine-nine call from Allie’s phone was logged at eleven twenty p.m.’ Donna glanced at Martin. ‘Was it made by our victim?’

‘No,’ he said. ‘Recording requested and received.’

‘Good. We’ll listen to that in a minute,’ Donna said. ‘A beat bobby responded at eleven twenty-five, checked for signs of life, reported a suspicious death, and secured the scene. Wet conditions meant we had to act quickly to document the wider area. The cause of death is likely to be due to blunt-force trauma. A post-mortem will be carried out later today. Here’s our scene.’

A slideshow of images unfolded on the projection screen.

Donna observed the reaction as people absorbed the graphic images of Allie. The close-ups of her face, pulpy and misshapen, of her ruined hands. The pattern of violence stippled across her limbs. The response was muted, a straightening of the spine, someone touching an earlobe, a quiet exhalation. Death, violence and brutality were not new to those present, and no one could afford to become too emotionally wrapped up in the cases they worked on, but they were all human.

Donna looked at the final picture. Allie on the cobblestones, before the tent had been erected, before Donna had first seen her. One foot bare, silver nails and bloodied fingers. The stains on her dress like black clouds. Hours earlier, this girl, like one of her own daughters, had been painting those nails, styling her hair, choosing her earrings. Not knowing what the night held. How it would end. It was this photograph that stuck in Donna’s head. That she would carry with her as they went about their work.

‘Allie and her friends, Betsy and Helena, had been at their

sixth-form prom at Mansion's House. At eleven fifteen Allie left to go looking for Betsy, whom she mistakenly thought was outside. That's our last sighting. Nothing untoward occurred during the evening and we've found no recent history of antagonism, in the real world or online, between Allie and anyone else. No boyfriend or girlfriend. We will, of course, be trying to verify all that. We recovered the victim's phone and bag at the scene. At this point there is nothing to suggest anything was stolen. Her purse was in her bag. There were no obvious signs of sexual assault but we'll know more after the post-mortem. Given the absence of known threats or animosity, we may be looking for an attacker or attackers who were not known to the victim. Family are father Steve and sister Teagan, age twelve. Mother deceased. Once we have formal confirmation of identity, hopefully this afternoon, we'll be making a statement to the media and issuing a public appeal for witnesses.'

'We've already got stuff being posted on the web,' Jade said.

Donna shook her head, exasperated but not surprised. 'We can't close it down, not immediately. Just pray there's nothing circulating that could affect any prosecution.'

'Thinking about other witnesses. Town would have been busy last night,' Martin said.

'Heaving,' Donna agreed. 'Someone must have seen something. CCTV might have picked something up. Martin?'

'On it,' he said. Meaning he had already begun contacting the city-centre control room to alert them of the incident and of the need to retrieve footage in the geographical area for that time. 'There may well be security cameras at the venue too,' he added.

'Yes, let's hope so. I'd like to set up a mobile incident unit on New Mill Street and use that to canvass people who work in the area at night: waiters, cleaners, bar staff, cabbies, bouncers . . .'

Mentally checking off each strand of the investigation, Donna turned to the next item. 'Forensics are in hand regarding trace material from the scene. That'll be coming back to us in fits and starts. The lab is, as always, snowed under.'

A groan rippled round the room. Donna grinned. 'You and me

both. But we work with what we have. Remember, communication is key. We'll have updates morning and evening but please don't stand on ceremony. If something comes in, flagged as a priority, and it lands on your desk, don't sit on it. Get it to Martin or me. Likewise, if something strikes you as significant, use your initiative. Your information packs have all relevant phone numbers and email addresses as well as maps of the area, victim photos and details and so on.' She turned to Martin again. 'Can we hear that nine-nine-nine call?'

The room hushed and Martin played the file, his bright blue eyes on Donna's as they listened. The operator's voice first: 'Emergency services, which service do you require?'

'Ambulance, ambulance.' The voice was male.

'Putting you through, caller.'

'Ambulance service here. What's your emergency, caller?'

'Yes, ambulance. She's very sick – they beat her.' The accent sounded African.

'Can you give me your name?' the operator said.

'Come quick. And police. They beat her. It is Swing Gate Fold, Swing Gate Fold.'

'I'm passing that through now. Please stay on the line. Are you at any risk yourself?'

The line went dead.

'African?' Jade said.

'I think so,' Donna said. 'We can get some help on that. There's a foreign-languages professor at the university. We've used him as an expert witness before. I'll find his details. Jade, see if he can help.'

'Yes, boss.'

'He says *they* beat her so this might be an eyewitness and it sounds like more than one person was involved in the attack,' Donna said. 'We may well be dealing with a hate crime.'

'He could be one of them,' Jade said. 'It goes too far and he freaks out, makes the call.'

'It is possible,' Donna said. 'Anything's possible, so open minds. Questions, anyone?'

Nobody spoke.

'OK, let's not cock this up. We've come a long way since the "cesspool of their own making" days and we're proud of that.' She saw nods and wry grins but Jade seemed puzzled. Too young to get the reference. She really did look like a teenager. Donna had gone so far as to check her file – which stated she was twenty-five and had served four years since her probation.

Earlier Donna had watched with a mix of amusement, envy and horror as Jade had downed a huge fry-up at the café. 'Heart attack on a plate, that,' Donna had said.

'Nowt wrong with my heart,' Jade had announced, stuffing fried bread and sausage into her mouth.

She was so skinny. Was she bulimic? Hardly the sort of thing you could ask a colleague, but Donna decided to keep a wary eye open. She took the health and well-being of her officers very seriously.

'Let's get to work,' she said. She switched off the slideshow and closed the meeting. People moved quickly, fired up, eager to start. The words from the tape echoed in her head. *They beat her. They beat her.* Now all their efforts would be channelled into finding out who 'they' were and why they had stolen a life.

Jade

'What was all that cesspool stuff?' Jade asked the boss, waiting in her office for the language expert's details.

'Our beloved Chief Constable James Anderton's opinion of the homosexual members of our community *circa* nineteen eighty-something.'

'Seriously?' Jade said.

'I kid you not. God had told him, apparently. God's got a lot to answer for,' the boss said, peering through her glasses at her computer and scribbling on a Post-it note.

'So you're not—'

'What?' the boss said, looking up.

'Catholic,' Jade said.

'Eh?'

'Well . . . five kids . . .' Jade said.

'Let's just leave that there, shall we?' the boss said, with a bit of an edge, handing her the note.

'Totally.' *Fuck.* Jade hadn't meant to say anything, but five kids was a bit excessive, wasn't it? Maybe the DI had had four boys and had been trying for a girl or the other way around. But Jade hadn't meant to get personal. She'd hate it if the boss started nosing about in her private life.

'I'll get on with this.' She waved the note with the language expert's details.

'Good. Do you want to attend the post-mortem?'

Did she! 'Yes, boss.'

'Twelve o'clock at the mortuary.'

'Yes, boss.'

'Meanwhile, any queries, if I'm not around, go to DS Harris.'

'Yes, boss.' Detective Sergeant Harris was the exact same guy who'd taken over Jade's first dead body. And here she was working alongside him. How cool was that?

The professor of languages didn't mind being contacted at the weekend. In fact, he seemed delighted to hear from Jade and asked her to forward a copy of the file immediately.

He came back to her within half an hour. 'You're looking at Horn of Africa, possibly Somali or Sudanese. I can't be more specific but that's your region.'

She logged the information on the system and would relay it to the boss when they met for the post-mortem.

Meanwhile she was writing up statements from last night: Steve Kennaway, Betsy Millington, Helena Jones and the teacher, Mrs Fallon. Best to do it while the details were still fresh. Those involved would need to read and sign them as a true account. Jade wasn't overly fond of paperwork, and this was harder than a lot of the other form-filling. You had to get all the critical facts in without waffling on too much. When you showed witness statements to people, they'd start moaning, *I didn't say that exactly*, or *I wouldn't put it like that*, and Jade was tempted to say, *You bloody write it then,* but she'd worked out that the way to deal with it was to ask if there were any inaccuracies, any facts they wished to change. Of course the statements sounded police-y, not like a normal person would talk, because that was how they were taught to write them: they had to get it down in terms that would be clear for trial.

The phones were going off all the time, mingled with the chatter of calls from the people staffing them, but she managed to zone them out.

A woman with stylish blonde hair, wearing a trendy, tweedy skirt-suit, came in to see the boss. DS Harris, who was lining up CCTV strategy at the desk next to Jade's, clocked the visitor and said to Jade, 'Press Office.'

Probably planning the press release for later, Jade guessed. She stretched her arms over her head, tugged one hand against the other: she was stiffening up after so many hours without sleep. Eyes getting gritty. Moments of light-headedness, too, that she mustn't ignore.

'Where were you before?' DS Harris asked, and Jade felt a stupid little glow of warmth. Sergeants were a mixed bag, senior officers, a rank hard won, so some of them liked to sling their weight around, ride the junior officers hard. They were the closest thing the police had to a sergeant major in the army, keeping the lower ranks in order. But some had the common touch, acted halfway human, like this one, even if he did look like he should have been pensioned off a while back. Grey hair, big belly, taut like a punchbag.

'East Manchester,' Jade said. 'Gorton.'

'Not an easy patch.'

'Nightmare. Never boring, though,' Jade said.

He grinned and went back to his screen.

Jade completed Steve's draft statement and began on Helena's. She entered her own name, badge number, and the crime number that had been allocated in the sections at the top of the page. Then the witness's name, date of birth and address. *Allie, Bets and I got ready at Allie's house for our sixth-form-college prom* . . . What bloody awful memories they'd have of it. Even worse, once the full facts came out, the way she died. Shit, totally shit. Jade kept writing. Every so often she'd feel a little kick inside, the thrill of what the day had brought. Not just the murder and shadowing the boss, but now going to the post-mortem an' all.

Martin

Martin parked on the double yellows towards the bottom of New Mill Street and put his permit in the windscreen so he wouldn't get ticketed. The crime-scene cordon was visible across the start of Swing Gate Fold, the narrow street that lay about seventy yards up the road on the opposite side. Metres, he corrected himself. Seventy metres – well, near enough. Close by, a mobile incident van was being manoeuvred into place.

The rain had stopped and the sky was hazy, the sun fighting to get through.

He walked up New Mill Street, past Swing Gate Fold, where the tent preserving the scene was still in place, rounded the bend and crossed to Mansion's House. There was plenty of activity going on there: roadies unloading flight cases and boxes at the side door and, when he reached the main entrance at the junction with Deansgate, more people carrying plastic crates and cardboard cartons up the marble steps.

Glancing up he saw the small black nose of the close-circuit television camera. Just the one, pointing sharply down over the entrance. It didn't look as if it would cover the pavement beyond, and anyone passing by. But, hopefully, it would help them establish exactly when their victim had left the building, what state he was in, whether he was alone and what direction he took.

The reception area was plush, done out in art-deco style, peacock blue and green patterned carpets, fluted plasterwork and wall sconces. Elaborate wallpaper in the same blue with silver and pink geometric patterns. There was nobody at the desk so Martin rang the bell and waited. The receptionist was on the ball when she arrived, and rang straight through to the building manager, who took Martin along a narrow, drab corridor and downstairs to a small windowless room at the back of the building. Two monitors were showing feeds: one from the entrance and one from the alley off Deansgate that ran parallel to New Mill Street at the opposite side of the building.

'Just the two cameras?' Martin said.

'Yes. It's a pretty sedate clientele – private functions, civil ceremonies, bar mitzvahs. The management charges a hefty deposit. If anyone kicks off, the hosts will sort it more often than not.'

'Were you working last night?' Martin asked.

'Yes, all quiet. Sat here and read my book.' He jerked a thumb to the copy of Bill Bryson's *The Road to Little Dribbling* on the desk.

'You were alerted to the disappearance of one of the students?' Martin said.

'About quarter to twelve. I checked the building, then outside round the block. There was no sign . . . It's awful,' he added, after a moment.

'You're still using tapes?' Martin saw the bulky VHS system.

'Not much point in upgrading,' the man said. 'They do the job.'

Martin got out an evidence bag. 'Can you give me the ones from last night, for the whole of the event?'

'Can do. They're all labelled.' There were four video cassettes, each three hours long. It was years since Martin had used VHS. Everything had gone onto DVD, movies and so on. Then with Dale's generation they didn't even have those, just electronic files, downloads, MP3s for their music. Even so, there was something reassuring about a physical format, tangible, solid.

Before he left, he asked the bloke if any other premises would have been open on New Mill Street of a night.

'No. It's a desert down here out of office hours. No one can rely on passing trade, like they can on the main drag.' He meant Deansgate. 'Further down is a kebab place, and round the corner there's a club, Fredo's. Rumours are it's on its last legs but I think it's still limping along.'

'What about intruders? Any problems with anything like that?' Martin said.

'Nothing. Now and again someone tries to doss down in the alley. I move them on.'

'Rough sleepers?'

The man nodded. 'Bad as it ever was. It's crazy. You don't realize something's improved until it gets worse again. Cuts, isn't it?'

'Tell me about it,' Martin said. There was a recruitment freeze on in the force, and they'd already lost dozens of officers through natural wastage. 'What about soliciting?' he said.

'Not so as you'd notice. I think they're mainly up around the back of Piccadilly station.' That fitted with what Martin knew: city-centre prostitution focused on the station. Other red-light areas were further out of town, Cheetham Hill or Levenshulme.

'Anyone in the alley last night?' Martin said.

'No.'

'Thanks. If you can sign here . . .' Martin handed him a receipt for the evidence taken and gave him the carbon copy of the form.

His next job was to walk the area, taking photos as he went, looking for any other CCTV cameras or addresses where there might be witnesses. He walked down the length of New Mill Street. The run of buildings on the left where he'd parked his car were offices, all empty on a Saturday. There was a large plot of land, which had been taken over by prefabricated buildings, used as a storage business and surrounded by chain-link fencing. The gates were locked. Beyond, there was a pub, derelict and boarded up. And then the kebab place the building manager had mentioned. It was on the left-hand corner at the T-junction with Water Street.

More light industrial units edged this road and between them, incongruous and shabby in the daylight, the club Fredo's. With shutters over the windows and the door, you'd be forgiven for thinking it had already had its last gasp but a poster in a frame advertised the current month's events.

Martin walked back up the other side of New Mill Street.

There was an old warehouse, which appeared to have been refurbished as offices (he couldn't see any balconies or bicycles, laundry or curtains), and next to that stood a block that was yet to have a facelift.

The mobile incident van, a Portakabin, was in place now, with officers preparing it for the public.

He stopped when he reached Swing Gate Fold and had a word with the officer guarding the cordon. The CSIs were still there, picking over the ground and emptying a skip near the end of the alley. It was a grim site, the cobbles oily and the walls dank, as if they never saw any sunlight. Blood was visible on the ground. A horrible place to die. A brutal way to die. The tent seemed incongruously clean and bright amid the grime.

What had he been doing, wandering around like that, this boy tarted up like a girl? What had he been thinking, taking off and not sticking with his mates inside, where he was safe? How come an eighteen-year-old lad got it into his head that he wanted to be a lass in the first place? Just wasn't natural, was it?

CHAPTER FOUR

Steve

His sister called. 'Steve, it's Emma. Mum just rang. I'm so sorry. I can't believe it.'

'I know,' he said.

'Where was . . . Where did it happen?'

'In town. She was . . . It looks like she was attacked.' He could hear himself speaking, the words echoing round his head, but he felt as if it wasn't really him talking. Some Robot Steve still acting like things made sense. He rubbed at his eyes until they hurt.

'What was in town?'

'The prom.'

'Al— Allie . . .' she still stumbled over the name '. . . was . . . what? Attacked at the prom?'

'Outside. They don't know who it was. They don't know yet. They don't know why.'

'Well—' She stopped short.

'What?' His back prickled with heat.

'It's just . . . If she was, you know, dressed up, well . . . some people . . . It's not very safe, is it? In public.'

'Fuck off, Emma. Just fuck off!' Steve hurled the phone at the wall and Teagan yelped.

Yun came in quickly. 'Problem?'

'It's my auntie Emma,' Teagan said. 'She's a complete twat.'

Steve began to laugh. And cry. Teagan picked up his phone

and checked it. She told him the screen was cracked but it still worked.

When he'd stopped shaking, he said to Yun, 'I don't want her here, my sister, not now. I can't cope with her on top of everything else. If she shows up . . .'

'She will, Dad,' Teagan said. 'She'll want to be here.'

'Text her,' he said. He held out his phone to Teagan, 'Just say . . .'

'Not up to any visitors?' Teagan said, then wrinkled her nose. 'But she'll know Nanny and Granddad are coming.'

Yun said, 'How about saying your parents are coming but you can't cope with anyone else right now?'

Teagan nodded. 'That'll do.' Her thumbs tapped out the text and she sent it.

His bloody sister. Sarah had always found Emma as difficult as Steve did. 'She ought to think before she speaks, and then she should keep her gob shut anyway,' Sarah had once said, after yet another of Emma's blunt pronouncements had ended in an argument.

When they'd finally told Emma that Allie was transgender, she had reacted with predictable horror. 'Christ. Look, I know you have to say you support your kids and everything, but seriously? It's probably just a phase.'

Steve was beyond relieved that they had decided to broach it without Allie being present.

'It's not a phase, Emma,' Sarah said steadily. 'It's not a problem. It's a fact.'

'But you must be concerned. I mean—'

'We're happy for her,' Sarah said.

Emma snorted, and Steve wanted to throttle her. He spoke up: 'She's clear about who she is, and what she wants. For a lot of teenagers that's a real struggle.'

'But the risks, the bullying—'

'Are you suggesting she should hide?' he said. 'That because other people are bigoted—'

'It's all very well getting all PC about it,' Emma interrupted, 'but he's only fourteen.'

'She,' Sarah said.

'How can anyone possibly know anything at that age?'

'She does,' Sarah said. 'She does and so do we.'

'Well, I don't know what Mum and Dad are going to say.' Emma picked at an imaginary hair on her cashmere sweater.

'They're fine with it,' Steve said. 'We told them at Christmas. Allie wanted some money for clothes – dresses and a good wool coat. We explained then. They chipped in.' Was it petty to savour the pinch that Emma's mouth had made, the spots of colour on her cheeks?

'They'd have to say that.' Emma tossed her head.

'Look,' Steve said, 'it takes a while to get used to the idea. It did me. And it's a surprise, I know. It's just how things are.'

Sarah said, 'Allie's a lot happier now she's come out to her friends, and the school has been brilliant.'

Emma had stared at them, eyes dripping scepticism, and that had been the last time the topic had been discussed with her. Family gatherings, two or three times a year, were awkward, Emma persisting in regarding Allie's identity as some perverse and wilful behaviour designed solely to irritate her aunt. At one point Steve had even suggested they stay away for his mother's birthday but Allie had insisted they go. 'I'm not letting Auntie Emma boss us about.'

'She's so uptight about it, Allie, I just wish she'd lose all the sideways glances and the barbed remarks,' he said.

'It's her that's got the problem,' Allie said. 'Just ignore her. Or call her out on it.'

'Maybe not that,' Steve replied. 'Well, not today, anyway, for Nanny's sake.'

'Dad,' Teagan said now, and Steve was yanked back to the present.

'Yes?'

'It feels weird, laughing.' Her eyes glittered with tears.

'I know, kid.' Steve nodded. 'But it's OK.' He cupped her head, felt her hair thick and springy, the heat beneath it. 'Whatever we do, it's OK. No right or wrong. OK?'

She gave a sniff and a sigh, her shoulders rising and falling. 'OK. I think I'll have a bacon sandwich, then. Do you want one?'

Jade

'First time?' the boss asked Jade.

'Yes, boss.'

They were dressed from head to toe in blue scrubs, gloves and hats, with masks at the ready. The pathologist, a woman who reminded Jade of some Hollywood star – Sandra Bullock or Angelina Jolie but with a Brummie accent – was running the show, helped by her assistant, a man who had small hands and a beard, with a net over it so he wouldn't shed any confusing evidence on the body.

The room was all stainless steel and shiny equipment, with a sealed floor underfoot that could be hosed down. The smell of bleach hung in the air.

The bag containing Allie lay on the trolley, and before the procedure began they each had to introduce themselves. Everything was recorded by a microphone suspended from the ceiling.

'How are we dealing with gender?' the boss said to the pathologist. 'I've been looking at the guidelines and she had begun to live permanently as a woman but had not yet applied for a gender-recognition certificate.'

'Legally male,' the pathologist said.

Jade spoke up: 'But if she was a woman at college and at home, just because she hasn't got a piece of paper—'

'Protocol,' the pathologist said. 'This body is the property of the coroner—'

'Yes, but—'

The pathologist showed her teeth, too many, too big, like a horse. 'And I have the authority to carry out this forensic post-mortem on their behalf as I see fit.' Ice cold.

'There must be room for interpretation,' Jade said. Now the boss was staring daggers at her, too.

'This is a legal procedure,' the pathologist said. 'Legally, the deceased is male.'

'But it—'

'DC Bradshaw,' the boss snapped. Eyes like lasers, nostrils flaring. So much for championing their victim.

'Post-mortem commenced on the fourth of June at twelve seventeen p.m.,' the pathologist said, rapid-fire. She listed those present. 'Deceased is Aled Kennaway, male, date of birth the twenty-fourth of April 1998. Eighteen at time of death. Jonah, prepare for radiography.'

'Jade.' The boss signalled they had to leave. The body would be X-rayed before it was unwrapped.

Jade didn't have any chance to challenge the boss about caving in to Dobbin because the pathologist followed them out while Jonah rigged up the X-ray cameras and used a remote control to take the images. The process was repeated twice to cover different sections of the body. The X-rays showed several broken ribs, a fractured wrist, broken jaw and fractured skull.

They all returned to the room and put on their masks. Jonah cut open the body bag, then drew it apart.

Jade felt a swell of pity as she saw Allie on the table. The mess of her, the bruises and bloodstains even darker than on photographs from the scene. She still lay in a similar position on her left side, her dress stained, damp and creased.

Jonah took some photographs from a few feet away, presumably to get the whole body into the frame, before moving in for close-ups.

Jonah and Dobbin removed the bag from underneath the body, and he took it to one of the wide benches that ringed the room and searched for any trace of material before wiping it with swabs, then sealing the swabs and the bag in separate containers.

When he'd finished, he helped Dobbin turn Allie over to photograph her back. 'Rigor has passed so he's easy enough to manipulate,' Dobbin said.

She.

They cut away the dress, removed the shoe and the underwear. Each item was tagged and bagged but Jonah left the dress on the side.

'Why hasn't he put it in a bag?' Jade said quietly, to the boss.

'It needs to dry out, so it doesn't deteriorate.'

They weighed and measured Allie's body and the pathologist summed up her appearance. 'Well nourished, skin white, eyes blue, hair light brown.'

Jade thought it was more of a dark blonde but she didn't interrupt.

Methodically they photographed all the cuts, bruises and other marks, each time placing a small ruler in the shot to show the scale. Dobbin continued her running commentary. There were lots of anatomical and medical terms, some of which Jade recognized; the rest she had to guess at.

Next Jonah began to wash the body, the wipes he used turning rusty with the blood. Jade could see the injuries more clearly now. There were bruises on the soft flesh of the abdomen, and on Allie's thighs more purple marks bloomed. Jade saw the penis, soft and small, no pubic hair visible. Allie's arms and legs were smooth too. Waxed, perhaps.

It took some time for every mark on the body to be recorded. Then Jonah and Dobbin each used a magnifying glass to search for smaller marks, such as injection sites. At one point Dobbin coughed, turning away from the table.

The boss barely moved.

Jonah combed Allie's hair, collecting any debris dislodged. He pulled several hairs from her head and put them into a bag.

Internal swabs were taken of the victim's mouth, ears and nose. Jonah sealed and labelled every item individually. The doctors worked quickly, but the number of stages, the attention to every little detail, the painstaking documentation, meant the post-mortem took time. With no role apart from observer, Jade didn't get bored exactly, more impatient.

'See here?'

Jade woke up at the change in the pathologist's tone. The pathologist traced her fingers a couple of inches above Allie's stomach. The boss followed her direction, leaning in, Jade at her elbow. 'The contusion. I think that's a footprint.'

'He stood on her?' the boss said.

'Stamped?' Jade said.

Dobbin didn't speculate. 'Another here.' She pointed to the outside of the right thigh. 'And . . . Jonah, on the left side.' They rolled the body over and Dobbin said, 'These arc shapes, I think they're from the toe of a shoe.'

'Kicking?' the boss said.

'Yes. No sign of any other instrument being used, bat or brick.'

'Could all these injuries be down to fists and boots?' the boss said.

'Yes. Tests will tell us more.'

He kicked her to death. Jade cleared her throat. *They.* Remembering the 999 call. *They beat her.* Fucking bastards.

The pathologist returned to cataloguing her findings. 'Examining the teeth, one filling to the upper left six, upper right one, maxillary central incisor knocked out, present in the mouth.' Using tweezers she removed the tooth. 'Lacerations to the tongue.' Jade could see the gap in Allie's front teeth, and the split lip. She closed her eyes, imagining the blow that had caused those injuries.

In a practised routine, Jonah took scrapings from under the nails. He clipped them and kept the clippings, then did fingerprints.

'Lacerations and grazes here on his palms, possibly from breaking the fall.' Dobbin addressed the boss.

When he knocked her down, Jade thought.

'And this series of wounds on the forearms, and these along the shins, are consistent with a defensive posture. Curling up, arms over his face . . .'

Her face.

'. . . knees drawn up to protect the abdomen.'

Swabs of the genitalia and the anus came next and the pathologist said, 'External examination complete.' She turned to the boss and

Jade. 'You might want to step back a bit now. We'll start the internal exam.' She lifted a blade.

I will not faint, Jade told herself. I will not. There was little blood as Dobbin made the Y-incision. 'There are the broken ribs,' she said.

Jonah approached the table with a saw. The buzz of the machine filled the room as they cut through the ribcage.

It was the colours that were most surprising to Jade. The browns and reds and pinks of the organs. With each one the pathologist began by recording any physical injury before surgically removing an organ, weighing it and taking samples for further analysis.

Jade let the words flow around her. 'Blood in the pericardial sac . . . rupture of the spleen . . . partially digested food in the stomach.'

The buffet at the prom.

Dobbin turned her attention to the brain. 'We need a close look at that scalp before we go in,' she said.

They wanted to shave her head. The boss looked at her, made a face, sad, resigned. Gave a small shrug. Jade took a breath. The smell of bleach caught at the back of her throat. She rubbed her neck.

Shorn, Allie looked smaller, even more vulnerable.

Jade thought of her neighbour, Mina, crying, 'Your hair.' Nothing can hurt her now, she told herself.

The pathologist described the wounds on Allie's scalp, then made a cut right around the head, and pulled down the face.

Saliva thick in her mouth, Jade looked up at the ceiling but that made it hard to swallow.

Nothing can hurt her. She's gone. It's just a body.

'Deep contusions. Fracture to the cranium. Proceeding to remove the calvaria.' The pathologist used the saw to cut off the dome of the skull. 'Trauma to the dura.' Then she was lifting out the brain.

Jade turned and strode to the door, her stomach convulsing, spasms rippling up into her throat making her gag. Desperate to reach the toilet in time.

Afterwards she splashed her face and neck with water and stared at herself in the mirror. *You fucking wimp. Fuck. Fucking. Fuck.*

Then she went back to face the music.

Sonia

The house was quiet when Sonia got in from work. Oliver was still in bed, she guessed. She'd leave him be. He hadn't been that late last night. It had been not long after twelve when she'd heard him come upstairs. But he could still sleep all day, given the chance, like most teenagers. Getting him up for seven thirty in the week, so he'd be on time to his apprenticeship at the other side of town, was a struggle. When would that change? How much longer would she have to be his knocker-upper as well as chief cook and bottle washer?

Her phone rang: her friend Rose. 'You fancy a drink tonight?' Rose said.

'I would if I'd any money. We could stay in, bring a bottle, download a movie.'

'I need to get out,' Rose said. 'Four walls, you know? My treat.' Rose lived with her dad, who was disabled with a lung condition that had him on oxygen. She had been married for all of five minutes as a seventeen-year-old and moved back home after. When her mum left, Rose became her dad's carer. She worked a few hours a week as a classroom assistant at a primary school and was desperate to have a family of her own but hadn't met anyone worth considering in years of trying. She kept upbeat mostly, but now and then the mask cracked and she confided in Sonia how lonely, how unhappy she was.

'Rose, I can't let you pay—'

'Course you can, don't be daft. You'd do the same for me.'

'Yeah. Don't hold your breath, though.'

Rose laughed.

'Are you sure?' Sonia said.

'Positive. There's karaoke on at the Swan.'

'We like a bit of karaoke,' Sonia said.

'That we do. Eight o'clock?'

'See you then.'

Sonia made herself a sandwich and a cup of coffee, had a fag. She should try vaping again, she thought, shivering slightly as she stood outside the back door. Bloody cold for June. Cold wind. In fact, she *would* try vaping again. Soon. It wasn't the same, whatever people said. She reckoned you had to accept that and get used to the difference. Different smell and taste, a different physical kick.

When she went upstairs to use the loo and get the laundry, she saw there was daylight showing under Oliver's door. She knocked and, getting no answer, went in. Bed empty, curtains drawn back. Out somewhere.

Curious, she texted him: *Where u? Back 4 tea?*

Park. Yes. He replied straight away.

Back in the kitchen, she loaded the washing-machine and saw the new pack of detergent had been opened, the old one gone. He must have done some washing. Wonders would never cease. Did he actually know how to operate the thing? She checked in the back room where she had the clothes horse and, sure enough, there was a load of his stuff hung to dry. Maybe it was a thank-you for the fifty/sixty quid. He was a good lad, really, beneath the teenage strop and sulks. He was. She saw newspaper on the floor by the window and peered over the rack. His good shoes were sitting on the free advertiser, the paper sodden. She reached down and felt them: dripping wet. Had he actually put these in the machine too? Daft bugger. Still a way to go yet, then. She fetched more paper and stuffed them with it.

Well, at least he'd made an effort. Smiling to herself, she went back to her own washing, her mind turning to the evening ahead and what she might wear.

Donna

Donna had told Jade to wait outside, get some fresh air, before going back to the incident room. She found her by the exit to the car park, biting her nails.

'I'm sorry,' Jade said.

'No problem,' Donna said. 'Most of us have been there, or come close.'

Jade turned to go, stuffing her hands into her jacket pockets, then hesitated.

'What is it?' Donna said.

'The pathologist, the identity stuff. You never even—'

'Whoa! Are you telling me how to do my job?' Donna said.

'No, but—'

Yes, you are. Tight with irritation, Donna kept her voice level while she laid out her thinking. 'Look, I could tell she wasn't going to negotiate. I could tell she'd dug her heels in. And I could accept that what goes down on that form, what's on the post-mortem and on her death certificate and in the register of births, marriages and deaths, is accurate according to the letter of the law. I hadn't got a leg to stand on. But it's not what's most important. What is most important is that *we* acknowledge her identity, in keeping with her wishes and those of her family, so *this inquiry* talks about Allie, not Aled, she not he, her not him. Like I said this morning. When I make a statement to the press and media later this afternoon, that's what I'll be doing.'

Jade studied her boots. Was she taking any of it in?

Donna went on, 'Same as her family will describe her as Allie in any notices in the paper, in their memorial or funeral arrangements, on her headstone or remembrance plaque. She died as a transgender woman. She possibly died *because* she was a transgender woman and, yes, it's frustrating the post-mortem report won't reflect that, but that's where we are. Accept it and move on.'

Jade glanced at her, eyes narrowed against the light, head tilted, silent. Sulking? Possibly. But Donna had had more than enough practice with sulkers, thanks to her kids. Not a good look for a junior officer, though. Donna hoped it wouldn't be a regular occurrence. 'Now, you've got work to do?'

'Yes, boss. The witness statements,' she said flatly.

'Good,' Donna said. 'Soon as you can.'

'Yes, boss,' Jade said, and stalked off, hands jammed into her pockets and shoulders up, the message clear. Don't mess with me.

Donna met Steve Kennaway, his mother and the family liaison officer, Yun Li, in the relatives' lounge at the mortuary prior to the formal identification. It was a carefully bland space with neutral colours, dark grey carpet, beige walls and brown upholstered chairs. There were tissues on the coffee-tables and a drinks machine in the corner.

Donna checked if Steve would be accompanied in the viewing room.

His mother, Mrs Kennaway, spoke up. 'Yes, I'll be with him.'

'I need to prepare you for what you will see,' Donna told them. 'Allie will be covered from the neck down, her hands visible by her sides. Her head will be covered and her face visible.' Donna sketched the shape around her own hairline. They would not need to see the shorn skull or the worst of the injuries. 'You will see her face is bruised and swollen. She has some cuts and grazes. I will ask you if this is your daughter and I will give her name and date of birth. You tell me if it is Allie.'

Steve looked away, closed his eyes. Donna waited a moment. 'Is there anything you want to ask me?'

He took his mother's hand. 'No,' he said.

'You are welcome to stay in the viewing room if you wish. That is completely up to you,' Donna went on. 'Yun Li and the mortuary technician will also be present for the identification. But we can give you time alone after that, should you wish, and you don't have to tell me yet. Are you ready now?'

Steve nodded and got to his feet.

The mortuary technician led them into the viewing room, Donna after him, then Steve and his mother, and finally Yun Li.

Donna heard a soft gasp from Mrs Kennaway and saw Steve hold his hand over his mouth.

Through the glass, Allie's body looked small on the trolley. The left side of her face, the side they could see, was less badly injured but still daubed with bruises and grazes, her lip torn and misshapen.

Donna spoke: 'Is this your daughter Allie Kennaway, date of birth the twenty-fourth of April 1998?'

'Yes, this is Allie,' Steve said.

'Thank you. Would you like some time here?' Donna said.

'No,' Steve said, his voice hoarse. He turned, stumbling slightly. He linked arms with his mother as they went back to the other room.

The two of them sat side by side, Steve covering his face and breathing unsteadily. Mrs Kennaway, eyes full of tears, was trembling.

'Thank you,' Donna said, after a few moments. 'I can only imagine how hard that must have been. Yun here will take you home when you're ready to go but please take as long as you need. We'll be making an official statement to the press and the public this afternoon. There is likely to be intense interest and it may be advisable to stay with family or friends until things calm down. We can arrange to book a hotel for you, if you'd prefer.'

'I want to stay at home,' Steve said.

He'd no idea what was coming, Donna realized. 'What's likely to happen, Steve, is that the media will be camped outside your house, filming anyone entering or leaving, asking for comments and statements. It can be highly intrusive and unwelcome at a time like this.'

'I want to stay at home,' he repeated.

His mother looked worried, a frown across her forehead. She opened her mouth to speak, then closed it.

'See how you go on,' Donna said. 'We'd ask you not to speak to anyone at this stage, no comments at all, because it could compromise the investigation.'

'Fine,' he said, but he seemed distracted, rubbing at his knuckles, rocking slightly.

'There's something else I need to tell you about. We've had the preliminary results from the post-mortem,' Donna said.

Steve turned to face her, his eyes clouded.

'They confirm what we suspected. That Allie died as a result of blunt-force trauma, a catastrophic brain injury.' Donna paused to see if Steve or his mother would want to know any more but neither of them spoke. 'Any questions you have, anything at all, if you need any help or advice, please ask Yun Li. I'll keep him updated.'

Mrs Kennaway nodded.

Steve's eyes were still unfocused. He was barely present. She thanked them both. Yun Li nodded to her: he'd keep an eye on things.

She was glad to get out of the building, away from the emotional overload, the atmosphere that made her feel claustrophobic, bitter grief and heartbreak choking the air.

Donna put on some make-up before the press conference, foundation, mascara, a touch of blush. Her hair needed a wash but a brush was all it would get. She had thick hair, which she was glad of. It didn't need much attention – a trim every few weeks, the fringe tidying up, and highlights to mask the grey.

She checked her teeth looked clean, no shreds of spinach stuck between them from the wrap she had eaten between the post-mortem and the formal ID. Like all officers at her level, she'd had some media training and had done enough public speaking not to feel nervous in front of the cameras.

Harold Jenkins, the chief constable, was in attendance. He sat between the press officer and Donna in front of the banner with the police-service logo. Screens either side carried a projected photograph of Allie Kennaway in her prom dress, taken by her father hours before her death. Eyes bright, wide-open smile.

The hall was crammed with journalists and photographers, film crews ranged at the back, their cameras raised on tripods to get a clear line to the stage.

Most of those present would have picked up on the rumours haemorrhaging across social media, but most would have held off reporting the murder until this official announcement. There was a volley of flashes and a battery of sounds as they took their seats.

Without any hesitation Donna read out her statement, remembering not to mask her face with the paper and to look up at those assembled as often as possible. 'Imagine you're talking to your family, asking them for help,' she had once been advised. 'Keep it warm, keep it real. The language may be formal but you need to be sympathetic and human.'

'Last night at eleven twenty p.m. police were called to Swing Gate Fold, off New Mill Street near Deansgate in the city centre. On arrival they found the body of Allie Kennaway, aged eighteen, a transgender woman.' She heard whispers at the word 'transgender', an extra dimension to the 'story'.

'Allie was attending her sixth-form prom at nearby Mansion's House. She left the venue at around eleven fifteen and shortly after was attacked and beaten by a person or persons unknown. She died at the scene from a catastrophic brain injury. Her family have been informed and our thoughts are with them. We would appeal to the general public to assist us in apprehending and prosecuting whoever committed this savage and senseless attack. If you were in Manchester last night, if you saw anything, heard anything, or remember anything, no matter how small or apparently insignificant, or if you have any other information that might assist us, please contact the inquiry or call Crimestoppers in complete confidence. Thank you.'

'Was it a hate crime?' somebody called, even though they'd been briefed there'd be no Q and A.

The chief constable nodded to Donna and they stood to leave.

The press officer reminded everyone that an official press release was available and thanked them all for attending. People began to move, scraping back chairs or dismantling their equipment.

'Bloody awful,' the chief constable said, as they waited for the lift. 'I know things are stretched to breaking point, but if you find yourself too short of resources on this one, you come to me.'

'Yes, sir,' Donna said, impressed by his offer. She didn't know him well and he came across as conservative and straitlaced. So his interest, his commitment to this case, pleased and surprised her.

'Eighteen,' he said, shaking his head.

'Yes, sir. It is awful. Her whole life ahead of her.' A cliché but, oh, so true.

CHAPTER FIVE

Martin

At the evening briefing, Martin showed them the significant sections from the CCTV he'd brought back from Mansion's House.

'Allie goes outside, with both friends here, at nine fifteen. They head right into New Mill Street out of sight and return at nine twenty-three.'

'There's a side door down there, recessed. That's where they'd been smoking weed,' Jade, the new DC, said.

'Right,' Martin said. 'They come back at nine twenty-six.' He watched with the rest of them as the three girls walked into shot and up the steps, talking and laughing. The one with short blonde hair, Bets, stopped and took a photograph of her friends, who blew kisses to the camera phone.

You couldn't tell by looking, Martin thought, that Allie wasn't a girl. If you knew, maybe you'd see the hands were larger, the feet too, but you'd easily be fooled. He couldn't imagine it, having a kid who wanted to swap sides. What a horror show. Not just playing on the other team but the whole medical shebang. The thought of it, of surgery, made his balls shrivel.

'Then here at eleven oh seven, as reported, Betsy Millington appears, again heads left, away from the crowds on Deansgate, and returns at eleven twelve. Three minutes later, at eleven fifteen, Allie appears.' The room watched as their victim walked down the steps. Martin paused the tape. 'No sign of incapacity, the gait is steady enough, no apparent distress or anxiety. And that's where we lose her.' Martin had to keep reminding himself to call the victim 'her'. He set the tape to resume playing and Allie disappeared to the right of the screen.

'Five minutes later the nine-nine-nine call is made,' Donna said. 'Anything from CCTV on New Mill Street?' she asked.

'No, no cameras,' Martin said. 'We've recovered footage for Deansgate for the evening and we've a team will start scrutinizing that while the rest of us get some kip.'

There were deliberate yawns from some of the staff and good-natured banter – 'You've no staying power, you lot . . . You don't know you're born.'

'We're looking for any sighting of our victim, and for sightings of groups of two or more people who leave Deansgate and go down New Mill Street or who appear on Deansgate and whose behaviour or appearance gives us cause for concern,' Martin said. 'Concentrate on footage between eleven p.m. and midnight. Depending on the results, we'll widen the search area.' He indicated the map. 'There are other ways to get to and from Deansgate.' He traced the web of interconnecting roads.

'Thanks, Martin.' Donna picked it up. 'I know you're all shattered and I won't keep you much longer. Other information before we conclude. Our unknown nine-nine-nine caller is believed to be East African in origin, Sudanese or Somali. Forensics should be coming in thick and fast in the morning but a promising heads-up is the identification of blood at the scene that does *not* belong to our victim.'

A subdued cheer rippled round the room. Martin saw Jade give a little victorious fist pump. 'Maybe she hurt one of them,' Jade said.

'Maybe,' Donna said.

Martin thought of the lost shoe. Had their victim kicked out and broken skin, or bloodied someone's nose? Had he tried to run? He'd not have got far in stupid heels like that.

Donna interrupted his thoughts and wound up the meeting: 'Thank you, everyone, and good night.'

Martin stood and rolled back his shoulders, shagged out and glad the long day was finally done.

At home, his wife Fran had lasagne ready to heat up for him. He took off his jacket and tie and sank onto the sofa.

'Is it that teenager?' she said. 'Allie Kennaway?' She passed him a lap tray.

'Yes,' he said.

'Horrible.'

'Is Dale out?' Martin said.

'Gone for a run.'

'At this time?'

'You know how keen he is,' Fran said.

'He doesn't want to overdo it,' Martin said.

'I know, but you try telling him that.'

Martin scooped up some food, scalding the roof of his mouth with the first bite.

'I just worry . . .' Fran said.

'What?'

'Well, if he doesn't get selected he'll be devastated.'

'That's the way it goes,' Martin said. 'But he's fitter than he ever was. He's got a good shot at it.' He ate another forkful – he was famished. 'Did he have a good night?'

'Yes.' She smiled.

The news came on and Martin turned up the volume. Their murder was top story, probably a combination of the youth of the victim and the novelty of him being transgender.

'Have you met the family?' Fran said.

Martin shook his head. They never talked much about his work. Fran always knew what case he was on and the information that was in the public domain but that was it. After the fact, when cases had been put to bed, and if they were socializing, Martin might trot out some tales about the weird and wonderful world of Major Crimes but never when a case was unsolved.

Fran said, 'Five or ten years ago you couldn't imagine anyone that young being . . . you know . . . changing sex but now it's everywhere. It was just drag queens, back then, wasn't it? Lily Savage and Dame Edna Everage. Or there's thingummy.'

He looked at her.

She made circular motions with her hand by way of encouragement. 'The comedian, the marathons.'

'Eddie Izzard.'

'That's him,' she said.

'Not sure he's a drag queen,' Martin said.

'I don't know. But things have gone too far the other way,' Fran said. 'I mean, you must be off yer head to start getting bits chopped off. Like mutilation.'

The thought made him want to heave. 'Fran.' He pulled a face.

'Well, exactly.'

He gave her his plate and watched some spokesperson from a local LGBT charity quote statistics about violence towards sexual minorities and the need for education and understanding.

He sipped at his whisky as the news continued, mind returning to the case. If it was an attack by people not known to the victim, like it was shaping up to be, then any forensic evidence was crucial because there was no pre-existing relationship to make connections, to point to motive. He hoped the lab would have something for them in the morning, like Donna promised.

Next thing he knew Fran was shaking him awake, telling him he should go to bed and that he really could do with a shower as well, unless he wanted to sleep on the sofa.

Steve

One of the detectives, the young one, had been round, asked Steve to check and sign his witness statement. He'd steeled himself to go through the document. It had been bizarre reading it, like a film script, his story written by someone else. He agreed it was accurate and signed his name.

Now he was looking at photographs, him, his parents and Teagan. Old prints, crammed into a shoebox, of Allie when she was young. He and Sarah had always been going to get an album, put everything in order, labelled and dated, but it had never happened. And more recent photos, the last seven or eight years, were all digital. Teagan had helped set up the laptop for those so they could have a slideshow.

Seeing all the images, the hundred or more pictures of Allie, helped counteract the dreadful sight of her at the mortuary that was burnt on the back of his eyeballs.

Was it normal, this steeping themselves in memories? He couldn't recall the days after Sarah died with any clarity, though he knew there had been some looking back to pull together material for her memorial service. Anyway, he chided himself, when did normal ever matter? If he'd learnt anything from Allie it was that 'normal' was a dangerous word.

'Look at that,' his mum said. 'Pause it, Teagan. When was that?'

Steve looked at the screen. Allie in a bad fairy outfit, black net skirt and shiny black wings, red tights, purple lipstick, talons instead of nails.

'Halloween?' Teagan said.

'That's right. She'd be twelve then,' Steve said. 'Still got her braces on.' A mouthful of metal.

Not long before that, Sarah had come to Steve and said, 'I think Aled's a cross-dresser.'

He'd laughed, taken aback. His son liked dressing up, fancy dress, but that wasn't the same as . . . it didn't mean . . .

'He's seen some dress online that he wants me to buy for him. I asked him if he liked dressing as a girl and he said, yes, he feels good like that.'

'Jesus,' Steve had said. Not sure what it meant, or how to respond.

It was Sarah who had guided him. 'So I've ordered the dress and I said we'd like to talk to him about it, so we can understand what he wants and how we can help.'

Steve must still have been looking worried because she'd gone on, 'It's OK, Steve. He's not hurting anyone, just finding his way.'

And they'd had the conversation with him one afternoon when Teagan was out playing at a friend's. Aled had flushed a little as he'd begun to talk. He hadn't said much, only that he felt better when he dressed as a girl and he wanted to do it more often.

So he had. At home initially and then with those friends he trusted.

The first few times Steve had seen him in a pleated skirt and stretchy T-shirt top or a dress and tights and black pumps, wearing make-up and earrings, he'd experienced a rush of love for this astonishing child and a swirl of unease. The unease wasn't distaste but anxiety, a fear that Aled was putting himself at risk.

He thought of Emma's words earlier, *It's not very safe, is it? In public.* Steve had been taught by Allie's example to learn to control those fears and put them into perspective. Had he been so wrong? Had he put Allie in harm's way? *Jesus.* Her big night: should he have told her not to go? Not to wear what she wanted? But she was with friends – she was at the prom. How could anyone have known?

The bloody statistics were in the A–Z project: *84 per cent of transgender people have considered taking their own lives and 35 per cent have attempted suicide. For young people under 26 the figure rises to 48 per cent attempting suicide.* Steve had come across similar figures when he'd needed to know more, to understand Allie's situation, and he had browsed transgender issues online. He recalled that painful quickening of his heart, the churn in his stomach at the stark numbers: *19 per cent have been physically attacked for being trans and 62 per cent have experienced transphobic abuse in public.* The irrational thought: if this was what being transgender meant, he didn't want his child to have that identity.

'It's not a choice,' Allie had said to him once, after Sarah died, when they were discussing her transition: when she started sixth-form college, she'd be attending as a girl. 'The only choice is whether I'm true to myself or not. If I hide or not. I don't want to hide any more.'

'Dad?' Teagan said.

He was wrenched back to the present. He must have made some sound: Teagan was staring at him with concern.

He couldn't speak. Instead he shook his head, eyes hot and aching. The savage pain, the crushing bitter misery of Sarah's loss had been tempered by time. But it was still there, deep and strong. This called it all back.

'You should get some sleep,' his mum said. 'Both of you.'

Steve stared at her.

'Rest, then, even if you can't sleep. Lie down and rest. We'll come back in the morning.' She glanced at Steve's dad, who nodded his agreement, his eyes red and watery, face grey and dotted with liver spots. His dad had barely spoken the whole time he'd been here. And Steve realized he was only just holding it together. That his silence and absent behaviour were a bulwark against the enormity of his loss.

'OK,' Steve said. 'We'll rest.'

'Dad, remember when I used to have a nest on the floor?' Teagan said, as they went upstairs. For years, she'd slept at the foot of their bed as often as not, woken by bad dreams or lonely in her own room.

'You want to do that now?' he said. *Oh, Teagan.* How could she bear this? How could she bear any of it?

'No, it's OK.'

'Sure?'

'Yes,' she said.

He couldn't tell if he was glad, or if he'd have liked her company. Everything was unstable, shifting, hard to fathom.

'Give us a hug,' he said, on the landing. And she put her arms around his chest, her ear to his breastbone.

He breathed in the smell of her, chocolate and salt and a trace of rose shampoo. 'Love you,' he said. 'See you in the morning.'

'Love you too. Night, Dad.'

He was still awake when she came in an hour later, dragging a sleeping bag and a pillow.

'Dad?'

'It's fine,' he said.

'Night night.'

And he lay on his back with his eyes closed and listened to the steady rhythm of her breathing.

Donna

Donna loved the contrast. Coming home after a long, demanding day of steering the juggernaut of a murder inquiry, with a thousand things to think of – coming from that to the hum of domesticity, the smaller and simpler concerns of home.

Of the kids, only Bryony was still up when Donna got in, doing something creative to her nails with glitter and stickers, while watching *Damages*, a legal thriller, on Netflix. Bryony was three years younger than Allie, three years older than Teagan. There was something adult, mature, about Teagan. Perhaps she'd had to grow up more quickly, losing her mum as an nine-year-old.

Jim filled Donna in on their day. The cinema trip had been a partial success but Matt had freaked out at some sound effects, which he was sure was thunder. Jim had had to take him into the foyer and walk round the complex for the rest of the film.

'I thought we were getting over the thunder,' Donna said. 'Did he clean the hamster out?'

'After a fashion. It'd probably be more accurate to say he played with Morris while I did the job.'

'Maybe next time you should play with Morris.'

'No fear,' Jim said. 'That animal's feral. I've still got scars – look.' He pointed to the silvery line on his thumb. 'Oh, and Lewis wants a snake.'

'That's not going to happen. Though maybe a snake would solve the Morris problem.'

'Harsh,' he said. 'You're obviously mixing with the wrong type of people.' He yawned.

'Am I keeping you up?' she said.

'Definitely.'

It was only as she got into bed beside him and heard the clatter of Morris at play that she realized she'd forgotten again to get Matt to move the cage. She was so tired, too tired to get up and do it now. But tomorrow she'd ask Jim to do it. She'd remember to do that, she promised herself. She definitely would.

In the hour since reaching her desk, Donna had sifted through the emails, messages and reports from the various parts of the inquiry, bringing herself up to speed, identifying what needed sharing with the team and what required further action.

At a little after eight thirty, she took her seat in the briefing room, her notes in order. Martin sat at her left, Jade at her right. She noticed Jade was left-handed: the hand holding the pen was twisted at an angle over the top of her daybook. Donna could smell Martin's after-shave and fabric conditioner from his clothes. Refreshed, like the rest of them, bright-eyed and raring to go. Energized, like herself, not least because she had received significant new evidence.

'Good morning, everyone,' she said. 'Our appeal generated a substantial number of calls from the public. One flagged up as urgent is a potential eyewitness. Jade, you and I will follow up on that. As I hoped, it's a bumper day for forensics. There's a summary of results, which you can download, but I'll take you through the most salient facts.

'To date, three separate DNA profiles have been identified at the scene. Profile one, consisting of blood on the ground, and blood and fingerprints on the victim's phone, has led us to a full match on the database.' There was a stir of excitement at this and, beside her, Jade gave a little jump in her seat and muttered, 'Yes!'

Donna smiled. She pulled up the details on the projection screen. 'The prints match those of Mahmoud Jamal Bishaar, a Somali national and failed asylum-seeker, missing since July 2015, when he absconded after the failure of his appeal. More than likely this individual is our nine-nine-nine caller. We will be actively looking for Bishaar. Given he fled the scene and is here illegally, it's highly doubtful he'll come forward voluntarily.'

There were nods and murmurs of assent.

'We'll circulate his description to the force but at this stage I'm not releasing his details to the public. If he's still in the area, a move like that could spook him and send him further afield.'

Martin scoffed. 'He'll already be long gone.'

'How?' Jade said. 'He's illegal, he's no cash.'

'That doesn't stop them,' Martin said. 'Jump on a lorry.'

'Anyway,' Donna interrupted them, 'I'd like the CCTV team to see if we can find Bishaar on camera, alone or with others.'

She looked back at her summary. 'Profile two has been drawn from saliva on the victim's face, and skin under the victim's fingernails, with further traces of DNA material on the upper arms and the clothing. We know it's a male but there is no match on our database.' In effect the person had no prior record of criminal activity. 'There were traces of cocaine and alcohol in the saliva.

'Profile three, also male, was retrieved from short red hairs on the victim's clothing and from skin cells at the scene. This individual is not on our database either. We also have traces of fibres on both the victim and at the scene, and these are undergoing further testing. And we have partial footwear impressions from three different shoes.'

'Then Bishaar could have been in on the attack,' Jade put in.

'Anything is possible,' Donna said, aware it sounded like a mantra. But she didn't want anyone getting fixated on a particular hunch or hypothesis to the detriment of other scenarios. Jade seemed keen to finger Bishaar and Donna made a mental note to keep an eye on that, make sure the young DC didn't start trying to make the evidence fit her pet theory.

'Any progress with potential suspects on CCTV?' she asked Martin.

'Barely scratched the surface. The short hair of one individual that you've outlined should help narrow potential sightings down but it's still going to be a long, hard slog with no further description of them.'

The public had a false impression of working with CCTV, imagining it took a matter of hours to isolate footage of suspects, when it was often weeks or even months. The recordings were frequently grainy, the quality of the images affected by factors like rain and light or the lack of it. Distance, camera angle, the number of people in the area, the wearing of caps and hoods, all influenced whether or not you could pick out an individual, whether you could see their face, if it was in focus, the features clear enough to read, if it was anything more than a blurred disc.

'If they kicked and beat her like that, they'd have had blood on them,' Jade said.

'They would,' Donna agreed. 'Reported sightings of Allie are being checked up on and eliminated where they contradict the hard facts. We've only five minutes between the footage of her leaving Mansion's House and the nine-nine-nine call. GPS coordinates confirm that the call was made from Swing Gate Fold itself. So in five minutes she's not going far. It's most likely she went directly down New Mill Street to Swing Gate Fold. We just don't know why.'

'We know she was looking for Bets,' Jade said, 'so she'd go down to the side door recess, expecting her to be smoking there. That was when something happened.'

There was a moment's quiet, everyone imagining what that 'something' had been.

Donna checked her notes. 'The pathologist tells us our victim had consumed cannabis and alcohol but not in amounts likely to seriously impair her faculties.' She surveyed the team. 'Early days yet but we've made a good start. Thank you all, and let's get to work.'

Jade

The witness, a young woman with pink and blonde hair and several nose-rings, had been asked to come into the station and now sat with Jade and the boss in a small meeting room.

They'd seen a transcript of her call to the investigation but now they needed to hear from her at first hand and, as long as she wasn't a time-waster, get a written statement.

Before they went in the boss suggested Jade do the interview while she take notes. Jade felt her skin tighten. Yes! But that also meant the boss would be observing her, assessing her, so she had to get it right. Open-ended questions, no leading, no pressure. A general outline, then the details and clarification when needed. And all the formalities done in the right order to make sure it was legally sound.

The witness confirmed her name, Louise Hill, her date of birth and address.

'You rang the incident line last night. Can you tell us what you'd seen?' Jade said.

'Yeah, two lads on Deansgate.' She coughed. 'They were walking quickly, then one stops and he looks upset . . . Well, I think he was.' She stopped, as if Jade might confirm her opinion.

Jade just said, 'Go on.'

'Then the other one – he was arguing with him. He grabbed him and made him walk on. I think that's why I remember it – because I thought there might be some bother.'

She was nervous, fiddling with her hair and clearing her throat so often Jade wished she could give her a Fisherman's Friend or something.

'What made you think that?' Jade said.

'Just the vibe between them at first. And then they hailed a cab and it pulled in and the one who was arguing, I could see these marks on his sleeve . . . like blood . . . Well, it could have been . . . That's what I thought. So, the cab pulled in and they got in.'

That was the bare bones of it. Next Jade walked her through each step of the account, pinning down facts and figures. The time, the direction she was coming from, the distance between her and the lads on the opposite side of the road. With the help of a street-view application, she got Louise to point out where she had been when she saw the men and where they'd picked up the taxi. A black cab.

Next came the work on identification of the two suspects. Age, race, height, build, hair, clothing. 'I'm sorry,' Louise said eventually. 'I'm just rubbish with faces. That's all I know.'

Jade summed it up: 'So they were both white and the first man, the one who seemed upset, he was about six foot tall, average build, shortish light-coloured hair. And you can't recall his clothes.'

'Right.' She gave a hacking cough.

'The other man, the one who was arguing and making the first man walk on, he was average height, average build. You don't know what colour hair.'

'Sorry,' she said.

'He wore a light-coloured, long-sleeved shirt, which had dark stains on the sleeve. Can you remember anything else? Shoes or trainers on either of them?'

'No, I'm sorry.'

'Any tattoos or scars?' Jade said.

'I don't know . . . I don't think . . . Oh, I don't know.'

'Was either of them smoking?'

'I don't know.' She looked like she was going to cry.

'Was either of them carrying anything?'

She shook her head.

Before Jade could continue, the boss barged in: 'Thank you, Louise, that's very helpful. DC Bradshaw will type this up for you to check and sign. If you do remember anything else, anything at all, please get in touch with her directly. One thing I'd like to ask is whether you'd be willing to meet with one of our artists. They work on photo-fit sketches in cases like this and they're very experienced in helping witnesses build a clearer picture of what they've seen. Would you be happy to give it a go?' She'd had to come steamrolling in. So much for leaving it all to Jade.

'Yes. I'm not sure I'll be any good, though.'

'Don't worry,' the boss said. 'If you don't mind waiting here for a few minutes we'll find someone to work on that with you while your statement's prepared. And thanks again for coming in.'

'Thanks,' the witness said.

They didn't speak on the way upstairs, not even a 'nicely handled' or a 'well done' from the boss, until Jade said, 'I'll get this written up, then. Do you want me to talk to the artist?'

'I'll do that,' the boss said. 'A word in my office first.'

Oh, crap.

Once they were in there, the boss took her time getting comfy behind her desk.

Like school. The head's office. Time and again.

'OK. The witness interview. Anything you'd change?'

The witness. 'I don't think so.'

'She was a bit anxious, wasn't she?' the boss said.

'I know.'

'I didn't see you doing anything to reassure her. You didn't thank her, not once. You didn't even thank her for coming in. You didn't tell her she was doing well. You didn't say anything positive for the duration of the interview.'

'Well, she wasn't exactly on the ball,' Jade said.

'You don't know that.' The boss was scowling. It made deep grooves above her nose, chiselled deep lines either side of her mouth. 'You can't possibly know that. Any of those small pieces of information, the light-coloured shirt with blood on it, the different build of the two men, their location, the fact one had short hair when we already have short red hair recovered from our crime scene. There's a wealth of material there. Any one of those items could be gold dust. But even if there had been nothing, a half-baked story with no useful detail, we should still treat every witness with respect, appreciation and gratitude.'

'Fine,' Jade said. She wanted to take the fancy snow-globe paperweight with its photo of gap-toothed children inside and smash it over the DI's head.

'You don't have to get all touchy-feely, Jade. It's simply a matter of making the person feel that what they're doing is valued and valuable. Because it is. That's how we get the best results. OK?'

'Yes, boss.' The boss was staring at her: she expected more. She could whistle for it.

Then Jade imagined her writing this up, some management-speak about failure to progress in the area of interpersonal skills, so she swallowed her resentment and added, 'Sorry, boss. I'll remember that next time. It makes sense.'

That worked: she was released. She escaped to the toilet and swallowed a couple more tablets. Practised mouthing *thank you*, *thanks*, *thank you so much* and smiling at the mirror, then leant closer and told her reflection to just fuck the fuck off.

Martin

Martin spent the day tracing the taxi driver who had picked up the two men from Deansgate. With it being a black cab, there was a central booking office where all the records were kept. But because they'd hired the taxi on-street it would take longer to identify which driver had caught the fare.

When he spoke about it with one of the operators, she said, 'It might be quickest if I circulate a notice rather than go through the log. I can ask anyone who was covering Deansgate at that time to call me. Could be teatime before we hear, if it's someone on nights, still in bed.'

'Let's try it,' Martin said. 'You've got my number.'

'I have. You any photo-fits?' she said.

'No.' They had tried to get something from the witness Donna and Jade had interviewed but there was so little distinction between the two faces that the boss had decided it was better to wait, in the hope they might get something stronger from somebody else. A misleading sketch could do more harm than good, steering people who *had* seen the suspects to distrust their memories because they didn't look anything like the police impression.

Martin was hoping the cab would have CCTV fitted: some of them did now, and there was a move under way at the city council to extend it to all black cabs.

He was eating a late lunch when he got word back with details of the cab driver, currently at home up in Moston. Martin arranged to meet the man straight away. He informed the boss and drove north out of the city centre.

The cabbie, Feroz Hassan, was British Asian, a middle-aged man, with a bigger pot-belly than Martin's, 'tache and huge eyebrows. The house was smart, new-build detached. A log-burning stove sat in the fireplace, a huge mirror above it, and on one wall a professional photograph of Hassan with his wife and four kids. None of the clutter you usually got in family homes. Maybe the kids weren't allowed in the living room.

Martin declined the offer of tea and, once he'd explained their interest in the passengers picked up on Deansgate, Hassan said, 'I thought there was something off. You think they did it?'

'We're just making inquiries at the moment. Why do you say there was something off?'

'The atmosphere – you know? Not talking to each other, like they'd fallen out. I thought perhaps they'd been in a fight. One of them had blood on his shirt.'

Martin nodded. Nice one. Hassan had seen blood, same as the other witness.

'I wouldn't have picked them up if I'd noticed that,' Hassan went on. 'I said to them, "Had some bother?" He said he'd had a nose-bleed.'

'Where did you take them?' Martin said.

'Chester Road, outside the tram station.'

Martin had been hoping for a residential address. 'Did they both get out there?'

'That's right.'

'Have you got a camera in the cab?'

'No. They reckon it'll improve security but would you want every hour of your working day on record?' His eyebrows sky high in disgust.

Martin grunted. 'They're bringing in body-cams for us too, front-line officers.' He wouldn't be expected to wear one, thank God. 'Can you describe the passengers?'

Hassan rubbed his moustache with a fingertip, obviously thinking. 'The one who talked, who gave me the destination, he was the one who had blood on his shirt. He'd got dark hair, clean-shaven

– they both were clean-shaven. It's hard to tell age but I'd put them at around twenty or so.'

'Can you describe the other guy?'

'Ginger, crewcut, freckles. Bit podgier. More than that I can't tell you.' The hair fitted but their earlier witness had said the short-haired man was taller and average build. Still, discrepancies were par for the course with eyewitnesses. It was a bloody miracle anyone ever got ID'd and taken to court.

'Anything about their faces, features?' Martin said.

'No. I only remember that much because I thought they might be trouble.'

Martin would run it past the boss but he couldn't see it was worth putting Hassan in with a sketch artist.

'How did they pay?' Martin said.

'Cash.' So, no credit-card trail to follow.

'Where's the car now?' Martin said.

'John's got it. We share the licence.'

'We need to get in touch, examine the vehicle,' Martin said.

'Well, how long's that going to take?' Hassan objected, clearly worried about his livelihood.

'Couldn't tell you.'

Hassan gave a dramatic sigh.

'This is a murder investigation . . .' Martin said.

Hassan dropped the injured act. 'Fair enough.' He rang John, who was doing a run from the airport. 'Where do you want him?'

Martin took the phone and gave John the address of the garage the police used for forensic vehicle examinations. 'I'll meet you there, sort out the paperwork.'

'When did you last clean the inside?' Martin said to Hassan.

'I swept it out Saturday morning before John picked it up. Wiped the seats down. Nothing worse than starting work in a dirty car or having to clean up after the other fellow's shift. We have it valeted every month, unless someone's been sick, so it's not due for another couple of weeks.'

Promising, very promising.

* * *

Martin's day got even better when an initial examination of the cab's passenger area, using luminol, showed blood traces on the carpet, traces that had not been visible to the naked eye. Martin watched the blue light, the chemical reaction and felt a punch of satisfaction. He knew he had to bide his time: this pair might not have had anything to do with Allie Kennaway's murder. Sometimes it turned out like that – suspects faded away as evidence eliminated them. But so far it was looking pretty damn sweet.

CHAPTER SIX

Jade

Jade didn't go home at the end of the day but instead began a trawl of the arches and back alleys around the canals where some of the city's homeless slept.

She picked her way between rotting rubbish and the remains of campfires, stopping to ask people nursing bottles of booze or puffing away on whatever they could get their hands on, weed or baccy, if they'd seen DD. No one spotted her for a cop: her brown skin and leather jacket served as camouflage. All she got was vacant stares, shakes of the head and a smattering of fuck-offs until one guy, Polish at a guess, said, 'You looking to buy?'

'Only from DD. You know where he's dossing?'

'Maybe,' he said.

'You asking me for money?'

'Maybe.' His fingers were bitten raw, his lips scabby. The stink of skunk hung round him.

Jade turned away. 'We'll see what DD says about that, then.'

'Wait,' the bloke called after her. 'No need to be nasty. He's down the river, Chapel Street, near the old flyover.'

At the river basin, a horrible stench of burning plastic hit Jade's throat. It was coming from a fire in an old oil drum. Some of these rough sleepers had cheap tents, the sort discarded by festival-goers, and outside the largest she spotted DD. A couple of lads with him, money changing hands.

‘A’ right, J?’ He rose. ‘Later, lads.’ His customers melted away. ‘Long time no see. You’ve had your hair done.’

‘A’ right, DD.’

He hadn’t changed much in the last three years, still ‘hench’, as the slang went, powerful shoulders, muscles straining against his V-neck sweater. Bare chest beneath. Black-haired, like Jade, but with pale skin and green eyes. DD had Roma blood. Jade had grown up with him. At fifteen he’d started living on the streets. He sold drugs to the homeless. He sold information, too, for a price. At least, he had to Jade in the past, and that was why she’d come looking for him now.

‘You here on official business?’ DD said.

He sat, and she lowered herself onto a pink plastic stool covered with stickers of cartoon rabbits. ‘Semi-official.’ She’d considered making DD an official community informant but he’d not been interested. Not one for rules and regulations. Or obligation.

‘I’m working the murder,’ Jade said. ‘Allie Kennaway.’

‘Fuckin’ disgrace,’ DD said.

‘We want to talk to this man.’ She showed him Bishaar’s photograph. ‘Failed asylum-seeker. Somali. We think he’s been sleeping rough.’

DD studied the picture. ‘He a suspect?’

‘Not sure. He’s definitely a witness. He made the nine-nine-nine call. He saw it.’

‘You got a name?’

‘Mahmoud Jamal Bishaar.’

‘How much?’ DD said.

‘Fifty,’ Jade said.

‘Another hundred if I find him.’

‘You’re shitting me. What happened to mate’s rates?’

‘Them is mate’s rates.’ He pocketed the cash and began to fill an e-cigarette with herbs from a small tin.

‘That Spice?’ Jade said.

‘You want some?’

‘No way. You got a death wish?’ Legal highs had recently been criminalized, so a whole glut of dodgy new drugs was flooding the market, no ingredients listed, no quality control. People were collapsing, ending up in A and E, or the mortuary.

'This is the real stuff. I stocked up. And, going forward, I trust my chemist.' He blew out a stream of smoke. 'You'd rather have weed?'

'I'm good,' she said.

'You weren't always that way,' he said.

'Yeah,' Jade said. 'I remember. I was there.' Not eager to start reminiscing about the bad old days.

'You doing a' right, then?' The jokey tone gone.

'Yeah, not bad. I'm still on the same number,' she said, getting ready to leave. 'Send me yours.'

Someone was coughing their lungs up, the gurgle of phlegm turning her stomach. A train rattled over the bridge nearby, making conversation impossible for a moment. 'The sooner the better,' she said.

'I get a bonus for express service,' he said.

'Do one, DD,' she said, keeping her face straight and walking away.

Donna

Donna had spent half the night dreaming about the case. Nonsense most of it. She'd arrested their window-cleaner in one episode, and in another Jim was the victim and he was now a girl in a prom dress like Allie Kennaway's.

That had woken her. She'd let the emotions of panic and sadness drain away, then counted her blessings or did a tally of sorts. It was a habit she'd got into years ago, not about material possessions but about her family. A review of each child, the pleasures they brought, the worries too, any crises going on.

Bryony was the most unsettled, these days. At fifteen her eager, open personality had transmuted. Now she was full of sarcasm and derision, everything an effort. As yet there had been no big problems with drugs or drink or sex or online bullying, or any of the other hazards modern teenagers encountered, and for that Donna was truly grateful. If only Bryony could make it through the next three or four years unscathed.

Robin and Lewis, the twins, had each other and that seemed to be all they needed. Thirteen-year-olds, they were changing shape rapidly, limbs lengthening, feet and hands spreading. Keeping them in shoes was costing a small fortune. They were popular and sporty at school, doing just enough to get by in class, and she couldn't imagine them being apart for any length of time. What would separate them? Romance? University? Work?

Ten-year-old Kirsten had always been hard work. Needy in ways that Donna, when she was being ruthlessly honest, found tiresome. Quick to anger and to tears, Kirsten always saw herself as hard done by, endlessly falling out with friends and classmates. Donna dreaded her move up to high school. Where would she find the resilience to deal with the demands and treacheries of the new social environment? Kirsten's one solace was her music. She played the piano with a talent that had come out of the blue. And Donna and Jim did all they could to encourage her.

And baby Matt, already eight, a peaceful, dreamy child, who needed chivvying every other minute but who had sudden dramatic fears that paralysed him. Nightmares of monsters and zombies, a lifelong fear of spiders (which Donna suspected Kirsten had schooled him in), of flying insects, of cats and thunder.

Jim started snoring, revving up louder with each breath. Donna shoved him and he turned over without waking, mumbled, 'Pen,' and fell quiet. For how long? What chance did she have of getting back to sleep when he was roaring like a bloody steam engine? She rolled onto her back, tried to relax her shoulders.

Were any of their kids gay? Lewis, perhaps – he had more of a feminine side to him, was more talkative, more sociable than Rob. But wouldn't it be clearer by now, if he did like boys? And if one of them, Kirsten, say, came out as transgender what might that be like?

Would she and Jim handle it as well as the Kennaways seemed to have? It would be a hell of a shock, she was sure of that, and a source of worry. But if Kirsten wanted to change gender, have surgery . . . Donna couldn't imagine it, the complexity of it, the emotional upheaval for the whole family.

Jim went to the toilet. Donna was aware of him coming back but he didn't get into bed, just sat on the edge in the dark.

'Jim?'

'It's OK,' he said, but his voice sounded strained.

She put the light on and sat up. 'What is it?'

'Nothing. Indigestion, I think.' Had he been calling 'pain' not 'pen'?

'Do you want some heartburn stuff?' Donna had some at her bedside.

'OK.'

He was whey-faced, covered with a sheen of sweat. *Heart attack?* She felt her own heart contract in response.

'Where does it hurt?' she said.

He rubbed at the centre of his chest.

'What about your arm?' She'd learnt some first aid as part of her job.

'Don't,' he said, giving her a look.

'What?'

'Jump on the nuclear option.'

'I'm ruling it out, not ruling it in,' she said. 'Here.'

He took the bottle from her.

'Wait. Maybe aspirin would be better,' she said.

'Do we have any?'

'Not sure. Are you hot?' She put a hand to his forehead, then the back of his neck. Felt him tense. He was cold, cold and wet. She didn't like it. 'Stay there.'

Downstairs she went to the medicine cupboard but they had no aspirin, only ibuprofen and paracetamol.

'It's easing off,' he said, when she got back upstairs.

'You sure?'

'Yes.'

'I think you should ring the doctor in the morning.'

'I'll see how I feel,' he said.

'It can't hurt to get it checked out.'

'It's indigestion,' he said. 'I'm sure of it.'

His reluctance to see the GP about anything, ever, drove her round the bend. 'Promise you'll tell me if it happens again.'

'I'll tell you if it happens again,' he parroted, but there was a sharp undercurrent in his tone that stung.

It was ten to four when she turned the light off. Two hours and forty minutes until her alarm would ring.

Jade pounced on her as soon as she came into the incident room. Only the two of them there as yet.

'Boss, I've got Bishaar.'

'What?'

'He's downstairs waiting for interview.'

'When did this happen?'

'Last night. Well, early this morning. He was holed up in an abandoned warehouse on Sherborne Street.' Jade could barely keep still. Dancing on the spot like a runner waiting for starter's orders. Eyes glittering.

'Tell me you've not arrested him.' *Please.*

'No, boss. I invited him to come and talk to us as a witness.'

'And he followed you like a little lamb, did he?'

Jade gave a tip of the head – trying to avoid the question, perhaps.

'Well?'

'Mention of Visas and Immigration might have helped,' Jade said.

'Christ, you didn't promise anything, did you?' Donna could imagine a whole horror-show unfolding, accusations of coercion or bribery.

'No, boss. I simply gave him the option. Talk to us or talk to them.' Her legs still working. Was she high? Buzzing with the kick of the collar or on something else?

'He'll have to talk to them anyway, eventually,' Donna said. 'You know that? Well, I doubt there'll be much talking. They'll stick him in a detention centre and then on the first plane back home.'

'Unless he's actually involved in the murder,' Jade said.

That again. They couldn't rule it out. He had been at the scene and three different footwear marks were found on Allie's body. But what the hell had Jade been thinking, tripping off like some bounty hunter with no word to anyone on the team?

'What happened to communication, Jade?'

The girl's face closed down. 'I'm telling you now, soon as you got here,' she said.

'I have a phone,' Donna said.

'It was late.'

'Christ! I'm a big girl,' Donna said. 'I'm senior investigating officer. I'm not going to throw a tantrum if one of my officers wakes me in the night with breaking news about a critical development. "Take the initiative," I said, and it seems you did. But the other part of the message was *sharing* information, not sitting on something, not keeping it to yourself, or for yourself. I'm very happy for you to show initiative but not at the expense of being a team player. We clear?'

'Yes, boss,' she said tonelessly.

'Hand over the details to DS Harris when he gets in. He can run the interview.'

'Boss.' Jade's brown eyes flashed.

'Yes?'

'I brought him in. I should—'

'This isn't *High Noon*, Jade. What was I just saying about team work?'

Jade's chin was up, hands in her pockets. Donna could see how hungry she was for it. She considered sticking with her choice of Martin, denying Jade the interview in order to teach her a lesson. For all of ten seconds. Passive-aggressive wasn't her style of management.

'Any other bright ideas, you tell me. Have you got that?'

'Yes, boss.'

'You do not go off flying solo. You understand?'

'Yes, boss.'

'You lead the interview, then. You in with DC Thwaite. Do we need an interpreter?'

'No, boss.' Face alight again, energy back in her voice. 'He speaks English and I checked he's no medical problems that need immediate attention.'

'How did you find him?' Donna said.

'Asked around – it seemed likely he was sleeping rough. Took his photo.'

'You were lucky.'

Jade glanced down. Embarrassed, perhaps, by the compliment. Or was she hiding something? 'Case like this, people want to help,' she said.

Martin arrived then, phone in hand, obviously reading something. 'The cab,' he said, his face alive with interest, electric blue eyes blazing. 'The blood traces on the floor in the back. It's Allie Kennaway's.'

CHAPTER SEVEN

Steve

He'd woken in the night, gasping, flooded with terror. Something crushing his chest, squatting on him. He couldn't breathe, couldn't move. Finally something broke and he gulped in air, shifted up onto his elbows, the green digital display of the alarm clock a niche of light in the blackness.

Then he remembered, the truth slamming into him so violently he lost his breath again.

Downstairs he made tea and listened to the blackbird sing, clear and cool in the dark.

His eyes moved over the photographs on the kitchen wall. They had become so familiar he didn't really see them any more. But now he took his time with each one, trying to recapture more of the times they represented. To stretch beyond the snapshot and recall the different rhythms and textures of their family life, of his working life, in various periods. The exhaustion after Teagan was born when she was awake several times a night. He'd escaped some of that, working away, travelling to France and Germany in his job as patent adviser. The picture of Allie and Teagan, taken in his parents' back garden – that was the summer they'd moved. Allie was piggy-backing Teagan, both of them laughing. Teagan, barefoot with shorts and a sun hat, was about two years old. She had her head flung back. A sprinkler was on and the spray created a wide rainbow behind them. That was the day Teagan had been stung by a wasp and the gathering had broken up early, her arm swelling like a balloon.

And the one of Allie holding the dog dated from around the time she'd told them she was transgender. Not just that she liked wearing female clothes but that she felt like a girl inside.

'Is he gay?' Steve had asked Sarah, shortly after.

'I don't think so,' she said.

'I've sometimes wondered if Teagan might be,' Steve said, 'but never Aled.'

'We'll ask him.'

And they had. And he wasn't. Or she wasn't. It had taken Steve some time to understand it all. Time to begin thinking of Aled as Allie. Of his son as his daughter. The name change was the hardest point for Steve.

Aled, as he was then, had broached it on the way back from holiday. 'I've been choosing a new name,' he said. 'A girl's name.'

'OK,' Sarah said.

Steve's hands tightened on the steering-wheel.

'You could be Savannah or Cassidy,' Teagan said.

'I don't think so.' Aled laughed. Teagan was seven. Savannah and Cassidy were the names she'd given her guinea pigs.

'Everyone at school calls me Teapot,' Teagan said. 'It's not fair.'

'Have you picked one, then?' Sarah said to Aled.

'I quite like Allie.' He spelt it out. 'It's similar and I'd still have the same initials.'

'What about Sally?' Teagan said.

'No,' Aled said. 'Definitely Allie. I want you to call me Allie. And "her" and "she".'

'Even when you're in boys' clothes?' Teagan said.

'Yes. All the time.'

'We'll have to practise,' Sarah said.

Once they were home, with the first load of washing on and the kids' uniforms sorted out for the following day, Steve had joined Sarah to watch some television but he couldn't concentrate on the drama unfolding onscreen. It seemed trite, irrelevant.

'I'll walk Dix,' he said.

'Again?'

'Just round the block.'

Sarah was still up when he got back. She said something about the shopping. Then, 'What is it?'

'Aled, Allie. It feels so permanent. Like there's no going back.' He tried to explain. 'It probably sounds daft but I feel like we're losing him, Sarah, our son. We won't have a son any more. It's sinking in and I'm not sure how I feel about it . . . Our boy.' His eyes stung.

'Yes, I know,' Sarah said.

Huge relief that she understood and wasn't belittling his fears.

'We won't have a son any more. We'll have another daughter,' she added. 'But it's the same person for all the changes. It's still our child. And this is what he wants. She.'

It had never mattered greatly to Steve, the sex of their children. They'd never chosen to find out whether they were having a boy or a girl in advance of the birth so it was a surprise and a joy each time. He knew some parents were desperate to have a son first, or to have one of each, or any other combination, and he hadn't understood any of those impulses. But now?

Sarah came closer and put her arms around his neck. 'It's her life, Steve. Her happiness. It's not about us. If he—' She pulled away. 'God. Maybe we should have a pronoun box. Fifty pence for every mistake.'

He hugged her again. He felt shaken, weak.

He kissed her. Then some more. He wanted her. Wanted to stop thinking. Wanted the comfort and escape of sex.

'How tired are you?' she said, a gleam in her eyes.

How he loved her. 'Not too tired,' he said. 'Never too tired for you.' And he took her hand and led her upstairs.

Sonia

'Oliver.' Sonia knocked on his bedroom door again. 'You'll be late.'

'I'm not going.'

'You can't just not go.'

'I'm ill,' he shouted. He didn't sound ill. No wheezing or sneezing.

'With what?'

'Flu. I don't know. I can't go.'

She could hardly drag him out of bed and force him. 'Have you rung them?' She felt stupid calling through the door but she never barged in any more. He was entitled to some privacy. 'Can I come in?'

A grunt, which she took as a yes.

The room was dark and smelt of vinegar. She put the lights on and Oliver pulled his pillow over his head. A jumbo bag of crisps sat open on the side.

'Have you got a temperature?'

'I don't know.'

'Let me see.'

He flung the pillow away, a churlish five-year-old.

She reached over. He did feel hot but nothing extreme. 'Are you shivery?'

'Yeah,' he said.

'Have you been sick? Diarrhoea?'

'No. But I feel sick.'

'You must ring them. I'll get you some water. How were you yesterday?' She'd not seen him. She'd done eight till four at the store. It didn't open until ten on a Sunday but she'd been put to work in the delivery hall at the back first, which was freezing cold even in summer. When she had got in he'd been up in his room playing video games and he'd gone out after that.

'OK,' he said.

'Is this because of Friday night?' she said.

'What?'

He had a strange expression on his face. She couldn't read it. 'Overdoing it in town and still suffering for it?' She dreaded to think what he might have got up to, drugs and drinking games, lads egging each other on.

'No.' He scowled.

'Did you go on to a club?'

'No, just a bar. Near the restaurant.'

'So?' she said.

'What?'

'Have you any change, then?'

'I got take-out last night.'

'This is down to some dodgy kebab, is it?'

'Dunno.'

He'd been sick before, eating one, but it hadn't put him off.

'Oh, Oliver. Let's hope it's just a twenty-four-hour thing. It won't look good if you miss any more days. Paracetamol,' she said. 'Paracetamol and water. And what happened to your shoes? You're not meant to wash leather.'

'I didn't wash them. It was raining and there was a big puddle.'

'They look like they've been in a bloody fountain, never mind a puddle. Next time stuff paper in them to soak it up. Don't leave them sopping wet.'

No response. 'Do you hear me?'

'Yes!'

He'd yelled so loudly that she flinched. The tendons in his neck were up like wires. She wanted to shout back but he was ill and it wouldn't do any good anyway. 'I'll get that water,' she said, her jaw tight. 'And if you do feel sick, don't eat anything until it's passed.'

He had never been a happy patient even as a little boy. But at least back then she could give him a cuddle, read him a book or settle him on the sofa with a DVD to watch. Now sometimes it felt like they were enemies, but she didn't know what the battle was, what the war was all about.

She'd told Rose about it on Saturday night. How touchy Oliver was, these days, how bloody rude. How being angry seemed to be his default position. She didn't know whether he was like that with his friends. He no longer knocked about with the lads from school, and this new crowd, with their odd nicknames, Foz and Seggie, were strangers to her. He never brought any of them home. No girls either, not for a while.

'And he's probably watching porn online, like they all are, before he's even met anyone serious. God knows what he'll expect. Mind, he's not exactly Prince Charming at the moment. I wouldn't wish him on anyone.'

'Not with you, he isn't,' Rose had said. 'Perhaps he's like Superman, transforms.'

'Or Jekyll and Hyde,' Sonia said. And felt a stab of guilt. This was her Oliver: she didn't want to be putting him down. 'I love him to bits but . . .'

'Give him time,' Rose said, and nudged her over their karaoke choice. 'What'll it be, "These Boots Are Made For Walking" or "Single Ladies"?'

Jade

Mahmoud Jamal Bishaar had a burst blood vessel in his left eye, a red spider against the blue-white of the eyeball. Jade thought of hard-boiled eggs, that same odd white. Cuts to his cheek and lip were scabbing over. His nose was swollen, puffed up, like he'd been thumped.

When Jade had surprised him at the warehouse, as he sat reading by the light from a small fire, he'd legged it. Or tried to. There was only one way out of the building and the uniformed officers she'd brought with her had been ready and waiting for him. Her heart had skipped a beat when she saw he was wearing trainers, a style similar to the type that had made one of the footprints on the body.

Bishaar hadn't said much since, an air of defeat coming off him.

At the station his clothes and shoes had been removed and pictures had been taken of his injuries. He'd been given canvas pumps and a navy blue jumpsuit, which swamped him, skinny wrists jutting out where he'd rolled up the sleeves.

She began the interview by establishing his details. According to his records, he was thirty-two. He looked older. 'We believe you were witness to a serious incident on Friday night at Swing Gate Fold. An incident resulting in the murder of Allie Kennaway. What can you tell me about that?'

He didn't speak.

Jade said, 'UK Visas and Immigration know you're here and that we want to question you as a potential witness. But if you're not going to cooperate I can send you to a removal centre now.' She was betting he'd rather be here than there.

'There was a fight.' He spoke so softly that Jade had to lean closer to hear. 'Two men, they were grabbing this girl, pulling her, and they knocked her down. And they were kicking her, over and over.'

'Where were you?' Jade said.

'I was by the bin.'

'What were you doing there?'

'Sleeping,' he said.

'What happened then?' Jade said.

'I went to stop them, and one of them hit me. He got me and hit me and hit me and threw me on the floor. And the other one, he kicks me.'

'Where did they hit you?'

'Here.' He pointed to his nose and his mouth. 'And here.' The side of his head. 'And in the stomach.'

'Then what?' Jade said.

'They are both kicking her again. One of them, he spat on her . . .' *Saliva at the scene* '. . . and they ran off. She wasn't moving.' He bowed his head. When he looked up again, his eyes were watery. The red spider trembled. 'Her phone was on the floor. I rang nine-nine-nine.'

'Why not use your phone?' Jade said. Everyone had one, these days. OK, not old Bert, who lived opposite her, but the rest of the planet. Even refugees like Bishaar had them as a way of finding out where they could cross borders and to stay in touch with family. There'd been one in his pocket when Jade had brought him in.

He was silent for a while, staring at his hands. 'My application for asylum was refused. The police . . . I used her phone. I couldn't stay with her. Perhaps if I had stayed . . .'

Was he looking for reassurance? *Don't worry, nowt you could have done, mate, too late.* He wasn't getting any from Jade. Guilt would keep him cooperative, she hoped.

'You didn't touch her?'

'No.'

'You didn't check if she was still breathing?'

'No,' he whispered.

'Did you touch any part of her?'

'No.'

Was he lying? He didn't know they had the footprint, yet. Had he joined in the attack? And then what? Had a crisis of conscience?

She needed to take him through it, move by move, the whole choreography of it, but first she said, 'The two men, tell me what you remember about them.'

'They were white. One had dark hair and a yellow shirt. Dark trousers. Most of the time he was away from me.'

'Away?' Jade said.

'Facing away. He was . . .' Bishaar raised his shoulders, pushed out his chest. 'Like he goes to the gym a lot.'

Jade thought of DD, the fashion for six-packs, for bulked-up pecs and biceps. A look that left her cold. 'And the other man?'

'Very short hair, red hair.' Like the cabbie had told DS Harris.

'What was he wearing?'

'A short-sleeve T-shirt with a collar. He was more fat.'

'How fat?'

'A little fat, not huge. And tall.'

'OK, so we'll call the first man, the dark-haired one, Man A, and the second Man B. Tell me who was doing what when you first saw them.'

'Man A, he was calling and pulling her.'

'Calling what?'

He raised his eyes, the red spider jumped. 'Like, "Come on, girl, come on, you little slag. Don't be a bitch."'

'And Man B?'

'He was going, "Yo, yo," like cheering him on. Then the Man A, he is grabbing at her skirt.' Bishaar pointed to his own lap. 'Grabbing her and he screams, "Fucking freak."' Bishaar stumbled over the swear word. '"Slut. Fucking prick." Lots of words like this. Lots of other things, I can't remember them all, and he punches her hard and she goes into his friend and he hits her too. I am on my feet. He pushes her and she falls, slides. The ground is wet.' Bishaar skids his hands in the air. 'And they are kicking. One each side. Like she is a football. And Man A, he spits on her.' Bishaar broke off, turned his head away.

This guy was good. Total recall. And she reckoned he was telling the truth. The chance that he'd been one of the attackers faded.

'And I am running to them and shouting to stop and they turn on me. The Man A he grabs my head and pulls me and gets me like this.' Bishaar curled his arm against the side of his body to form a circle, mimed a fist punching at the head. 'I'm bleeding, my nose and my mouth, and he drags me round and throws me down.' *The reports of blood on one of the suspect's sleeves.*

'And Man B?'

'He kicks me in the stomach.'

'Did either of them speak?'

'Man A. When he was hitting me. "Nigger. Nigger." And swearing.'

Still no mention of the shoeprint, though.

'We have forensic evidence that suggests someone wearing shoes like yours kicked the victim. Can you explain that to me?'

For a moment he looked terrified. 'No, no. I did not do this.'

Jade waited, letting him sweat it. His face cleared, his hands flew apart. 'When he pulled me, first pulled me, he pulled me over her.' He gestured with his hands. 'That must be it.'

'When he pulled you, you stepped on her, that right?' Jade said.

'Yes,' he said.

'Do you know which part of her body you stepped on?'

'I think . . .' He hesitated, pressed his index finger between his eyebrows. 'I think, near the middle, maybe her leg or her hip.'

Near enough.

'Anything else you remember?'

'They'd been drinking. I could smell it.'

'Yes.'

'They laughed. When they ran off, they were cheering, shouting.' He looked pained.

'How tall were they?'

'Man A was taller than me. I am one hundred and sixty-eight centimetres so he is one hundred and seventy-three, I think. And Man B is taller. Six, seven centimetres, more maybe.'

'Did you see which direction they went in?'

'They went right.'

'Away from Deansgate?'

'Yes.'

'We're going to get your statement written up and I'll use a scale plan to mark exactly where you were. I'd like you to work with a police artist to create photo-fits of the men.'

'Do you have a pencil?' he said. 'Some paper?'

So you can stab me in the eye and make a bid to escape? She stared at him. He met her gaze, gave a half-smile, the red spider in his eye shifting.

Curiosity won. Jade turned to DC Thwaite taking notes, who shrugged. 'Only a pen.'

'Pen is OK,' Bishaar said.

He took it in his left hand and effortlessly he sketched an oval, divided it into sections, drew in features, eyes, mouth. He was like those portrait artists on Market Street. He added short hair, largish ears, a smattering of freckles, thick eyebrows.

'This is Man B?' Jade checked.

'But the nose isn't right. With a pencil it's better.'

'You an artist, then?' Jade said.

'Illustrator. Back home, graphic designer. Once,' he said, regret and bitterness in that last word.

And he'd be going back. Jade didn't know the ins and outs of his situation but she reckoned there'd be no warm welcome for him on his return to Somalia, no flags and fatted calves.

'Man A, he's not so clear,' Bishaar said. 'Most of the time he was away from me.'

'Have a go anyway, with our photo-fit artist,' Jade said.

She ended the recording and was at the door before she remembered. And hesitated – it wasn't like he'd come in of his own free will. She'd had to track him down, drag him here. Still, for the sketch alone it was worth playing nice. 'Thank you,' she said. 'Thank you for all your help.'

CHAPTER EIGHT

Martin

Jade came to him after the Bishaar interview. Donna was tied up in a meeting with the press office. Yesterday there'd been headlines in all the Sundays. *Trans Teen Tragic Murder* probably took the medal for the punchiest.

'I've let the boss know Bishaar's given us enough for photo-fits,' Jade said. 'The descriptions aren't far off what Louise Hill and Feroz Hassan told us.'

He listened to her summarize the witness testimony.

'It all chimes with the forensics,' she said, 'right down to where he was when he was losing blood, and how he stepped on the victim. But he says the two lads went right, away from Deansgate, so that might change the focus for the CCTV.'

Martin touched his screen, pulling up the mapping software, which showed locations flagged with key facts and times.

He used the cursor. 'OK, here's the nine-nine-nine call from Bishaar at eleven twenty, and here, at eleven thirty-five, is where Louise Hill saw them hail a cab on Deansgate.'

'Fifteen minutes,' Jade said.

'So they could have gone round the houses and joined Deansgate here or here or here.' He highlighted the possible junctions. 'We've been focusing on the junction with New Mill Street. I'll pass that on.'

Jade was almost shaking with the thrill of it. He wondered if she was like him, enjoyed the chase and the hunt, a piece of the action. He guessed she'd yet to discover that most investigations were slow, steady. Evidence came grudgingly. Some was misleading, or wasn't there for the taking, or was contradictory.

'It isn't always like this,' Martin said.

'Like what?' she said.

'Productive, making progress. You got a lucky break, finding Bishaar, a witness to the whole thing with a good eye for detail.'

'Might hit a brick wall yet, if no one IDs our photo-fit,' she said.

Where was she from? Well, where were her parents from? What did they think about her working in the police? How did the rest of her community see her? And the short hair, were they allowed to do that? The name 'Bradshaw', what was that about? Had she married out? No ring on her finger, though.

There'd been a lot of Asians at Dale's school, cliquey, stuck to themselves. Only one of them ever played in the football teams. Keener on cricket, probably. Some people said they were put off by racism in soccer. Same argument people trotted out about the police. But if the talent wasn't there, or if people couldn't cope with the real world and a bit of banter, that was their own look-out.

He glanced at Jade, hunched over her desk, working away. She probably did have the skills needed. She'd done all right so far but whether she could stick it for the long haul was another matter. He'd seen others like that, smart and ambitious but not committed to the job. Using it as a stepping-stone to a career in public service. Either that or turning round and biting the hand that fed them, crying racism at the first clash of values, the lost promotion or the poor progress report.

His phone rang. The boss.

'Martin, the photo-fits are ready and we're releasing them with a public appeal. Can you make sure everyone on the investigation is briefed, and tell the incident unit to get posters up on the van and in key locations around Deansgate.'

'Will do.' He switched to a call waiting from Dale, answered it before his voicemail cut in.

'It's Saturday, Dad – they just told me. They want me to try out on Saturday.'

Martin grinned. He felt like punching the air. 'Brilliant! I'm not sure I'll be able to get away.'

'It's cool,' Dale said, breathless. 'I just wanted to tell you.'

'Brilliant, mate. Now, don't go mad. Train today and Thursday. But you should rest tomorrow, Friday as well. Just do your stretching. Don't go mad. Right? You can do this. See you later. Good lad.'

He must have raised his voice. Jade was watching. 'Our Dale,' he said to her, still grinning. 'Trying out for the league. Footie. Been out of the running with an injury for long enough. Hoping he gets picked up.'

'Great.' She smiled, and that was it. Not her thing but he didn't let it take the edge off his buzz. He could see himself now in the VIP box, Dale man of the match. Captain maybe, one day. A natural. Like Marcus Rashford at Man United, like Beckham or Best.

Brilliant.

Steve

There were piles of cards, dozens of them. Steve told Teagan she could open them with Nanny. His father had been sent out shopping for essentials. When he'd left the house they'd heard a chorus of questions from the reporters who clustered around the drive. They put Steve in mind of a nest of chicks shrieking for food.

'What do they want?' he asked Yun Li.

'A story. Anything they can get hold of, but we'd still advise you not to speak to anyone yet.'

'Are they allowed to do that? Isn't it harassment or something?' his mother said.

'Free speech,' Teagan said.

There was a ping: a notification from Allie's Facebook page. It had become an online shrine.

Teagan dropped the envelope she was opening and turned her attention to the computer. Her face clouded and reddened. 'Oh, my God. That is so horrible. People are leaving horrible comments.' She looked at Yun. 'Can you stop them?'

'We can report them to the moderators but it could still take a day or two to be taken down.'

'Don't read any more,' Steve said.

'But—' Her face was twisted.

'Don't read any more. Turn off the notifications.'

As he said it, there was another ping. Teagan leant closer. 'They're going to do a vigil,' she said. 'A candlelit vigil for Allie. I want to go.'

'Who are?' her grandmother said.

'The LGBT Foundation. On Friday. Eleven till midnight. Can I go, Dad?'

Christ, he didn't know. Was it a good idea? He could barely remember what month it was, what year. Couldn't decide whether to eat or not, let alone something like this. 'Let's talk about it later.'

'Coffee?' Yun offered.

Steve said yes. Maybe it would help cut through the fog.

'These are lovely,' his mother said, her voice husky with tears as she set down a card. He couldn't bring himself to look at them. Not yet.

There was a clamour again outside and the sound of the door opening and closing but it was Emma who came in with Yun, not his father.

'Oh, Steve,' she said.

He rose and she came forward to him. Her embrace was hard, fierce. The perfume she wore was strong, sickly sweet – he didn't like it.

'I'm so sorry,' she said, releasing him.

'Would you like some coffee?' Yun said.

'Coffee'd be great,' Emma said. Then, to their mother, 'Where's Dad?'

'Shopping, which could be a mixed blessing. I asked him to fetch some watercress last week when he was out getting petrol and he brought salad cress.'

'What's the difference?' Teagan asked, and his mum explained.

'Cards,' Emma said.

'You can look,' Teagan said, pushing a pile over to her aunt.

'Thanks.' She picked one up but didn't open it.

The sun came out, lancing through the window, making shadow play of the leaves on the silver birch outside. Steve watched them jitter and tremble.

Yun returned with coffee, and when everyone had been served, he said, 'I've had some news from DI Bell.'

Steve put down his cup. A shiver spread across his back.

'We've been able to speak to the person who made the nine-nine-nine call and as a result of that we have drawn up descriptions of two men we want to speak to.'

His mother made a sound, a whimper in her throat.

Steve stared at his hands, then at Teagan's. They were like his, peasant's hands. Allie's had been slimmer, the fingers longer.

'These photo-fits will be publicized at a press conference in about an hour's time. We'll be asking the public to help us identify who they are.'

'That's good, isn't it?' Emma said uncertainly.

Teagan got up, left the room, her face set.

'Teagan?' Emma called.

'Leave her,' Steve said. 'I'll go in a minute.' He looked at Yun, fighting to concentrate. *Two men we want to speak to*. 'Are they the ones that did it?'

'We believe so.'

'You don't know?' Steve said.

'We believe they are,' Yun repeated. 'And if we do apprehend them we can test that suspicion against all the evidence we already have.'

Steve tried, and failed, to picture the two men. When he imagined the scene, Allie in her dress in the rain, two strangers approaching, his mind recoiled, as if he'd exposed it to a live wire. Aversion therapy. Images came into his head from *A Clockwork Orange*, of eyeballs and head restraints. Operatic violence. He felt nauseous. The coffee smelt wrong, oily or burnt.

He was a coward. His daughter had gone through the most brutal of attacks and he couldn't even bear to think about it.

They were all huddled round, quietly watching, when the pictures came on the television. Steve felt nothing. An emptiness. His eyes ranged over the images as the newsreader spoke with the right measure of solemnity, giving the facts of height, colouring, build and so on. How very young they looked to be. Swiftly an immense sadness filled him. Sadness for the waste, the loss, for his bright, beautiful girl, and for these boys, who had done such a terrible, terrible thing.

Sonia

Oliver was in bed when Sonia got back from work. He said he still felt sick, so she made herself an omelette for tea. Perhaps he had some gastric bug, *E. coli* or salmonella, though he hadn't actually thrown up. Or it could be something mechanical, couldn't it? A problem with his stomach, an ulcer, perhaps. Did teenagers get ulcers? She decided if he wasn't better by Wednesday, if two days' rest hadn't got him back to normal, she'd make him see the doctor.

Her feet ached from standing up – that was one bad thing about the laundry compared to the supermarket: you were on your feet all day. Cynthia had varicose veins like tree roots climbing up the back of her legs.

After she'd tidied round, fed the cat and cleaned its litter tray, she put her feet up while she watched *The Good Wife*, enjoying the way the central character navigated all the demands on her time, lusting after her clothes and make-up, her cool assurance, her strength.

When the recording finished she switched over to the news. They were talking about the plans for Muhammad Ali's funeral on Friday, which was to be screened worldwide. What a character. She watched the piece and, in the scrolling headlines below, she read that police in Manchester had released photo-fits of two men they wanted to speak to in connection with the murder of eighteen-year-old Allie Kennaway. That was a horrible business. Even worse that there was more than one suspect. It tormented her, the idea of a group picking on one person. It made her think of those nature documentaries, lions in a pack hunting prey and singling out the smallest and the weakest.

There had been murders like that over the years that stuck in her head and she wished they wouldn't. Suzanne Capper, only sixteen, two years younger than Sonia at the time, was held captive and tortured, then doused in petrol and set on fire by a group of neighbours. Then, of course, there was Stephen Lawrence. And, more recently, a girl called Sophie Lancaster and her boyfriend had been beaten up in a park by a gang of teenagers. Sophie had died of her injuries. The couple were targeted because they were Goths.

As Sonia reached for her nail file, the newsreader moved on to talk about Allie Kennaway and two pictures filled the screen. Sonia felt the blood drain from her face. Her hand spasmed and she dropped the nail file. Oliver. The boy on the right was Oliver. She choked. Her vision swam. Don't be daft, she told herself. Don't be so stupid. Oliver would never . . . not in a million . . . Unable to look away, to silence the broadcaster or turn off the set, her eyes devoured the image. His face, his ears and mouth, his freckles and thick eyebrows. *No. God, no.* There had to be some mistake, a cock-up – there had to be. Maybe Oliver had been seen near to where it had happened and got muddled up in someone's mind.

He would never— Not her baby boy.

He'd washed his clothes. His shoes too.

Oh, Jesus.

Her heart was going to explode. She fumbled with the remote. Turned off the television.

Outside she lit a cigarette.

It was still light, just, the sky glowing violet over to the west. She drew in smoke as deeply as she could, thoughts piercing her like knives. The cat winding round her ankles.

He came home early. Been avoiding me. His shoes. Pretending to be ill. Never used the washing-machine before.

She smoked a second cigarette, her tongue dry, mouth sour.

She must be mad even to think it.

The cat mewed. 'I've fed you,' she muttered.

He was hiding.

But he wouldn't. Why would he do such a thing? How could he? He wasn't crazy – he wasn't violent. *This is insane.* She gripped her hair, pulled at it until her scalp stung.

She had to talk to him. She'd recognized him – so others would before long.

She wanted to ring Rose, to talk it through with her, but she knew she couldn't. She couldn't share this with anyone. It was too dangerous. Too shameful. It was a mistake anyway. It could not be true. So she must find out what the real story was and then she would work out what to do.

There was a burst of shouting from next-door-but-one.

'You're mad,' she said to herself.

She could not be thinking of her lad as a murderer. The word was obscene. They must sort it, get it cleared up. Figure out the mix-up.

She went upstairs, her throat thick. Her whole body felt as though something alien was in her veins, not blood but something chemical, toxic and thin.

'Oliver?' She banged on his door. 'I want to talk to you.'

'I'm asleep.'

She walked in. The room was dimly lit by the glow from his screen. He'd paused the game, two cars on a flyover, statistics at the side of the image.

She snapped on the light. 'Turn that off,' she said. 'Now. And come downstairs.'

She didn't wait for refusal or delaying tactics but quickly went back down.

There were sounds of him getting out of bed, going into the bathroom, then plodding downstairs.

'What?' He hovered in the living-room doorway in his oversized T-shirt and boxers.

'Sit down.'

He fell into the armchair, legs apart, hands loose on the chair arms. A sullen look on his face.

She felt a lurch of uncertainty. *This is stupid.* She should just send him back to bed. Forget all about it.

'Friday night,' she said. 'Tell me what happened.'

Something passed through his eyes, gone so quickly she wondered if she'd imagined it.

'What d'you mean? I went out.'

'Where?'

'To town.'

'Where in town?'

'To eat. A Cuban place on Peter Street.'

Each reply accompanied by a jerk of the shoulders up and down.

'Then where?'

'I told you, a bar nearby.'

'What bar?' Sonia said.

'I don't know,' he said. 'The Cavalier or something.'

'And after there?'

He threw his head back, spoke to the ceiling. 'Then came home.'

'Tell me the truth, Oliver.'

'That is the truth.' Offended, sitting up straight.

'Who were you with?'

'Seggie, Foz, some others.'

'Real names,' she said.

He snorted. 'Why?' Eyes fixed on her.

'You've heard of Allie Kennaway?'

He shrugged. His gaze fell from hers.

'She was killed on Friday night near Deansgate. It's been all over the news.'

'So?' he said. A flush stained his neck, the tips of his ears. She bit her tongue to stop herself crying out.

'Did you see her?'

'No,' he sneered.

'Tell the truth.'

'I am.'

'Tell me the truth,' she said.

'I said I am.' He stood up. 'This is mental.'

'Sit down,' she shouted.

He did so. His face like thunder.

'Why did you wash your clothes?'

'I stood in a puddle – I told you.'

'Your top,' Sonia said.

'I fell in it.'

'Don't lie to me.'

'I'm not. We were messing about – we were on the beer. I fell over.'

'Look.' She swiped at her phone. Pulled up the photo-fits from the news site. Zoomed into the image of Oliver. Got up and moved closer. Turned it to show him. 'Look at that.'

He stopped dead still. She saw the colour climb into his face again. He raised a hand, rubbed it over his hair. 'What's that?' His voice faltered.

'That's you. That's a photo-fit of you,' she said. 'The police want to talk to you about the murder.' She'd said the word aloud and it hung in the air between them.

'That's not me,' he said. 'That's nothing like me.'

'Stop lying! Oliver, whatever happened we need to talk about it, sort it out. You need to tell—'

'It's not me. You're fucking mental. You're accusing me of killing someone?'

'If it's not you,' she tried to speak calmly, 'then we need to go to the police and explain that someone's made a mistake.'

'No way.'

'Oliver.'

'That's not me.' He raised his voice. He jabbed a finger at her. 'I haven't done anything and I'm not going to speak to the fucking police or anyone else.' He stood up.

'Oliver, listen—'

'No! Just fuck off. You mad bitch.' He ran upstairs, leaving her shuddering.

Seconds later she heard him come down. The house rattled as he slammed the door. The phone was still in her hand, the picture of her son fading from the screen.

CHAPTER NINE

Donna

The morning's discussion centred around the photo-fits and responses to them. 'People are already coming forward,' Donna told them all. 'No names as yet, but we've a sighting, which sounds spot-on, from a club on Water Street at the bottom of New Mill Street.'

'Fredo's?' said Martin. 'I've seen the place.'

'That's it. The doorman there claims he has CCTV. You'll take that?'

Martin nodded.

'We've also heard from a woman who says she was harassed by men fitting these descriptions at the Cavalier bar on Peter Street. Jade, you'll follow up?'

'Yes, boss. Maybe the reason we're not getting any names is because people are protecting them.'

Donna considered the likelihood. 'Usually that happens when the perpetrators are involved in gang activity or are from families with connections to organized crime. I think we're looking at a different situation. Nothing to suggest it's payback or even a case of mistaken identity. From the testimony so far, we know these men held Allie Kennaway in Swing Gate Fold. Man A was grabbing at her and verbally abusing her. One interpretation of Bishaar's evidence is that the sexual harassment and abuse becomes more aggressive and violent once Man A grabs her crotch.'

'He realizes it's a man,' Martin said.

And when had Allie realized she was in real danger? The thought flashed in Donna's head and she pushed it away. She couldn't afford to dwell on that. It was indulgent and did nothing to advance their efforts. She said, 'We can't know whether the men intended rape when they seized Allie Kennaway, held her against her will, assaulted and abused her, but it would appear the discovery of Allie's biological sex, of her transgender identity, was the trigger for the murder. And that, as you're all aware, makes this a hate crime.'

Jade was silent, giving a sideways look, sceptical.

'It's not impossible someone is shielding these suspects,' Donna explained. 'All I'm saying is, I don't think we're dealing with members of a criminal fraternity where we might expect that behaviour as a matter of course.'

'Boss?' One of the incident-room receivers who'd been working the phones raised her hand, so Donna could see who'd spoken.

'Rhiannon?'

'We're getting some abusive calls saying Allie Kennaway deserved everything she got. Spouting crap.' *Oh, God.* It pained her to think of the vile things they'd be saying. 'Do you want us to do any more than log them?'

'Not for now.' They didn't have the resources to start looking into every vicious little troll that came crawling out from under its rock.

'One last item,' Donna said. 'There will be a vigil for Allie Kennaway on Friday instigated by the LGBT Foundation and with the active support of our Federation's Lesbian and Gay Staff Affiliation. You are all at liberty to attend if you so wish. Let's get to work. Let's find out who these two are. Thank you.'

Jade

Jade arranged to meet the witness at her home.

'I don't start work till twelve, so as long as I leave by quarter past eleven, I'll be fine,' the woman said.

Home was a room in a terraced house in Fallowfield. Most of the street was student accommodation and every other front garden bristled with To Let signs. Several houses were getting the annual make-over, with the year's students gone for the long summer break. The next batch would find freshly painted wood-chip wallpaper and new bottom-of-the-range mattresses on patched-up divan bases. Within weeks of occupation the mould would grow back and the condensation start to rot any fabric or paper.

Jade had lived in a place like that for a few months.

Candida Gallego – 'I go by Candy' – had a slight Spanish accent and spoke perfect English. She offered Jade coffee, which Jade refused. She never drank in other people's houses: who knew what it might taste like, if the cups were clean, the milk fresh? And you only needed one knobhead playing God with Rohypnol or rat poison to ruin everything.

'I saw those guys in town, in the Cavalier,' Candy said. 'They were horrible. Touching us, not taking no for an answer.'

'Did you complain to anyone?' Jade said.

Candy shook her head. 'The place was packed. It was crazy.' She wore a row of coloured bands on her wrist, the sort you got from festivals and charity events, which she pulled and turned as she spoke. Jade wondered if she wore them to work, if she took them off to sleep. Jade couldn't bear anything on her wrist, a watch or jewellery. Hated the sensation. The associations . . .

'We were going on somewhere anyway. The one with the dark hair, he followed us through the bar on our way out. He was shouting, you know? "Prick teaser, you need a good shag. Fucking lesbians."' She stretched one of the bracelets. 'He was nasty, very drunk. But there are bouncers on the door so he stopped when we got near there and we went out.'

'What about the other one?' Jade touched the image of the man with the short red hair.

'He said a few things. He put his arm around my friend's neck. She pushed him off. It was him I recognized first. The other picture, the dark-haired guy – it's not quite right.'

Bishaar had said he'd seen little of Man A's face.

'If you had to describe him what would you change?' Jade said.

'I think the mouth is too small, and the eyes are wrong, but he was nice-looking. Shitty man but nice-looking.'

'OK. What time did you leave the bar?' Jade said.

'Quarter to eleven,' Candy said.

'And how long were they bothering you?'

'Five minutes. Long enough.'

'And the touching?' Jade said.

'He grabbed my breast. Then between my legs. Prick.' She curled her lip.

'You could report it,' Jade said. 'That's sexual assault.'

Candy made a *pfft* sound.

'There are places you can get support.'

'I'm OK. Just idiots,' Candy said. 'It happens a lot.'

Well, it fucking shouldn't. Why do we let the dickheads get away with it?

Candy said, 'But if they did this, the murder, they should go to jail for ever.'

'Yeah,' Jade agreed. 'Can you remember anything else about them, anything they said?'

'The dark-haired guy, he said to the other one that my friend needed a good slap,' she said, letting go of the bracelets.

'Yes?'

'Yes. When my friend pushed him away.'

'Pushed this man?' Jade pointed to Man B.

'Yes. The man perving on me said, "Watch her, she needs a slap."' She grimaced, turning the bracelet again.

'Anything else? Their clothes?'

'Man A had a shirt on, a lemon colour. That's it.'

Same as Bishaar had described. 'Was the shirt clean?' Jade said. 'Any stains?'

'No, it looked clean.'

Jade thanked her. Thoughts already racing ahead. They knew now where the men had been before the attack and where they were afterwards. The net was closing, minute by minute. Soon they'd have names, surely. Even if someone was shielding them, there'd be loads of people seeing the faces on the news, in the papers. Some good citizen would come forward. They had to.

Candy's account had reinforced what they'd already learnt but all Jade felt was impatience. She wanted the scumbags in custody now, wanted to be confronting them in the interview room, making them sweat, piling the pressure on, drowning them in the evidence until they caved and spilt their guts. She couldn't wait.

Martin

Martin passed the incident van on his way down New Mill Street. Posters of the two photo-fits plastered the sides and more were hung on the boarded-up buildings in the area.

At the T-junction he turned left into Water Street and parked in front of Fredo's.

The man who answered the door matched Martin for weight and height but he was younger, a black guy. His close-cut hair had a pattern shaved into it. He wore a tracksuit and blinding fluorescent orange trainers. His nose had been broken at least once, judging by the way it bent to one side.

'Mr Clements?'

'That's me.'

'DS Harris. You rang the investigation hotline.'

'Come in.'

The club was lit by fluorescents and reeked of stale alcohol. A cleaner was wiping down banquette seats with some spray, yellow gloves up to her elbows. The place was all mirrored columns and fake landscapes on the walls, painted deserts, mountain scenes, rocky coves. Martin couldn't work out what the style was meant to be. It looked like reject backdrops from *Game of Thrones* and *Doctor Who* mashed together.

'This way.' Clements took him round the side of the bar and through a door marked private into a small room.

'You were on the door on Friday?' Martin said.

'That's right.'

'On your own?'

'Me and Zandra. She's away for the week, Ibiza. I knew them as soon as that picture came on the telly. Man, clear as day.'

Martin felt hope growing. With live footage of the men they'd be so much closer to clinching an identification.

Clements switched on a video-player. 'Still analogue,' he said. 'I keep telling the boss we should go digital, better resolution, but her angle is she'd rather spend the money on good door staff and stop trouble before it starts.'

Martin had imagined the boss was a man. He wondered briefly how a woman had ended up running a club like this and whether she'd chosen the décor. 'How come you recognized these two?' he asked.

'Turned them away,' Clements said.

'Dress code?' They knew Man B had had a short-sleeved polo shirt on, and most clubs had a strict no-sportswear policy, assuming that putting the clientele in shirts, ties and proper shoes would improve their behaviour.

'No, we're relaxed about that, as long as they're clean and presentable. This pair were pissed, coked up, too, I reckon. Started with the language as soon as I asked a couple of questions.'

'You see any ID?'

'No. I didn't care how old they were, they were trouble. You let someone like that in, it ruins the night for the rest of the customers.' He was fast-forwarding and reversing to get to the right point on the tape. 'Here we go.'

A grainy image filled the screen.

Martin's mouth went dry. A buzzing filled his ears. He pressed his hand against the edge of the desk to steady himself as he watched the film, saw the attitude of the two men, their obscene gestures, faces contorted, obviously spitting abuse.

'I'm going to take this with me,' Martin said, as the footage ended with the two suspects moving out of frame.

'No worries,' Clements said.

Martin held his breath walking back through the dance hall, saliva clagging his mouth. The smell of spilt beer was intolerable.

A hundred yards down the road he pulled the car in and scrambled out, barely reaching the gutter as the vomit, hot and bitter, forced its way out of his mouth and nose.

He drove straight home, the video on the seat beside him, his rage burning, growing, stifling the fear biting at his throat, the confusion and bewilderment that gripped his bowels. The rage was blooming and, with it, the need to lash out, to hit and punch and kick and crush and destroy someone.

CHAPTER TEN

Steve

Steve was making toast. The others had gone, only him and Teagan left in the house. The freezer was stuffed full of stews and casseroles but neither of them fancied a full meal. He fetched the peanut butter and jam. At the sound of the fridge opening Dix clambered out of his bed and limped across to Steve.

'You stiff, boy?'

The dog whined.

Steve checked the time, then decided it didn't really matter: if Dix wanted to eat he could. He must have picked up on the atmosphere, the fact his humans were sad. That one of them was missing. Steve fed the dog and washed out the can, then dried his hands.

Turning back to the counter he saw the planner stuck to the side of the fridge. Allie's exams. Today was English literature. He had a vision of the hall at college, serried ranks of desks and one empty space, a blank exam paper. He felt dizzy, and leant his forehead against the wall cupboard. She'd miss them all, English literature, media studies, Spanish and sociology.

Loughborough University – he'd have to let them know. Was there a procedure, an easy way of telling the university she would not be getting her 240 points, not be taking up her place to study Communications and Media or moving into halls? And what about student finance? Christ, doing applications for that had been a marathon. The company kept writing to Steve asking for proof of his income. Proof he had already sent. Getting through on the phone was a mammoth achievement, getting any sense when you did a question of luck.

Would Yun Li know about any of this?

Bets and Helena would be in there now, sweating over *Wuthering Heights* and Toni Morrison. Poor kids. Perhaps they'd be able to delay the exam, given the trauma they'd suffered. They'd been such good friends to Allie, right from the start of high school. And when Allie had been targeted by bullies in year nine it had been Bets and Helena, with Allie's agreement, who'd reported it to the head of year.

He remembered Allie crying at the tea-table when Sarah asked her what was wrong. It had all come out then, the deliberate shoving and pushing in the corridors, the nasty comments. The graffiti in the toilets. Allie was only dressing as a girl some of the time then and she used the toilets appropriate to what she was wearing.

The text messages and the comments on Facebook were the worst.

U shd kill urself freak.

Shemale slag.

Girls have cunts, boys have dicks, sicko.

Ur so fake.

Ladyboy. Hope you get AIDS and die.

Tranny trash, slit your wrists.

Queer prick.

Ugly fucker.

Cock girl.

You can't ever be a real woman with a freak face like that. LOL.

The head of year had implemented the school bullying policy, and students had organized a special assembly on LGBT rights. Steve had insisted Allie change her phone number and they altered her Facebook account to the most private settings.

Teagan had not heard all of it, just enough to get upset on Allie's behalf. 'They're stupid idiots with no brains,' she'd told her sister. 'They should be expelled and locked in prison for ten years.'

'I think that's a bit extreme,' Sarah had said.

Steve recalled how impotent he'd felt. How his impulse had been to lash out and hurt those who were hurting his child.

That was another bloody statistic: trans people experienced even more transphobic attacks than gay or lesbian people experienced homophobic attacks.

Sarah had done her best to explain it to Teagan, and Allie. How people who were threatened or disgusted by different sexuality or gender identity were probably insecure themselves. Hating people who were different, abusing them, was a way of proving their own masculinity or femininity, their heterosexuality.

'That's bonkers,' Teagan had said.

Sarah had laughed. 'You're right there.'

What had they been thinking, the men who had killed her? He tested the words. The men who had killed her. Where had it come from, that hatred? Had they known she was a trans woman? Had they followed her, chased her, even? The pictures in his head were revolting, appalling, but he couldn't stop them unfolding. Did they not have sisters, or girlfriends, or mothers they cared for? Could they not see that Allie was just another girl, really, finding her way?

Had she said anything? Had she spoken to them? Had she sensed they were hostile and tried to appease them, or challenge them, or plead with them?

'Dad!' He was jerked back to reality by Teagan running in. There was an acrid smell in the air and he began to cough. 'Dad! The toast!'

Sonia

Sonia went to fetch clean suits for a customer and the snap of static plastered the thin protective bags to her arms. She was alive with static today, all the hairs on her body standing to attention. And it felt like that was all there was in her head, in her guts, the hiss and sizzle of electricity.

She dealt with payment and returned to ironing, on automatic pilot as she pressed cuffs and shoulders, pleats and hems.

Oliver hadn't come home at all last night. It wasn't the first time he'd stayed out without warning her but it was the first time he'd done it in the wake of such a massive falling-out.

Her texts and calls had gone unanswered. She'd no idea where he'd slept. If he'd slept. With one of those new mates, on a park bench or in a doorway?

She folded pillow slips and stacked them with matching sheets, bound the lot together in polythene, again the static biting at her fingers.

Across the road she saw the paper delivery van stop. The driver jumped out and took a bundle into the newsagent's. The lunchtime edition. He came out and changed the poster on the sandwich board. She could read it from here. *Allie Kennaway Murder, Suspect Photos.*

Jesus.

His picture would be on the front page. Of course it would. Cynthia was off this afternoon at the dentist, then going for her mammogram. But how long before she or Rose or someone else Sonia knew said to her, 'Have you seen that picture?' And what would she say then?

She put the sheets on the shelves, ready for collection, transferred washing into one of the dryers and set it for an hour. Another dryer had finished and she pulled out the load, the chemical smell of the conditioner harsh in her throat, her hands smarting with the heat. The radio was on, set to Radio 2, but the chatter, even the music, grated on her nerves, so she switched it off.

In the small backyard she had another cigarette, propping the door open with a tub of dry-cleaning fluid so she could hear if any customers came into the shop. She was smoking too much. Her head was pounding, a shard of pain stabbing through her left eye, and she knew the fags made it worse but she was desperate.

Where are you?

She checked her phone again, just in case.

Back at the ironing station she began the next batch.

What if he'd done something stupid? Thrown himself into the Irwell or necked a load of tablets?

She worried away at the situation all afternoon, but however many times she reran the conversation with Oliver, his flat denials and his outrage, she could not bring herself to believe him. Instead she clung to the hope that whatever he had done wasn't quite as bleak, as brutal, as she feared. Perhaps he'd witnessed the attack. Perhaps he was just covering up for someone. He'd never been a leader, Oliver. Even as a little boy he'd been a follower. Finding someone he thought was better in some way, stronger, cleverer, funnier, and treading in their footsteps. There'd been scraps at school when he'd gone along with some daft plan because he wanted to belong, to be part of the gang.

But he wasn't malicious, Sonia thought, as she cashed up and put the takings into the safe. He never got any pleasure out of hurting people, not in itself. Did he?

It was raining heavily as she walked home, thunder growling overhead and lightning flickering near to Old Trafford. Perhaps the storm breaking would finally ease the tension in her head.

The house was quiet, apart from the spatter of rain on the windowpanes. She called, and went up to his room to look for him. She was on her own, yet she had the sense he had been back. He usually left a trail of evidence, like a dog marking territory – cups and plates, clothes on the floor, trainers dropped in the hall, the cable from charging his phone. But there was none of that. Was it just her wishful thinking?

She went into the back room to look for the cat and saw straight away that Oliver's good shoes had gone, along with the clothes he'd washed. All of them, gone.

Donna

Donna paused in her work to text Kirsten, who had a piano exam that afternoon. Jim would take her and bring her back. Since his turn on Sunday night he'd insisted he felt well. Nevertheless Donna had put aspirin on the shopping list, and would continue to nag him to see the GP. Recalling the colour of his face and the clammy feel of his skin, she knew it hadn't been indigestion.

'It's called preventive health care,' she had argued, the previous evening. 'A radical new idea. Amazing results. You wouldn't hesitate if it was one of the kids. Or if it was me.'

He never got to justify his reluctance then because the twins burst in, high on winning their interschool basketball competition.

She couldn't remember when Jim had last seen the doctor. He didn't seem to understand her concern wasn't just for him but for all of them. *I need you. The kids need you. If you have a heart attack or stroke we're all affected.*

'You're being melodramatic,' was what he'd say.

I'm being realistic, I'm being pragmatic, and so should you be.

Jade knocked at her office door.

'Come in,' Donna said.

'Confirmed sighting,' Jade said. 'In the Cavalier at ten forty. The witness, Candy Gallego, and her friend left five minutes later. The men were still there. She says the picture of Man A isn't accurate.'

'OK,' Donna said. 'Can she suggest what needs changing?' She wouldn't necessarily redo the photo-fit yet: it made it look like they were clutching at straws, too scattergun. *This one? No? How about this one, then?*

Jade shook her head. 'Said he was good-looking and that the mouth's too small, the eyes aren't right. But what was interesting was that the men were being abusive, harassing her and her mate.' Jade's eyes glittered. It gave her an impish quality, particularly with the choppy fringe and the dimple that accompanied her quick smile.

Puck, Donna thought. A Mancunian Puck. 'That gives us another location,' she said.

'I can see if there's any CCTV at the Cavalier,' Jade said.

'Good. Hang on a minute.' Donna raised her hand to stop her leaving. She brought up their timeline on the computer.

'Come,' Donna said, gesturing Jade round to her side of the desk. The mounting excitement of finding another part of the picture made her feel expansive. 'So, if we put our suspects here at ten forty-five . . .' she looked to Jade to double-check and Jade gave a nod '. . . our next known sighting is at Swing Gate Fold at eleven twenty. So what were they doing in between? That gives us thirty-five minutes.'

'They might have stayed at the Cavalier, drinking. Gone to Swing Gate Fold from there. What about the club on Water Street?' Jade asked.

'I'll see what DS Harris has got.' Donna rang Martin.

'Boss?'

'How'd you get on at Fredo's?'

'A waste of time,' Martin said. 'The bloke needs to get himself to Specsavers. Wants his eyes examining. Or his head. Two chancers he turned away on the door. One was a black guy and the other looked nothing like either of our photo-fits. Didn't tally with any descriptions.'

Donna felt a wash of disappointment.

'Any news your end?' Martin said.

'We've a confirmed sighting of the suspects acting obnoxious before the attack.' She relayed the facts. 'So we might have them on film at the Cavalier, be able to get a proper look at them and see when they left. Jade is going to call down.'

'I can do that,' Martin said. 'I'm not far from there now.'

'Are you sure?'

'Yes, no problem.'

'Great,' Donna said. 'See how you get on and we can catch up in the morning.'

'Thanks, boss.'

Donna told Jade Fredo's was a dead end and Martin would take the Cavalier. A shadow darkened Jade's expression and her mouth tightened. Donna saw she was resentful because someone else had got the ball. Just when Donna thought Jade was beginning to get the message. 'You have a problem with that?' Donna said.

'No, boss,' Jade said, barely this side of rude. The shine gone from her eyes. Face blank.

'Good.'

Jade was already moving to the door.

'Teamwork, Jade.'

'Yes, boss.'

She was erratic, switched the . . . What was it? Not charm as such but energy. Switched the energy on and off like a teenager or a toddler and that wasn't a good MO for a detective. It didn't help the work. Did she realize her career, her progress could be hampered if she didn't develop a better attitude? She must. You had to have some smarts to get into the police service, these days. Competition was fierce. Jade had potential in the Major Incident Team but only if her outlook improved. Only if she embraced working as a team. And if she didn't, Donna would make no bones about recommending Jade return to uniformed operations.

Martin

Martin sat in the car at the edge of the parking area near Barton Moss. Only one other vehicle there: a man walking two lurchers, who had parked up half an hour ago.

Occasionally Martin saw a jogger lope past, through the gap in the trees, or a cyclist. People not put off by the wet weather or the encroaching dark. Chasing fitness or glory. Like Dale, on his run.

I'll pick you up at the car park, Martin had texted him. And now he waited.

He watched the dog-walker return, his form and that of the sway-back dogs distorted by the rain streaming down the windscreen.

Martin's mind was on a loop, running and rerunning the images from the CCTV, the salient facts of the investigation. Round and round they came, punctuated by the hammer blow of the question stuck in his head. *Why? Why? Why?*

He saw movement, a pale shape by the path, then Dale emerged and gave a wave before pausing, bent over breathless. After a moment he walked over to the old shelter. A bus stop once, a concrete bunker, open-fronted, and began his warm-down. Leg stretches, knee bends.

Martin knew the routine by heart.

Three more days to the trials. If Dale didn't get selected this time, his chance to shine would probably be gone. He'd maybe get by playing in the local league, going into coaching or fitness training or sportswear sales. *Why risk all that? Why?*

Exercises done, Dale ran towards the car and Martin got out, moved round to intercept him.

'Hi, Dad.' Dale went to open the passenger door but Martin was on him, hand on his throat, face inches away.

'What the fuck have you done?'

The smile fell. Dale blinked rapidly. His skin was hot from running, damp with sweat and rain.

He began to speak. 'I don't know—'

Martin let go of his neck and grabbed his chin. 'Don't say another word. *I know!*' he roared. '*I know!* You stupid fucker.'

Dale blanched.

Martin wanted to belt him, thump him black and blue, make him weep. Instead he shoved him away, almost knocking him down. 'Get in the car,' he said. The anger pumping his heart too fast. 'Get in now.'

Dale obeyed.

Martin stood in the rain, breathing heavily until he trusted himself to behave with restraint. Then he joined Dale.

Dale didn't look at him: he was turned away. Martin could hear him swallow, saw small tremors travel across his skin, chill setting in on top of the shock.

'Friday night,' Martin said. 'What happened?'

'Dad, I swear—'

'No!' Martin slammed his fist on the dashboard. He spoke quietly, staring ahead at the trees, black in the rain: 'You and your mate were at the Cavalier. We have a witness. You were giving her grief apparently. You went from there to Fredo's on Water Street. You were caught on camera, the pair of you, drunk and drugged up. You were barred. Next news you're on Swing Gate Fold where an eyewitness saw the whole fucking thing. We've evidence from the scene there, shedloads of it. Including your DNA. You spat on him, you daft twat. You spat on him after kicking him to death. Your shoes left marks on the body. A mark like that is as good as a fingerprint. You hailed a cab on Deansgate. We traced the driver. The victim's blood is in his car. You are that close to being arrested and charged with murder.' Martin held his finger and thumb a fraction apart. 'You'll get a minimum of fifteen years. Minimum. For a hate crime, that increases. You could be doing thirty years. No football. No fucking future. Thirty years sucking some old guy's cock or taking it up the arse. For what?'

Acid in his throat, the burning in his gut.

Dale was sniffing hard, wiping his nose on his sleeve. Martin looked back at the dark, saw white movement in the trees, a blurred face staring his way. A barn owl.

'So tell me. Tell me all of it,' Martin said.

Silence, apart from the whisper of rain on the roof of the car.

'Tell me.'

'We – we were – we were hammered,' Dale said, stammering. 'It was just a bit of fun. We had a . . . We hadn't got anywhere earlier . . . Then we were sacked off trying to get into the club. We were having a laugh that's all, just messing and . . .' His voice trailed away.

'All of it,' Martin said.

The owl swivelled its head, the big moon face ridiculous.

'We were – we were just messing. I thought it was a girl. We were just messing. I grabbed him . . .' He made a retching sound in his throat. 'Fucking tranny. They shouldn't go around like that, tricking people. He needed to be taught a lesson, that's all. I never meant anything bad to happen. Just teach him a lesson. Fucking pervert.'

Martin thought of the photographs, of the list of injuries from the post-mortem, of Dale's fitness and his strength. 'And your mate?'

'He did it too.'

'Did he grab her?' Martin said.

'No.'

'You hit the African?'

'We never saw him there. Then he was coming at us. It was self-defence.'

Martin almost laughed. Dale hadn't got a fucking clue. 'Your mate, what's his name?'

'Oliver. Oliver Poole.'

'Can you trust him?'

Dale hesitated, and Martin's guts twisted.

'I think so,' Dale said at last, shivering.

Not good enough.

'Call him,' Martin said.

'Are you going to arrest us?' Dale said.

'Just call him,' Martin said.

'Dad, please—'

Martin swung round to face him and Dale reared back, banging his head against the passenger window. The cowardly move inflamed Martin's temper but he didn't touch Dale. He watched as his son began to cry, snot bubbling from his nose, his lips swelling, sobbing and begging, 'It was a mistake. He shouldn't have tried to con us like that. Making us look like queers. Fucking freak. It was a mistake. Please, Dad, please.'

Martin said nothing until the blubbering had stopped. Then he spoke, his bowels on fire. 'From now on you do exactly what I say. No questions, no excuses. You obey me. You don't open your mouth, you don't make a move, you don't take a piss unless I tell you to. Do you understand?'

Dale nodded, another spasm shaking his frame.

'It's not just your life on the line any more, you stupid little tosser.' Martin raised a finger. 'Not a word to your mother, or to anyone else. Nothing. You don't blink unless I've told you to. Now call Oliver and arrange to meet him. Not at his house. And don't tell him I'm with you.'

Martin let his head fall back onto the headrest. He listened to Dale talk, and watched the owl rise from cover and take off on large pale wings, a ghost in the night.

Jade

Jade kicked her front door shut with more force than necessary, bolted and locked it.

Irritation at the boss ran under her skin, like a virus. It was as if the DI didn't trust her. Jade had brought her the witness from the Cavalier but it was DS Harris who got to follow up on their CCTV.

Was it favouritism? Probably. The pair were obviously old pals. Maybe they hadn't started out together – DS Harris had a few years on DI Bell – but they'd clearly worked plenty of cases side by side.

Jade opened the freezer and stared at the snowscape inside, corners of ready-meal boxes sticking out here and there, like rocks in a glacier.

She hated ready meals but she hated cooking even more. And the new unpredictability of her working hours meant there was no way she was going to start peeling and chopping and boiling stuff when she did get home.

Was she hungry anyway? She usually was but now she felt sick every time she thought about work. She was supposed to eat little and often, regular meals. If she didn't, things would only get worse.

She tugged at one of the cartons, the ice crystals that smothered it squeaking in response. Chicken Chow Mein. She shook her head and wrestled with the carton beneath, until it came free, and brushed off the frost. Macaroni Cheese. That'd do.

And she'd brought them Bishaar, an eyewitness. A fucking *eyewitness*. That was the biggest breakthrough they'd had. His testimony was platinum. With that and the DNA, they'd have a case as soon as they'd ID'd the suspects.

Jade slipped the food container from the cardboard sleeve and stabbed the plastic film several times with the fork, then stuck it in the microwave.

It was like the boss had her on a lead, one of those extending ones: she'd let Jade run so far, then yank her to a halt and reel her in.

Should she say something? The thought made her neck prickle. She tried to frame the words. *Why couldn't I do the Cavalier visit?*

Because I sent Martin.

She should have said something at the time, something that sounded positive, not like she was moaning. *Boss, I'd like to follow through on the Cavalier line.*

Teamwork, Jade. She trotted that out whenever Jade did something she didn't like. Or said something she didn't like.

I know what teamwork means, but where's the continuity in letting DS Harris take over the Cavalier when I spoke to Candy, and I know what we've got so far?

The microwave pinged and Jade pulled out the container, steam scalding her fingers. She peeled back the film and stirred the contents.

Mina had offered to cook for her, as soon as they'd got acquainted. 'I always make too much . . . You're skin and bone . . . Can you eat pork? . . . Or I could make vegetarian?' Trying to guess if Jade was a good Muslim or a Hindu, maybe. Jade had turned her down: she didn't need someone to feed her up or cluck over her. All that fuss.

Nowadays, every time Jade went into Mina's she'd be force-fed pastries or a plate of biscuits. Polish hospitality. It was an Irish thing, too, wasn't it? Not that Jade actually knew anything of being Irish, but in *Father Ted* the housekeeper was always desperate to make tea, to serve the priests. Perhaps it was a countryside thing. A human thing? Pain in the arse, whatever it was.

The food was bland, synthetic-tasting, but she ate it as quickly as she could and had almost finished when there was a thudding on the adjoining wall from Bert's flat.

Not again. She sighed and rubbed her head, took her tablets with a gulp of water from the tap and headed next door.

Steve

Steve could tell there was something wrong even before Yun Li spoke. He saw it in the expression on the man's face, mouth tight, eyes cast slightly away and down, in the set of his shoulders as he took a breath, in the way he steepled his fingers.

'What is it?' Steve thought of the photo-fits. The two young men. Had the police found them? His knees went weak so he pulled out one of the kitchen chairs and sat down.

Yun joined him. 'There's been an article in one of the tabloids. About Allie.'

Steve took a moment to comprehend that this wasn't what he had imagined and experienced a sensation almost of relief. He blinked to clear his vision. 'What does it say?'

'They've interviewed Emma,' Yun Li said.

'What?'

The police officer gave a small shake of his head.

'But she knew we weren't talking to the—' Steve stopped. Did she? Had anyone made that clear to her? The prospect she might somehow have jeopardized the efforts of the police hit him. After all, that was the reason they'd been given in the first place: talking to the press might compromise the inquiry. 'The investigation?' Steve said.

'They steered clear of that. It's more of a profile piece, human interest, about Allie and Emma.'

Christ! And Emma? Who was Emma to talk about Allie? He stood so quickly the room spun. Heat flew down his back and his arms. 'Is it online?'

'I have it here.' Yun Li opened his briefcase and handed Steve the tabloid, already open on page five. *An exclusive.*

Before Steve caught more than the headline *Too Much Too Young*, his phone rang. He picked it up and saw Emma's name, hit the end-call button.

He began to read, his eyes snagging each time he saw the name Aled, each time Emma referred to Allie as 'he'.

> 'Of course I was concerned when I heard about Aled wanting to wear girls' clothes. I'm not sure where he got the idea from. It all happened too quickly,' Mrs Emma Moore tells our reporter. 'He was still a child. How can a fourteen-year-old boy really know what he wants? I was terribly worried for him. The health risks alone associated with hormone treatment and surgery should give any parent pause for thought. On top of that there's the danger of psychological problems. It's hard to know how much he was doing it for attention or whether he was being unduly influenced by peer pressure. I felt he was putting himself in danger. Sadly, events have borne that out.'

Christ! She was blaming Allie for endangering herself. And, by extension, Steve for allowing her to transition. Blaming the victim. Outrage brought heat to his face, made his heart quicken.

> 'I think this confusion about gender is an unfortunate symptom of wider social breakdown. Young boys need stronger role models. Men need to retain respect and authority.'

There were two pictures: the one of Allie they had released to the inquiry and one of her before transition, wearing a suit. He realized it was from Sarah's funeral. Emma must have given it to them. He felt like weeping with rage.

'How could she?' he said.

'The press can be very persuasive – words twisted, taken out of context.'

'Oh, it's all in context,' he said, throwing down the paper. He knew he'd have to read it through but his throat was tight with anger.

'She's the last person in this family to talk about Allie. Is there anything we can . . .' He let the sentence drop, knowing it was pointless. Right of reply, or calls for retraction, would fall on deaf ears. There was nothing strictly inaccurate in what he'd read so far, and all the references that grated were attributed to Emma, but it was Allie's story seen through the prism of prejudice and ignorance. Smeared and distorted.

'Ignore it,' Yun said.

Does it matter? Steve asked himself, as he looked for clean clothes after his shower. But he knew it did. Set against the enormity of Allie's death, Emma's comments might seem trivial but Steve knew, he had learnt from his daughter, there was an unbreakable connection between language and representation, and the oppression and violence suffered by trans people.

He was coming downstairs when the doorbell rang. Expecting his parents, he opened it to find his sister there. She began talking quickly – he could tell she felt some measure of guilt, some responsibility for the article. 'I should have asked you first but—'

'There's a word for what you did,' Steve said. He didn't shout: he was cold and clear for a moment. 'It's called dead-naming.'

She looked perplexed.

'When you use a trans person's birth name, when you call Allie Aled, when you call her "him", or she "he", it's dead-naming. She would hate that. I hate that.'

Emma frowned. She said quickly, 'Well, I didn't know and—'

'No, you didn't. How dare you speak about Allie at all? You had no right. All that shit about it being too young, too fast. Blaming her. Blaming us.' His head swam, and his insides were churning. 'I can't talk to you now,' he said. He shut the door and leant back against it, eyes closed, dry and aching. And eventually he heard Emma's footsteps as she walked back down the drive.

CHAPTER ELEVEN

Donna

There was a message for Donna, marked high priority, when she arrived at work. One name had been given three times in calls to the hotline. Anthony Mayhew. A name! *Yes!*

There'd been little further information: all the people who had come forward had chosen to remain anonymous, but one had mentioned an area too, claiming Mayhew lived in Newton Heath on the north side of the city.

Donna had to force herself to take off her jacket before she got down to work, reorganizing her strategy to accommodate the new lead.

She saw Jade arrive, early again. Trying to show willing? Donna asked her to check for that name on the database. Jade looked wan, with bruised shadows under her eyes, but her face lit up at the news, as if she'd suddenly been plugged in.

She was back in moments, holding a printout, and began to speak before Donna had finished emailing a reply to the lab concerning a comparison between the shoe marks on the body and the trainers confiscated from Bishaar.

'One minute,' Donna said, holding up her hand.

She heard the faint *snick-snick* sound as Jade picked at her nails. A tic Donna had noticed before. It set her teeth on edge. Jim bit his nails, always had, and Donna hated that too. Nowadays she'd clear her throat or, when she was close enough, touch his arm and he'd stop, for a few minutes, anyway. What with that and the snoring, she spent half her time with him feeling irritated. Or bored. The thought came from nowhere and she tried to quash it. All marriages had dull patches, didn't they? Doldrums.

He'd been up in the night again but said he just couldn't sleep. He'd still not seen the GP, claiming he hadn't been able to get through, but Donna wasn't convinced. How persistent had he been? Had he even tried? He seemed to resent her asking about it. When Donna attempted to lighten the mood, asking him about his day, whether he had lessons booked, he didn't answer, feigning distraction over some letter from school that he needed to check. She'd let it go.

Donna pressed send and sat back, took her glasses off. 'Tell me.'

'Anthony John Mayhew, date of birth, the nineteenth of January 1988. Lives on Summer Drive in Newton Heath.'

Twenty-eight. A little older than Donna had expected.

'He's got a string of offences to his name: theft, affray, domestic violence. Most recently he's served three years for rape. He was released on licence two months ago.'

'Let's see.'

Jade passed her the sheet of paper. There was no striking resemblance between Mayhew and the descriptions they had. Mayhew had a round, chubby face, a crewcut and thin lips. Dark hair and eyes. Could possibly be Man A.

Donna considered whether to pick him up now or wait for a comparison of the DNA. She decided to go ahead. 'Bring him in,' she said to Jade. 'But don't arrest him. Invite him to attend an interview as a person of interest.'

'Which he could decline,' Jade said.

'He's out on licence so his status is precarious,' Donna said. 'Let's see if he'll cooperate. And if the DNA matches we'll do a video ID with Bishaar.' She felt a swirl of elation. This could be one of them. The man who'd beaten and kicked Allie Kennaway, who'd spat on her as she lay dying.

* * *

Martin came in and Donna signalled to him from her office.

'Coffee?' He held a polystyrene cup in each hand.

'How did you guess?' Donna said.

'Psychic.'

'You're a star.'

Donna took a sip. Martin looked tired too, like Jade had. Was she pushing them too hard? Expecting unreasonable hours? But that was the reality of a murder case. And some of us aren't as young as we were, she tried to reassure herself. All the same, she said, 'You OK?'

'Never better. At least once I get this down me.' He raised his coffee.

'Well, we have a person of interest,' Donna said.

'Seriously?'

'Anthony John Mayhew,' Donna said. 'Three different callers.'

'So what do you think?' Martin said.

'I'm not going to jinx it but . . .' Donna grinned and took a long drink of coffee.

'Let's take a look.'

Donna brought up the Mayhew file,

'Not much like our photo-fits,' Martin said.

'It's definitely not Man B, though the short hair fits. Could possibly be Man A, if he's grown his hair a bit. It's four years old, after all,' Donna said. 'And we already know Bishaar's description of Man A wasn't as accurate as Man B. Jade's bringing Mayhew in for a chat, all being well.'

'Nice work,' Martin said. 'Not wanting to burst your bubble . . .'

'Oh, what now?' Donna put her coffee down.

'The Cavalier, the CCTV wasn't working.'

'On a Friday night?'

'They'd had a problem with electrics the previous day, blown fuses. Anyway, they prioritized getting the tills and the kitchen up to speed. CCTV wasn't back on until the Saturday.'

Shit. Every time Donna felt the lift, the sense that she was gaining ground, something came along and dragged her back down. 'That's why you brought coffee,' she said.

‘Not much in the way of compensation,’ he said.

‘No. Still, we have Mayhew, there’s hope yet.’

‘Always,’ Martin said, as he left.

Yes, Donna thought, there is hope. And we’re moving forward. We are.

Jade

'What?' Anthony Mayhew demanded, when Jade knocked him up, his eyes flicking from her to the constables accompanying her and the police car parked outside.

He'd put on weight since his mugshot, grown a double chin, a paunch, and doubled the width of his limbs. Prison food obviously suited him.

Jade explained his name had come up in connection with an ongoing investigation.

'I haven't done anything,' he said.

'Then it shouldn't take us long,' she said.

'Fucking joke.' He shook his head.

Who's laughing?

'If you want to get dressed . . .'

He was wearing a navy vest and some thin, grey sweatpants that had shrunk in the wash and ended halfway down his shins.

He stood his ground.

Oh, come on, don't be an arse.

'What's going on?' A woman's voice came from the back of the flat. Mayhew ignored it.

He gave a heavy sigh, muttered, 'Fucking joke,' again, and wandered back into what Jade guessed was a bedroom. She heard the exchange of voices, the woman's sharp and agitated, his weary, cutting her off with blunt responses.

Jade wondered if this woman was the one he'd been convicted of hurting, if she'd waited for him to do his time and come home. Or if she was a new partner, someone who hadn't been put off by his convictions for domestic violence and rape. Perhaps she thought he'd been rehabilitated. That he'd learnt his lesson. Or that she could change him. Jade wasn't sure people could change, not that much.

Once they were established in the interview room, Jade cut to the chase. 'Can you tell me where you were on Friday evening?'

'Friday?'

'That's right, Friday.'

'Home.' He didn't elaborate but held eye contact. A challenge. Jade matched him, gave it three beats before she blinked, and said, 'Anyone confirm that?'

'The girlfriend.'

Not the strongest of alibis.

'Her name?'

'Michaela Swan.'

'And what were you and Michaela doing that evening?'

He gave a leer, chuckled and rolled back his shoulders. A sniggering kid. *Twat.*

'Did you go into the centre of Manchester?'

'No.'

'Did you leave the property at all?' Jade said.

'No.'

A brick wall.

She didn't think there was any point in pressing him until they'd spoken to Michaela about his alibi, keeping Mayhew here while they did so he couldn't coach her. It was likely he'd already schooled 'the girlfriend' in what to say if the police ever came snooping.

Michaela reminded Jade of a bird: scrawny, with a small beak of a nose, she made quick, jerking movements with her head and neck as she answered Jade's questions.

'Where were you on Friday evening?'

Head back. 'Here.' Head jutting forward.

'And Anthony?'

'Here too.'

'Between what times?'

'From four. Why?'

'Did either of you leave the house?'

'No, we was in all night. Why?' Head cocked to one side. 'What's going on?'

'You're certain?' Jade said.

'Yes.' Michaela folded her arms, puffed out her chest.

'Did anyone call round?'

'No. I don't know what you think he's done but he was here.'

'OK,' Jade said. She turned to go.

'Is that it? What about Anthony? Where is he now? When's he coming home? What you picked him up for?'

'I can't tell you that at the moment. All I can say is, his name has come up in connection with an ongoing investigation.'

A little shimmy of her head back and forth a couple of times. 'What investigation?'

Jade kept quiet.

'Is he under arrest?'

'No, he's not under arrest.'

'Good. Because he a'n't done owt.'

We'll see about that. Jade had no idea if Michaela was telling the truth, or whether Mayhew was guilty, but the woman's confirmation of his whereabouts certainly wasn't strong enough to rule him out. Three people had seen the police appeal, seen the photo-fits, and rung in giving the same name. That had to mean something.

The tiredness that Jade had been keeping at bay, thanks to the rush of progress at work, crept back through her as she returned to the station. It had been eleven thirty when Bert banged on the wall. And after three o'clock by the time he had finally been lifted and restored to an upright position by the emergency falls service, then had fought and won the debate about whether or not he needed to be checked over at the hospital.

He'd gone down on the threshold between his living room and bedroom, smacked his temple on the chest of drawers and his nose on the floor. His face was covered with blood, and he looked like an extra from a slasher movie when Jade answered his call for help.

'We can't keep meeting like this,' he'd said, when she arrived.

'Too bloody right.'

'There might be concussion,' one of the falls team had said, as they argued about hospital.

'Date of birth, twelfth of November 1926,' Bert rattled off. 'Prime minister still a bloody Tory. Do you want me to go through the months of the year backwards?'

'I think that's the dementia test,' Jade said.

'How many fingers, then, go on,' Bert said, exasperation making his voice quaver. The whiskers on his chin were all white. If he stopped shaving, he'd have a white beard. Old men with white beards were usually fat, like Father Christmas or Captain Birdseye, but Bert was as thin as a stick.

At long last, with Bert in bed, cup of tea to hand, Jade had told him she was going.

'Thanks,' Bert said. 'Sorry for all the bother.'

'So you should be,' she said. 'Just watch where you're going. Pick your feet up. I told you last time.'

'You did.'

'You stay in bed. I'm not coming round here again tonight if you do your falling-log act.'

'Understood.' She had her back to him but she could hear the smile in his voice. Daft old sod.

Sonia

After a sleepless night, Sonia had texted Cynthia at daybreak, claiming she'd got the bug that was going round and wouldn't be in for work. There was always a bug going round.

Still no word from Oliver and she was sick with worry, her nerves strung so tight she thought she might snap. Fly apart. In bits.

She ached to see him, to sit him down and tell him how much she loved him, how much she cared for him. And after that? What would she say next? *I'm your mum. It's my job to look after you, to provide for you, to protect you, to raise you right.* That was where things got tricky.

If love was unconditional, then shouldn't loyalty be, too? Could she defend him when he might have had a part in something so horrific?

'He wouldn't,' she whispered. 'He couldn't.'

Fighting tears, she made herself go on the police website and read the appeal, staring again at the pictures of the two men wanted for questioning. She played the video of the woman in charge, DI Bell, asking for help. She studied the photograph of Allie Kennaway.

Perhaps Oliver should go away travelling, like a lot of kids did, these days. Wait until it'd all settled down. She might be able to get a loan from the Credit Union to pay for it. Then she imagined being found out, the shame of it. Sonia had never done anything wrong in her life.

The cat yowled and she let it jump onto her lap. Running her fingers over its head, she could feel the fur slide over the bony skull. 'What am I going to do, Puss?' *What the fuck am I going to do?* She couldn't carry on like this. It was killing her.

* * *

Halfway to the bus stop she saw Nicky, one of her neighbours, waiting there with the baby in the pushchair. Nicky's head was bent as though she was using her phone. Sonia turned back sharply and walked instead the extra mile to the tram station, paying more to make the journey into town. But she couldn't risk chatting to someone who knew her, and knew Oliver.

The sun had come out, and the trees that lined some sections of the route were lush after all the recent rain. A riot of green. Part of her wished it was still raining: the sunshine, the clean blue sky, made her own preoccupations seem even sicker, more warped.

A woman with a small child got on at Trafford Bar. She had dark coppery skin and wore African dress. A turban-style wrap on her head, a long skirt and tunic in a brilliant red and yellow print.

The child was tired. He sat on his mother's lap, his head bobbing lower and lower with the motion of the tram. The woman stroked his back over and over. Sonia remembered her own mother used to do that, stroke her back and sing. So very long ago. She had a keen desire to be a child again, to see her mum. A pang of loss. She closed her eyes and waited for the journey to end.

Sonia smoked two cigarettes while she watched the comings and goings at the police station across the road. She tried rehearsing her lines but the words blurred and stuck, backing up together, like boxes blocked on a conveyor-belt.

The city centre was busy and everyone she saw using the police station, or passing by, looked so ordinary, so normal. Some were carrying coffee or ice cream or shopping, others, tourists, pointing and shooting everything with their tablets, phones and cameras. A crocodile of schoolchildren in smart blue uniforms went past, skipping as they chattered.

Only the appearance of a lad begging, a scarecrow of a kid with torn clothes, reminded her that everyone wasn't living in some bubble of contentment.

Sonia got out another cigarette then put it back. Her tongue was like pumice.

The lad begging reached her. 'Spare change, miss?'

She gave him fifty pence. There were posters up saying you shouldn't give them money, that it made it harder for them to get help, to get off the streets, but she always felt so mean ignoring them.

When the lights changed she crossed the road and walked inside the building. In the reception area two men behind the counter were laughing about something, but as she got closer they stopped and the younger one asked if he could help.

'I'd like to—' She couldn't get her breath. She coughed, sucked in air. Her face was greasy with sweat. 'I'd like to talk to DI Bell.'

'What's it in connection with?'

Her head was buzzing. She didn't want to say, 'Allie Kennaway', she didn't want to say 'Murder'. There was a poster on the wall, appealing for help, that picture again – the girl in the green dress, with her wavy hair. Sonia pointed to the sheet.

'Can I have your name?'

'Sonia Poole.'

'Please take a seat.'

The younger man went out through the door behind Reception. The older one nodded and smiled at Sonia as she sat on one of the chairs. She looked away, unable to control the muscles round her mouth, to force a smile.

There were cat hairs on her trousers and she hadn't done her hair. She must look a right mess.

The noise from outside was muffled in there. The man at the desk was typing on a computer, making a soft, clicking sound with his tongue as he worked.

Sonia wanted to move. She felt constricted, trapped in her seat. All she could do was drum her feet lightly on the floor.

Finally the younger man came in and said, 'There'll be someone down to see you shortly.'

What would Oliver do – what would he say? – if he knew she was here?

His face, his words came back to her. *You're fucking mental. Accusing me of killing someone. Just fuck off. You mad bitch.*

She was betraying her own child.

Your own flesh and blood. That was what people said, didn't they? And *Blood is thicker than water.*

But hadn't he already betrayed himself, betrayed her, chosen to do wrong, to deliberately hurt someone? Let it be a mistake, she pleaded. Let it be some huge, stupid mistake. She didn't believe in God but she did believe in living life the best way you could, looking out for each other, working hard. She believed in kindness. It tore at her heart to think of the cruelty behind what had happened, to imagine Oliver capable of such violence.

'Mrs Poole?' A big man with grey hair, wearing a suit and a striped tie, stood inside a door to the left of the seating area. 'Will you come this way?'

She followed him into a small room where he invited her to sit down. He opened a notebook. He asked her name and address, her date of birth. She managed to answer but could feel the pressure swelling in her throat, and when he said, 'You want to talk to us about the Allie Kennaway inquiry?' she began to cry, gasping and unable to make her words clear.

'Take your time,' he said, as she shuddered and wiped her face with her hands. He didn't say anything else, just waited. She appreciated his patience. He wasn't pushy, and he didn't seem embarrassed by her display.

'I'm so sorry,' she said, when she could talk again. 'My son, Oliver . . .' She paused. She got out her phone and opened the gallery, showed him a photo of Oliver from Christmas, swiped to a second. Oliver with the cat, Oliver grinning straight at the camera: the cat had done something funny, but she couldn't recall what now.

She thought the detective might react to the photos, make some comment but he said, 'Go on.'

'He was in town on Friday . . .' She told him everything in fits and starts. About Oliver acting oddly, about not knowing whom he'd been out with, about him coming home earlier than expected, missing work, avoiding her, about him washing his own clothes, and his shoes, about seeing his face on the television and their argument, and how he'd run away, come back when she was out and taken those clothes and shoes. 'I don't know what he's done, I can't believe he'd do . . . not that . . . not to anyone. I didn't know what to do.'

'You've done the right thing,' the man said. 'Have you any idea where Oliver might be?'

'No. We've no family in the area, and I don't know these new friends.'

'It's clearly a very worrying situation for you but thank you for coming in and alerting us. If Oliver comes home or contacts you, please let me know immediately. Day or night. I'll give you my direct line.'

'I'm worried he might have hurt himself,' she said.

'Why?'

'If he was involved then . . . Oh, I don't know. I don't know that he could live with it. He's not that sort of person. I think there's been some awful mistake. He's a good boy. He really is.'

'It's impossible to be sure what the facts are at this stage,' the detective said. 'And that's what we deal with at the end of the day, hard facts. Until we speak to Oliver we simply don't know the whole truth of the situation. I can tell you that your visit here will remain confidential. It will only be shared with those staff on the investigation.'

'Will you be giving his name out?' she said. She imagined the shock as that news ripped through her community, her friends and neighbours, the staff at the supermarket, Rose and Cynthia.

'We'll be making every effort to find him but, Mrs Poole, our priority is to make sure no further harm is done. To Oliver or anyone else. So, for now we won't release his name. I can't go into any details at this stage but I can tell you we are currently questioning someone else about the incident.'

The other man? Had they found the other man? Was he one of Oliver's friends? 'Oh, God.' The room tilted. 'Other people, people who know us, they'll have seen the pictures in the news.' She could hear herself babbling. 'What if anyone asks me?'

'It's important the information you've given me is not shared with anyone else,' he said, looking deadly serious. 'It could compromise our work. We want to make sure everything happens according to proper protocol. You understand?'

Did she? What was he saying?

'I'm not—' She stumbled to a halt.

'As far as anyone else is concerned, you've not been here. Oliver's off with friends for a few days or something like that.'

Keep it all secret? Could she do that? Go home and drive herself mad with worry? She thought coming here would be the end of it in some way and now it felt like the beginning. 'I don't know if I can do that.'

'We would appreciate your cooperation,' he said. 'What we do in a situation like this is proceed with care and caution. We wouldn't want to panic Oliver, for example, and push him into doing something stupid. It sounds like he's vulnerable, as it is. I do understand it's not easy, but if you can do as I ask, at least until we've found Oliver and have had a proper talk. Meanwhile if he does come home, call me straight away. And as soon as I hear anything, I'll let you know.'

'OK,' she said. 'Thank you.' But she was deflated, the anxiety still gnawing away at her, the fear for Oliver just as strong.

They exchanged numbers and he thanked her again for coming in.

Their goodbyes in the reception area were stiff, made more awkward when a young Asian woman wearing a leather jacket opened the door from upstairs onto Sonia and almost knocked her over.

Back outside, the sun beat down, harsh, malign, and a band of pain tightened around Sonia's head in response.

The lad who had been begging had gone.

She lit a cigarette and walked towards the tram stop.

Had she done the right thing? If she had, why did she still feel so guilty and distressed? Why did she still feel so very scared?

CHAPTER TWELVE

Steve

Yun Li's phone rang. He picked it up and moved to the kitchen out of earshot.

Teagan was petting Dix and browsing on her phone. She stilled, alert, waiting to see if there was news. Her attention, her vigilance worried Steve. 'We should take that animal out for a walk,' he said. 'He's not had one all week.'

'It's raining,' Teagan said.

'If it stops.'

Yun came back in and took a seat. 'The inquest will be opened tomorrow.'

Steve drew in a breath. 'What time? When do we need—'

'You're not expected to attend,' he said.

'Why not?' Teagan was frowning.

'It's a formality,' Yun said. 'Because there's an ongoing investigation, the coroner will open and adjourn the inquest until that's complete. Once it is, a full inquest can be held. At that stage families and friends usually do attend. It's entirely up to you.' He opened his palms. 'But nothing more will happen tomorrow.'

'What's it for, though, if the police are finding out what happened anyway?' Teagan said.

'The inquest looks to establish who the deceased is, when, where and how they died but not who was responsible. That's for the courts to decide, if a case comes to trial.'

'That's stupid,' Teagan said.

'It might feel like that.' Yun smiled. He turned to Steve. 'The coroner will send an interim death certificate to the registrar and that's important because it means the coroner will be able to release Allie's body in due course.'

Steve swallowed, pressed his hands between his knees. 'Soon?' he said.

'Not necessarily.' Yun looked apologetic. 'It's usual to wait until the police have charged someone because the defendant . . .' He hesitated, glancing at Teagan.

'Go on,' Steve said. He couldn't imagine anything Yun Li said now could be harder for Teagan to handle than what she'd already heard over the last few days.

'The defendant has the right to arrange an independent post-mortem.'

Oh, God.

Teagan gave a sharp sigh.

'And what if you don't charge someone? What if you can't find them?' Steve was angry – irrationally so, because he knew the family liaison officer had nothing to do with the rules of the law or even the hunt for the suspects.

'In a complicated case, where we can't establish who is responsible so no charges are brought, a decision can be made to carry out a second independent post-mortem anyway and release the body.'

'Why do they have to do two?' Steve said.

'The post-mortem supplies forensic evidence, scientific evidence, but at trial there might be different interpretations applied to that evidence,' Yun said.

'Like what?' Teagan said.

Yun paused for a moment. 'A bruise on someone's knee, say. Did someone hit them or could it have been caused by them tripping and falling?'

Teagan was intent on him, dark eyes solemn beneath her fringe, brown hair framing her face, apparently wanting more. She needed to understand, Steve could see that. She needed to find sense in the middle of this senseless mess.

'Or if someone had been hurt with a knife,' Yun added.

'Stabbed?' Teagan said.

'Stabbed, and say the police found a knife at the defendant's house. They'd want to see if the independent post-mortem raised any doubts about that being the weapon.'

'How can they tell?' Teagan said.

'From the shape of the wound. But expert witnesses might disagree about that.'

'And if there was blood on the knife?' Teagan said.

'That would strengthen the prosecution case,' Yun said, 'if it was the right blood.'

Steve didn't like to think about the blood, about Allie's injuries. He knew he needed to face it eventually – hiding from the facts wasn't sustainable: the horror would only divide and multiply, a canker in the dark of his imagination – but he wasn't ready, not yet.

Yun was still talking: 'But perhaps the defendant would say the victim attacked him so he got the knife to protect himself and the victim fell on the knife. Then the experts might use the post-mortem findings to debate whether the stab wound might have happened like that or not.'

Teagan seemed satisfied. She rolled over and tickled Dix between his ears.

'We can expect some press coverage tomorrow,' Yun said.

'It can't be any worse than Emma's little intervention,' Steve said.

'What?' Teagan sat bolt upright.

'Emma was interviewed about Allie in one of the papers,' Steve said.

'What did she say?'

'A load of rubbish.'

'Why didn't you tell me?' Teagan said, standing, hands on her hips.

'I didn't *not* tell you,' he said, 'I just—' He looked at Yun. 'Have you got it there?'

He went to fetch it.

'And before you get upset or cross about it, I've already had a go at her,' Steve said. He was shattered. He rubbed at his chin, the stubble rough. When had he last shaved?

When Yun returned with the paper, Teagan took it from him and disappeared upstairs.

Minutes later, music blared from her room. David Bowie's 'Rebel Rebel' at full volume. Teagan's riposte to her aunt.

When they were first going out, Steve and Sarah had danced to that song, and years later he'd watched Allie dance to it too. Bowie, one of those icons who had played with gender and sexuality, who'd shaken things up. Outrageous to some at the time, a lifeline for others. Back in January, when Bowie had died unexpectedly, his *Greatest Hits* album had been on repeat in their house for days.

It was hard to listen to the music now. Bittersweet. His throat ached but he couldn't cry any more. He went and closed the door, muffling the song, though the beat still thrummed in his head, like the pulse of his blood.

Jade

Down in Reception, on her way to grab a sandwich, Jade nearly smashed into DS Harris and the woman with him. The woman looked stressed out, shaky, her face a mask of worry.

As Jade waited in the coffee shop, she wondered who the woman was. Another witness? Or maybe someone else with suspicions about Anthony Mayhew, like the callers to the hotline. If only they could find some evidence to contradict Mayhew's alibi that he was at home shagging his girlfriend.

Coming back into the station with her lunch, Jade asked at the front desk who the woman was. Sonia Poole. The reception staff wouldn't know all the ins and outs of the woman's visit so she sought out DS Harris. She found him sitting at his desk, bent over his work. She saw the roll of flesh spilling over his shirt collar, his thick neck. The broad shoulders. Did he have to shop at one of those specialist outsize shops?

'Any news?' Jade said.

He turned from his paperwork slowly, seemingly reluctant to break off. 'No.'

'The woman downstairs?' Jade asked.

'A waste of time.'

'How come?'

'A psychic, reckoned she could lead us to the killer. The victim was talking to her, along with a bunch of angels and a side order of leprechauns. Complete nutter.'

'Oh.' Jade was disappointed. 'Have you come across her before?'

'No. Why?' He spoke sharply. A flare of annoyance lit his eyes a penetrating blue, the colour of gas flames, and Jade felt her cheeks warm.

'Just I heard they made a habit of it,' she said, 'psychics, pitching up and offering their services.'

He didn't reply but went back to his work. Jade should have left it at that. She knew she should let him be but she kept talking. Wanting to provoke. Poking the bear. 'What did she say about him? The killer? Did she only mention one person?'

'It was a load of shite, which I am in the middle of copying up, if I could only get a minute's peace.'

'Right,' Jade said.

'A coffee might help.' His tone softened and now he was smiling at her.

Jade wanted him to get his own fucking coffee or maybe fetch him one and throw it in his big, fucking face but knew that wouldn't be a wise career move. *Teamwork, Jade.* 'How do you have it?' Jade said.

'Milk and sugar.' He held out a fiver. 'And your own.'

'Ta.'

The vending machine was on the other side of the building. The windows along the corridor gave views over the city centre. A mish-mash of fancy Victorian stone edifices and modern glass and steel creations, all hazy with rain. A plane was circling south towards the airport. Trams and trains carved their way between the buildings.

What had Bishaar made of the place when he arrived from Somalia? Thankful to be alive, she guessed. But the weather, the damp and the cold, would have been a shock. And the city itself? Presumably he'd lived in a town or city over there, if he worked in graphic design. Not much call for that in the desert or plains or whatever they had. Jade found it hard to imagine an African city with coffee shops and cinemas, malls and traffic jams. All you ever saw on the news were images of soldiers and trucks, goats and scrubland, shacks and huts, and people with malnutrition, AIDS or Ebola.

Back in the incident room she saw the DS was with the boss in her office. She put his coffee on his desk.

Had the results of Mayhew's DNA test come through? Could they match him to the crime scene?

At her own terminal, she opened the investigation log but there was nothing about it there. She clicked through to reports of information received, wondering how the sergeant had described Sonia Poole, what language he'd used to sum up the unreliability of the woman and the pointlessness of looking into her claims. *Mentally challenged? Mental-health issues?*

When Jade couldn't find any entry she searched the other folders, then checked back chronologically. Nothing. She tried using 'Poole' as a search term. No results. Perhaps DS Harris had given up, not even bothered to enter the most basic facts. He was a detective sergeant, maybe he had that discretion. But it ran counter to all Jade had been taught. Everything was potentially valuable until the investigation revealed otherwise. So every item of information had to be documented, recorded and kept on file. If someone like Jade neglected to upload an informant's details like that, she'd be in deep shit, given a right rollicking, if anyone ever found out.

He might have been interrupted. If the boss had called him in as soon as Jade had gone for coffee, he might not have had time to register the entry.

A psychic. You heard stories of coppers who lost it, who ended up in thrall to clairvoyants when proper police work had failed to get results. Poor bastards. What a scam. The dead were dead and gone, as far as Jade was concerned. Spirits, good or evil, gods or ghosts, were the product of a delusional mind, along with tooth fairies and vampires and Father Christmas.

Donna

'You got a minute?' Martin said.

'DNA?' Donna took her glasses off.

'No.'

She saw worry in his expression. Trouble at home? Something wrong with his wife, Fran? Would that account for how washed out he looked?

'Come in, sit down,' Donna said.

He closed the door and sat, squeezing his large frame into the office chair.

Donna waited. He cleared his throat and said, 'Jade Bradshaw. Have there been any problems?'

Not what Donna had expected. She thought for a moment . . . Jade blowing hot and cold, her tendency to go off and do her own thing, arguing with Donna, the sulking. 'What sort of problems?'

'With anyone on the team?' Martin said.

'Not that I'm aware of. Why?'

Martin picked a large paperclip from her desk, turned it end over end as he spoke. 'I hoped to sort it out myself. I'd rather that than add to everything you've got on your plate but I'm not sure that's going to be possible.'

'You've lost me,' Donna said. 'Is there a problem with Jade's work?'

'Yes,' Martin said. 'And that's not the half of it. Her work, her attitude, her behaviour.'

Oh, hell. Jade was prickly, truculent at times, but as far as Donna could see she'd made a good enough start as a DC.

'I have tried talking to her about it but . . .' He shook his head, twisted open one end of the paperclip. 'Let's just say that made it worse.'

Donna was still trying to understand. What exactly had Jade been doing? Was it a clash of personalities or approaches? Donna could imagine it: Jade, young and impulsive, wanting to rush at things, Martin trying to rein her in, set her straight, Jade taking that as criticism. 'I need specifics,' she said. 'Her work?'

'Sure. Half the time she's not sticking to the task she's given. She's making it up as she goes along. She's uncooperative.'

Donna recalled Jade bringing in Bishaar, her failure to inform herself, or anyone else, of her plan until it was a *fait accompli*. Jade pushing herself forward to interview him. Her resentment when Martin had gone to get the CCTV from the Cavalier.

'I'm not saying she hasn't got what it takes as a detective but at the moment she's cherry-picking. Take the grunt stuff,' Martin said. 'She's sloppy, disorganized. I asked her to take the tape from Fredo's to the evidence store and get it booked in, even though it's neither use nor ornament to us. She said she would. Next thing I find out that it's missing.'

Oh, Jesus.

'And Jade's denying she ever had it. Crazy.' He shook his head. 'I tried talking to her about it and she went ballistic—'

'You couldn't have got the wrong end of the stick?' Donna said, eager to find an explanation, a way to put this right.

'She lied to me, Donna. You can check with the evidence store. They never got it.'

'Of course.'

'And then she was—' He broke off, exhaled loudly. 'God, I hate this.'

'She was what?' Donna said, a chill inside her.

'If I could have handled it myself—'

'She was what?' Donna repeated.

'She was abusive. Badmouthing you, the way you run the inquiry, the way you dress, everything. Saying you had a little clique, you gave all the best work to your mates and they got the recognition for it, and you didn't give a toss for anyone else. Said you were a bitch with a reputation for bullying other women. That you couldn't stand the competition.'

Jesus! Donna felt the sting of outrage, then an eddy of uncertainty. *I'm not like that, am I? I don't operate like that. I don't. Do I?* She'd prided herself on being scrupulously fair, on mentoring the younger women in her team, on setting an example. Her mind flew back over her recent interactions with Jade. Had Donna been bitchy? She was worried about Jim, stretched to her limits by the case, but had she said anything, done anything Jade could have read as bullying? She had been, perhaps, a little sharp with her last night over who would check out the CCTV at the Cavalier, but this morning she hadn't sensed any lingering resentment.

'I'm sorry,' Martin said. 'Then she starts claiming I'm racist.'

Donna groaned, put her head in her hands. *I really do not need this.*

'I know,' Martin said. 'I couldn't reason with her.'

'When was this?'

'This morning. There'd been a few moments before that, when there was something a bit off.' He bent open another leg of the paperclip. 'I couldn't see why she was acting like that. No boundaries, no professionalism. Like some sort of kamikaze mission. Bizarre.'

Donna thought of Jade, her face going blank when she was disappointed or denied something she wanted, her eyes lighting up when they made a break. Yes, there were shifts, and there was something mercurial about her, but the backstabbing, the negligence Martin described, came as a complete shock and a very nasty one. Jade had indeed needed reining in, needed guidance, but Donna had admired the younger woman's appetite for the work, and her eagerness. She had savoured that energy, believed Jade showed promise, if she could improve her social skills and learn nuance and patience.

Could Martin have misread the situation in some way? Donna knew he could be blunt at times, forceful. If Jade had felt patronized, or intimidated, she might have let rip, saying things she didn't mean. It didn't explain the lost evidence, though. That was disturbing.

Donna needed to talk to her, see if Martin had got things out of proportion. If she had an explanation for the tape getting lost. Perhaps Martin felt threatened by her, her youth, her gender or ethnicity. It wouldn't be the first time an old-school copper had found the diversity within the ranks hard to handle. Was he exaggerating?

'Well, I say it's bizarre,' Martin said, 'but then I found something that made sense of it all. But I was out of my depth. I know there are procedures to follow, and it's all in the handbook, but I wasn't sure whether to instigate anything myself or whether it'd be best coming from you.'

There was more? 'Go on,' Donna said.

The paperclip was one straight length of wire. Martin folded it in half.

'She's on medication,' Martin said heavily. 'Olanzapine. It's an antipsychotic. I went to borrow her stapler and it was there in full view. Almost like she wanted to be found out.'

'Oh, Jesus!'

'You didn't know?' Martin said.

'Of course I didn't. She wouldn't be here if I knew.'

'She's ill,' Martin said. 'It explains it all. Nothing on her medical?'

'No, she'd not have made it through,' Donna said. That first day on the case, Donna had wondered if Jade was bulimic. Then there was the way she couldn't stand still, the reckless behaviour. On Monday Donna had speculated whether Jade was high, and put it down to excitement about her collaring Bishaar. *Antipsychotics?*

'You're sure they're hers?' Donna said.

Martin held out his phone, showing a photograph of the medicine, Jade's name visible on the pharmacy label along with the prescription date, just last month.

Christ! 'This is confidential, Martin. We have to deal with it so carefully. The last thing we want is a wrongful-dismissal case or anything like that.'

'Yes, totally. But it all adds up, the trouble concentrating, the paranoia. She thinks you and I are out to get her. If this came out . . . her health status or what happened with the tape . . .'

'I know,' Donna said. Her staff had to be competent, fit for work; they had to follow procedure to the letter, be beyond reproach. Any breach, any failure – for example, to protect the chain of evidence – could be seized on by the defence to undermine a prosecution. Thank Christ the tape wouldn't form part of their case for the prosecution.

'If it had been anything more significant than a false sighting on the tape . . .' Martin echoed her thoughts. 'I'm sorry, if I could have dealt with it, I would.'

'You did right to bring it to me. Bugger!' she said. 'She's a lot to offer on paper and it wasn't all plain sailing but this . . .' She felt nauseous, her mouth sour. Jade badmouthing her and accusing Martin of racism were cause for concern, her losing evidence even more so, but her being mentally unwell was the most serious issue. Jade had concealed the fact, lied in effect. The situation was untenable. The medication was an irrefutable problem.

'I'll have to talk to her, get her version of events,' Donna said.

'Of course,' Martin said.

'I'd like to think there's some other explanation for it all. But I can't see how she can justify coming to work on a script for anti-psychotics. She must know that's a red card.'

Donna's email pinged. She tore herself away from the conversation and squinted to read the subject heading. 'DNA,' she said. Her eyes scanned the message and the hope for a match between one of the crime-scene profiles and Anthony Mayhew guttered and died. Her stomach sank. 'Shit. Mayhew's clear on that score, no match,' she said. 'But let's cross all the Ts. You get Bishaar to look at a photo ID parade with Mayhew in the mix. If Bishaar IDs him, we talk to Mayhew again under caution.'

'And if he doesn't?' Martin said.

'We eliminate Mayhew. Send him on his way.' That was what Donna thought would happen. A key candidate for the killing was steadily losing plausibility. 'Three people named him as of interest. Why would anyone do that if there wasn't some truth to it?' she said.

'Revenge? Drop him in it. Make life difficult,' Martin said.

Murder inquiries did attract hoaxers, giving misleading

information. Hoping to see their enemies or rivals take the blame for an offence. But three separate people? That must have been coordinated. And in all probability it meant the team had wasted precious time on a dead end.

She sat back. 'So, Jade. I'll deal with it. Well – I'll talk to her, see what she has to say for herself, then pass it on to HR.'

'Sorry,' Martin said.

'Yeah. Don't say a word – to anyone,' Donna told him.

'Of course not.'

When he left, Donna reached over, picked up the mangled paperclip and dropped it into the bin.

She could see through the window to the outer office that Martin was leaving. Jade was still at her desk, fingers twisting the strands of hair at the nape of her neck.

The prospect of confronting her weighed heavily on Donna. The shitty side of managing people. How to tackle it? The overriding concern was Jade's use of medication for a mental-health problem. That in itself rendered her unfit to work – unfit for police work anyway. It was the key issue. If at all possible, Donna would avoid getting into Jade's abusive remarks about her leadership and the accusations of cronyism, racism and misogyny. And perhaps the girl would come up with reasons to satisfy Donna, though for the life of her Donna couldn't think what they might be.

Fully aware she was procrastinating, Donna decided to update the investigation log before doing anything else. Maybe she'd have lunch next, then deal with Jade. No, she chided herself, lunch afterwards. Face the nastiness first, then get out of the building for half an hour, walk, breathe, debrief.

Bargain made, Donna put on her glasses and began to type, trying to ignore the worm of apprehension in her belly.

Martin

Martin had been tempted, sorely tempted, to steer Bishaar towards fingering Mayhew as Man A. There were strict rules to an ID parade, covering everything from the laying out of the six numbered photographs to the way the question was framed. And the whole event was filmed to prevent any coercion. So the only way Martin could have rigged the result was if he'd had the chance to bribe Bishaar beforehand, offer him an opportunity of escape, or immunity from deportation. (Not that Martin could guarantee any sort of immunity, no way.) Interfering in that aspect of the investigation could all too easily come back and bite him on the arse. Bishaar might refuse the bribe or suspect a trap. And having the man at large was a risk – he might be caught again and betray Martin. All speculation now. Martin was waiting to be called into the ID suite, any chance to intercept Bishaar, before he arrived from the remand centre, long gone.

Martin took a swig of the antacid he'd bought, his guts aflame with bile, his mind roaming round, lumbering into all the problems that still threatened Dale, and by extension himself. Focus, he cautioned himself, prioritize. Bishaar *wouldn't* pick out Mayhew, and Mayhew would be sent home, but at least putting the man in the ring had bought Martin some time. Time to think through the strategy of damage limitation.

All their cards rested on preventing the identification of Dale or his mate Oliver. If they could spin that indefinitely, then as long as neither of them ever crossed the line and got picked up by the police, they could carry on with their lives, no one any the wiser.

Oliver's mother was a potential spanner in the works but she'd no real proof her son had done anything. And Oliver had denied it all, thank fuck. Though the lad wasn't too bright in other regards. At least Dale had had the sense to destroy everything he'd been wearing, knowing it could so easily incriminate him. Yet when Martin had asked Oliver about his clothing and his shoes, when they were sitting in the car in wasteland near the Ship Canal, far from cameras or prying eyes, Oliver had said, 'I washed it all.'

Washed it, for fuck's sake. 'Burn it, or bury it somewhere no one will ever think to look,' Martin said. 'There'll be blood in the seams of your trousers, in the stitching on your shoes. The tiniest trace is all we need. Do you get it?'

Oliver nodded.

'Phones,' Martin said, holding out his hand.

'My life's on that—' Dale started.

'Your life's on the fucking line,' Martin snapped. 'These show where you were, who you talked to, what sites you visited, text messages sent and received. From now on you use these.' He gave them each a cheap handset, paid for in cash from a place in Rusholme. He'd bought them along with the ones he'd used to tip off the hotline.

'You don't go home,' he said to Oliver, 'not yet. You don't talk to your mum.'

'Suits me,' Oliver said. He was crashing on a friend's sofa. The friend worked nights handling baggage at the airport. It sounded like a good arrangement to Martin, the lads seeing little of each other. Oliver had sacked off his apprenticeship. Martin had considered telling him to go back, carry on as normal, but then the lad's mother might go looking for him there and ruin everything.

He gave Oliver fifty quid for food and told him to find something cash-in-hand, try the car-wash places and the takeaways. Off the books was better for now. Had the kid the gumption to sort out some work? Maybe going hungry would concentrate his mind, as long as it didn't send him home, crying to his mother.

Dale looked to be sulking about the phone. Martin felt his temper simmering, coming to the boil. 'You sure you want to do this?' he asked them both. 'Because I can drive you both to the nick right now and hand you over. Your choice. You got any doubts, any problem with my way of handling things, any yen to confess, you tell me now and I start the car. Yes?'

'No,' Dale said. Oliver echoed him.

'This is not a game,' Martin said. 'I'm risking my own neck, my livelihood, my reputation, my fucking pension for you, so you do exactly as I say. You put a foot wrong, you'll pay for it. I have a lot of friends, a lot of contacts. Not all good people.'

Dale shifted in his seat and Oliver nodded quickly, his eyes moist, his Adam's apple bobbing as he swallowed. Martin saw beads of sweat on the lad's upper lip and his forehead. Had he the balls to get through this? To stay loyal? He was an unknown quantity but they were saddled with him.

Martin let the silence hang for a moment, then said, 'I want to see you again tomorrow night. Oliver, get yourself to Trafford Bar for eight. I'll pick you up there.'

'What for?' Dale asked.

'We'll talk about it tomorrow,' Martin said. 'Now, Facebook, WhatsApp, Instagram, Twitter – either of you put anything on there?'

'No,' they said in unison.

'Glad to hear it. Stay clear, keep your heads down. Anyone talks to you about the murder, you play innocent, then change the subject.'

Now his chain of thoughts was broken as he was called to the room for the ID parade. He went through the motions. The African looked at the photographs and shook his head, said no, for the recording, he couldn't see either of the people he'd witnessed during the attack on Friday night in the photographs shown to him.

As they sat there, Martin did his best to conceal his hatred. If Bishaar hadn't been dossing on the streets, living here illegally, like a parasite, evading the authorities, then no one would have a real clue about the Kennaway killing. It was him and his fucking Good Samaritan act, then his Leonardo da Vinci number, that had screwed everything up. And even if he were out of the picture, even if Martin did manage to get to him, get shot of him somehow, his written statement and his sketches could be used in his absence at any trial. There was no way round it.

Bishaar nodded politely after the ID parade was finished and Martin felt like decking him. Muslim scum. He'd been at the scene. He'd witnessed the murder. He'd a coherent account of what had happened and it matched the forensics. But, and it was a very useful but, he had fled the scene. He was a criminal, a destitute. So, if push came to shove and Martin's plans unravelled, if Dale or Oliver was apprehended, then those facts just might be given a different spin. Plan B. That was why Martin would spend another evening in the car, in the dark, with Dale and Oliver. Walking through Plan B, in case everything else went tits up.

CHAPTER THIRTEEN

Steve

'She's your sister. You can't avoid her for ever,' Steve's mum said, pushing the newspaper back across the table to him.

'Pity,' he murmured. 'She just never seems to learn. She's got her view of how things are, and if anything doesn't fit into that, it's wrong. Sarah thought she was a narcissist.'

His mother raised her eyebrows.

'Has she spoken to you?' he said.

'Yes.' She didn't elaborate.

'I can imagine,' he said. '*I* wouldn't listen to reason. *I'm* overreacting. *I* wouldn't let her explain. *I* shut the door in her face. It's all my fault.'

'My lips are sealed,' his mum said. 'I'm not getting in the middle of it. It never does any good.'

His dad arrived, dressed in a boiler suit and gumboots.

'What have you come as?' Steve said.

'Thought I'd have a go out there.' He nodded to the garden. 'Tidy up.'

'Isn't it raining?' Steve said.

'Slackening off.'

Clearly he needed to keep busy. Steve wished he could join in, find some sanctuary in simple, manual work, but he knew he hadn't the wherewithal. Each time he made a start on something, with the washing, say, or clearing the fridge, mindless tasks he'd done a thousand times before, he kept losing track, his concentration shot. Not just mental incapacity but physical too: his coordination was off, his muscles weak. Diminished.

'Where's Teagan?' his dad said.

'Upstairs,' Steve said.

'I'll see if she wants to help.'

'Have you thought at all about the funeral?' his mum said.

Steve shook his head. 'We don't know when they'll release the body.' He hated describing her like that, 'the body', but how else to put it? *Allie's body?*

'That doesn't mean you have to wait,' his mother said. 'You can still make plans. It'll give you something to do.'

'You think I need something to do?' Steve said.

'Yes,' she said simply. 'Remember when Sarah died, making all the arrangements? It's a way of doing something for the person, thinking about how to . . . celebrate them.'

That period of intense, frantic activity had been a blur, so much to sort out, and when it all stopped after the funeral it was like he crashed and fell. He'd found himself in an awful yawning chasm of loneliness and desolation. He'd hauled himself through it, hour by hour, for Allie and Teagan. And his daughters had been stunned, stripped raw. Nights of weeping. The endless seesaw moments when normal life tipped into wretched unhappiness. Teagan howling, pushing him away, small fists beating at him. Raging against the universe. Allie, withdrawn, impassive, the light gone from her eyes. They'd pulled through, stumbled forward together. And now this. He wanted to weep. He knuckled his eyes. 'You're probably right.'

'You can't control anything else,' she said, 'the papers, this investigation. But you and Teagan can work out what you want for Allie.'

'Yeah,' he said.

'She's busy.' His dad came through the kitchen.

'What's she doing?' Steve said.

'Writing something.' He let himself out of the back door.

'I don't even know what Allie would want,' Steve said. 'Cremation or burial. She was eighteen. It's not something you ask your kids, is it?' There was anger bubbling deep inside beneath the sorrow.

'Would she want to be with her mum?'

Sarah had been cremated and they'd taken her ashes to Lathkill Dale, a valley in the Derbyshire Peak District. It was where Steve had proposed to her. Later it had been a place for picnics and walks with the children. Sarah had chosen the spot, making her wishes known once they'd been told no treatment could save her.

'Or you might decide you want her closer, here at home or in the cemetery,' his mum said.

'No.' He couldn't bear to think of Allie lying with all the dead or of her ashes in an urn on the bookshelf or at the garden of remembrance beneath a polished granite plaque. Maybe with Sarah wasn't such a bad idea. 'Teagan wants to go to this vigil on Friday,' he said.

'You don't?'

'I'm not sure. It's good they're doing it but . . . we're the ones who lost her. I don't know that I want to share it with strangers. All these people who never knew her.'

'They're not strangers.' Teagan was there. He hadn't heard her come in. 'Not proper strangers. It's a community. Allie was part of it. I want to go.'

'You can,' Steve said. 'I'm not sure whether I will.'

'I can take you,' his mum said, 'if your dad decides not to.'

'Good,' Teagan said. She tucked her hair behind her ears and held out a piece of file paper to Steve. 'I've done this.'

'What is it?'

'A letter to Allie. I want to post it online, so people don't just hear Auntie Emma's side of things.'

'Will it make me cry?' Steve said.

'Probably,' she said.

His eyes scanned the page, caught random phrases, *Dear Allie, You were six when I was born . . . I'm proud of you . . . You were scared of pigeons . . . funny, kind . . .* Then Teagan made a noise and he saw her face crumple and she was crying. He opened his arms and shuffled the chair round so she could come to him, as Dix whined and struggled to his feet.

Jade

'Can I see you for a minute?' The boss stopped at Jade's desk.

'Sure.' Jade picked up her daybook and phone, then locked her desk drawer where she kept her bag. There were signs around the room, warning people to protect their valuables, which was pretty ironic, given they were all meant to be upholders of the law.

'What are we going to do about Mayhew, given there's no match with the DNA?' she asked.

'That's not what I want to talk to you about.' Something edgy in the way she said it as she ushered Jade into her office and closed the door.

The boss went round to her side of the desk and settled in her chair.

'Please, sit down.'

I'd rather stand. Jade felt like bolting. Something was wrong. Her mind flew back over the last twenty-four hours – the visit to Candida Gallego, picking up Anthony Mayhew – searching for any mistake she'd made, any act that triggered unease when she thought of it, and came up blank.

Sitting, Jade forced herself to meet the boss's eyes. Was she angry? She didn't look angry, not happy either. Sad, maybe, or disappointed. Perhaps she'd had bad news and this was about her, not Jade. Could that be it?

The boss tilted her head but it wasn't one of those pitying gestures, not like she was sorry for Jade, but a tilt the other way, like she didn't want to get close. A distancing.

'How are you finding work?'

Trick question. Say as little as possible. 'Fine.'

'It's very demanding,' the boss said. 'A lot to take in, steep learning curve.'

'That's fine,' Jade said. 'It's what I want to do.'

'It can be stressful,' the boss said. 'Not just the hours and the intensity but the emotional toll it takes on all of us.'

Jade didn't know what she was supposed to say to that, so she said nothing.

'It's crucial everyone on the team has the resilience required.' Was she talking about teamwork again? Was this some sort of pep talk?

Jade nodded to show she was listening. Hands in her lap, out of sight, she picked at the skin around her thumbnail.

'Mentally as well as physically,' the boss said.

Mentally. Did she know? What did she know? Thoughts scrabbled over each other, all claws and teeth. Jade stared at the snow globe. When the silence stretched out she glanced up. The boss was studying her with steady eyes, her mouth turned down, deep creases at the sides. A chill slithered across Jade's skin.

'You completed a medical on entry to the police service and it was a condition of employment that you notified us of any serious illness, or anything that might impact on your ability to do your job.'

Fuck! Jade's heart thumped out of rhythm. 'There's nothing wrong with me,' she said.

'I need you to be honest.'

'I am.' Jade tugged at the strip of skin and felt the sting of pain.

'Jade, it has come to my attention that you have been taking medication at work,' the boss said.

'That's personal!' How did she know? How the fuck did she know?

'Not when it affects your performance.' The boss looked sad, her eyes hooded.

'It doesn't. It *doesn't.*'

'I can't ignore this. If you're being treated for a mental illness, given the pressure you're under—'

'I'm fine,' Jade said. Her body humming with indignation. Dark spots dancing at the edge of her vision.

'I don't think so. You need time off. You need to speak to Human Resources, look at a referral to Occupational Health, and see if you can agree a plan. I'm not saying you can't eventually come back—'

'You're sacking me from the team?' Jade was on her feet, heart banging in her chest. 'Don't do that – you can't do that! Look, I got you Bishaar, that interview. That interview made the case, gave us suspects, an eyewitness account. That's all good. OK, thanking people, I'll get better at that and I know teamwork matters . . .' She could hear herself gulping air, rabbiting on. *Calm down. Slow down.*

'Jade, if it has an impact on your work—'

'How? How has it impacted on my work? It hasn't.' She was shouting. She shouldn't shout but she had to make the boss listen.

'The video from Fredo's on Water Street, losing that, losing evidence. Then lying about it to DS Harris.'

A kick to the stomach. '*What?* I never!'

The boss blinked, shook her head. Despairing.

Harris. *The bastard.* 'I never had the video. I never!'

The boss held up her hand. 'To put into evidence.'

'No! Was it DS Harris told you all this?'

'I'm not prepared—'

'Why does he want rid of me?' Jade said. 'Have you asked yourself that? There must be a reason.'

'I'm sorry, Jade,' the boss said quietly. 'But you've misled me. You've failed to disclose a serious health condition. I can't ignore that.'

'He's fucking me over and you can't even see it cos you're so fucking pally.'

The boss's face pinched with disapproval. 'Jade, don't.'

'Best mates together, isn't it? Closing ranks. What a joke. He's setting me up. He's a fucking liar. And you're a stupid bitch.' Jade hit at her own head with her fists.

'DC Bradshaw!' The boss's tone was hard as steel. 'Enough.'

Jade was trembling, eyes burning. She wanted to lunge and turn over the desk, pull down the filing cabinet, hurl the chair through the window, savour again the delicious release of letting go. Letting the rage out. 'You don't know what you're doing!' she yelled, fury howling inside her.

'You need to calm down. This is not helping.'

'You won't even listen to me. Fuck you, then! Fuck you all!'

She ran out, her teeth clamped together, her breath thin and tight. At her desk she grabbed her things and, ignoring the sideways glances from some of the other staff, walked out.

The air was soft and warm. The sky showed patches of blue between the pale grey banks of cloud. She stared at the cars in the car park, the riot vans at the far side, the patrol cars, saw the coppers swapping banter as the shift changed. This was her life.

The bristle of anxiety came, seesawing with her anger, like a rash spreading over her skin, burrowing into her organs. She took some tablets. The medication kept a lid on it all, just about.

She looked back at the buzz of activity in the car park. Now what? What the fuck was she going to do now?

Sonia

Rose was on the doorstep. 'I rang the shop – they said you were off sick.'

'Yeah,' Sonia said. 'Fluey, you know. You don't want to catch it.'

'I'll be all right. I won't stay long.'

'Rose, really.' She wanted to close the door. How could she do that? Shut out her closest friend.

'Really nothing,' Rose said. 'I knew something was up when you didn't answer your phone. It's not like you.'

'Sorry.' Sonia caved in, stood back and let Rose past.

'You sit down. I'll make a brew.'

Sonia watched as her friend, relaxed and at home in her kitchen, filled the kettle, fetched mugs and coffee.

Rose kept talking as she spooned out coffee, opened the milk. 'They've cancelled Dad's outpatient appointment again. It's the third time. I feel like wheeling him down there and chaining myself to the radiators, or whatever, refusing to leave until they've seen him. And the GP's been out to us because this new drug Dad's on is making him feel sick so I want them to try something else.'

Had Rose seen Oliver's picture? Was she building up to it? Was that why she really called round?

'You should be in bed,' Rose said, putting the drinks on the table.

'I was, not been up that long.' Sonia hated lying, had never been very good at it. She preferred to face things head-on, the same as Rose did.

Rose got out her e-cig and Sonia picked up her fags. Without need of any discussion Sonia opened the back door and they went out. There was a moment of silence as they both smoked.

Say it, Sonia willed Rose. *Let's drop the pretence.*

'Last time I had flu was that holiday in Lanzarote. Bloody awful. You remember?' Rose said.

Sonia murmured in agreement. Rose had managed to get a carer who would call in on her dad twice a day so she could have a break. Oliver had been eleven, just finished at primary school. He'd been lovely at that age, happy to play in the pool all day long, and he soon made friends with some of the other boys, Sonia calling him back every couple of hours for food or more sunscreen. His fair skin burnt badly if she wasn't vigilant. Even so, by the third day his nose and the tips of his ears were red and peeling, but it hadn't spoilt his enjoyment.

They had gone out on the first night, she and Rose sharing Sangria with their paella, Oliver wolfing down chicken nuggets and chips and angling to buy an inflatable octopus for the pool. Rose had felt grotty, wanted to get to bed early, and she didn't get up again, other than to use the bathroom, till the journey back.

'I don't suppose Oliver's been bringing you cups of tea or anything,' Rose said now.

Sonia waited, expecting her to go on and start talking about the news or the police. But she didn't. 'No,' she said. She began to cough, sounding like she really did have some virus. When the spasm stopped, she sipped her coffee. She thought about what the detective had told her to do, then said, 'He's away, actually.' She felt a rush of heat in her cheeks.

'How come? Where?'

'It's a residential thing, part of his course.' More lies. 'A couple of weeks. Team building.'

'Camping and outdoor stuff?'

'Yes.'

'Hope the weather stays nice for them. Sounds great, though,' Rose said. 'At least you don't have to worry about him while you're ill.'

Oh, Christ. She longed to tell her, to crumble and let the truth spill out, to have someone to share the dreadful feeling with, to reflect the shock back at her.

Rose would understand. Rose knew Oliver, had known him his whole life. She had cuddled him and tickled him, teased him and treated him to birthday and Christmas presents. She'd listened to his chatter about Angry Birds or his fantasy football team. She'd been his auntie and his godmother. Only in these last two or three years had her role in his life waned, as Oliver grew more independent. And more awkward.

'Rose.' Sonia turned to her friend, cigarette smoke catching her eye, making it sting.

'Yeah?' Rose said.

'There is . . . erm . . .' But the truth was lodged solid beneath her breastbone. Leaden. Dangerous. 'I . . . I think I'll go back to bed.'

'Course. You poor thing. But keep me posted.'

Inside, Rose poured away the remainder of her coffee. 'Text me if you need anything. Promise?'

'Sure,' Sonia said.

'We'll have a proper catch-up when you're back on your feet.'

'Yeah,' said Sonia. But she couldn't imagine it. She was losing everything – that was what it felt like – respect for herself, trust in her son, and now her friend, their relationship tainted by secrets and lies.

CHAPTER FOURTEEN

Donna

Donna was shaken by her confrontation with Jade and saddened that Jade's reactions, her refusal to accept she was in the wrong regarding the medication, the attack on Martin, the lie about the tape, appeared to confirm everything Martin had said. Donna needed to frame an email for HR about the situation but she'd find it easier when she was calmer.

Could she have handled it differently? She'd tried to keep things professional, formal, wanting to give Jade space to address the concerns, but Jade had simply exploded. Emotions out of control. *Fucking bitch* and *Fuck you* now rang in Donna's head.

She was on the point of leaving to get something to eat when a call came through, an unknown number. She hesitated. If it was important they'd leave a message, wouldn't they? But . . . Before her voicemail picked up she swiped to answer the call.

'Mrs Bell?'

Not work, then. 'Yes.'

'This is the Accident and Emergency unit at the Manchester Royal Infirmary.'

Oh, Jesus. Kirsten? One of the twins? A sporting accident? 'Yes?'

'Your husband, Mr Bell, was brought here, an hour ago, after a traffic accident.'

'Oh, good God.' *Oh, Jim.* Donna's vision swam. She leant against her desk and closed her eyes, waiting for what came next. 'How is he? What happened?'

'He's conscious and we're ordering tests to make sure there are no internal injuries. He's got a fracture to the right leg and some cuts and bruises. His blood levels indicate he may have had some sort of heart event.'

Heart event?

'All being well, he will then be admitted to a ward, either cardio or orthopaedics. He asked us to call you.'

'Yes.' *The children. School pick-ups – Matt and Kirsten finish at three*. 'Do you know what happened?' Donna said.

'He has no clear recollection of the collision. Has he been experiencing any dizziness or blackouts recently?'

'He complained of chest pains.' She'd *told* him to see the GP, time and again. The stupid man. She was so angry with him. 'I'll come down,' she said. *Collision?* 'What did he collide with?'

'I'll tell you what we know when you get here. Ask for Dr Vaughan.'

She rang Martin straight away. 'Jim's been in a car accident. He's OK, a broken leg. I need to see him, sort the kids out.'

'Donna, I'm so sorry to hear that.'

'Can you act as senior investigating officer until I'm back? Arrange for Mayhew to be taken home.'

'Yes, of course.'

She parked in the multi-storey at the hospital and walked through the site to the main entrance. A and E was not unfamiliar territory, though Jim had probably done more trips here with their various children than Donna had.

Building work had been going on around the complex for years. There was now a new children's hospital and a new eye hospital, glossy buildings with clean, sleek interiors that put the main entrance and the older parts of the building to shame.

Donna passed a clutch of smokers and made her way through to A and E reception.

She gave her name, and Jim's, and asked for Dr Vaughan.

The doctor was a young man with a squat build, a plump, polished face and a rich Welsh accent. 'Come through here, please,' he said, 'where we can hear ourselves think.'

'Here' was a tiny office off one of the corridors. Dr Vaughan opened the door and gestured for her to go in.

At that moment someone called his name and Donna saw two police officers approach.

'Ah, come in,' the doctor invited them. 'This is Mrs Bell. She's just arrived but hasn't had the full picture.'

'What picture?' Donna said.

No one answered, but Donna took in the serious expressions, the thick silence, and sweat broke out across her skin in response. *Jim?* Was there worse news about him?

'Please have a seat, everyone. We should be able to fit, if we put this one here and . . .' The doctor fussed about arranging chairs until the four of them were crowded around the small desk.

'Mrs Bell,' the doctor said.

'Detective Inspector Bell.' She wanted them to know she was in the job. One of the officers, the older man, gave a nod and she saw a flicker of surprise in the eyes of the other.

He's dead. Jim's dead. That's why they're here. She could see cup marks glinting on the table top. Old tea or coffee. Her throat was dry and cracked.

'As you know, your husband was involved in a collision this morning,' Dr Vaughan said.

'Yes.'

'He was brought here by ambulance.' His cheeks shone, squeaky clean.

He's dead. Just say it, she wanted to scream.

The doctor looked over at the older police officer who took up the story. 'His car mounted the pavement on Audenshaw Road and collided with a pedestrian. A young man. An ambulance was called but I'm sorry to say he was pronounced dead on arrival here.'

Not Jim. Not Jim, then. Relief made her weak, then came the backwash of shame at the relief. 'Oh, my God,' she said. 'Does he know? Does Jim know?'

'Not yet. We thought it best to wait until we were sure he was not in any danger himself and until somebody could be here when he's given the news.'

Oh, Jesus.

'There was no one in the car with him?' Donna said. 'He wasn't giving a lesson?'

'No.'

'We're satisfied he has no internal injuries, so Mr Bell will be referred to our cardiology department and his leg will be set in a cast. He's on the assessment ward at present. If we can go down there.'

The scraping back of chairs followed and the manoeuvring to get out of the confined space.

On the way, Donna spoke to the older of the two officers, Sergeant Williams, trying to gather more details to surround the image she had of Jim slumped over his air bag and a man prone on the pavement. 'Had he tried to stop, to slow down, do you know?'

'We don't know yet. The traffic investigators should be able to establish that in time.'

'Who's the young man?'

'I can't tell you at this stage. His family have still to be informed.'

All the times she had said those exact same words. 'Were there any witnesses?'

'I believe so.'

And a man on the ground with – what? His head smashed or his torso crushed?

'How long did the ambulance take?'

'Six minutes.' Within the agreed targets.

When she first saw Jim she couldn't speak. His face was bloodied and cut, his complexion beneath sallow. Eyes closed, he looked to be in pain.

She swallowed hard. 'Jim?'

He opened his eyes. 'Donna.' His lips twitched and she thought he was trying to smile. There was a haunted look in his expression. Did he know? Had he guessed?

'They think you had a heart attack,' she said.

'That's right,' Dr Vaughan put in. He drew the curtains round the bed.

Jim's leg was visible, crushed and misshapen below the hospital gown. They must have cut his clothes off. She saw something glinting in his hair. Glass? Fragments of glass.

Donna pulled up a chair and took Jim's hand.

'I explained to your wife that we'll be getting Cardio to take a look at you and get this leg strapped up as soon as we can. You've had some pain relief?'

He nodded. Said tightly, 'I could do with some more.'

'I'll have a word with the nurse.'

Jim's eyes moved to the police officers. 'I don't remember a thing,' he said. 'The last thing I remember is leaving the ring road.'

'I've got some difficult news, Mr Bell,' Sergeant Williams said.

Jim glanced at Donna. She pressed her fist to her mouth, looked away.

'Oh?' Jim said. Wary. Frightened, she thought. Of course he was.

'Your car mounted the pavement on Audenshaw Road after you apparently lost control and . . .'

Donna couldn't watch Jim's face as the officer continued to speak. She looked at his hand in hers, flecked with rusty smears. She put her other hand over it. *Hold tight.*

'No!' Jim said, when he heard about the fatality.

Donna met his eyes then. He looked as if he was asking her to deny what he'd just been told. 'A terrible accident,' she said, her voice dry.

'Who?' Jim said.

The police officer gave the same answer as he had to Donna: the victim's family had to be told first.

A terrible accident. And if Jim had seen the GP? If he'd done what she'd asked him to? The thought was hateful, traitorous, but she couldn't suppress it.

And how long before Jim, lost and shattered, thought it too?

Jade

Jade drove. No destination in mind, only the desire for movement. She barely noticed the traffic or the road conditions, her mind cartwheeling back to the argument in the boss's office.

She increased her speed as she joined the motorway, hogging the outside lane, but no matter how fast she went she couldn't outrun the scene playing in her mind.

Teamwork, Jade.

Where was the teamwork in firing her? Harris had crucified her. Not only grassing her up because she was on prescription meds but inventing stone-cold lies about her work. The missing tape, for fuck's sake.

A large 4x4 powered up to hang on Jade's tail. She thought briefly of braking, giving the guy a scare, knew it wasn't the best idea she'd ever had and moved into the centre lane, flicking him the finger as he streaked off, gunning his engine. Dickhead.

Jade had never even seen the CCTV tape from Fredo's, let alone lost the thing. But the boss hadn't listened to her. She was set on getting shot of Jade. Why? When Jade tried to argue her corner, the boss had shouted her down, loyal to her old pal. It was beyond unfair.

To think Jade had been pleased to be working alongside Harris, that she considered him a role model, someone to respect, with his bravery awards, his years on the job. Someone to learn from. And he'd killed her career just like that.

Why?

The tape. She kept coming back to the tape. She'd never seen it. Had anyone? Did it even exist? Had Harris messed up collecting it and used her as a scapegoat? Had he lost it himself, or never had it in the first place? It didn't make sense. None of it.

What if she could find the tape? Prove to the boss that it had never been in her possession. Would Jade be listened to then? The pair of them were thick as thieves. They were claiming she wasn't fit for work because she'd ballsed that up, lost evidence, but if she could show them it wasn't true . . .

That would be something, wouldn't it?

A chain of custody existed for every item of evidence. She would start at the beginning. Work out exactly when and where the CCTV recording had disappeared. That was her only option. That, or sit at home going mental.

The next exit was two miles ahead. She took the slip road and skirted the roundabout until she was heading east, back to Manchester, ignoring the speed limit. Too riled to give a fuck.

At Fredo's, Jade found a band unloading their gear. A poster on the wall advertised tonight's bill as *Rising Stars: Doors open 8 p.m.*

Jade spoke to one of them, a girl in a tartan skate-dress and black suede knee-high boots, asking if she knew where the manager was.

'Not sure. Clements let us in. I'll get him.'

The girl came back with Clements, a big, buff Afro-Caribbean guy, patterns shaved into his hair. He told her he was security. There was a thump as one of the band dropped a reel of cable onto the floor. Jade asked if there was somewhere quieter they could talk.

'Sure.' He jerked his head in the direction of backstage and took her to his office. The CCTV monitor gave a live feed of the activity on the pavement as the band continued to shift their equipment.

'I'm following up for a colleague,' Jade said. 'You contacted us with information about the suspects in the Allie Kennaway inquiry.'

'The tape, yeah.'

So the tape did exist.

'You thought the people on the tape fitted the descriptions of the suspects?'

'Spitting image,' the man said. 'I showed him.'

'Yes. Just to be clear . . .' Jade drew out her phone and clicked on the photo-fits. 'The two men looked like these two?'

'Bang on.' Excitement burst under her skin, stinging, sizzling. Jade recalled overhearing Harris's scornful dismissal. *Wants his eyes examining . . . One was a black guy and the other looked nothing like either of our photo-fits.*

'They were both white?' Jade said.

'Yes.' Clements looked at her as if she'd lost the plot.

What the fuck was Harris playing at? 'You remember what time they were here?'

He narrowed one eye. 'It was just after eleven, five past, ten past. It's on the tape – there's a time-stamp.'

'How were they behaving?'

'Out of order. Pissed up, coked up, giving loads of abuse when I barred 'em. I told the other guy all this.'

'Yes,' Jade said. 'We wondered if you'd remembered anything else since then.'

He shook his head. 'No.'

'Did you get a receipt for the cassette?'

'No. Should I have?'

Yes. 'Not necessarily.' Jade fudged it. 'I'm just following up, like I said.'

'It's hard to believe, you get me?' he said, showing her out. 'Two idiots like that, worse for wear, potty-mouths but kids. Half an hour later they've killed someone. Shocking.'

'Yes,' Jade agreed. *And that's not the only thing that's shocking, believe me, mate.*

Steve

At the police station reception desk, Steve asked for DI Bell in person. He saw the polite flicker of interest pass between the staff there when he gave his name. Them putting two and two together.

One of the men made a phone call, then said DI Bell wasn't available, but if he'd like to come back tomorrow . . . Putting him off. Seriously?

'DC Bradshaw?' Steve remembered the young detective's name but not much more than that, except she'd been striking to look at, a gamine beauty with dark eyes, smooth brown skin and sharp cheekbones. And very young. Was she a trainee of some sort? He wanted someone who knew the score, who could tell him exactly what was being done. Not a novice.

The man spoke to someone on the phone and said, 'She's not available either. If you'd like to call back in the morning, sir, or we can ask DI Bell to contact you when she comes in.'

His frustration boiled over. '*No!*' he shouted. 'I want to see someone now and I'm not leaving until I do!' He slammed at the counter with the heels of his hands.

An officer in uniform coming through the door moved towards him, glaring, his hand going to the baton on his belt but one of the men waved him away. 'It's OK, mate.' To Steve he said, 'If you'd like to take a seat?'

'I don't want to take a seat. I want to talk to someone. Have they all gone home? Is anyone actually doing anything to get the bastards who killed my daughter?' He could hear the anguish and rage in his voice but felt helpless to modify his tone. 'Is there anyone actually here? Where is DI Bell? Why isn't she here? She clocked off early, did she? My daughter—' He was going to explode. He turned away, walked a few steps to the row of chairs by the windows. 'Get me whoever is in charge,' he said. 'Now.'

More phone calls. Steve listened to one side of it. 'Yes, sir . . . Steve Kennaway . . . In Reception . . . Wants to see someone now . . . Yes, I have explained that . . . Yes, sir . . . Yes, will do.'

Steve watched a couple outside, walking with a toddler between them. The child stopped suddenly, let go of their hands and turned to his father, who almost stumbled over him. The child had his arms raised, wanting to be picked up. His mother said something but she was smiling. Steve hated them for their happiness, their well-being. The father scooped the child up and set him on his shoulders. *High as the sky.* That's what Teagan had called it when she was little. *High as the sky, Daddy.* Steve or Sarah must have used the phrase at one time or another for her to adopt it.

The couple passed by, the dad holding the child's ankles, the little one with his hands wrapped around his father's neck.

Not too tight or you'll choke me . . . Was it Allie or Teagan who had held on too tight?

'Mr Kennaway?'

Steve turned.

'If you come with me, sir, I'll take you to see the acting SIO.'

Steve frowned at the acronym. 'The what?'

'The acting senior investigating officer.'

Steve was shown into a room with sofas, coffee-tables and a box of toys in the corner. A lounge without windows or a television.

'He'll be with you soon,' the man said. 'Can I get you a drink?'

'No,' Steve said, still angry. 'I don't want a drink. All I want is to see someone in authority.'

'You will.'

Left on his own, Steve circled the room as the minutes ticked by. Two. Then five. Then seven. He was building up to finding his way back downstairs to scream at them about the wait when a man entered.

'Detective Sergeant Harris.' He held out his hand, shook Steve's.

A firm grip. Warm skin. Big hands, big-framed. A thick neck, grey hair. Experienced, then.

The sergeant sat, pulling at the knees of his trousers. A smart grey suit. Steve took a chair opposite him, the fury still travelling up his spine in waves.

'First of all, my condolences,' DS Harris said. 'It's a tragedy, what's happened. A terrible waste. But how can I help?'

'I want to know what's going on,' Steve said. 'What's being done to find the people responsible?'

'You were allocated a family liaison officer?' DS Harris said.

'Yes.'

He folded his hands together and leant towards Steve. 'Their role is to act as a link between the investigation and yourselves.'

'I know that.' Steve struggled to keep his voice level. 'But it's not enough. Have you found any more witnesses? Has anyone else come forward? We're getting told nothing.'

'We all want the same outcome, Mr Kennaway, justice for your family. You must understand we never share operational information while we're still actively investigating leads. But I can tell you we've received significant help from the general public and everyone here on the team is working one hundred per cent to trace and apprehend the suspects.'

'Have you arrested anyone?' Steve asked him.

'I'm not at liberty to say.' Did that mean they had?

'I'm her fucking father!' Steve yelled.

The man stared at him for a moment, neon blue eyes steady, then went on in the same calm way: 'As soon as we can release any information your FLO will be briefed and you'll be the first to know. But I'm not going to lie to you. These things take time.' He splayed his palms upward, a little apart, bounced them as though weighing the burden of the work. 'It could be weeks, it could be months. But we won't rest until we get a result.'

Platitudes. What had Steve expected? Inside information, a slew of revelations about tip-offs from the public, names to match the photo-fits? A tour of the incident room?

'Now, I really should get on,' DS Harris was saying. 'If there's nothing else . . .'

'I want her back,' Steve said.

'I can only imagine—'

'No. Allie's body. I want her back. Now. So, if there needs to be a second post-mortem can you just get on with it? Give me my daughter back.' His voice shook and spit flew from the corners of his mouth but he didn't care.

'I'll pass that through to the coroner's office,' DS Harris said, smoothing his tie. 'We'll see what can be done.'

Steve didn't want to leave. He felt cheated, short-changed, but there was nothing else he could say. Biting the inside of his cheek, his back like a board, he followed DS Harris down the stairs. The detective moved nimbly for such a large man, keeping up a brisk pace.

In the reception area, he put out a hand to shake goodbye. Steve ignored it.

'DI Bell, she is still involved?' Steve said.

'Oh, yes,' DS Harris said. 'Just out of the office at the moment.'

'Right. And DC Bradshaw?'

The detective's smile faltered for a second. Then he said, 'She's not in today.' He seemed pissed off that the young DC wasn't there. Maybe she was ill or something. Or perhaps DS Harris was just irritated by Steve taking up his time. He went on, 'I'll speak to the coroner and, any news at all, Yun Li will make sure you're updated.'

Outside, the sun was breaking through the clouds. *High as the sky, Daddy.* It was Allie who had held on too tight, he was almost certain. Time was, he'd been able to ask Sarah to sharpen the focus of his memories.

I want her back, he thought. I want her back. I want them both back.

CHAPTER FIFTEEN

Donna

Kirsten greeted Donna with a look of astonishment when she saw her waiting at the school gates. 'Mum? Where's Dad? Why are you here?'

'Dad had an accident in the car. He's in the hospital.'

'No! Is he OK?'

'Yes . . . well, a broken leg.'

Donna scanned the streams of children weaving through the playground. She was looking for Matt.

'Are you making tea?'

'Yes. No. I don't know,' Donna said.

'We are having tea?' Kirsten said, a familiar note of sarcasm creeping back into her voice.

'I expect so,' Donna said. Then, seeing Kirsten's face, 'Of course we're having tea. I wouldn't let you go hungry.'

Matt collided with Donna, shouting, 'Mum!' His jumper was inside out.

Kirsten told him about Jim.

'Has he got crutches?' Matt said. 'Has he got a big plaster thing on?'

'Yes. Well, he should have by now. Come on, I've parked over the bridge.'

Donna only half listened to their chatter on the way to the car, her mind occupied with working out how to manage the next few days. If she could drop Matt and Kirsten off, perhaps Bryony could pick them up and walk them home. They would complain. The walk was a couple of miles. Or a taxi? Bryony could get a taxi from her school to the kids' and then back to the house. Unless they used their bikes. Were the bikes all working? She could imagine Bryony's response. 'No way am I riding a bike.'

Anyway, if they sorted themselves out with a snack Donna could get back by, say, seven and make tea. It'd have to be something quick and easy, pasta or pizza from the freezer. Continue with her most urgent work in the evenings. The weekend wouldn't be so bad – she could do some work from home in between ferrying the kids to their activities.

How long would it be till Jim was up and functioning? Christ, she felt guilty for even asking the question. Bones, legs, took weeks, didn't they? Weeks till he could drive and carry and . . . Oh, God.

Perhaps they could find someone, an au pair or something, to help out.

'You'll have to look after us, then,' Matt said, as if he was reading her mind, 'till Dad's better.'

Ain't going to happen. She was not about to start being a housewife and stay-at-home mother. Besides, there was absolutely no way she was giving up her role leading the Major Incident Team in the middle of a murder inquiry.

'I was thinking we might need help,' she said.

'What sort of help?' Kirsten said suspiciously.

'I don't know yet.' Could she ask Bryony to take it on? And what was *it*? Meals to be sure. Donna could sort out packed lunches for the little ones. They could all get their own breakfast so it was teatimes. And the twins could do all the dishwasher loading and emptying. And the bins. They were meant to load the dishwasher anyway but invariably 'forgot'.

'Can we go and see Dad?' Matt said.

'Soon, not today,' she said.

'Aw,' Kirsten complained.

'He'd love to see you but they're moving him today and we have to wait and find out when visiting hours are.'

Donna could cover the laundry, even if it meant loading the machine when she got in from work. Fit in a big shop at the weekend, fill the freezer. How hard could it be?

After they'd eaten, she laid out her plan and got them to agree to their various roles. After some dissension from Kirsten about walking home (and a swift veto on bikes from Bryony), it was agreed that if it was raining they could get a taxi and if dry they would walk.

'It'll be good exercise,' Donna said.

'Why don't you walk to work, then?' Kirsten said.

'That's, like, ten miles,' Rob said.

'Is it?' Kirsten said.

'More like seven,' Donna said.

'What's that in kilometres?' Matt said.

'Work it out, dummy,' Kirsten said.

'There's something else I need to tell you,' Donna said, lowering her voice so they stopped bickering and paid attention. 'Dad's accident happened because he had a heart attack. He's all right,' she went on quickly, seeing panic on Kirsten's face, 'and the doctors will be checking his heart to see what they can do so it doesn't happen again.'

'Like a bypass?' Lewis said.

'Yes, or medication,' Donna said. 'It depends what they find. So, anyway, he lost control of the car and hit someone, a man, and hurt him very badly, and he died.'

'Oh, no,' Bryony said.

'Will Dad go to prison?' Matt said.

'No, stupid, it was an accident,' Kirsten said.

'You're not stupid,' Donna said to Matt. 'And it was an accident so they won't punish Dad. He couldn't help it. He didn't do anything wrong. But because someone died they have to have an investigation and explain what happened for the man's family.'

Was he married? Had he children? Even now the coroner would be giving permission for a post-mortem, and the police would be tasked with getting a formal identification. All the same steps as happened with a murder, with any sudden death.

‘He won’t be able to do his driving lessons, though?’ Matt said.

‘Not till he’s better,’ Donna said. How badly would this hit his insurance premium?

‘When can we see Dad?’ Bryony said.

‘Tomorrow, all being well. But they won’t let us all in at once. They have rules. Two or three visitors at a time.’

‘We’ll have to take turns,’ Matt said.

‘Yes.’

The disruption to ordinary routine meant the children hung around the living room longer than usual, clinging together instead of separating off into their rooms or, in the case of the older ones, going out to see friends.

With *Masterchef* on the television, Donna’s thoughts returned to work. Their early success in finding Bishaar, in getting descriptions of the attack and the assailants, had led her to expect a swift conclusion, especially given the plethora of DNA from the scene. But now, with Anthony Mayhew eliminated, the whole inquiry had stalled.

On top of that, tackling Jade had been every bit as unpleasant as she’d feared. At one point she’d thought Jade was going to physically attack her. Donna had sensed the aggression, the change in the air. It was a sad business, but thank God it had come to her attention before any more harm had been done.

Calls were still coming in, in response to photo-fits and the appeal, so perhaps they just needed to wait it out until one of them came up trumps.

What else have we got? she asked herself. What’s solid? Nothing yet on CCTV, which was disappointing, the recording from Fredo’s being irrelevant (even if it did turn up again after Jade had lost it) and the one from the Cavalier non-existent. But we do know what they look like. We have their DNA. We can trace most of their movements before and afterwards. We have a chillingly detailed account of the killing from an eyewitness. All we need now are the suspects’ names but, given they’re not on the system . . .

It came to her then – another way to approach the problem.

She went upstairs for privacy and made the call.

'Harold Jenkins. Hello?'

'Sir, this is DI Bell. Sorry to call so late.'

'Not at all, Donna. What can I do?'

'You remember you said if I needed more resources for the Allie Kennaway murder . . . ?'

'I do.'

'Well, we've not been able to put names to our suspects yet. They've no existing criminal records and no one has identified them so far.'

'Go on.'

'I know it's a long shot but I'd like to go back to the lab, sir, and order familial DNA testing. Perhaps we might find a relative on the database and trace the suspects that way.'

Martin

'You training again, Dale?' Fran said. 'You should have a day off. You don't want to overdo it.'

'Maybe tomorrow,' Martin said. 'Tonight I can give him a lift. Tomorrow could be tricky.'

'He doesn't need a lift – he can get the bus, or he could just go round the park if all he needs is a run.'

'When did you get your coaching certificate?' Martin said.

'Oh, go on, then,' Fran said. 'I just don't know why you're ferrying him about all of a sudden.'

'I don't often get the chance. Anyway, it's no bother,' Martin said. He wished she'd keep her nose out but knew he mustn't react in any way that increased her curiosity or aroused suspicion.

Martin drove in silence. Dale was quiet too, probably sensing his father was in no mood for any blather.

The evening was dry and dull, no sunset visible, only a fading of the light through various shades of grey.

Oliver was waiting, as instructed, and Martin pulled in long enough for him to slip into the back. He drove to the outskirts of the Trafford Park, a spot on the edge of the sprawling industrial zone, with its factories and warehouses, shipping containers and cranes. He used to come here to meet one of his community informants back when he was investigating vice. Then, Martin knew, there had been no cameras along the road; now, he drove up and back double-checking before he parked the car.

'You found a job?' he said to Oliver.

'Not yet.'

'Try harder. Now – question for you, the pair of you. What are you going to do if you're arrested?'

Dale threw back his head.

'Are they going to arrest us?' Oliver said.

'Not if I can help it,' Martin said. 'But if they do, what do you say?'

'No comment?' Dale said uncertainly.

Martin scoffed. 'Yeah, right. Any better ideas?' he said to Oliver.

The lad blushed as he spoke. 'We didn't do it. We weren't there.'

'That right?' Martin leant in closer towards the back seats. 'Your DNA is at the scene, and we've an eyewitness saw you clear as day – he could pick you out of a line-up with his eyes half closed. Your kick marks are on the victim's body. We know you were there. We can prove it.' Martin turned to Dale. 'Prove you kicked him, spat on him, tracked his blood into a cab.'

Dale glanced back at his mate, then stared ahead out of the front windscreen. 'So we're fucked,' he said. 'If they arrest us.'

'Well and truly,' Martin said.

'We could go abroad,' Oliver said.

Martin stared at him. 'What the fuck do you think this is? The bleeding Bourne Conspiracy?'

'So what are we doing here?' Dale said hotly. 'Is this just so you can make us feel like shit?'

Martin moved forward swiftly and Dale jerked away. 'The reason we're here is that you two stupid pricks kicked someone to death. You think I want to be dragged into this fucking mess? But here we are. And if you do get arrested, either of you, there's some things you need to understand. First, and most importantly, we never had this conversation, or any conversation. I never knew anything about your part in the crime or your attempts to cover your arses. Clear?'

Both boys nodded.

'I am pure as driven snow. If you are arrested . . .' he looked at Dale, who was nervous, twitchy, a muscle working on the edge of his jaw '. . . I'll have to step down from the investigation. You'll be on your own. It'll be down to you two.'

'What will?' Dale shook his head. 'You just said we'd be fucked. So what can we do?'

'I'll tell you. You listen to me. I'm going to tell you what happened on Friday night and you learn this step by step. And we none of us go home tonight until you have. Off by heart and back to front. So, first off, you go into town, you have the meal, your other mates go off to the party – they're on the guest list, you two weren't. Next, you walk down to the Cavalier . . .'

Their eyes were on him, soaking up every word. If the world smiled on him, they'd never need to repeat any of it. But if everything went to shit, then learning this story, sticking to it line by line, insisting it was the truth, would be their only chance to escape conviction.

Steve

He should go to bed. He knew that. He ignored the thought and poured another measure into his whisky glass.

By the light of the table lamp, he'd been attempting to go through the emails that had piled up in his inbox. Finding himself overwhelmed by the task, he closed his laptop.

Beside him on the sofa, Allie's *A–Z of Being T* lay open. *Lola – a song from the olden days (1970) by The Kinks. A young man meets the beautiful Lola in a London . . .*

He didn't usually drink whisky but they were out of beer so he'd brought the bottle down from the top of the fridge. It had been a Christmas present. This year? Last year? Either from his parents or his sister.

Emma. Just thinking of her lit a small flame of indignation in his solar plexus.

You can't avoid her for ever.

Couldn't he? Other people were happily estranged from members of their family. He wouldn't care if he never saw her again.

Had there ever been a time when there'd been peace between them? Hard to recall one. As children, their fights had been protracted and bitter. With only two years between them they might have been playmates, but all their energies were directed into rivalry, into trying to get the better of each other or the rival into trouble. It must have driven his mother to distraction. She was the only one around, most of the time, to dispense discipline or arbitrate. Emma had a facility for crying at will and was able to switch on the outrage. She'd a Machiavellian mind, quick-thinking and opportunistic, could dream up justifications and downright lies in a heartbeat. Tactics that left Steve speechless, impotent to challenge the injustice of it all.

His mother wasn't a fool and could often see through Emma's histrionics but other adults were regularly conned. Was it simply jealousy – the cliché of Emma's nose being put out of joint when Steve came along, resulting in a lifelong competition for love and attention?

Still, he let her get under his skin. Five minutes' contact and he was four years old and bawling because she'd wrecked his line of cars, so carefully arranged to follow the pattern on the dining-room carpet. Or he was six and she'd ruined his birthday party, winning Pass the Parcel and Pin the Tail on the Donkey, and leaping to join in when he didn't blow all of the candles out in one go. And sneering when he got upset.

Fights consisted of Steve shouting and Emma mimicking him, calling him a cry-baby, a cissy. They were reasonably matched for strength and it usually took an adult to prise them apart as thumps, kicks and slaps were exchanged.

Would it have been different if Emma had been a boy? Or Steve a girl? They said sisters fought but in the next breath claimed to be the best of friends. And brothers, they could be vicious rivals, couldn't they? From Cain and Abel down to the pair in Oasis, the Gallagher brothers, with their well-publicized slanging matches.

He drank some of the whisky and felt it warm his gullet. The house was quiet, only the occasional snoring of the dog and the ticking of the joists as they settled with the cooling night.

He didn't want to waste his time, his energy, dwelling on Emma. He was sick of it. Sick of his Pavlovian responses.

The things she'd said about Allie. *Young boys needed stronger role models. Men needed to retain respect and authority*. Implying what? That Steve had failed in some way. That he was a loser, not enough of a man? His thoughts jumbled. What did it even mean nowadays to be a man? In his father's time most of the workforce in his section at the plant were male, the women given different jobs. Work was men together, sports too – the football or the cricket

– pub the same, save for weekends when wives and girlfriends joined in.

But that world was long dead. At work Steve had equally good relationships with men and women. Probably a quarter of his clients were women.

In his schooldays, a boy's worth was gauged by strength but also by skill. A boy with a comic wit and a facility for making the class laugh was valued, or the one who led the soccer team or played in a band. There were anxieties about height, penis size, acne and being thought homosexual (no one came out back in his day, not at his school anyway). A real man wasn't queer.

He drained the whisky, wincing as he swallowed. He should eat something. He should go to bed.

He'd never questioned his manhood, his masculinity or his sexuality. He'd asked Sarah once if she'd ever been attracted to women.

'Lesbian tendencies? No, not really. Maybe I've not met the right woman.' She laughed. 'As a kid I wanted to be a boy – I wished I'd been born a boy.'

'Why? I'm glad you weren't.'

'The usual. Boys had more fun, fewer rules. They could go off exploring while the girls had to bake bloody cakes or entertain the aunties or whatever.'

'Chained to the kitchen?' Steve said.

'Not exactly that but there was a line. My father never used the washing-machine, never cooked a meal. If I'd had a brother he'd never have lifted a finger either.'

'Does it matter, in a relationship, if you're happy with the arrangement?' Steve said.

'Ah,' she said, 'there's the rub. I bet you'd get different answers from men and women about that.'

All the stereotypes: men don't do housework, women aren't good drivers, men are no good with feelings, women can't wire a plug. Women are from Venus, men are from Mars.

What role model had Allie had in mind when she'd talked about changing gender? What was a woman in her eyes? The only image

Steve had in his head of trans women back then came from drag queens, who seemed to play up the stereotype of the ultra-feminine at a time when many women were trying to break away from all that.

It's hard to know how much he was doing it for attention. Why was it so hard to forget about Emma, to put her and her snide comments in a box marked 'Reactionary Claptrap' and lock it away out of sight? To let it go.

He refilled the tumbler.

A narcissist: that was what Sarah had said, a personality type that could never be persuaded by anyone else's opinion if it didn't reflect their own. No real sense of empathy.

But why couldn't *he* have some perspective on it? He knew the truth was there, behind the fog in his mind. The reason his feelings about his sister were so powerful, why he overreacted. If only he could dig it out, like a pebble in the mud. All the things she'd said. *He was still a child . . . putting himself in danger . . .* He closed his eyes, rooted around some more, grasping at possibilities. Then he had it. The answer to why her comments hurt so. The reason he objected so vehemently, out of all proportion, was because in the first unguarded, untutored moments, in the immediacy of learning about Allie's desires, her intentions, her real identity, Steve had experienced those exact same thoughts. *How can a fourteen-year-old boy really know what he wants? The health risks alone.* Loathed himself for it. And suppressed them.

He sighed and rubbed his face with one hand. He ought to put the glass down, switch off the lamp and go to bed. In a minute, he promised himself. In a few minutes.

Jade

A note had been slipped under her door. Mina's shopping list. *Shit.* It was too late to go now so she'd have to try to fit it in first thing. She should never have suggested it. There were home helps out there for that sort of thing. But after finding Mina breathless, lugging carrier bags up to their floor and giving her a hand time and again, there'd been one day when Jade was late for work. Rushing to get the woman and her groceries up the stairs, she had snatched a bag, which had split, sending tins and potatoes and milk bouncing down the stairs. Jade had wanted to chuck the rest down after it. And Mina too.

Instead she'd said, 'Next week I'll do the shopping. You write a list.'

'No, I couldn't—'

'You could. You will. I've got the car and that's the end of it.'

Now Jade put the note into her bag and shook off her jacket. She was wired, her head buzzing and pulse tripping fast. Nowhere near ready for sleep. But she had plenty to be getting on with.

First she opened the styrofoam container, wolfed down the kebab and chips she'd brought from the parade, choking when some pitta caught in her throat. The smell of raw onions filled the flat. She washed her hands. Then, sitting cross-legged in the old armchair, she connected her phone to her tablet and uploaded the files she'd got from the Cavalier.

When she'd gone into the pub and told them she was following up on an earlier visit, all she'd met was a wall of confusion. Rather than keep banging on that door, she'd changed tack: 'Sorry, must have got my wires crossed. It's CCTV footage from Friday evening we're after.'

The lad who was manager must have been practising his customer-service skills and couldn't do enough to help: navigating the system's hard drive, locating the time period, copying the files from three separate camera feeds into one folder, which she could upload to her phone.

Jade selected the feed that came from the entranceway first. Candida Gallego had encountered the two men at ten forty. Jade started the footage a couple of hours earlier and set it playing on double-speed looking for the suspects arriving, reckoning she could pause and take a closer look for any likely sightings.

There! She stabbed pause and rewound, holding her breath, and there they were. *Oh, God.* At nine thirty-three. Nods to the door staff. The film was in colour: she could see the dark-haired man wore a lemon shirt, while his mate was clearly a redhead and instantly recognizable from the photo-fit. Candy had been right: Man A had a bigger mouth and different eyes from the ones on the police image. She reran the section, stopping it at the point where both men were most clearly visible. Staring at them for long enough, her stomach churning. *Gotcha.* Yes, there was still the need to put names to faces, to hunt them down wherever they were hiding, but here they were, the pair of them. The men who'd killed Allie Kennaway.

Thirsty, she fetched herself a can of Red Bull and sat down again. Jumping forward in time Jade saw Candy and her friend leaving the Cavalier and then, ten minutes later, the two suspects came out. Another waymark for the timeline. Jade drank her can in three long swallows. Burped and caught a taste of lamb fat.

Over the next hour she traced the movements of the two men while they were in the Cavalier. She tagged them getting drinks at the bar twice and going into the Gents together. That could have been when they'd done some lines – Clements had said they were coked up when he barred them.

The angle of the cameras and the crush of people meant that the altercation with Candy and her friend was not recorded but Jade could see Candy's back at one point, see her shaking her head and slashing her palm crosswise as if she was cutting off the approach.

Jade paced the room as she listed what she now knew. DS Harris had taken the tape from Fredo's and pretended that Jade had lost it. He'd failed to collect any CCTV from the Cavalier. He'd lied about both items. Why? Was he having a breakdown? Or was it booze, maybe? Though usually you could smell a boozer even if they sucked mints or swigged mouthwash: the alcohol seeped through the pores. It drew veins across the face, ballooned the nose and set hands trembling.

Maybe he had other problems – gambling or money troubles, an affair gone nasty, something that was sucking up his time and attention while he pretended to be working the case.

It didn't add up, though. Harris could have left her to do the Cavalier but he had volunteered. Why volunteer if you're not capable? Was he sabotaging the investigation? Why? Was he dirty? Was someone paying him to derail their efforts? Or pressurizing him to pervert the case?

Or was it something closer, more personal? He had a son, didn't he? *Trying for the football.* How old would he be? She stood stock still, hands braced over her head. That was crazy! Football, they started them young, didn't they? Primary school. Could one of them be his son? She picked up the tablet, looked at Man A, frozen on the screen. She couldn't see any resemblance between him and Harris. Nothing – different build, different hair colour, features, different eyes. Same with Man B. The only thing he shared with Harris was his height.

Fact: Harris had interfered with the CCTV line of inquiry. Had he done anything else? She thought about the woman who had come in, the medium. Harris hadn't liked Jade asking about her, and he hadn't entered her details in the system. Poole. Sonia Poole. The psycho psychic.

Jade shivered and rubbed her arms. Back in her seat she searched online for that name and found an entry in Firswood.

It was two in the morning. She couldn't reasonably turn up on someone's doorstep until – what? – eight? Not unless she was arresting them. Shit. Itching with impatience, she circled the room.

Either Harris was losing it, falling apart on the job, or it was something more intentional. Whatever, the boss needed to know. *I'm a big girl. I'm not going to throw a tantrum if one of my officers wakes me in the night with breaking news about a critical development.* Jade had to make her listen. Listen long enough to get over the fact that Jade had carried on as though she was still part of the team, had kept working even though she'd been told to step down and see HR.

She rehearsed what she'd say. 'Boss, I need to talk to you. There've been some serious irregularities in the investigation. You need to see them.' No mention of the DS for now or the boss might cut her off. Jade dialled but it went to voicemail. She said her piece and added, 'Can you ring me back as soon as you get this?'

Please, please, ring me back.

CHAPTER SIXTEEN

Donna

As she made her way downstairs to sort out breakfast and packed lunches, Donna listened to the voicemail from Jade with a sinking feeling. Which part of *Step down and see HR* did she not understand? *Irregularities in the investigation?* When Jade herself had been instrumental in compromising evidence. Donna couldn't ignore the message: that would be irresponsible. At the very least she needed to know what Jade was on about but she was wary of encouraging any paranoia, if that was what was going on.

There was no bread. How could there be no bread for sandwiches when there was almost a full loaf last night?

Donna rummaged through the freezer but there was none in reserve. Kirsten was already up so Donna sent her to the corner shop, which should just be open. Kirsten came back empty-handed. 'They didn't have any.'

'How can they not have bread? Bread, milk, biscuits, loo rolls, papers.' She counted off the basics that people would spend over the odds on for convenience.

Could she fob the kids off with crisps and fruit? Doubtful. 'We'll buy you a sandwich on the way,' she said.

'Cool.'

Donna looked at the clock. 'What time do the twins get up? And Bryony?'

Kirsten shrugged.

'Go and wake them all, and Matt.'

Before long she heard banging overhead and Bryony shouting, 'Don't take all day.' Obviously beaten to the bathroom. Bryony came in and peered into the bread bin. 'There's no bread,' she said.

'Funny. Someone must have eaten it all,' Donna said.

'Well, it wasn't me,' Bryony retorted.

'There's cereal,' Donna called at Bryony's departing back.

'She doesn't like cereal,' Kirsten said.

Since when?

'Can we see Dad today?' Matt had surfaced, his hair sticking up at all angles.

'Hope so,' Donna said. 'I'll ring the hospital a bit later, find out when visiting time is.'

'Where's my PE kit?' Kirsten said.

'I don't know,' Donna said. 'Where is it usually?'

'I don't know.'

'Well, go and look for it.'

'Dad would know,' Kirsten said.

Donna gritted her teeth. 'Dad's not here.'

Kirsten sighed, and her thin shoulders slumped.

'Kirsten, it's not going to magically appear out of thin air. Look in your room, then check the hall and the utility room. Now!'

Kirsten threw her a malevolent glare and stomped off.

'Hurry up and eat that,' Donna said to Matt. 'Then get dressed.'

He mumbled something to her, his mouth bulging.

'Say that again, without the granola.'

'It's dirty.'

'What?'

'My uniform,' he said.

Oh, Christ. 'You've got a spare.'

'It's my old one. It's too small.'

'Up to you,' she said. 'Dirty or small.'

He pressed his spoon into the milk in his bowl, lifted it slowly, did it again. Daydreaming.

'Matt!'

'What?'

'Go now. Put one of them on.'

She had to go in search of Kirsten who had emptied all her drawers onto her bed and was sifting through the contents. 'It's not here.'

'Then you'll have to leave it. We're going to be late. I'll write you a note.'

In the hall, Kirsten took an age putting on her shoes and Donna knew she was doing it on purpose but resisted challenging her and prompting a full-blown hissy-fit.

She chivvied Matt and Kirsten into the car, then went back into the house to give Bryony taxi money in case it rained. By then Bryony was in the shower. 'I'll leave it on the table,' Donna shouted to her.

They stopped at a Tesco Express on the way to school. She let Kirsten and Matt pick out their lunches, and chose something for herself to eat at her desk. She scooted to the bakery shelves and put two large loaves into the basket, one white, one wholemeal.

'Nobody likes brown,' Kirsten said.

'I do,' Donna told her. 'The twins do.'

'They don't,' Matt chipped in.

'Oh, for Christ's sake!' Donna erupted, shouting at the top of her voice. 'Why are you all so bloody picky?'

Kirsten burst into tears. 'I hate you,' she wailed. 'I want Dad.'

Don't we all.

Donna ran to swap the loaf, ignoring the black looks she was getting from the cashier. Crap parent out of control, no discipline. Kirsten's sobs grew louder. *Oh, pack it in.*

In the car, Donna simply said, 'That's enough now, Kirsten. It's hard for us all without Dad, and if he were here I think he'd want you to be as helpful as possible. Don't you?'

Kirsten coughed and sniffed and gradually quietened, and Donna concentrated on the traffic, eager to get them to school and off her hands as quickly as she could.

* * *

'Boss?' Martin put his head round the door. 'How's Jim?'

'Comfortable, they say. They're doing tests today.' Donna sighed. 'There was a fatality. He lost control of the car and drove into a pedestrian. A young man.'

'Oh, Christ.' Martin stepped in and shut the door behind him. 'Should you be here? I can manage.'

'Thanks. I'd rather be here. It's not as if sitting by his bedside is going to solve anything and the kids are all at school so . . .' She gave a shrug. *Should* she be at his bedside? Wouldn't a loving wife be there, helping him through this? But there are visiting hours, she told herself, with a sense of reprieve. She had rung the hospital and written them down. She'd go on her own before lunch, then with the kids in the evening. 'I'm going in for eleven-ish if you can cover for me until I'm back.'

'Sure.'

'Guess who called me in the middle of the night.'

He grimaced. 'She didn't?'

'She did. Left a message. I think she may have been pursuing the case,' Donna said.

Martin looked askance. 'That is way out of order.'

'I know. I'll deal with it.' Donna had returned Jade's call but Jade hadn't picked up so Donna left a carefully worded message inviting her to come in as a witness and give a statement to someone separate from the inquiry about any 'irregularities'. Donna wanted to keep Jade at a distance to protect the investigation.

'So,' she said. 'Anthony Mayhew – done and dusted?'

'Yes,' Martin said. 'Taken home as soon as you left yesterday. I told the team we'd have a briefing this morning. Do you still want to go ahead with that?'

'Sure, yes. We could say ten o'clock or—'

Her phone rang, the forensics lab, and she signalled to him to wait so they could agree a time. 'Hello?'

'The familial DNA tests you requested in the Allie Kennaway investigation . . .'

'Yes?'

'We have a hit, a familial match to Man A.'

Yes! Donna felt the sizzle of adrenalin spark her nerve endings. 'Excellent.' She pulled her notebook over, pen ready.

'I'm sorry, ma'am.' Something in the way he said it gave her pause and sent shivers up the back of her neck. 'The match is to a serving police officer.'

'Oh, Christ.' It was regrettable when an officer's relative was involved in a serious crime but not unheard of. Police officers' DNA profiles were routinely included on the database so if they accidentally left traces at a crime scene they could be discounted. She looked across to Martin, standing by the door, concern visible on his face.

'The markers indicate a paternal connection,' the voice at the other end of the line was saying. 'We're looking at father and son.'

'OK,' Donna said. So Man A's father was in the service.

'The match is to Detective Sergeant Martin Harris.'

A punch to her guts. *Martin!* Donna couldn't speak for a moment, her mind locked in confusion. A blur of heat filled the back of her skull. A rush of vertigo made her feel like she'd swoon. 'Thank you.' She ended the call.

'You OK?' Martin said. 'Is it Jim?'

'No.' Her tongue was thick in her mouth. 'Martin . . .' The blood was beating in her ears. She felt unsteady. Did he know? He must. Her thoughts knotted, jumbled. *Serious irregularities in the investigation. Why does he want rid of me?* Jade's words.

Donna forced herself to speak. 'Last night I requested another look at the DNA. Specifically, familial testing.'

'Good idea,' he said.

She pressed her knuckles together for a moment, hoping to hide the tremble in her hands. 'There's been a positive match.'

'But that's brilliant.' His eyes shone, blue lightning, a smile on his lips.

'A match to you, Martin, a match between you and Man A.'

He looked puzzled. The smile fell away. Then he staggered, crumpling, catching the edge of the chair opposite hers, which rocked and slid beneath him before tipping him onto his knees.

'Jesus!' Donna ran to help him up until he could sit. 'I'll get a first-aider,' she said.

'No.' He rocked forward and back, gave shuddering breaths, his hands clamped to his knees.

He had one son, she knew that. Dale. The light of his life.

Martin looked at her. Tears stood in his eyes. 'He wouldn't,' he said. 'He'd never do something like that. Never.'

What could she say? The evidence was there. His son had been at the scene. Martin must have known. And covered up the fact. All the stuff with Jade, was there a connection? Was it a smokescreen, a distraction? The evidence she'd allegedly lost was meaningless. *Martin* had said it was meaningless. Donna had never seen it. Oh, shit. She felt sick, and there was a rushing sensation in her head.

'Martin, I'm going to have to ask you—'

'Yes, of course. I'll have to withdraw. Understood. There must be some mistake, Donna. There must be. Our Dale—' His voice broke. He was still breathing heavily.

'I'm sorry,' she said. 'And I have to ask you to remain here at the moment.'

While we go and arrest your son.

'Yes.' His face was working with emotion.

'Can I fetch you some water or would you like some fresh air?'

'Fresh air, maybe.' He stood and Donna waited to see if he'd keel over again. He looked shocking. 'You'll want my phone,' he said, 'my notebook.'

'Just for now. And I'll have to notify Professional Standards, even if there's no—'

'Of course.' His eyes filled again.

His visceral reaction and his patent shock were compelling. Had he really been working alongside her, sitting in the meetings, talking to witnesses, allocating tasks, knowing all along who they were looking for?

'He'll be at home now,' Martin said quietly. At the doorway, he paused and looked back at her. 'I'd have known if he was involved.

I'd have seen it. He's got his trials on Saturday. It can't be right.' He was dazed.

Donna didn't speak. She watched him leave. A ruin of a man.

And a traitor.

Sonia

As soon as she'd woken, after a night of ugly dreams and restlessness, the dread came rushing back. She checked her phone, at the side of the bed, but there was no word from Oliver.

Carry on as normal. That was what the detective had said. *How?* She tried to imagine turning up at the laundry again, recovered from her twenty-four-hour bug, making chit-chat with Cynthia, banter with the regulars, waiting for the talk to turn to the murder, to the suspect who looked like Oliver. She couldn't do it.

She sent a text: *Still sick, sorry. Will text u when Im over it. Maybe Govinda can fill in?* She'd not heard if Govinda had found any other work.

After a shower, she had coffee and smoked. No appetite. The thought of swallowing made her want to heave. The jittery feeling wouldn't settle, her blood fizzing in her veins, her head light.

She needed to move, to keep active, shake off some of the tension and tire herself. Fetching the vacuum-cleaner she began with the stairs. Above the whine she heard thumping and it took her a moment to understand that someone was at the door.

Usually Sonia could place the people who turned up unannounced when she saw them, a combination of their clothing and manner that defined them as officials, odd-jobbers, Jehovah's Witnesses or Mormons, meter-readers, charity collectors, or sales advisers flogging windows, plastic guttering, or a better deal for dual fuel. The woman on the doorstep was impossible to categorize. Asian with a punky haircut wearing a leather jacket. Was she collecting for something?

'Sonia Poole?'

She knew her name. 'Yes.'

'Detective Constable Bradshaw.' The woman showed her ID card in a leather wallet, a shield at one side. The police. Sonia's stomach flipped. They'd found Oliver. *Oh, God.*

'Can I come in?'

'Is he all right?' Sonia said.

The woman didn't reply as she stepped inside, which panicked Sonia further. 'Have you found him?'

'Found who?'

She should know. Didn't these people talk to each other? 'Oliver. My son.'

'Can we sit down?'

'Yes. Sorry.' Sonia took her into the kitchen, moved the cat off one chair and let the visitor have the other. Thought then, 'Or we could go in the living room?'

'Here's good.' DC Bradshaw placed her phone on the table. 'I'm going to record our conversation so I can make sure I don't leave anything out of my notes.' Sonia wasn't sure whether she was comfortable with that but the woman didn't give her any option. 'You came into the station yesterday?' She opened her notebook, the same type as the man had had.

'Yes.'

'You spoke to DS Harris?'

'I didn't get his name.' Did she? If he had told her it, Sonia didn't remember.

'A big man, in his fifties. Grey hair, blue striped tie.'

'Yes,' Sonia said.

'I'm following up on your visit.'

'So you've not found Oliver?' Sonia's hope and the fear matching it ebbed away. *Where was he? Where on earth was he?*

'No. We haven't,' the constable said. She sounded a bit unsure.

'I can't imagine where he is,' Sonia said. 'It's been three nights. Not a word.'

The woman was staring at the shelf above the table, the one

with cookery books on it and the framed photo of Oliver. 'That's Oliver?'

'Yes,' Sonia said.

'Recent?'

Something was off. Sonia didn't know what it was but she felt wary. 'Two years ago.'

'And you came in because of the appeal . . . to talk to us about Oliver?' Like she was guessing, making it up as she went along.

Perhaps Sonia should call DS Harris, ask him if it was OK to talk to this colleague. He'd told her to keep quiet but did that include other people in the police? Surely not. Perhaps DS Harris had sent this DC Bradshaw. Maybe she was a bit slow at her job.

'Why are you here?' Sonia said.

'To follow up, like I said. See if you've thought of anything else since yesterday.'

'No,' she said. 'Nothing. Will you excuse me a minute? I just need the loo.'

'Of course.'

Sonia went upstairs, climbing over the vacuum hose, closed the bathroom door and dialled the number that DS Harris had given her. There was no answer. She didn't leave a message because she couldn't think of what to say.

She flushed the toilet for effect and went back to the kitchen. The police officer didn't look as if she'd moved a muscle. 'If you could go over the facts again for me?' Her gaze was intense. She didn't smile and Sonia felt uncomfortable.

'Why?' she said. She sounded narked. She hadn't meant to but the woman had her rattled.

'There's been a bit of a mix-up in communication so we need to get your statement again.'

A bit of a mix-up? 'So no one's been looking for him? Nothing's happened?'

There was no reply for long enough. Sonia looked at the way the woman held her pen so tight, her nails ragged and bitten down.

'I'm sorry,' DC Bradshaw said. 'The sooner we get this done, the better.'

Sonia shook her head, a bitter taste in her mouth.

'It was very good of you to come forward,' DC Bradshaw said. 'That can't have been easy, your own son. All we want is to find Oliver and make sure he's safe. Tell me what you told DS Harris.'

'He . . . he was in town on Friday and he came home a bit earlier than I thought and then, it was weird, he'd washed his clothes and his shoes. He never does any washing. When I asked him about it he made up some story about falling in a puddle. Then when I saw the photo-fits—' She stopped, her heart aching.

'Did you talk to Oliver about it?'

'I tried. He went ballistic, said I was crazy. He left the house. That was on Monday.'

'And no contact since?'

'No.' Sonia was overtaken by sadness, tears leaking from her eyes. She wiped at them with her fingers and then the backs of her hands. 'I'm sorry.'

DC Bradshaw's phone began to ring, then cut out.

'Do you have the clothes?'

Sonia looked at her: she didn't seem to know anything. Had she even talked to DS Harris? 'No. He came back,' Sonia said. 'He came back sometime on Tuesday when I was at work. They've gone, them and the shoes.'

'OK.' The constable wrote more notes and said, 'We're going to need some more detail but this is good for now. You have Oliver's phone number?' Sonia gave it to her. 'And you've no idea where he might have gone?'

'No. None.'

'Do you know who he was with on Friday night?'

'Not really. Just their nicknames. Someone called Foz and another lad, Seggie. That's all I know.'

'And can you tell me how you left things with DS Harris at your meeting yesterday?'

'Why don't you know?' Sonia said. 'Didn't he tell you?' It was weird. She was being messed about in some way but she couldn't put her finger on it.

The woman stared at Sonia, her eyes almost black, and said. 'DS Harris was taken ill last night so we're trying to work out where he was up to with everything.'

'Oh, right.' If he was ill that would explain why he wasn't answering his phone. Sonia said, 'He told me to carry on as normal and that you'd keep looking for Oliver. He said if anyone talked about the . . .' she didn't want to use the filthy word but she steeled herself '. . . about the murder, I was to change the subject, and if people asked about Oliver to say he was away. He said there was already someone else being questioned, a suspect. I don't know if that was the other one from the photos.'

The constable was writing quickly, and Sonia could see her lips pressed tight together. Was she angry? What right had she to be angry? Sonia had done all she could to help and it sounded like one big cock-up.

'I don't know what to do,' Sonia said, the enormity of it all bearing down on her. 'It's a nightmare. I thought you were all out there looking for him. Anything could have happened to him.' She was furious with them, with the police and with Oliver. Was he sleeping rough? Taking drugs to help him forget what he'd done? He'd no money. Had he already thrown himself in the canal? 'Why weren't you looking for him? While I'm sat here going out of my mind. Why weren't you trying to find him?'

Sonia's phone rang. Unknown number. She answered it.

'Mum?' He was alive! Her heart flew into her mouth. She jumped to her feet. 'Oliver? Oh, God, Oliver, are you all right?'

'Mum, I'm at the police station, the main one. I've been arrested.' He sounded subdued, young and scared. None of the swagger and scorn of late.

'Oh, love.' Her hand went to her throat.

'I didn't do it,' he said, his voice shaking a little. 'I told you, I didn't do it. I've got to go now.'

'Oliver, I love you,' she said.

'Yeah. Me too.'

Sonia looked across to DC Bradshaw. The officer was watching her carefully.

'He's been arrested,' Sonia said, tears running down her cheeks. 'He's at the police station now.'

CHAPTER SEVENTEEN

Martin

'Why have they arrested him? What the fuck is going on?' Fran screeched. She'd been there when the police arrived, had seen them read Dale his rights and bundle him into the back of a squad car. Martin had had to wait it out at the station while Professional Standards were informed of his close connection to a person of interest in the investigation. It also served to prevent him warning Dale or trying to interfere in his apprehension.

'You know as much as I do,' Martin said.

'I doubt that,' Fran said. 'What have you done?'

'What have *I* done?' His temper flared hot through his torso. 'It's not what I've done. I'm not the one they've nicked, you stupid bitch.'

'And you knew nothing?' she said, all sarcasm.

He wanted to lamp her, wipe the smirk off her face. He turned and swept a backhand across the side table, sent the glass vase with its bouquet of roses and lilies halfway across the room to shatter, showering water and flowers everywhere.

Fran was silent then. He could just hear her breathing. Fast and shallow.

He rubbed at the back of his neck. He walked to the French windows, stared out at the garden. The patio with its teak furniture, the smooth green lawn, the first apples coming in on the tree, the water feature bubbling away in the corner. All picture perfect. Like the house. Paid for by years of work, of long shifts seeing what the worst dregs of humanity had to offer. Twenty-eight years' paying for the house, the holidays, the landscaping, the new car every year.

Two years to retirement. And now this.

'Murder, they said,' Fran began again. 'There's only one murder I'm aware of. And you're working it.'

'It's a mix-up,' Martin said, still staring at the view, watching birds on the feeder, goldfinches and coal tits. 'Our Dale hasn't killed anybody. No way.'

'Can't you do something?' she said.

'I've got him a solicitor,' Martin said. 'Other than that I can't go anywhere near him.'

'He's just a kid,' she said, beginning to cry, the strange, huffing sound he hated.

'He's eighteen, legally an adult.' He turned. 'Fran, I hate this as much as you but I believe in him. He's not a killer.'

'So why is he arrested?'

She needed to know that side of it or she might get suspicious that Martin hadn't told her. 'The DNA found at the crime scene, there was no match to anyone on the database. They ran familial DNA tests. That led them to me, which gave them Dale.'

'Oh, Christ.' She sat down, patting at her chest.

'All it proves—'

'Oh, fuck,' she said.

'All it proves is Dale was there,' Martin said.

'Yes, it proves he was there,' she said. 'And if he was there, then—'

'It doesn't prove who did what,' Martin said. 'Can you seriously see our Dale kicking someone to death? Because that's not my boy.'

'I don't know what to think,' she said.

'Mistakes get made,' Martin said.

'You think that's what this is? Some mistake? It's a pretty big fucking mistake,' she said. 'Can't you speak to someone? Sort it out.'

He crossed to her. Crouched down. She leant away. Stock still.

'I can't be involved,' he said. 'Use your brain. All we can do is sit tight, let the solicitor do his job. It's a long, long way from arrest to charge. And even further from charge to trial, if it comes to that. We're nowhere near that. Right?'

She gave a nod and he patted her knee.

'Can I see him?' she said.

'No. Not yet.'

She started on with the crying again. *Huff, huff, huff.* Martin stood, and squeezed his eyes shut. 'There's going to be an explanation,' he said. 'We just have to wait.' He rolled back his shoulders. Made a decision. 'I'll be back later.'

'Where are you going?' she said, panicky.

'Stretch my legs.'

She opened her mouth. He knew she wanted him to stay and he couldn't. He couldn't face the neediness, the endless questions. He looked at her dead on. And she thought better of it.

'You could go to Mel's for a bit,' he said, 'till things are clearer.' Better off at her sister's than here on his back twenty-four seven.

She gave a nod.

He went to fetch his coat. Familial fucking DNA. He could have throttled Donna. Why hadn't she run that past him? Strictly speaking, *he* was acting SIO when she'd put that request in. If he could have dissuaded her, it wouldn't have come to this. Dale would be getting ready for Saturday's trials and the inquiry would be stalled. How could Donna do that? Go behind his back. Something slithered in his guts. Had she suspected him at that point? Had some part of Jade's lunatic raving made Donna question his behaviour? No. He rejected the thought. Donna believed his story about the CCTV tape. She'd acted on it, after all. Donna wasn't a problem. Jade had been but now she was out of the picture, a manipulative little slag off her box on meds. One problem solved.

Donna running to the lab without consulting him had completely fucked up all his efforts to spare Dale and Oliver from coming onto the radar, but at least Plan B might save his son from a lengthy jail sentence.

He wanted a drink and decided it would be best to find a boozer where he wasn't known, take a paper, avoid conversation. Sit there long enough to drown his sorrows. By then Fran should have shifted to Mel's and he'd have the place to himself.

At the very least Donna would let him know if they brought charges. And what they were. Wouldn't she?

What a bloody mess. All of it. A fucking nightmare.

Steve

'Dad!'

His first thought was danger. She needed him. He was halfway to his feet, trying to get his bearings, before he saw Teagan, arms crossed, staring at him.

'You slept on the sofa?' she said, like it was a betrayal of some sort.

There was a pounding in his temples, a ripple of pain through his skull. 'I didn't mean to.'

'Have you got a hangover?'

'Yes.' Honesty was the best policy with Teagan. He closed his eyes. His mouth was full of paste.

'Are you going to be sick?'

'Only if you keep talking about it,' Steve said.

'Shall I get you some breakfast?'

Oh, Teagan. I should be doing that, looking after you. 'I'll make toast. Just get a quick shower and wake myself up.'

'We could go for a walk with Dix,' she called, as he went upstairs.

'We could.'

The shower helped a little, but when he went to brush his teeth, the sensation of the toothbrush in his mouth made him gag.

He managed a slice of toast. Coffee. Paracetamol. But the ache in his head seemed to pulse with every beat of his blood. Serves me right.

'Yun Li rang,' Teagan said. 'He won't be here today but we can call if we need him. I told him we were going out.'

'What about the reporters?' Steve said. He'd walked through them, tight-lipped, yesterday on his way to the police station. Registering but not replying to every quick-fire question.

'Tell us about Allie, Mr Kennaway.'

'How are you bearing up?'

'Do you think someone's sheltering those responsible?'

'Are you happy with how the police are handling things?'

'They've all gone,' Teagan said.

He looked out of the front door. She was right. He wondered what new tragedy they were flocking to. Like scavengers after carrion. That wasn't fair. After all, publicizing Allie's murder was part of trying to find those responsible.

'Where shall we go?' Steve tried to summon some energy, inject a note of anticipation into his voice.

'Lyme Park,' she said.

'OK.'

Steve had to lift Dix into the back of the car. 'Lost your spring, boy, eh?'

The deer park was a fourteen-mile drive away. A rolling estate surrounded the grand house and gardens. The day was fine, a clear blue sky and warm winds. Steve felt fragile, raw at being outside and away from the cocoon of the house, the headache still gnawing behind his eyes.

They walked up through the pine woods, the air rich with the smell of loam and vegetation, cool and watery in the shade. Teagan showered encouragement on the dog and stopped every so often to photograph items of interest, pine cones, the trees, the canopy silhouetted against the sky.

'What's that for?' Steve said.

'I don't know yet,' she said.

He tried to empty his mind, to focus on the present, as they climbed over the stile at the far end of the copse onto the open heathland. He noted the colours of the grasses and the meandering drystone walls, the sounds of birds, the burble of the rivulets that streamed down the hillside, and the drone of engine noise from an occasional jet passing overhead.

Their descent took them into a gully between two slopes. The path was narrow, treacherous, a morass of mud and stones. At times they had to use their hands as well as their feet to navigate the steepest stretches.

Dix was slow climbing out on the far side and Teagan called him on. The three paused for breath at the top.

There was a tree in flower, small white stars. Steve didn't know its name. Sweetly perfumed. *Allie*. Longing for her – for her and for Sarah – swamped him. He put a hand on the tree trunk, turning away from Teagan, his composure fissuring, splitting like the patterns of the bark, like the patterns on the skin of his hand.

'You go ahead,' he said. 'I need a pee.'

He scrambled back round the crown of the hill until he was out of her sight, then knelt, his knees instantly soaked by the waterlogged peat. Covering his face, he sobbed until the worst of the pressure had eased and he felt capable of walking again, his head still banging with every step.

Donna

The mood when Donna walked in was radically different. People were sombre, silent, barely relating to each other, turned in on themselves. Disbelief, anger, mistrust about Martin had undermined morale.

Donna needed to motivate them, to reassure them, to bring them back together in some sort of unity and restore trust. People talked about cops being like family. And you were. You shared the most testing, most horrific, most dangerous experiences, peering into the pit of savagery, loss and cruelty, and then you switched off, went home and acted halfway sane for your other family. So, when someone took that bond, that camaraderie and trust, and shat all over it, the blow was visceral. A betrayal of kinship.

'I'm not going to speculate about whether DS Harris had prior knowledge of his son's suspected involvement in this case. That would be a waste of my time and yours. If evidence comes to light, and we *will* actively be looking for such evidence, Martin Harris will be subject to due process like anyone else.

'This is an unpleasant situation for us all. It's easy to feel undermined, to lose heart. We're not going to do that because we have a job to finish and you are a bloody good team. Look at what we've achieved: Dale Harris and Oliver Poole are here in custody, awaiting interview. Later today I'm confident we'll be able to match their DNA profiles to our scene of crime. Look at what else we have. Four witnesses, who will help give us a narrative for the events of Friday night. Candida Gallego, sexually assaulted by Dale Harris in the Cavalier, Mahmoud Bishaar, who witnessed the murder itself, Louise Hill, who saw the men arguing and told us about the blood on Dale Harris's shirt sleeve, and Feroz Hassan, who had the men in his cab, where they left traces of Allie Kennaway's blood. On top of all that we have substantial forensic evidence from the scene that perfectly fits our eyewitness account. This is the home run,' she said. 'And I'm asking you all for a final push.'

Donna lifted up the photograph of Allie Kennaway. 'This is why we're here and I believe we're *so* close to establishing who killed this young woman. Focus on that. Continue to work as meticulously and with as much energy as you have been so far, and continue to share information. Check and double-check evidence as it comes in. I know you're as committed to solving this murder as I am. If mistakes have been made, I have to hold my hands up and take the fall.' She saw glances of sympathy and felt a softening in the air. 'But I'm *not* going to let that distract me now, and neither should you. From here on in, everything will be handled in an exemplary fashion. Our work will be irreproachable. Please don't discuss the situation with anyone outside the room.' There were nods of agreement. 'And I promise to inform you all as soon as we know anything more about how things stand. Thank you.'

Her phone rang as she walked to her office.

'DI Bell,' she answered.

'Sergeant Williams here, ma'am.' Donna waited for him to say more, wondering if it related to their arrests. 'I'm ringing as a matter of courtesy, ma'am. We're about to announce the identity of the victim in yesterday's road-traffic incident, involving Mr Bell.'

Shit. She hadn't recognized Williams's name.

'Yes,' she said. 'Thank you.'

'The deceased was Aaron Drummond, aged twenty-eight. Customer service assistant. Mr Drummond was married with two young children.'

Oh, God. Donna closed her eyes. 'Thank you,' she said again. 'Thank you for letting me know.'

'Will you be seeing your husband?'

Do I have to do everything? It was all too much. The case, the kids, Jim's trouble. This dead man and his children. His poor children. His wife.

'I'll tell him,' she said.

Visiting was eleven to midday. She'd arrive at half eleven, get someone to drive her, save time trying to park, and if she spent twenty minutes with Jim, she could be back to resume interviews by just after twelve.

She rang down to the custody suite. 'Where are we up to with lawyers for Dale Harris and Oliver Poole?'

'We've Thomas McKinney on his way for Dale Harris.' One of the city's biggest defence lawyers. Martin must have arranged that. She'd go to someone like him if one of her kids was in Dale's position. She tried to imagine it: Rob or Lewis in a cell, blood on their hands. What would she do if one of hers had hurt someone, killed someone? She couldn't imagine hiding it, lying. Had Martin felt any qualms when he learnt his son was responsible? Had he hesitated at all before choosing to corrupt the investigation?

'Oliver Poole has requested a duty solicitor, who is meeting with him now.'

'I'll start with him, then. No time to waste. Inform Poole and his solicitor that we're conducting an initial interview soon as they're ready.'

'Yes, boss.'

Knocking at her door. She looked up to see the chief constable.

Astonished, she got to her feet. 'Sir? Come in.' She was flustered, her breath catching.

'Just passing through,' he said. 'But I wanted a word. This business with DS Harris, the arrest of his son.'

'Sir?'

'Is it going to be a problem for us?' Any warmth in his manner had evaporated. He regarded her steadily.

Well, what do you think? She wanted to defend herself, defend the team and their work, but it would be wrong to pretend things weren't close to disastrous. 'I don't know, sir. DS Harris alleges he was completely in the dark about his son's potential involvement, and he stepped down straight away. Professional Standards have been informed. I imagine they will want to audit his input.' *At the very least.*

'You check his work on the case so far. I want to know where we stand before they descend on us.'

Donna thought about the missing tape from Fredo's. What had Martin put in his notebook about that? Accusing Jade of losing it was obviously a fit-up. And Jade had talked about irregularities – plural. What else was there?

God, he had fooled Donna so comprehensively. Sure, Martin had a reputation for a quick temper, for being a little heavy at times, jumping in. There'd been the odd fist-fight after a boozy night with the lads. The sort of night that Donna avoided or, if she had to show her face, left before it got raucous. Common enough for some coppers, handy with their fists. And that quality, the physical bravado, had served him well as a bobby, when he was facing real danger. When he piled in and disarmed a gangster with a handgun, or wrested a knife off a scally. Two awards for bravery. But beyond that there had never been any gossip that Donna had heard. No whispers about violence in the marriage, no whiff of dodgy dealings or unsavoury connections.

The chief constable said, 'I must ask whether you feel your existing relationship with DS Harris might impede any such assessment as regards impartiality and so on.'

Her stomach clenched, her jaw too. The slimy bastard.

'Our existing relationship is a professional one, sir. And I have no reservations about my ability to be impartial. I hope you don't.'

He didn't reply, just gave a nod, then said, 'And your husband? With this workload, if we need to bring someone in to take the reins . . .'

'Thank you, sir. No, sir. I can manage.' No way were they going to take this off her. Not now. This was her investigation, her team, what was left of it. And she would see it through to the end. Bitter or sweet.

* * *

Oliver Poole looked younger than his eighteen years, puppy fat in his face, though he was six feet tall. She'd put him at sixteen if she had to guess. He seemed withdrawn, hunched over and staring at the table, avoiding eye contact. Terrified, probably. He'd never been in trouble before, and now here he was, accused of the most serious of crimes and not allowed any contact with his family or friends. His solicitor and Donna were the only people he'd speak to in the immediate future. Donna had to make him feel safe, feel listened to. She had to get him to trust her, at least enough to tell her the truth.

She ran through his rights for him, ensured he understood his situation and the grounds on which he was being questioned. The duty solicitor, Jeremy Chortle, whom Donna knew from previous interviews, sat with pen poised ready to make notes. Beside Donna, DC Thwaite did the same, a record of the session to accompany the video-recording already rolling.

'Can you tell me where you were last Friday evening, Oliver?' Donna said.

'In town.' He spoke quietly. She could barely see his face, head bent so low she was looking at the crown of his head, his ginger hair cropped close and bristly.

'When did you get to town?'

'Around half eight.'

It was important to lead up to the event slowly or he might shut down altogether. Few people who killed were undamaged, emotionally and mentally, by the act. And for someone so young it would be even worse.

'Where did you go?'

'A Cuban restaurant on Peter Street,' he said.

'Who were you with?'

'Dale and Foz and Seggie,' he said. The fact he was answering questions and wasn't choosing to say, 'No comment,' gave her hope that they could make significant progress with him.

'What happened after that?'

'We went to the Cavalier.'

'All of you?'

'Just me and Dale.'

'What happened to the others?'

'There was a private party on. Seggie's brother got them on the guest list but he couldn't get us two on.'

'How long were you in the Cavalier?'

'Don't know.'

'Do you know when you left?'

'No.'

'Where did you go when you left?' she said.

'Nowhere. We just walked around for a bit.'

'Where?'

'Just around. Deansgate and that.' He began to tremble, the whole of his frame shaking, muscles twitching. He knew what was coming.

She tried to calm him. 'Thank you. Do you remember anything about the Cavalier?'

'Not really.' No mention of the harassment of Candida Gallego. Hiding it? Or oblivious? Nothing out of the ordinary. Just a bit of everyday sexual assault.

'You were drinking?'

'Yes.'

'What did you have to drink?' she said.

'Cider.' Back in fashion. You could get dozens of different flavours now.

'How many?'

'Two rounds, I think.'

'You're not sure?'

'No.' The shaking had subsided.

'Did you take any drugs?'

He hesitated. She stayed silent. 'Yes,' he said eventually.

'What did you take?'

'Some C.' A quick glance up at her, anxiety in his light brown eyes.

'Cocaine?' she said, matter-of-fact.

'Yes.'

'OK,' she said. 'So, you've told me that you were in the Cavalier and you had some cider to drink, you took some cocaine, and when you left you wandered around town near Deansgate. Is that correct?'

'Yes.'

She was circling closer to the crime, hoping he wouldn't freeze up or break down. 'Thank you. At that point what was your state of mind, your capability, given the substances you'd taken?'

'Pretty much out of it,' he said, sounding ashamed.

'OK. Now I want to ask you about an incident that happened at around eleven fifteen that night, on Spring Gate Fold, a small side street off New Mill Street.'

He trembled again, his breath audible, harsh and quick.

'That was the site of an attack on a young transgender woman called Allie Kennaway. I think you know something about that. I think you can help us. What can you tell me, Oliver?'

A drop of fluid landed on the table, then another. Was he crying?

'Oliver, can you look at me, please?'

He lifted his head. He was pale but dripping with sweat.

'Would you like a drink of water?' Donna asked him.

'Yes, please.'

She signalled to DC Thwaite to fetch one. When the officer returned, Oliver took the paper cone and drained it.

'You were there at Spring Gate Fold, weren't you?' Donna said.

'Yes,' he said.

Whoa! It was a significant admission. She'd anticipated denials, an instinctive twisting and turning while she steadily worked on him, laying out the evidence they had, tying the noose tighter, but he was pliant, cooperative. Perhaps he was sickened, sorry for what he'd done. Wanted to make amends by finally taking responsibility.

'Was Dale Harris with you?' Donna said.

'Yes.'

'This is a picture of Allie Kennaway,' Donna said, placing the photograph they were using for the investigation on the desk, facing Oliver. 'Did you see her there?'

'Yes.' Almost a whisper.

'Can you tell me where she was when you first saw her?'

'There, in the alley.'

'In Spring Gate Fold?'

'Yes,' he said.

'Had you seen her before that?' Donna asked.

'No.'

'She was already there when you and Dale reached Spring Gate Fold?'

'Yes.'

'Why did you go to Spring Gate Fold?' Donna said.

'We heard someone calling for help.'

Donna's back stiffened. 'You heard someone calling for help. Is that right?'

'Yes.'

'Where were you when you heard someone calling?'

'New Mill Street.'

'Going where?'

'Nowhere, really. We just didn't want to go home yet.'

'So you heard calling, someone in trouble. Is that correct?'

'Yes.' He wiped his sleeve over his face, mopping at the sweat.

'And what did you find when you got there?'

'This bloke – he was after her, you know. He was trying to rape her. She was screaming and we tried to get him off.'

Oh, God. 'You and Dale?'

'Yes. And he knocked her down and he pulled out a knife.'

'OK. Can you describe this man?'

'He was black, like, African.'

Oh, Christ. He was blaming Bishaar. Donna felt tension lock across her shoulders. Her heart jumped. 'How old?'

'I don't know.'

'How tall?'

'Smaller than me, I reckon, maybe five seven or five eight.'

'What else can you remember about him? What was he wearing?'

'One of those shirts without a collar and trousers, like cargos, khaki.'

All the details were consistent. Too consistent. Too easily recalled.

'And you say he drew a knife?'

'Yes. One of those big hunter's knives. He said he was going to kill us. Then he grabbed me and held the knife to my neck. He told Dale to kick him.'

'Kick Allie Kennaway?'

'Yes.'

'Where was she at that point?' Donna said.

'Still on the floor. Not moving.'

'What did Dale do?'

Oliver shook his head, wiped at his nose with the back of his hand.

'What did Dale do?' Donna said again, keeping her voice level.

'He kicked him.'

'He kicked Allie Kennaway?'

'Yes.' Half the time he referred to Allie as 'her' and the rest as 'him'.

'Where did he kick her?'

'I'm not sure.'

'Why aren't you sure?'

'I didn't see it all. It was mental. The black guy had a knife at my throat. I was trying not to get cut. He kept shouting, "Again! Again!" and Dale had to do what he said.'

'How many times did Dale kick her?'

'I don't know. A few.'

'What happened then?'

Oliver's head was down again. He didn't reply. She repeated the question.

'He made me kick her as well. He still had the knife. I couldn't do anything.'

If this was true, if any word of this was true, why would Bishaar call 999?

'Did you kick her?'

'Yes,' he said. 'He walked me over there, he had the knife on me.'

'How many times did you kick her?'

'Two or three.'

'And after that what happened?'

'He said we'd killed her. And he said if we spoke to the police or anyone else he'd come and find us. He said he was a child soldier. He'd been a child soldier in Africa and there was a gang of them here. They'd hunt us down and torture us. He said that they'd – that – that . . .'

'Take your time,' she said, as he stumbled over his words.

'He said they'd cut out our tongues and cut off our pricks and then skin us until we bled to death.'

Child soldier? Torture? Jesus.

'And then?'

'He told us to go home. And never to say anything.'

'What did you do?' Donna said.

'We got a cab and we went home. We tried to cover it up.'

'How?'

'We got rid of our clothes and our phones. I'm sorry,' he said. 'We were scared.'

Maybe, but not of child soldiers and torture. Scared of being caught, of being found out. Scared of what they'd done. Oliver's story was a load of bollocks. But it fitted the crime scene. It fitted the evidence, if you twisted it far enough.

Evidence Martin Harris had been privy to. She was convinced beyond any doubt now that Martin Harris was up to his neck in it. It sickened her.

Donna decided not to challenge Oliver yet. Let him think she'd swallowed the story of the 'bogeyman' who 'made me do it'. And see what Dale Harris's version of events was. Then she'd find a way to undermine their devious little plan.

'That's been very helpful,' she said. 'A couple more questions before we take a break.'

Oliver looked across at her, eyes guarded, breathing still uneven.

'When you first saw Allie Kennaway, did you know she was transgender?'

'What?' Was he playing for time?

'When you first saw Allie Kennaway, did you know she was transgender?' Donna said.

'No. I thought she was just a normal girl.'

'So when did you realize that she was a transgender woman?'

He didn't reply at first. He blinked and licked his lips. 'I don't know.'

'Was it when you kicked her?'

'No. After. When it came on the news.'

'OK. And did you or Dale tell anyone else about this?' *Like Martin?*

'No,' he said.

'Did anyone find out?'

'Just you,' Oliver said. His tawny eyes drilled by fear.

CHAPTER EIGHTEEN

Jade

While Jade had been talking to Sonia Poole, DI Bell had left a message for her. Shit about coming in to make a statement. Not to her, though. The DI seemed hell bent on keeping Jade out of the running. But the boss needed to know what Jade had found out. And now. Did anyone even know Martin Harris's son was their Man A? Had they picked up Dale Harris as well as Oliver Poole? The boss needed to see and hear the evidence. To let Jade back into the team so she could help take down Harris, along with the killers he'd been shielding.

She'd turn up at the boss's office and refuse to leave until the boss had heard her out. What was the worst that could happen? Jade getting arrested? Possibly. *Obtaining information under false pretences. Impersonating a police officer.* Jade ran her fingers over her warrant card, the card she should've surrendered. What if there were measures in place to stop her getting into the building? And Harris. If Harris was there . . .

Shit.

Instead of driving to the official car park she left her vehicle a couple of blocks away in the multi-storey at the Great Northern shopping centre.

Nearing the station she grew self-conscious, felt anxiety grip her, expected to hear her name shouted out at any moment, to hear the rush of footsteps after her.

She lifted her head higher and dropped her shoulders, made

herself walk a fraction slower but just as purposefully. Owning the street.

The car park was at the back of the station. Through the chain-link fence she clocked immediately that Harris's Merc wasn't there. She looked more slowly for the boss's Volvo but that was missing too.

The boss had to come back here sooner or later but Jade could only hang about for so long before attracting attention.

Picking at her fingers, she winced as she caught a raw edge.

She looked up at the building. There, on the fourth floor, the Major Incident Team would be focusing on interviews with Oliver Poole.

Why wasn't the boss here? Had something come up already, some lead that required the personal attention of the senior investigating officer? What could be more important than overseeing the interview?

Jade stifled the urge to duck out of sight when she saw people passing the windows on the fourth-floor corridor.

Which gave her an idea.

The biggest hurdle would be getting through the front desk if they'd been alerted to Jade's new status (which was what? Nut-job? Head case?). Only one way to find out. If she was pulled up she'd tell them she had an appointment with HR on the first floor. Just hope no one wanted to escort her there in person.

She waited at the corner of the building, pretending to study her phone until she saw a group of uniforms, three of them, headed for the entrance. She tagged on behind them. Even so, when one of the men on the desk looked over and saw her she felt her legs weaken and her head buzz. Then he gave her a quick nod and she went through after the others.

From the third floor (home to offices for Crime Reduction, policy and administration, training and neighbourhood policing), in a seat near the drinks machine, she had a good view of the car park. Now it was just a question of waiting. Waiting and watching until the boss got back.

Donna

Donna was replaying the interview with Dale Harris in her head as she was driven to the hospital. He had come across as more collected than Oliver, none of the sweating or trembling. His replies were delivered in a steady monotone with only occasional hesitation.

Replies that painted the same picture as his friend had. Often using the same phrases. How the two of them had wandered around town, drunk and drugged up. How they'd heard cries and screams and discovered Mahmoud Bishaar sexually assaulting Allie Kennaway. How their attempts to protect her had enraged Bishaar and how he had forced them at knifepoint to kick the prone girl. And threatened them on pain of death to keep silent and to destroy evidence.

The thought of Martin Harris coaching them, telling them how to account for each element of the evidence, the shoe marks on the body, the skin under his son's fingernails, the spittle on Allie's face, made Donna feel murderous.

And while Donna didn't believe a word of it, it was hard to know what a jury would make of it. The word of two previously law-abiding young men versus that of a destitute African Muslim asylum-seeker.

Juries were always tasked with considering the evidence and only the evidence, and expected to leave all prejudices, assumptions and bias at the courtroom door, but in real life the behaviour of juries was nigh on impossible to predict. A serious crime of murder or manslaughter required the standard of proof to be *beyond* any reasonable doubt. If it came down to who was believed, to two against one, Donna wasn't sure a jury would convict.

* * *

The driver dropped her at A and E and she told him she'd call when she was ready to be collected around midday. Twenty minutes would be enough.

When she found the right ward and right bay, Jim looked even worse than he had the day before. The bruising on his face was a darker colour, the cuts had crusted over, and there was a lump on his forehead. His leg was encased in plaster up to the thigh. His eyes were shut.

She had brought him a wash-bag, toiletries and a dressing-gown. It would be some time before he needed other clothes.

Donna moved the chair round to face the bed, which roused him.

He asked after the kids and she told him they wanted to visit. She'd bring them that evening.

'They miss you,' she said. 'Me too.' Did she? Did she miss him? Really *miss him*, or just miss the convenience of him being there to look after the family? The thought was like a barb, caught under her skin. What was wrong with her? This was her husband, the man she'd shared twenty years of her life with, but what she felt for him now was closer to pity than love. She struggled to act normal. 'Is there anything you want bringing?' she said.

'Don't think so.' He seemed slow. Perhaps it was the painkillers.

'Have you seen the cardiologist?'

'Not yet. So maybe tomorrow.'

She took a breath. 'Jim, Sergeant Williams rang me this morning,' she said. 'They've released the man's name.'

'Right.' He screwed up his mouth.

She took his hand. 'You want to know?'

'Yes.' He blinked.

'He was Aaron Drummond. He had a wife and two children. He was twenty-eight years old. A customer service assistant.'

He turned his head away from her. She saw his chest rise and fall slowly. Once. Twice. Thought of the heart in there, frail, damaged. 'Right,' he said eventually.

'I'm sorry,' she said.

'Yes.' Curt. What was he doing? Trying to be brave? To be stoic?

Donna gave his hand a squeeze and he withdrew it, reaching for water at the bedside.

When he'd had a drink, Donna said, 'They'll want to take your statement, the police. Soon, probably. While it's still fresh.'

'I don't remember a thing,' he said. 'I left the ring road and next thing I'm in hospital. Nothing.'

'Then tell them that. It's all you can do. It was an accident,' she reminded him. 'A horrible accident.'

Jim didn't ask about her work and she didn't volunteer anything. She struggled to fill the last few minutes of visiting time with snippets about the kids. He was distracted. It was an uphill battle to get any reaction.

She put the chair away and he lay back, eyes closing.

She kissed his forehead, careful not to touch the cuts or the egg over his eye.

She thought about saying she loved him but the words wouldn't come. Why? Because she wasn't sure of her feelings for him any more? Because she was a coward and feared he'd not reply in kind? Had he stopped loving her? Was that the reason for the gulf between them? A gulf she didn't know how to bridge. Or was it her fault that she no longer felt any sexual attraction to him, any passion? Just familiarity, a vague fondness. *Christ!* She shouldn't be thinking like this. Not now.

Work was waiting for her. Overwhelming as it was, fucked up as it seemed to be today, work was where she wanted to be. Work was easier, safer than this.

'I'll see you later,' she said, and touched his hand.

She was calling her driver before she reached the main corridor.

Sonia

She shivered. Her arms were cold. She was cold all over. She rubbed at her arms, then her thighs. There was a fog in her head, dense, and every so often thoughts penetrated, sharp and dangerous as lightning.

The cat was yowling outside. Standing, Sonia felt stiff, as if her bones had been filled with concrete.

The cat slipped in and circled her feet. Sonia looked at the feeding bowls. There were still some nibbles left. 'Finish that first,' she said.

The cat sniffed at the remains, then walked away, tail held high.

An image kept coming to her of Oliver in a cell, huddled on a bench, knees drawn up, head down. Oliver, alone and frightened.

All she wanted was to see him. But DC Bradshaw had explained she wouldn't be allowed to. No one could have any contact with a person in custody, not until they were either released or charged. The detective had told Sonia that Oliver could be held for four days at the very most before they'd have to either let him go for lack of evidence or bring charges. 'If he is charged, he'll go to prison on remand. Probably Manchester.'

'Strangeways?' Sonia had said.

'Yes. Then you can arrange to visit him,' DC Bradshaw had said.

'Could he get bail?' Sonia had asked.

'Not for a charge this serious.'

Eighteen years of growing, of learning, of discovering the world. Eighteen years of care and love, of having a home, food on the table, friends and family. All lost. For what? What had led him to do such a thing? To hurt someone, to deliberately gang up on someone? When had he become the sort of person who did that?

He's not, she thought. He's not. She knew him better than anyone. There had to be some mistake, a proper explanation. Something that would actually add up, would make sense and fit the character of the boy she'd raised.

If he was guilty, if they found him guilty, he'd be locked up for years.

Everyone would know. They would look at her and nudge each other and say, 'Her lad was one of them that killed Allie Kennaway.' And because she was his mother, she would share some of the blame. There'd be gossip about whether she'd let him run wild or neglected him, saying she'd not been tough enough on him. She'd be doubly to blame for being a single parent. Comments about the lack of a man, no father figure in the household. Would it make any difference that she'd gone to the police? Tried to turn him in? That she'd tried to do the right thing?

Who would want to know her? People would hate her for having a son who had killed someone. A murderer. People would hate her for betraying her own flesh and blood to the police. She might have to move, leave everything and everyone she knew and live somewhere else. Tell lies when she was asked if she had kids. Hide her visits to him.

She was almost out of cigarettes. No way could she face Aseef at the corner shop so she'd have to go to the petrol station. If she hung on until dark there'd be less chance of running into someone who'd stop her for a natter. Sonia couldn't trust herself to do that and not shatter, crumble into a million gibbering pieces. She felt trapped – cold, lonely and trapped.

She picked up the phone and, before she could have second thoughts, called Rose.

'Hi, you any better?' Rose said.

'Can you come?' Sonia said. 'I need you, Rose. I just—' She choked and began to sob.

'I'll come as soon as I can,' Rose said, swift and clear, not even asking for an explanation. 'I'll sort Dad out and then I'll come round. OK, darling? It'll be all right.'

Steve

Steve left Teagan at his parents' and drove from there to his sister's. Emma worked from home, doing business translation for two large clients. She was fluent in Italian and French. One thing they had in common, Steve thought, a love of languages. And Emma sometimes travelled, too, but not as widely as Steve did with his patents work. He'd been worrying lately about how the Brexit referendum might affect his work. Not that a leave vote was likely. Now that seemed so irrelevant, part of his life that no longer had meaning.

Emma's house was small and smart. A modern townhouse in a row of six, opposite a park. It had an integral garage and curious stained glass in rectangles, green and yellow, which Steve could never decide whether he liked or not.

Her husband had moved out four years ago just before Sarah was diagnosed. There hadn't been anyone else involved in the break-up. Emma always claimed it was mutual; the marriage wasn't working any more.

She opened the door to him, glasses on top of her head, and he wondered if she'd slam it shut on him, echoing his treatment of her yesterday.

'Can we talk?' he said.

'Come in.' She gave a rueful smile.

The ground floor was open plan, kitchen area at the back, dining in the middle, lounge at the front. Emma had redecorated after Troy had left, replacing the beige and brown with pale blue walls and gold-coloured curtains. The sofa was pale blue leather. A sand-coloured rug filled the living area. Desert colours. It looked fresh and welcoming and extremely tidy. Magazines were lined up neatly on a side table, cushions set at perky angles on the sofa.

'Tea? Coffee?' Emma said.

'Tea would be great, thanks.'

Steve sat on the rocking chair while she made their drinks. She had some photographs propped on the TV stand. One of her and her friends at a party, probably back in her university days, another of Steve and family after Teagan was born, and one of their parents on their fiftieth wedding anniversary. Steve had an identical copy of that one at home.

Was she lonely? Now Troy wasn't here? She seemed to have a busy social life by all accounts.

'You don't want sugar?' she said.

'No, thanks.'

She brought the drinks, passed him his, put hers on the side table, on a coaster, and sat on the sofa. He held his cup between his palms until the heat grew too fierce.

'I want to talk to you about Allie,' he said. 'About yesterday. Why I reacted like I did. So you can understand.'

'I do understand,' she said.

'No,' he said.

'You seem to think—'

He heard criticism, spiky, in her tone, and interrupted, irritation blooming: 'Emma. Please. Hear me out. Just let me talk until I'm done and then you can say whatever you need to say.'

'If you're here to lecture me—'

'For God's sake.'

There was a painful silence. Triple-glazing insulated the room so the only sound was from inside, the fabric of Emma's clothes rustling as she moved her legs, the creak of the rocking chair under Steve's weight.

He looked at her. 'Will you listen? Please? Will you just listen?'

'OK.' She pursed her lips, crossed her ankles.

'It's true Allie had been confused for a while, about how she felt. And frightened. She was miserable, depressed, even. Times she'd break down in tears. It was horrible. Sarah and I, we didn't know how to help. But the counselling Allie had helped her through. Finding someone who got it, who understood, who completely accepted her. After that, Allie was clear. She was so clear. And so much happier. She knew who she was, she knew what she wanted, and how she wanted to change herself physically . . . outwardly . . . to reflect what was true inside. The fear about whether she was crazy or freaky or sick to want this had gone. The only fear then was about the rest of us, about how the world would react. What we would say and do.' He took a breath, rubbed his hands along the smooth wood of the chair arms. 'Look, the things you said in the paper – things you've said in the past, like feeling uneasy about it, thinking she was too young, misguided, hoping it was a phase – I thought them too. All of those things. And others. How could she do that? How could she want to deny all those years of being a boy? Of being my son? And the prospect of . . . I don't know, some alien creature taking her over. Some parody of a woman that people would ridicule. And the worries about her health, the risk of side-effects when she finally started on the hormones. All of that.'

'So why did you go along with it?' Emma said.

Steve looked up, stared at the lampshade, a golden globe. The room was airless, a tomb. A smell caught at the back of his throat, air freshener or some cleaning fluid. He was stifled. 'Because it wasn't about me or Sarah,' he said. 'Or you. Because the most important thing in the world was Allie's happiness. And she'd been so desperately, profoundly unhappy. And then to see her—' He couldn't speak. He took a gulp of tea, then another, as he framed his thoughts. 'I've made mistakes. Of course I have. And I'll make more.' Did he sound pompous? He didn't want that. 'What I'm trying to say is we can't control how we feel, we can't police our emotions, I get that. But we *can* take responsibility for what we say and what we do. Do you see the difference?'

'So I'm not allowed to speak freely?' Emma said.

Christ. He couldn't reach her. Couldn't get beyond the posture, the little England outrage, to anything deeper. Humility, she had no humility.

'What if Allie was black?' he said.

'What?' Emma said.

'What if she was Jewish, I don't know . . . Would you still want to be able to say whatever you liked?'

'Apart from the fact that that's impossible, I'm not racist or anti-Semitic. Besides, people don't choose their race or their religion. They're born into it.'

'Allie didn't choose this. It's not some lifestyle choice.'

'I don't agree,' she said.

'Can't you see—'

'It's taking things to extremes. It's not natural. It's just following some bizarre fashion, some trend. Teenagers always like to shock.'

He couldn't sit any longer. 'My daughter is dead. Your niece is dead. Very likely because of who she was and for no other reason. Don't you see how it all connects?'

'Steve, I'm as devastated as you are. I'm grieving too.' Tears shone in her eyes. 'What happened was terrible. Outrageous.'

But? There was a 'but' filling the space between them. He willed her not to say it.

'And whoever's responsible should be locked away for the rest of their lives,' Emma said.

'It'll keep happening,' he said. 'Until people like Allie are properly accepted. Don't you see? You going to the papers, acting as if you had any right to talk for us—'

'I wasn't claiming—'

'You had no right. And the stuff they print, that feeds into it. It feeds the disgust and the hatred.'

'You're being melodramatic,' she said.

'Jesus! She's dead, for Chrissake,' he yelled.

'Because it wasn't safe.'

He stared at her, horrified. Blaming him, blaming Allie.

Emma ran her hands over her face.

'I can't do this any more,' he said. 'I don't want to see you again.

I don’t want to hear from you. I don’t want you in my life any more. Or Teagan’s.’

‘Steve—’

‘I mean it,’ he said. And he left without looking back.

Donna

Donna received an email on her way back from the hospital. The DNA profiles from the crime scene and from Allie's body matched both Dale Harris and Oliver Poole. It was all she needed to go ahead and arrest Martin Harris on suspicion of perverting the course of justice and assisting an offender. It chilled her to think of him in custody, in interview. A Judas in the team trailing the stink of corruption.

In Dale and Oliver's second interviews she would look more closely at their version of events, start to query and challenge what they said, pick out contradictions and inconsistencies, find holes in the story. She would need to use angles they wouldn't be prepared for and also probe for any weaknesses in the relationship. Who followed whom? According to Bishaar, Dale was the instigator of the attack, the more violent. It was also Dale Harris who had harassed Candida Gallego earlier in the evening. What did Oliver feel about that? And the brutal murder? How long-lived, how strong, was the friendship? What had the men argued about as they walked on Deansgate looking for a taxi? What capacity was there to drive a wedge between the two as a way of breaking through to the truth?

Nothing to date suggested the murder was planned. It seemed to be random, spontaneous. It was purely chance that Allie had gone out to look for her friend Bets, chance that Bets wasn't there, chance that Dale and Oliver had been on New Mill Street at that exact time.

Donna received a text message. From Bryony. *Hows dad? Whens visiting? Bx*

OK, Donna typed. *7 pm. You get tea first. Pick you all up at 6.40 xx*

It'd be easier to see Jim with the kids there as a buffer. The thought brought her up short. Was that how the pair of them functioned now, only as parents, no longer partners or lovers? She didn't want to think about it. Not now. There was too much other stuff jostling for space in her head.

Donna had just got out of the lift on the fourth floor, when a figure burst through the door at the top of the stairs, making her jump.

Jade Bradshaw.

The woman looked wild, eyes darting here and there, jaw set. Poised – for what? To run? To attack?

Donna spoke calmly, determined not to inflame the situation. 'Jade. Are you all right?'

'You need to listen to me,' Jade hissed. Obviously agitated.

'Look, you can't be here. Not like this. We've enough of a problem already. Go to Reception and I'll arrange for someone to take your statement.'

Jade threw her hands into the air, made a half-turn, which led Donna to think she was doing as she'd been asked. Wrong.

Jade lunged, grabbed Donna's wrists and began pulling her along the corridor.

'Get off me,' Donna shouted.

Jade was surprisingly strong for someone who looked like she hadn't had a decent meal for weeks.

Antipsychotics. Was she dangerous? Really dangerous? Donna moved to get ahead of Jade, putting out her foot to try to trip her over but Jade stepped round it and shoved Donna sideways through the door into the Ladies, letting go of her as the door swung shut behind them.

'Calm down,' Donna said. 'Calm down now.' She held up her hands, partly in defence. Jade stood blocking the door. Donna glanced at the cubicles, hoping there might be help from someone there but they were alone.

'Oliver Poole.' Jade said. 'Dale Harris.'

'I can't discuss that. You're on sick leave, Jade.'

'I'm not sick.'

'Well, you do a pretty good impression of it,' Donna said.

'Just shut the fuck up, will you?' Her eyes flashed.

Had she got a knife? Was she hearing voices or seeing things? 'Jade—'

'He knew. DS Harris. He knew it was Dale. He lied about the tape from Fredo's to put us off the scent. That's what he was doing with all that shit about the CCTV. He was getting rid of the evidence and blaming me. He lied about the Cavalier. They didn't have a power cut. I've been there. I've got the file.'

The bastard.

'And listen to this.' Jade put her hand into her pocket and Donna jerked backwards. But it was a phone, that was all. A mobile phone. A recording.

Jade's voice: 'You spoke to DS Harris?'

Then a woman: 'I didn't get his name.'

Jade: 'A big man, in his fifties. Grey hair, blue striped tie?'

The woman: 'Yes.'

'That's Sonia Poole,' Jade said.

Oh, Jesus. Sweat pricked Donna's scalp, her pulse galloped.

'She came here yesterday,' Jade said. 'I saw her in Reception. She was reporting her son was Man B from the photo-fits. You know what Harris told me? She was a psychic who claimed Allie and all the angels were talking to her. He *knew*, boss. Maybe not at first, maybe not even when the photo-fits came, but as soon as he went to Fredo's he saw Dale and Oliver on the tape, off their skulls and hurling abuse. He knew then. That's why he got rid of the tape or lost it or whatever he's done.'

The extent of Martin's betrayal hit Donna anew. He hadn't just betrayed the team, his colleagues, but the Kennaways too. The very people he was meant to serve, to protect.

'Here . . . from the Cavalier.' Jade tapped at the phone and turned it so Donna could see the screen. Dale and Oliver at the pub before the murder.

Donna watched the clip, saw the lads buying drinks. Evidence Martin had tried to prevent them ever seeing.

'Jesus,' Donna said. She held onto the basin for a moment.

'I'm not sick,' Jade said. 'He is. Those two fuckers are. Not me.'

It was enough to crucify Martin, but Jade had been removed from duty. The legality of the evidence was questionable at best. 'Jade, I don't know that we can use any of this.'

'Why the fuck not?' She glared at Donna, face incredulous.

'I sacked you, remember? You don't have the proper authority.'

Jade pulled out her warrant card. 'I had this, my notes back everything up. It's all solid.'

Donna felt breathless as if she had run too far, too fast.

'You were off the case.' Donna raised her voice.

'Who knew?' Jade demanded. 'Did you tell the team?'

'Not yet but—'

'HR?'

'No,' Donna said.

'Me neither. So, I'm back on the team. No one knows the difference.'

'Jade, I can't. You're being treated for—'

'It's none of your business,' Jade said. 'You'd never have known if Harris hadn't snitched on me. There's no problem with my work. I'm not the one who lost evidence. He is. He probably torched it, actually – that's what I'd do in his shoes. But you believed him over me.'

'I'm sorry,' Donna said, guilt ballooning inside her. 'I should have questioned it more. Gone deeper. But the fact remains you're on medication for a psychiatric condition. I can't ignore that.' It was a boulder blocking the way.

'You can. We go back to how it was before,' Jade said.

'Jade, I can't.'

Jade's face tightened, darkened. 'Or I go to the Federation, raise a case against you for unfair treatment, bullying, failure to listen to a serious complaint. I don't give a fuck, take your pick.'

'It doesn't have to be like this,' Donna said.

'No. We could just put our heads together and nail the bastards, all three of them.' She spoke bitterly, ferociously, and Donna sensed the need, the passion beneath words.

'You're a risk, Jade. If you're not well—'

'Fuck! How many more times?' Jade shouted. 'I'm fine. It doesn't affect my work.'

'Tell me what it's for, exactly? The medication?' Donna said.

'No.'

'Jade, what happened to you?' Donna said.

Silence. Jade's fingers busy, picking at her nails.

'Look. There's no way I can—' Donna said.

Jade turned away. 'Bad things happened. A long time ago. Antipsychotic, the clue's in the name.' Her head snapped round to face Donna. 'It's only a problem if I don't take them.' A bright anger in her eyes. And something else. Pain.

'Do you see someone? Have you ever had—'

'I need it. It works. That's all. I swear. No one need ever know. Take me back.' Jade's eyes, dark as ink, were locked on hers.

'I don't know if I can. If anyone ever found out . . .'

Jade flung out her hands. 'Sure you can, you're the boss. If you can't do that, then what the fuck are you for?'

Donna thought of what Martin had done to Jade. How he'd scapegoated her. The lies.

Jade waited, hands on hips, head tilted, fringe hanging over one eye. Scrawny, fierce, vulnerable. Donna saw she carried with her the power, the raw vitality that would make her a brilliant cop and a living nightmare to work with.

I must be out of my tiny mind. Donna gave a nod.

Jade returned it with a ghost of a smile, stepped back and held the door open for her.

CHAPTER NINETEEN

Jade

While the boss pulled together an arrest warrant for Martin Harris and notified all those who needed to know, triggering a series of detonations up the force hierarchy, Jade was given the job of interviewing his son.

The DI had told her the gist of what the lads were saying, basically dobbing Bishaar in for the crime and claiming to be in fear of their lives.

Jade watched the recording of the first interviews. Dale spoke as little as possible while appearing cooperative. He echoed Oliver's words. He was polite, outwardly calm.

Just as polite as Jade when she began the second interview by recapping what he'd said earlier in the day.

Then she said, 'There are a few things I'm finding hard to understand. You've been through this traumatic event, you're party to kicking a woman to death, then you're released by the man you say had a knife. Now, your father is a police officer, a detective, why don't you turn to him? Tell him what happened?'

'We were scared,' Dale said.

'I get that,' Jade said. 'But didn't you think the police might be able to protect you if you told us what had happened?'

'The African guy said not to tell the police.'

'Perhaps you thought your father wouldn't believe you?' Jade said.

'No. Yes.' He couldn't work out how to answer. So Jade kept at him.

'It's all a bit random, isn't it? Hard to believe. You're a sportsman, aren't you? Footballer? Fit? Strong?'

'I play football,' he said, guarded. Not bragging. Or lapping up the flattery. Jade wondered what that restraint cost him.

'And your pal Oliver is a big lad, six foot, well-built. So there's two of you and Allie Kennaway. I make that three against one. Mr Bishaar is five foot six, a flyweight,' she said. 'You could take him down.'

'He had a knife,' Dale said.

'Describe this knife,' she said.

'A big hunting knife, one of those with curvy edges.'

'And he pulled this knife on Oliver?'

'Yes,' Dale said.

'Where'd he pull it from?'

Dale pinched the end of his nose. 'His pocket.'

'Which pocket?' Jade said.

'In his pants,' Dale said.

'Which side?'

'The right,' he said.

'You sure about that?' Jade remembered Bishaar doing the sketches. He was left-handed like her. *Sweet.* A gift for the prosecution, if they went to trial.

'Yes,' Dale said.

'We've got a witness who ran into you in the Cavalier earlier that evening. She said you were harassing her, sexually harassing her.'

He scoffed, a laugh of disbelief, then cut it off, straightened his face. He was attractive, if you liked the glossy mag/male-model look. Jade didn't.

'It was a bit of fun,' he said.

'You touched her breasts, you touched her genitals. When she objected you called her a frigid bitch. Is that what passes for fun in your life?' Jade said.

'It wasn't like that,' he said.

Jade could feel resentment coming off him. His face was taut. He'd balled his fists but didn't appear to have noticed. 'What was it like?'

'Just a bit of banter. She took it the wrong way.'

'How should she have taken it?' Jade said. *On her back with her legs open?*

'We were just having a laugh,' he said. There was a flinty look in his eye, a spark of something beneath the clean-cut nice-lad image.

'And Allie Kennaway, when you ran into her on New Mill Street, was that just a bit of fun?'

'No,' he said quickly. 'She wasn't there. She was in the alley, Spring Gate Fold.'

'Once you'd dragged her there,' Jade said.

'No. We didn't.'

'The woman in the Cavalier had sent you packing. You tried to get into a nightclub and they told you to do one.' A flare of alarm ran across his face, quickly hidden. The abortive trip to Fredo's wasn't part of the script he'd learnt. His dad would have told him that was all tidied away. 'I think you were still looking for fun,' Jade went on. 'Pissed off that the night was turning out to be rubbish. You see Allie Kennaway. You determine to have some fun one way or another.'

'No,' he said. 'She was in the alley. The African was trying to rape her.'

'How could you tell?'

'What?' Dale said.

'How could you tell he was attempting rape?' Jade said. 'What was he doing?'

'He was grabbing between his legs – her legs. She was screaming.'

'Like you grabbed the woman in the pub?' Jade said.

'No, not like that,' Dale said.

'Explain the difference.'

'This was serious – he had a hand on her throat too. He didn't stop when she screamed.' Dale was describing himself, Jade was sure of it. His own actions now played out in Bishaar's name.

'You called him an African?' she said.

'He was,' Dale said.

'How did you know?' Jade said.

'He's black, isn't he? Coal black.' *How original. And what am I? Nigger brown?*

'Wasn't it because your dad told you he was African?'

That light in his eyes again. He didn't like it when she mentioned Harris. 'I don't know what you're talking about.'

'We never made his name or his ethnic identity public,' Jade said.

'I could tell from his colour, and the way he speaks, the accent.'

'What did he say? His exact words?' Jade said.

'He said, "Kick her! Kick her." Then he kept saying, "Again! Again!"'

'This knife . . .' Jade switched track, saw Dale swallow. 'You said he pulled it from his right pocket. Was it in a sheath or anything?'

'No.'

'You said it was a big knife. How long was it?'

'A foot or so,' Dale said.

'A knife like that, kept in a trouser pocket. Wouldn't it cut through the material?'

'I don't know. Maybe there was a sheath in the pocket.'

'I thought you said there was no sheath.'

'I didn't see one,' Dale said. His pupils shrank. A sign of anger. She saw him adjust his posture. He was struggling to keep calm now. She jumped to another topic. 'What were you and Oliver arguing about just before you got the taxi?'

'What?'

'You were seen arguing. Oliver had stopped. He was shouting at you. You pulled him, made him walk on,' Jade said.

'I don't remember,' Dale said.

'Really? You remember all those other details clear as day but not this. A barney with your mate?'

'I don't remember,' Dale said.

'How did you get the blood on your shirt?' Jade said.

He went pale. 'What?'

She felt a kick inside. 'There was blood on your shirt, on your sleeve. How did it get there?'

'I don't know,' Dale said.

'You told us you kicked Allie Kennaway six or seven times. Did you thump her too?'

'No.'

'Punch her or slap her?'

'No,' he said.

'But you did hit Mahmoud Bishaar?' Jade said.

'I didn't.'

'You held him in a headlock and you hit him several times. His nose was bleeding. And his lip. He was bleeding on your shirt.'

'No way. No. He had a knife. He had a knife on Oliver. That's all.'

'Have you got a girlfriend?'

'What?'

You heard. 'Have you got a girlfriend?'

'No.'

'Boyfriend, then?'

He turned his face away. She could see how tight the muscles in his neck were, like he was straining to remain seated. She imagined his teeth crushed together.

'Do you have a boyfriend?' Jade asked.

'No.'

'You watch a lot of porn, Dale?'

'Some,' he retaliated, turning to face her.

'Give you ideas, does it? How to be with a woman? How to have a bit of fun?'

'No,' he said. He scratched the inside of his wrist.

'Where's that shirt?' Jade said.

'I burnt it,' he said.

'Where?'

'In the woods,' Dale said.

'You can show us where?'

'I don't remember where.'

'Why did you burn it?' Jade said.

'He told us to.'

'Your dad?'

'The African.' He spat the word. She was getting to him.

'I think you burnt it because it was evidence. Because you'd committed a murder and you didn't want to get caught,' Jade said.

'No,' he said.

'Did your dad talk about work at home?'

'No.'

'Never?' Jade said.

'No.'

'You knew that he was investigating the murder?'

A pause. 'Yes.'

'But you didn't tell him you'd been there?' Jade said.

'No.'

'Then he found out?'

'No. No, he didn't.' He sat still, frame rigid, but Jade saw twitches he couldn't prevent flicker on his forearm, at the base of his throat, through his cheeks.

'We have evidence that he did. Hard evidence that he was trying to conceal your part in the murder.'

'He didn't know anything about it!'

'Your dad could use his role as a police officer to destroy evidence. Cover it up because he *knew* you were guilty.'

'No, no, he didn't,' Dale said. 'He didn't even know we were there.'

'He knew you were guilty, not Bishaar but you and Oliver.'

'No, that's not true. That's a lie.'

'Why else would he try to derail the same investigation that he's working on? To stop us finding you. You and Oliver. The people who killed Allie Kennaway.'

'That's a fucking lie.' His voice rose in agitation and he jabbed a finger at her, hatred vivid in his pinprick eyes.

Jade watched him, the nasty little scrote, for long enough, then said, 'I know you're not telling me the truth. We're going to go over it again and again until you start making some sense. Same with

Oliver. We'll get there. We won't have any trouble getting an extension to the time we're allowed to hold you. Not for a case so serious. With such overwhelming evidence against you.'

She picked up the file. 'Oh, yeah, and there's something else you should know. We've a warrant out for your father's arrest. It's all gone to shit, Dale. He can't help you any more. In fact, his interfering with the inquiry has only made it blindingly obvious to everyone that you're guilty as sin, you and your mate Oliver. And you perjuring yourself is only making things worse. You killed that girl and we're going to prove it.'

Martin

Martin saw the flicker of blue light coming from squad cars as soon as the taxi turned onto his crescent. Leaning forward, he said, 'Can you take me to the cashpoint at Tesco's on Chester Road. I forgot to get some earlier.'

A nod from the driver.

The taxi passed his house and Martin made out figures, shadowy, at the door. Only the hall light still on, so Fran must have left as instructed.

Someone had sent them after him. Had Oliver grassed him or Dale up? The thought made his bowels cramp. They couldn't arrest him without having found something out. There was nothing in his notebook to incriminate him. He went over it again: the tape from Fredo's he'd written up as a dead end; he'd also noted the time he had tasked DC Bradshaw with taking the video to the evidence store; his failure to retrieve CCTV from the Cavalier due to their power cut was cited in two sentences, nothing to send anyone sniffing round there; and no one would ever trace him to the anonymous tip-offs about Anthony Mayhew, he was pretty sure of that.

The visit from Sonia Poole? The failure to record that would be harder to explain. Had it come to light? Had the silly cow gone back to the station and had a second pop at fingering her son for murder? What sort of parent did that? What sort of loyalty, what honour, was there in sacrificing your child? Why ruin any more lives? Just for one mistake. She should be ashamed of herself.

His gullet was burning. A backwash of beer and whisky rose in his throat and he took a couple of swigs of the heartburn suspension to tamp it down.

He needed to know if Sonia Poole had done something stupid in spite of his advice. And if she hadn't, he must persuade her it wouldn't be in anyone's interest now to reveal what she'd said to him at the station. Not hers or her son's. But how could he account for the fact that her name was recorded in the log at Reception?

His mind gnawed away at the problem until, with a sense of release, he found the answer. She could say she *had* recognized Oliver in the photo-fit, was driven half mad thinking he was involved but when she reached the police station (and Martin smiled to himself at the simplicity of it) and was faced with the stone-cold reality of informing on him, of seeing Oliver's life ruined, she had bottled it. So when Martin spoke to her she pretended to be a psychic talking bollocks about messages from the afterlife. That could work. Yes, that could work very nicely.

So if Dale and Oliver held their nerve, if Sonia Poole did what he told her, Plan B could still pan out. If, make that *when*, Martin got arrested he would keep quiet and ride it out. He was a decorated officer, for fuck's sake, a distinguished career. But he needed to get Sonia Poole onside. Lay it out for her how Martin's way was the only option, if she wanted her son to have a chance at acquittal. Make her believe Mahmoud Bishaar was the real evil bastard in all this and Oliver just a pawn. Wrong place, wrong time. Martin would have to come clean and tell her he was Dale's father. That he knew how she must feel, that their lads had one chance at beating this, thanks to Martin. That Oliver needed her help, and she must do exactly what Martin said.

The cab pulled into the supermarket car park and drove up close to the cash machines. Martin withdrew two hundred. He checked the address for Sonia Poole on his phone. He'd made a note of it when the shit first hit the fan in case the lad had gone running home to Mummy with his tail between his legs.

Back in the cab he gave the Firswood address.

They were there in ten minutes. Martin paid the taxi and approached the Poole house. He swore when a cat ran between his legs almost sending him arse over tit. It waited by the door as Martin rang the bell and slid inside when the door was opened.

'Mrs Poole?'

She looked like she'd been slapped and left for dead, red eyes and pasty skin, hair like straw. Smell of fags coming off her. 'Can I have a word?' He smiled, hoping to get her to relax.

'They arrested him,' she said.

'I know. That's why I'm here,' Martin said.

'Sonia?'

Shite. Someone else was there, another woman. Appearing in the hall. 'You all right, Sonia?'

'It's the police,' Sonia Poole said. She turned and walked back into the house, leaving Martin to follow her.

This was not a conversation he could have with a third party present.

The two women were in the kitchen. A bottle of vodka stood on the table with two glasses, each with a slice of lemon. Martin's mouth watered and the reflux rose again, like water backing up a sewer. 'I think we'd better talk in private,' he said.

'Rose knows everything,' Sonia Poole said, her words slurred. 'Anything you want to say to me you can say to her as well. She's his godmother.' Her voice was close to breaking.

Martin prayed she wouldn't start wailing. He'd had enough of weeping women for one day.

Sonia Poole picked up her drink and paused, the glass halfway to her mouth, frowning. 'They said you were ill.'

'Who did? Did you go into the police station?' She *had* sold him out. *Sweet fucking Christ.*

'No. The one who came earlier. She said you were ill and she wanted me to go over it all again. Everything I told you. You haven't even been looking for him, not properly, from what she said.'

Had Donna been here?

'We were doing everything we could,' Martin said. 'That is the truth. Was it DI Bell you spoke to?'

'No. Bradshaw. DC Bradshaw.'

Fuck. Martin's heart thumped hard and his bowels twisted. It was Jade who'd fucked everything up. Jade, with some vendetta to sink him, to destroy him and his family. Skanky Paki bitch. It was like he was running from an earthquake, crevasses snaking over the ground, opening all around him. 'Glad she's seen you,' he managed. 'Bit of crossed wires there obviously.' *Shite!* There was no way he could enlist Sonia Poole to cover for him now. 'We'll keep you informed of any developments,' he said, retreating into the jargon. 'I'll see myself out.' His head was going to explode. His guts were roiling.

Jade Bradshaw. Who the fuck did she think she was? Did she imagine she could mess about with someone like Martin Harris and get away with it? Fuck that. She needed sorting out. And Martin was just the man to do it. Once and for all.

Donna

'Take a seat.' The chief constable gave a nod towards a spare chair. Donna had been summoned. She had never been in his office before. This wouldn't just be a bollocking then, it would be a disembowelling.

The room occupied the corner of the building with a view out over St Peter's Square to the library and the town hall. The chief con had a standing desk and remained upright, to one side of it, putting Donna in mind of a preacher. And herself a penitent. She heard the clock-tower bell chime a quarter past six.

'Harris has been apprehended?' he said.

'Not yet, sir. He wasn't at his home address.'

'Flight risk?'

Was he? Wouldn't he carry on with his bid to protect Dale? Or now, with his complicity unmasked, would he save his own skin? 'I'm not sure, sir. But I'd advise alerting the Border Force to be on the safe side.'

'What are the charges?'

'Conspiracy to pervert the course of justice, assisting an offender, tampering with evidence,' Donna said.

'And you had no idea?' he said coldly.

Donna's cheeks grew hot. Her instincts had failed her. She remembered the flickers of doubt when Martin had put in his complaint about Jade. She'd been negligent about it, trusting Martin because of their familiar working relations. The undeniable issue of the medication had coloured her reaction. It'd been a clever stroke, she realized. The medication was hard fact, and with that in the mix, Martin had invented the rest: lost evidence, negative, abusive comments. Jade's lack of control, her going into meltdown, when Donna had raised the concerns with her, had been grist to the mill.

'No idea, sir, no,' she said.

'A cock-up of this magnitude doesn't go away,' he said. 'Especially not when it relates to one of the most sensitive cases we've dealt with in years. The eyes of the public are on us twenty-four seven. You know that as well as anyone. Not only that but our performance, our behaviour, is being monitored and measured by an extremely vociferous LGBT community. We have a high-profile hate crime and a corrupt detective. It's a disaster of nuclear proportions.' He slapped his palm onto his desk.

'Sir, I'm sorry if—'

'Sorry doesn't cut it, Donna. It happened on your watch and you need to make it right, salvage this inquiry, and quick, or I'll find someone else who will.'

'We've made good progress and I—'

He raised a hand to silence her. 'My overriding concern is that this leaves any prosecution open to accusations of procedural failings. A botched investigation means the case is thrown out of court. Those two thugs walk away. And the good reputation of this police service is immeasurably damaged.'

The thought of that was haunting her but she fought to appear confident. 'It won't happen, sir,' she said. 'I'm going over everything now. Any exhibits or evidence handled by Martin Harris will be omitted from our case file but we will gather new supporting evidence to strengthen our position against Oliver Poole and Dale Harris but also against Martin Harris. We can prove there was conspiracy, sir. I'm sure we can. We can win this.'

'Donna, I'm not in the mood for platitudes or slogans. This is a spectacular fuck-up so don't spin it any other way. Not to me.' He spoke with such loathing that humiliation burnt through her.

'No, sir.'

'Talk me though the narrative so far.'

Donna did so while he stood listening, side on and arms folded, his profile outlined against the cityscape beyond.

Every so often he asked for clarification. When she'd finished, he exhaled loudly. 'You'll perhaps understand why I don't share your faith in a positive outcome. Any confidence in your work as SIO has been seriously undermined. You carry the can for this. It may be your family circumstances mean you've taken your eye off the ball.'

Had she? Was that why she'd made the mistakes she had? *And would you dare say that if I were a male officer and it was my wife who'd been in an accident?*

'Sir.' She spoke before he could say any more about replacing her, or rub her nose in the mess any longer. 'Let me get on with it. Now.' She stood up. 'I'm conscious of the time, and the sooner I get back to it, the more I can get done.'

He gave a nod of dismissal. Then a parting shot: 'Pray to God the media don't get a whiff of it until we have it all locked down, or there'll be a perfect shit storm and any chance of a fair trial will be out of the window.'

In the lift, Donna rang Bryony.

'Mum, where are you? It's a quarter past seven.'

'I'm stuck at work. I can't get back. I don't know when I'll be home.'

'Oh, great.'

'I'm sorry. You could still go to the hospital. Take a taxi,' Donna said.

'What with? I spent what you gave me.'

I don't fucking know. Get a bus. Walk. Donna couldn't come up with any practical solution. There had been a time when there was an emergency cache of money under the bowl in the hall where the spare keys lived. But the system had collapsed: too often one of them would use it and forget to replace it.

'I'll ring the hospital and get them to tell Dad you'll visit tomorrow,' Donna said.

In the background she could hear Kirsten: 'Is she coming?'

Then Matt: 'When are we going?'

And Bryony, shushing them: 'I can't hear.' Then, 'Mum's at work so we can't go.' Kirsten crying.

Donna's insides corkscrewed. 'I'm sorry,' she said. 'Tell them all I'm sorry.'

'She's sorry,' Bryony announced loudly, her voice thick with resentment. Then hung up. Not even a goodbye. Donna wanted to scream.

At her desk she sat with her head in her hands for a few moments. Then she stretched, feeling the muscles stiff in her back, frozen across her shoulders. She opened the investigation log.

It was going to be a long night.

CHAPTER TWENTY

Steve

Steve walked into the living room and found Bets and Helena on the sofa either side of Teagan. A tablet was hooked up to the TV, Allie filling the screen. One of the videos they'd made: Allie pretending to be a newsreader, a strange continental accent and lots of eyebrow action. Giggles turning into cackles.

Steve swayed. Moved to a chair.

'I invited them,' Teagan said, pausing the film, head raised, as if she expected him to object. 'Nanny's just gone.'

'Steve . . .' Bets looked petrified. And he could see Helena had been crying, tissues balled on the table next to her.

'It's fine,' Steve said. 'I'm glad you came. I'm not sure I'm ready for—' He waved a hand at the screen.

'We can turn it off,' Teagan said.

'No, no. You carry on. I want to make a couple of calls.' At the doorway, he turned back. 'Have you eaten?'

'No,' Teagan said.

'D'you want to order some Chinese? All of you?'

'OK,' Teagan said. Nods from Bets and Helena.

'What do you want?' Teagan asked him.

'Beef fried rice,' he said, the first dish that came into his head.

He put the milk, beer and pineapple juice he'd bought into the fridge. The very act of shopping had felt alien. He felt alien. Exposed and out of place, expecting at any moment to be recognized as Allie's father . . . the father of the dead girl.

He rang his mother and told her briefly what the situation was with Emma.

'Oh, Steve.' She sighed. 'I'm so sorry to hear that. Perhaps if you—'

'I don't want to talk about it, Mum. Tell Dad, will you?'

'Of course. I'll pick Teagan up at ten thirty tomorrow night, unless you need me in the day.'

'No. That's great. Thanks.'

Steve got a bunch of forks ready, glasses and drinks. He was so tired. He promised himself an early night but sleep was erratic, evasive still.

He rang Yun Li next, apologizing if it was late. 'I want to look into giving an interview,' he said. 'Something to counteract Emma's piece. You said there was a press office. Could they arrange something?'

'Yes, I'm sure. They'd probably want to have some input,' Yun said.

'No,' Steve said. They wanted to manage him, orchestrate what was said and done, and he wasn't having that. 'No.'

'The concern is that comments may be made that undermine the inquiry and—'

'I won't be talking about that,' Steve said. 'I'll be talking about Allie, what she was like. Yes, of course, about the shock of all this, the . . .' He sucked in a breath. 'But nothing about the police, nothing that could mess up your PR.'

Yun didn't respond immediately, so Steve went on. 'I could do it myself. Contact the *Indy* or the *Guardian*.'

'Let me talk to the press officer. She can speak to you directly – she's called Rowena Swift.'

The name brought back Sarah, teasing him as they tussled about naming Teagan on the day she was born. *Rowena, Morwenna, Myfanwy, Ffion.* Head thrown back and laughing when Steve said, 'Look, there's unusual and then there's unpronounceable. How will anyone ever spell it?'

Teagan was a compromise. Tegwin the Welsh name, Teagan, the Irish version.

'All Celtic, isn't it?' Steve had argued. 'Teagan I like. Tegwin sounds like some bozo from a sitcom, Tegwin the Tool.'

'Steady, boyo,' Sarah said. 'It means "beautiful". She is beautiful. Look at her.'

Teagan had a cap of fine dark hair, eyes almost black. Allie had been practically bald at birth, just a fuzz of downy fair hair for the first year. Aled meant 'child, offspring'. *Child.* He couldn't remember now what Allie meant. 'Harmony'? He looked it up on his phone. Yes, 'harmony'. Or 'stone'. Or 'noble'. Also 'fair, defender'.

Steve heard singing, Allie's voice reaching him from the living room. 'Mr Cellophane', from *Chicago*, one of the show tunes she'd liked. Singing was certainly never one of Allie's strong suits.

The doorbell rang and Steve took delivery of the food. He let Teagan dole it out and sat with the girls in the living room to eat. Teagan had paused the video, which was now showing Allie and Helena in the snow. An outrageously expensive skiing trip to France with school that Steve had been cajoled into paying for.

He ate his meal, aware that he was hungry, really hungry, for the first time in days. Enjoying the saltiness, the spice, which left his mouth peppery. 'Is this the one where you tumble?' he asked Helena, who nodded. 'Let's see,' he said.

Teagan set it playing and they all watched as the two girls laboured up the slope, turned round, painfully slowly, trying to manoeuvre the long skis. Then Helena began to slide before she was ready. Allie grabbed for her and the two performed a slow, clumsy glide round, arms and ski sticks whirling, until Allie fell, bringing Helena down with her. The screams of the pair were drowned by Bets's laughter – she had been filming them. Steve was saved from the tears that threatened by his phone ringing. He took it through to the kitchen.

'Mr Kennaway, Rowena Swift here.' Half-baked puns about her name and the speed of her getting in touch flew through his head.

'First of all, I'd like to say how very sorry I am for your loss. For you and all the family.'

'Thank you.'

'Your family liaison officer has spoken to me and I understand you'd like an opportunity to speak to the press. Is that right?'

'Yes,' he said.

'And you're interested in raising awareness by speaking about Allie's transition and what that meant for you all as a family.'

'Yes,' he said, after a pause. He hadn't exactly thought of it in those terms but it was part of what he wanted to do. He wanted people to hear about Allie. Not the Allie in the headlines now, not the victim, but the Allie from before. The Allie who couldn't hold a tune and nearly broke her neck skiing. The Allie he had carried on his shoulders and taught to dribble a football. The Allie who had then taught him so much. The person behind the label. The daughter who had been born a son.

'Excellent,' she said. 'Leave it with me. I'll sound people out and get back to you.'

Jade

Jade parked and got out, automatically glancing up at her windows, a matter of habit. Something shivered up her spine as she saw the bathroom light was off. The bedroom still glowed, a rectangle of sunshine yellow through the thin curtains, but the window to the right was a black hole.

Quickly she got back into the car and locked the doors, switching off the internal light. Was someone up there watching for her? Had they already seen her?

She started the engine and moved the car onto the street at the front where it couldn't be seen from her side of the flats.

Then she rang Mina.

'Jade! I knew I forgot something. Cooking oil.'

The shopping. *Fuck.* 'Mina, I can't do anything about that now.'

'You're not in the shop?'

'No. Look. Have you been in my flat?'

'No. But the fireman came.'

'What fireman?' Jade said, her skin crawling.

'Checking the smoke alarms. Mine's fine. And yours too.'

'You gave him my key?'

'It was very quick. Two minutes and he brought it back. It doesn't take long.'

'What did he look like, this fireman?' Jade dug her nails into her palm.

'Big,' Mina said. 'Nice-looking man. He can give me a fireman's lift any time.' She chortled.

'How old?' Jade said.

'Younger than me. Too old for you.'

'You reckon?'

'Oh, yes, grey hair.'

Jade swallowed. 'What time was this?'

'About an hour ago.'

'It's a bit late for calling on people.'

'Ah, no,' Mina said. 'I asked him about that and he said it's the best time to catch people in.'

'OK,' Jade said.

'Is everything all right?' Mina said.

'Yeah, fine.' Jade couldn't cope with Mina getting into a state on top of everything else. 'I'll see you later.'

Jade called Bert and asked him if anyone had called to check fire safety.

'No,' he said. 'Should they have?'

She wasn't going to get into it with him. 'Just wondered. Might be worth getting it done some time.'

'Jade?' he said, puzzled.

'Got to go. See you.'

Jade grabbed at her hair, trying to think straight. Her mind spooling too quickly, a sickly sensation. That bastard had come here, to her home. Blagged his way in, and now what? Was he there? Or had he left when he found out she wasn't home? There was no sign of his Merc anywhere nearby. Had he gone off to try to find her elsewhere? Left something for her in the flat, a warning, a booby trap? Was he waiting for her? To do what? Threaten her? Punish her? Silence her?

She shuddered.

She should call it in. Sit here like a lemon while the others stormed the steps and burst into her flat. But what if he wasn't there? If this was just a head-fuck? The boss had let her come back to work, but if Jade started acting paranoid, delusional, she'd get the sack again, wouldn't she? What if she was completely wrong? What if Harris was long gone and Jade cried wolf and dragged a load of coppers out, wasting time and money all because her bathroom lightbulb had blown?

Sack that. If he was there, she wanted to be the one to find and arrest him. The thought of slapping cuffs on him made her blood sing.

She saw the pathologist peeling down Allie Kennaway's face to expose the skull, lifting her brain, then herself running to spew up. And before that, the way they'd laid her dress on the side so it could dry and preserve the evidence. Allie's friends blunted by shock and her little sister, so fierce with everyone.

'You bastard,' Jade breathed. He'd known all of that and still he'd lied and bullied and bent to get his way, twisting everything so his lad would escape.

Jade imagined going up to her flat, up the stairs with the dodgy light. Opening her door. She hadn't even a knife on her to cut him down. She had some pepper spray, if she got close enough to use it.

Jade swiped at her phone and found the name she wanted.

'J? Someone else you want me to find?' DD asked. 'Getting to be a habit.'

'I need your help.'

'Where?'

She told him her address. 'I'm in the car outside, the Nissan Pixo.'

'They're not paying you enough,' he said.

The next ten minutes stretched out. Jade kept checking the time on her phone. The tension spiralling inside gave her stomach-ache. She reached for her tablets, then thought better of it. She needed to be sharp, even if that meant edgy and wired. She tore at her nails. She could be wrong. Maybe she was. DD would rip the piss out of her and demand more cash. Whatever.

At last a car pulled in behind her, headlights already off. Engine so quiet as to go unnoticed. She wondered where he'd got the ride, if he owned it, had borrowed it, stolen it.

She unlocked the passenger door and DD got in beside her. He wore dark clothes, hoodie and pants, beanie hat, the glint of gold from the chain round his neck the only thing to catch the light, apart from his eyes. Glittering eyes. For a second she thought he was laughing at her but then she saw he was excited. This, the whiff of danger, the sniff of illegality, the chance something might kick off was meat and drink to DD. Always had been. Way back, there'd been other nights, other fights, pacts made, scrapping and stealing, and Jade had been there at his side. Losing herself in the wildness, in the high of the moment. Two fingers to the world and never mind the bruises.

She told him the minimum. Dirty cop, spoiling evidence, son in custody. How they were trying to pin it on Bishaar, the guy from Somalia.

'That is well wrong.' Even DD had some moral code. 'And Plod's here why?'

'I caught him out, found proof. So my guess is he either wants to beat the shit out of me or get shot of me.' She didn't dare say there was a chance the flat was empty.

'And you want?'

To kill him. 'Collar him. Take him in.'

'I can't be here, once we're done. You know that?' DD said.

'Sure.' While DD wasn't on Greater Manchester's most-wanted list he was a known criminal and he needed to stay off the radar. Any discovery of his involvement in Jade's affairs would muck things up for her, too. In their history, their life as kids scrabbling to get by, the things they'd been, the things they'd done, that was all buried and no one else's business.

'You notice anyone else hanging around?' DD said.

'No. We just need him on the floor,' she said. 'So I can cuff him. I won't make the call until you've gone. You carrying?'

'Depends,' DD said.

'I'd rather you weren't. More risk.'

He nodded. He pulled a pair of thick leather gloves out of his pocket.

'You still spar?' Jade said. He'd been a boxer, taken it up at a time when he needed to defend himself. Developed a ferocious skill. DD's anger was slow to burn but unstoppable when roused. The discipline of the sport helped him control it. Some of the time.

'Keep my hand in. Try that.' He held out a glove. Jade took it. It weighed a ton. The knuckles filled with lead, she reckoned, the same principle as a cosh. A punch with one of those to your spleen or kidney and even the biggest man would be crippled by the pain.

'I think he'll be in the bathroom. The light's off. We go straight in there, fast. Try to catch him on the back foot. Aim high. He's tall.'

They got out of the car and Jade locked it. She led the way up the concrete stairway, DD right behind her, their footsteps almost silent.

Outside her door, Jade stopped and listened. The only sounds she could make out came from Mina's along the way, the natter of a television.

Jade looked over her shoulder at DD, who rolled his hat down, turning it into a balaclava. Jade readied herself, pulse bumping in her throat. She switched her phone flashlight on.

DD winked at her and Jade put her key into the door, pushing it wide open as soon as the catch gave and jumping aside to let DD ahead. She raced after him along the short hallway to the bathroom. DD flung open the bathroom door, fists up, Jade's light spilling on the basin and toilet.

Movement and bulk from the left and a crackling sound, then DD fell, collapsing back on to her. Jade dropped her phone. Harris lunged for her. She saw the stun gun, squat and black, in his hand and scrambled to her feet. DD was motionless.

Harris, grinning, came for her. His eyes shards of ice. His size filling the bathroom doorway. Jade ran but he was fast, grabbing her arm and yanking her backwards, swinging her round so she crashed into the wooden chair, falling over it, catching her mouth, her face, her hands. The wood splintered with a ripping sound.

A grunt alerted her. He was almost upon her. Jade rolled to the side, pulling part of the broken chair on top of her, thrusting it at him.

He snatched it away, threw it behind him.

Get up. Get up.

She scrambled across the space towards the window, to the television. Harris got his foot caught in the remnants of the chair, giving her a precious second to stand.

Blood thundered in her ears, her heart hammering like a piston.

She lifted the TV and held it up in front of herself. A barrier. Maybe a weapon. Staggering under its weight. She stepped towards him but the cables held and pulled her to a halt.

Harris slammed into the screen, knocking her off balance. The TV smashed down, glass shattering, flying across the floor.

He came closer, the stun gun raised. She was crouching, cornered. She sprang up and launched herself at him, judging the angle, tilting her head and leaping to head-butt him full on the nose. The crack of bone, the spew of blood hot on her face. At the same moment the gun made contact with her shoulder. Her body locked rigid. The charge sent her nerves into a frenzy, spasms of pain spurting through her arm, up her neck, in her mouth, across her face. Black flies swarming in her vision. Falling. His howl in her ears. Her own scream.

Jade played dead, stilled her limbs, held her breath. She heard him swearing above her, his voice thickened by his broken nose.

There was banging at the door, a voice calling her name. She heard Harris turn away from her.

Summoning all her strength, she raised herself halfway up, her arms jittering, any noise she made muffled by the calling and thumping from outside. She was dizzy, the room revolving, then dipping like fairground waltzers.

On her knees she could see he still held the gun loosely at his side. Close enough to reach. Jade snatched for it, and using her body weight for leverage, she twisted hard, forcing his wrist round so he had to let go. He roared. Wheeled at her. But she had the gun. She pressed it against his abdomen and pulled the trigger. He fell. Smashing into bits of broken chair making the floor rock and shudder. She leant over, jabbed it into the centre of his chest and pulled the trigger again. Saw the rictus grin as the electricity ripped through him. 'Damn your black heart,' she said. 'Damn you, you fucker.'

Jade's hand flexed on the trigger, the hunger to make Harris suffer, to keep him incapacitated, was too big to deny. She centred the muzzle. Squeezed again.

A hurricane in her head, released through the gun in her fist. A deep well of rage, liquid fire, stoked by other blows, other attacks, by horrors she did not name. Terrors that set her mind shrieking and her flesh crawling.

She leapt round as someone touched her back. DD. Conscious, upright, his own hands raised surrender style.

'Fuck off,' Jade spat.

'You want him dead or alive?' he said. 'I mean, if it was my call, I'd go for it, babe.'

Babe? Jade was panting. Her back ached and her heart was juddering. She was itching to zap Harris again. Or DD, if he didn't shut the fuck up.

'Might take some explaining, though,' DD said. 'And maybe you want to see him in court, see him banged up.'

Allie Kennaway on the cobbles in her prom gown, one shoe gone.

'Fuck!' Jade rocked back on her heels. She got to her feet, bent, bracing her hands on her knees. DD was right. She let the fury ebb away, a tide going out. She was sore everywhere, like she'd been hit by a tank.

The banging at the door was even more frantic. But she tuned it out.

Harris was too heavy to roll over so she knelt and cuffed his hands in front of him.

More thundering on the door. *I'm coming. Just keep your bloody hair on.*

'You all right?' DD said, rubbing his own chest. 'Fucking kills, doesn't it? And you've got blood.' He pointed to his own face.

'Not mine.' *Not most of it, anyway.* Jade nodded at Harris, still unresponsive. His nose streaming blood.

'Big fucker.'

Bang. Bang. Bang.

Jade staggered upright but DD beat her to the door. Bert was there. With a hammer. 'Bloody hell,' he said, when he saw Jade. His eyes swung round the flat, to Harris and the shattered furniture. Then at DD, looking every inch the psycho serial killer in his balaclava.

'Are you all right, Jade?' Bert said.

'Yeah, I'm good.'

'It sounded like someone was murdering you,' Bert said, eyes sliding back to DD.

'He was.' Jade jerked a thumb towards Harris. 'Least, he was trying.'

'He's a big bugger,' Bert said. 'So what's going on?'

'I'm out of here,' DD said, pulling off the balaclava. 'I weren't here,' he said to Bert. 'You never seen me, clear?'

'You never saw him,' Jade told Bert.

'What?'

'It's important. You heard the racket, you came round, found me and King Kong here. That's all.'

'Are you asking me to tell fibs?' Bert frowned.

'If you have to. Probably won't come to that.'

'How come?'

'Because I'm not pressing charges,' Jade said.

'Are you mad?' Bert said. 'You're a police officer.'

'So is he.' Jade gestured to Harris. 'And what he's already done is far more serious, believe me. That's what I'm arresting him for. Soon as he wakes up.'

'*If* he wakes up,' DD said. 'You might want to send for the priest.' He looked at her for a moment. Then he left without another word.

Jade asked Bert to go and tell Mina everything was OK.

He came back in a minute. Mina had been watching a *Harry Potter* film and she'd thought the noise was on the soundtrack.

'You think he needs an ambulance?' Bert said.

'I'll call one,' Jade said. 'And the police. After I've nicked him.'

A few seconds later Martin Harris sputtered and began to move, lifting his head an inch off the floor, trying to move his arms against the cuffs.

Slowly and meticulously, Jade recited the caution, relishing each word, savouring the loathing she saw in his eyes, the pulse of victory leaping in her blood, threading through the drumbeat of pain.

CHAPTER TWENTY-ONE

Donna

Donna was waiting in the custody suite. Jade had rung her minutes before. 'Boss, I'm bringing Harris in.'

'Where did you find him?'

'He found me,' Jade said, something dark behind the words.

Donna felt a spike of fear, thinking of Martin chasing Jade. 'Are you OK?'

'Yeah, I'm good. He's a bit woozy, I reckon.'

'How come?'

'Stun gun.'

'Legal?' Donna's mind raced over the implications. If Jade had an unauthorized weapon, an illegal import . . .

'Not mine, boss, so I couldn't say. Car's here now. The paramedics have checked him out and he's fit to be detained.'

Donna stifled a gasp when she caught sight of them. Martin in cuffs, flanked between two officers in uniform, his clothes dishevelled and stained. A rip in his shirt, bloodied face, blackened eyes.

After them came Jade, cuts on her cheek, swollen lip. Her eyes were blazing, her body taut, with an intensity that seemed too great for her slight frame.

When Martin's eyes met Donna's, he gave her a look of utter indifference before turning his attention to the desk.

Jade glanced at Donna, triumph shining in her eyes, and stepped forward to outline the charges against Martin to the custody sergeant.

Martin answered the standard questions. The handcuffs were removed, he emptied his pockets and was frisked. The atmosphere among those present was Arctic: icy disdain and procedural rigour. A barrier to contain the repugnance of facing corruption in one of their own.

Donna thought of the Kennaways, how they would come to hear about the bent copper who had tried to destroy their claim for justice. Again she felt the corrosive wash of shame at her failure to believe Jade, at her acceptance of Martin's lies.

The ripples from this would taint her reputation for ever. She'd have to prove herself over and over again, for the bosses, for the people of Manchester, for her colleagues. And there would always be rumours: *she must have known, it's never just one bad apple, she wasn't fit to lead.*

No time for self-pity now, though. They had to sort this out, redeem something from the mire Martin had led them into. From the inquiry that had been twisted and fouled.

'Come and see me when you're done here,' she said to Jade.

Donna moved to go, then turned back and touched Jade's arm. Jade flinched. 'Good work,' Donna told her. 'Excellent work.'

Jade gave a swift nod, and Donna also caught a glimpse of movement from Martin, his back to them, a flexing across his shoulders before he stilled. Like a horse dislodging flies.

When Jade had finished telling her what had happened at the flat, basically that Martin had ambushed her but she'd been able to use his own weapon to disable him, Donna said, 'Why didn't you call for back-up?'

Jade shrugged. 'I wasn't sure anyone was actually in my flat.'

'You went into a potentially life-threatening situation on your own and unarmed,' Donna said. How could she not see this was beyond stupid?

'I got him, though,' Jade said. As if that justified everything.

'He could have killed you, hospitalized you at the very least.'

'He didn't,' Jade said.

'We should add this to the charge sheet, breaking and entering, causing grievous bodily harm with intent, assaulting a police officer—'

'No.' Jade stuck her hands into her pockets. Studied her feet. Back against the wall.

'Why on earth not?'

'Because it's more important to go for the conspiracy to pervert, assisting an offender. That's the only thing that matters.'

'He could get extra time,' Donna said. 'I want to go after him for everything we can throw at him.'

'He's a slippery bastard, boss. He could twist it all, get into the stuff like before, how I'm off my head. It's too messy. I won't do it.' Chin jutting out in defiance.

'All the times we have to persuade people to come to us, to report crime, to press charges, to see it through, and you're waving a white feather?'

Jade glared at her. 'I won't do it.'

Exasperated, wondering if there were other reasons for her reluctance, if there was something she was hiding, Donna said, 'I think you're making a mistake.'

Another shrug.

Stalemate.

'Jade, I'm sorry,' Donna said. She was saying that to everyone, these days. *Sorry, sorry, sorry.* 'None of this would have—'

'Yeah, OK,' Jade said quickly, her skin flushing, darkening her complexion. 'What about Dale and Oliver?'

Donna pinched the bridge of her nose, turned her concentration to the two murder suspects. 'My money is on Dale being the stronger of the two, calling the shots. Agreed?'

'Yes.' Jade pushed herself away from the wall and came to sit down near Donna. Up close Donna could see dust in her hair, speckles of silver too. Glass? Like with Jim. No time for him now. She'd phone in the morning. Go in at lunchtime, if she could. It felt like a chore, one she dreaded. *You're avoiding him.*

Jade's hands were battered, flecked with cuts and grazes. From fighting Martin? Him twice her size.

'I also think Oliver is more scared,' Donna said.

'He's probably more scared of Martin than he is of us,' Jade said.

'Can't think why,' Donna said drily.

'Oliver's the weakest link,' Jade said. 'So we put the screws on, try and trip him up?'

'No,' Donna said. 'Nothing that smells of coercion. He's already been coerced by Martin, probably Dale as well. Threatened and pressured. I'm not saying we don't work on any contradictions, unpick the less plausible elements of the story, but he needs to believe the best thing for him is to tell the truth.'

'And grass up his mate?' Jade said sceptically.

'And make amends,' Donna corrected her. 'Look, from everything we heard he's from a loving, stable home. His mother had the guts, the moral courage, to come to us with her fears. In my experience, a boy like Oliver doesn't get involved in a serious crime like this and not be haunted by it. It's a nightmare for him. One day he's hanging about playing his Xbox and doing an apprenticeship or going out on the piss, the next he's covered in blood and there's a dead girl in the rain. He runs away from home, and his mate's dad, a detective, is telling him what to do, what to say and no doubt what'll happen if he doesn't play by Martin's rules. I'm going to show Oliver he doesn't have to play that game. That he can stand on his own two feet and take responsibility for what he's done.'

'And if he tells you where to shove it?' Jade said.

'Ye of little faith,' Donna said.

'Can I sit in?'

'I don't think so,' Donna said. 'You might want tomorrow off. Have a break.'

'I'm fine,' Jade said.

'I think I've got this covered,' Donna said.

'C'mon, boss,' Jade said. 'What happened to teamwork?'

'You've been assaulted. Look at the state of you.'

'And. I. Am. Fine.'

Donna sighed. 'You won't take no for an answer, will you?'

Jade smiled. 'What about interviews with Martin Harris?'

'Neither of us goes anywhere near,' Donna said. 'We maintain a clear distance at this point. I'll hand it over to someone of my rank. But he's going to go "no comment". I can't see him doing anything else.' She checked the time. 'You want to get out of here for a few hours? Clean yourself up? We'll start the Poole interview at eight tomorrow morning.'

'Maybe,' Jade said.

Donna yawned. 'I'll go home. Show my face. Check the kids haven't changed the locks.' *See if any of them are still speaking to me.*

Jade

Jade had slept on the sofa in the visitors' lounge. Not that she'd got much kip. Every time she nodded off, she'd jerk awake, little explosions inside, like a sequence of fireworks primed to run all night long. Her skin was greasy, scratchy, and the cuts itched. Her back hurt with each breath.

There was a staff shower, which she used, the water stinging the cuts. Without a towel she used paper napkins to mop up most of the wet. But she was still damp when she pulled her clothes back on. Her hair would dry quickly enough by itself.

Her stomach growled. When had she last eaten? Lunchtime the previous day?

She found a café half a block from the station, open early, busy with contractors in their boiler suits and chunky boots. She ignored the undercurrent of glances her way, people no doubt trying to guess who she was, what she was, what had happened to her face, why she'd washed up here among the regulars. She ate a sausage and egg muffin, drank coffee, took her tablets, then waited for the food, the drugs, to ground her, to neutralize the shocks still coursing through her, like the spit and crackle of a loose connection.

Jade was attending the Oliver Poole interview on the understanding she take notes and observe. Keep her trap shut, in other words.

Fine by Jade, as long as she was there, in the room.

Oliver was quite a contrast to Dale Harris. Much bigger for a start. He put Jade in mind of a squaddie or a halfback. He didn't have Dale Harris's boy-band good looks, not that he was minging or anything, but the round face and red colouring weren't fashionable. Jade sensed a softness to him, as though he could be bullied as easily as be a bully. There'd been kids like that in the home. One she remembered clearly – Titch, they'd called him. Massive kid. Bullied when he'd first arrived until he'd shut himself in his room and set it on fire. By the time Titch returned from hospital, treated for second-degree burns, his main enemies had been moved. Titch took over their role. He beat DD half senseless one time, in the park so the staff couldn't see. DD had refused to say who'd done it. He swore Jade to silence too.

After that DD had begun sparring. He'd learnt how to move, how to punch someone and incapacitate them. He'd taught Jade some moves. DD had bided his time, and when Titch slagged him off again, DD fanned the flames, taunting him until the big lad lost it. Then DD let rip. Fists like jackhammers. It took three staff to pull DD off him. Titch had never bothered DD again.

Now the boss finished the preliminaries and said, 'Oliver, there have been substantial developments since yesterday. Martin Harris, Dale's father, has been arrested on suspicion of perverting the course of justice and assisting an offender. And there may well be further charges to follow.'

He blinked fast, looking shit scared.

'You know Martin Harris?'

'No,' Oliver said, quick and low.

The boss didn't say anything for a bit. She was just looking at him. Not with a face on or anything, just looking, and she said, 'Let me tell you what I think, Oliver. I think Martin Harris learnt what you and Dale had done, that you had killed Allie Kennaway, and I think he offered to help.'

Oliver was shaking his head slowly, murmuring, 'No,' as she continued, 'He was a police officer. He was working on this inquiry. He could make evidence disappear, he could falsify evidence, and he coached you in a cover story in case you were arrested.'

'No,' he said more loudly.

'He probably told you he could protect you. He was wrong. He's downstairs now, in a cell. He'll be interviewed this morning. The offences he's committed could see him behind bars for years, possibly life. It's all gone wrong, Oliver.'

'We didn't do it. The homeless guy, the African—'

'I'm going to stop you, there,' the boss said. 'Because the story, and it is a story, you've been coached in is ridiculous. It's a farce. Three people against one. The supposed knife. How could anyone carry a knife like that loose in their pocket? We arrested Mahmoud Bishaar and it was not among his possessions. Dale was seen with blood on his shirt, blood from his attack on Bishaar. He held Bishaar in a stranglehold and punched his nose. Do you remember that? If you were forced at knifepoint to hurt Allie Kennaway, why not run to the police as soon as you were free? And, most significantly, why would Mahmoud Bishaar call for an ambulance and alert the police as soon as he could to try to save Allie Kennaway's life? That's not the action of a psychotic killer. Your story is a shambles, Oliver. Cooked up in desperation. It won't bear scrutiny. Now that we've apprehended Martin Harris and established his role in interfering with the work of the inquiry, it looks even worse for you and Dale. If you were innocent, as you claim, Martin Harris would have put his trust in the criminal justice system. The system he has served his whole working life. He'd have brought you in so we could learn the truth. So we could arrest the man responsible.'

'That is the truth,' Oliver shouted, his face creased, ears bright red.

Quiet again. Jade didn't know if the boss did this to think about what to say next or for some other reason. To calm him, maybe. To slow things down?

'I want you to think about something else now,' the boss said. 'You see, I think this is unbearably difficult for you. To find yourself here in a police station and charged with murder, the most serious of crimes. You never saw this coming.' She was talking so gently, like she was truly sorry for him. It gave Jade the creeps.

'When you went out with Dale you were expecting a good time, a meal with some mates, a few drinks, maybe clubbing. You never planned any of this. You never wanted any of this, did you?'

His nose went red and he looked down at his hands.

'You're not a bad person. You've never done anything like this before, not by a million miles. It all went so wrong, didn't it? Five minutes and everything changed. You never meant that to happen. And I think you'd give anything to turn back time. To wipe it all away.'

The boss kept on talking, like she cared more about Oliver Poole than anyone else on the planet. Oliver sat rigid, silent, still looking down. Jade kept forgetting to write. The boss's voice was hypnotic, like she was telling a bedtime story.

'But the past can't be changed,' the boss said. 'I think you tried to do the right thing, just after it had happened. You were arguing with Dale. I think you wanted to get help then. Because you knew it was wrong. You've probably been thinking about it over and over. What if you hadn't gone into town? What if you'd got into Fredo's instead of being turned away? What if Dale hadn't grabbed her, that girl, in the street? What if Mahmoud Bishaar had woken seconds sooner and frightened you off?' Another pause. 'She's dead. Allie Kennaway. The same age as you, and she's gone. Because you killed her.'

'I didn't fucking kill her,' he screamed, the cords in his neck standing out. Then he choked on his words: 'I never. I never did it.'

A beat or two and the boss said, 'You can't change the past but you can change what happens now. You can keep lying and cause more pain for that family, for Allie's dad, for her little sister. Or you can take responsibility for your actions and face the consequences. You can be a man.'

He was swaying in the chair, as if he was trying to soothe some unbearable pain, tiny sounds coming from him. All because of what the boss was doing, what she was saying and the way she was saying it. It was incredible.

'That is a terrible secret to keep. Imagine if it was you, hurt, killed in an attack. If it was your mother grieving, wanting to know the truth. Don't you think that's the least you can do? You can never make it right, Oliver, but you can be honest. You can stop making it worse for the people who loved Allie. The people who woke up this morning and remembered again that she wasn't there any more. That she was never coming home.'

Oliver broke. He was sniffing, crying. The boss stayed quiet. Jade cleared her throat. Oliver's hands went to his face.

'We should take a break,' his solicitor said.

The boss ignored him. She spoke to Oliver instead. 'You're very distressed, Oliver. You've been through an enormous trauma and you've been pressured to lie and to conspire to put another person in prison for a crime that you've committed. I don't think you could live with that. You don't owe Dale Harris or his father anything. Not loyalty or allegiance or a debt of gratitude. But you do owe the Kennaway family, and you owe your own family. You owe yourself. You never set out to kill someone. You made a dreadful, dreadful mistake and lying about it is only making it worse. And the only way to start to make amends for that is to own up to it.'

Silence in the room, apart from Oliver, still crying and swallowing, breath ragged. The boss stretched it out so long Jade thought she'd blown it. Then she said softly, 'Oliver, you didn't mean to do it, did you?'

'No,' he blurted. 'I don't know why we did it . . . I'm sorry . . . It's just . . . Oh, God.' He cried more loudly. Sobs that wrenched his shoulders up and down. Jade couldn't bear the sound. She bit her lip, felt the pain where the scab had formed.

'Thank you,' the boss said, when he'd calmed down enough to pay attention. 'I know how hard that must be. We'll take a break but we'll need to get a fresh statement from you.'

'Yes,' he said thickly.

'It's important for our records that what you're saying is clear and unambiguous so when you say, "I don't know why we did it", please can you tell me exactly what "it" is?'

'The killing,' he whispered.

'Killing Allie Kennaway?'

'Yes.' And he wept like a baby.

CHAPTER TWENTY-TWO

Sonia

Sonia hadn't replied to any of the texts from the supermarket wanting to know when she'd be back in work. She had no idea what to say. She couldn't stay off indefinitely or she'd be in a mess with the rent and bills.

Perhaps she'd go in tomorrow. The thought made her stomach cramp. But it wasn't as though anything about Oliver had been made public yet, apart from the photo-fits, which were anonymous. If she kept her head down, told people she was still a bit fluey, she should be able to get through her shift. It might even help to be distracted by customers and cock-ups with the scanners or the security-tag remover.

Rose had to take her dad for his podiatrist appointment but promised to call round after tea. She had been amazing. What would Sonia do without her?

The kitchen was a tip. The cat's bowl was crusted with dried-on food. Muddy footprints on the floor, cat hairs. The window over the sink mottled with splashes. And the hob spattered with grease. Sonia ran a sink full of hot soapy water and began cleaning.

Ten minutes in and her phone rang. It was DC Bradshaw. Sonia sat down heavily, her heart pattering fast.

'Oliver has been in a series of interviews this afternoon and has given us a new statement,' DC Bradshaw said.

'Right.' Sonia closed her eyes, concentrated.

'He's made a confession.'

Oh, God.

'As a result he's been formally charged and will be appearing at the magistrates' court in the morning.'

'He's been charged?' Her voice shook with shock.

'Yes. He's been charged with murder,' DC Bradshaw said.

'Oh, no. No. Please no.' Any slender hope Sonia had had that Oliver was innocent was ripped apart. She'd been right. He had done it. The room seemed to close in on her. Her head hummed with fear.

'The magistrate will refer the matter to the Crown Court and Oliver will be remanded in custody.'

'He confessed?' Sonia said.

'That's right. That means he'll probably appear as a witness for the prosecution.'

'And the other boy?'

'Dale Harris is likely to plead not guilty.'

'I can't believe it's Oliver . . . I think I knew but . . . it's like at the same time I didn't . . . I didn't want it to be true. How could he do that?'

DC Bradshaw said nothing.

'If he's confessed does that mean he'll go to prison?' Sonia said.

'Pretty much, given his involvement. But his cooperation probably means a lighter sentence and an earlier chance at parole. The conviction may be for manslaughter rather than murder because there wasn't any clear intent to kill.'

'But it'll be years?' Sonia said.

'Yes.'

'Did he say why . . . why they did it?' Sonia said. Part of her numb with disbelief. *This is not happening. Oliver. Murder.*

'He says they were both drunk and had taken drugs. He said Dale Harris grabbed Allie and sexually assaulted her. On discovering she was transgender he became violent and Oliver joined in the attack.'

Sonia couldn't speak.

'The officer you dealt with at the station, Detective Sergeant Harris, you should know that Dale Harris is his son.'

'What?' A chill ran over Sonia's skin.

'Dale Harris is DS Harris's son.'

Sonia thought of the man and his promises. The advice he'd given her. Then his appearance yesterday, talking about crossed wires. 'I don't understand,' she said.

'DS Harris has also been arrested and charged with conspiring to pervert the course of justice and assisting an offender.'

'He knew?' Sonia said. 'When I came in to tell someone about Oliver matching the photo-fits, when I saw him, he already knew?'

'I'm sorry,' DC Bradshaw said. 'He used his position to try to corrupt the inquiry.'

And Sonia had mistrusted this young detective when she'd come to the house yesterday. 'When you were here,' Sonia said, 'I rang him to see if I should talk to you or not. He didn't answer.'

A pause, then: 'The detectives dealing with his case will see that when they examine his phone and they'll want to talk to you about it. They'll also want to talk to you about how DS Harris dealt with your visit to the station. Just tell them what you told me. You may well be called as a witness.'

The thought made Sonia feel ill.

'You'll most likely hear from Oliver tomorrow afternoon. Once he arrives in custody he can make a phone call. You'll be able to arrange to see him.'

'Yes,' she said. 'Thank you.'

She didn't know much about prison, about what it was really like to be behind bars, but from the little she did know, the documentaries on television, the features in the paper, she thought it would destroy Oliver. Spit him out years later – how many? Fifteen, twenty? – damaged, stunted, broken. *Oh, Oliver. Oliver. Oliver.*

The cat jumped into her lap and she stroked its head, rubbed at its ears. Her tears fell on its fur as she wept for all that was lost.

Martin

Martin Harris let the questions wash over him, waiting only for the detective inspector to stop speaking each time before answering, 'No comment.'

He'd been at the other side of the table on countless occasions and knew that refusal to comment wasn't easy to sustain. There was a natural impulse to set the questioner straight, to rebut accusations and correct mistakes, to answer those seemingly innocuous questions, to defend yourself. Fatal.

In order not to get caught in any of these traps he tuned out as much as he possibly could. Imagined the bloke was speaking a foreign language, a jumble of nonsense, nothing to do with him. Listened to the rise and fall of the sentences for his cue.

Martin didn't know the DI – they'd probably shipped him in from North Manchester for that very reason. He was young, slight, nondescript, and wore rectangular wire-framed specs, more like an accountant than a copper.

It was a dance: Martin would repeat his moves as long as necessary, and then they'd charge him, if the CPS reckoned there was a strong chance of a successful prosecution.

His bowels tightened, thinking about that. It should never have happened. He wouldn't be here, dealing with this fuckery, if it wasn't for Jade Bradshaw and her devious fucking—

'Mr Harris? Would you like me to repeat the question?'

'No comment,' Martin said.

There was bile at the back of his throat, a sharp pain below his ribs. His nose was still blocked with dried blood. He needed more antacids. He wasn't allowed any medicine in his cell. It had to be doled out by the doctor. In minuscule amounts.

He had no idea where things were up to with Dale and Oliver, but as long as they stuck to the script there was still a chance.

For them if not for him.

'You spoke with Mrs Sonia Poole yesterday. Is that correct?'

'No comment.'

Fran didn't know he was here yet. Martin had used his phone call to get himself a solicitor. She'd find out soon enough. *Christ, what a fucking mess.*

He should have rammed the stun gun into the Paki bitch. Into her gob. Full power till the battery died. Till she was quiet.

He'd kill her. He would. If they sent him down, he'd do his time, and when he got out he'd turn her inside out, make her suffer, make her scream. Make her disappear.

'No comment.'

The inspector inhaled loudly and trotted out the next question.

And the Muslim fucker. It was Bradshaw brought him in. Without him in the picture they had nothing. No witness, no photo-fits, nothing. Dale would still be gearing up for his trials.

Bradshaw was toxic, a psycho, but Donna, the two-faced bitch, had seen fit to let her work again. Arresting him. It was a joke. *Bradshaw* arresting *him*.

'No comment.'

She'd pay for this, the skanky bitch. She'd pay, with interest for all the time he'd have to wait.

The acid lapped at his throat. His mouth flooded with saliva.

'Mr Harris?'

He swallowed. 'No comment.' And he stared past the DI to the wall opposite as the next question rolled over him.

Donna

Donna had briefed Yun Li that she wanted to talk to the Kennaways in person to tell them about the latest developments. Only then would the press office release a statement, announcing the names of those charged with the murder and associated offences.

Yun answered the door and took her into the living room. Steve Kennaway reached to turn off the television. Donna caught a glimpse of an African landscape, a herd of giraffes. Teagan sat beside her father, legs crossed under her.

Donna looked from father to daughter, and said to Steve, 'It might be better if we speak in private.'

'Dad,' Teagan complained.

'It's all right,' Steve said to Donna.

Teagan stared at her, unblinking. Her serious face was framed by dark hair.

Donna broke the silence. 'We've made significant progress today,' she said.

Teagan slipped her hand into her father's.

'Two men have been charged with Allie's murder.'

Steve Kennaway made a sound, indistinct. Creases furrowed his brow.

'Dale Anthony Harris and Oliver Poole, both eighteen.'

'Same age as her,' Steve Kennaway said, his voice thin.

'It's likely to be several months until they come to trial,' Donna said. 'There will be various stages to the judicial process. Yun can explain those to you over the next few days. He'll remain a point of contact for you indefinitely.'

'Thank you,' Steve said. 'Why did they do it? Do you know why?'

Donna wiped her hands on her trousers, took a breath. 'Only one of them, Oliver Poole, has admitted the crime. According to Oliver, it was Dale Harris who began sexually harassing Allie and allegedly became violent when he realized she was transgender. In effect a hate crime.'

'Dad,' Teagan said.

'Oh, God,' said Steve Kennaway.

'The other man, Dale Harris, claims to have interrupted an attack on Allie by a man called Mahmoud Bishaar, the one who helped us with the photo-fits. Dale Harris alleges Bishaar then drew a knife and forced him and Oliver Poole to assault Allie, leading to death.'

Steve Kennaway gasped, and Teagan looked at her father, an expression of confusion on her face.

'Initially that account was given by both suspects but Oliver Poole altered his statement this afternoon.'

'So the other one is lying?' Teagan said.

'We think he is,' Donna said. 'And we're charging him with conspiring to pervert the course of justice.'

'Good.' Teagan nodded for emphasis. 'What about Mr Bishaar? He called the ambulance?'

'He did.'

'And he tried to save her. He should get an award or something.'

If only it worked like that.

'I'm afraid Mr Bishaar is a failed asylum-seeker,' Donna said. 'He will remain in a detention centre until the trial, but then he'll be deported.'

'That's not fair,' Teagan said. 'That's so not fair. How can they do that? We should do something.'

Steve Kennaway looked at Donna.

'I'm not sure anything can be done,' she said.

Yun spoke up: 'There may be the opportunity to launch a fresh appeal for asylum. We could get some legal advice.'

'Yes,' Steve Kennaway said.

Teagan echoed him, 'Yes, do that.'

'There is more, I'm afraid,' Donna said, her breath catching.

'We've also charged one of the officers on the team with conspiracy to pervert the course of justice. DS Martin Harris. He's Dale Harris's father.'

Steve Kennaway stared at her. His mouth slack. Then he said, 'What are you—' He stood swiftly, letting go of Teagan's hand. The dog raised its head. 'But I spoke to him.'

He moved away from the sofa. 'I talked to the man. I was desperate to know what was happening.' He began to shout: 'He sat there. You're telling me he fucking sat there, knowing?' He kicked out at the coffee-table, toppling it.

Teagan shouted, 'Dad! Dad, don't.'

'Get out!' Steve yelled at Donna. 'His son did that to my daughter. He was working for you. The fucking bastard. I went to him and begged for her body. To him!' His face was blotched with red. His hands raised, an angry supplication.

Donna felt his rage, his sense of impotence, shared them. She felt wretched that she had failed the family, failed to discern Martin was manipulating her, that Jade, even if she had lied at her medical, was to be trusted.

'I'm so sorry,' Donna said. Service policy was never to apologize, never to admit culpability or accept blame. When those seeking redress were persistent, when every other avenue had been exhausted, an expression of regret was made. A full and frank apology was extremely rare. The chief constable and the Federation would spontaneously combust if they could hear her now. 'I should have known. I should have found out sooner. So I will do everything—'

'Get out,' Steve Kennaway said again, cold and quiet.

Donna went without another word, her throat and chest tight, her eyes stinging.

At the front door, Yun said, 'Are you all right, boss?'

'No, not really.' She shivered. 'Look, tell them everything you can. Stay close. Go the extra mile. God knows they deserve it.'

'I will.'

'Tell them about the complaints procedures too, though it'll have to wait till after trial.'

'Sure.' Yun opened the door. 'DS Harris . . . He always seemed so . . . How could he turn like that? When this gets out . . .'

'I know,' Donna said, looking up at the cloudy sky, the colour of steel and bone. 'I know.'

'But Oliver Poole confessed. That changes everything,' Yun said. 'There's no way a jury will believe Dale Harris now.'

'Yes,' Donna said. 'Let's hope so.' She felt drained, no sense of triumph or achievement, but he was right. When the case came to trial it was more than likely that just verdicts would be reached: the men who had killed Allie Kennaway would be found guilty and punished for the crime.

Jade

On her way home, Jade remembered Mina's shopping. *Shit, shit, shit.* She'd no idea where the list was. She made a detour to Aldi and got some basics, the things Mina always asked for: bread, crumpets, milk, biscuits, cheese, eggs, pork, potatoes, bananas, tins of tomatoes.

When she knocked on Mina's door there was no answer. That wasn't right. Mina never went anywhere bar the GP's, certainly not at night. Maybe she'd the TV on too loud but when Jade pressed her ear to the door she couldn't hear anything.

Jade put the shopping down and got her own key out. She walked swiftly along the corridor, holding her breath.

Scraping sounds, voices. From Jade's flat. Someone in there. Fear scrabbled up her back, dug needle fingers under her skin. Who? Friends of Harris? She couldn't call DD – it would be a good while, if ever, before she had the balls to ask for DD's help again.

How had they got in? The door was closed, no damage. Still the clatter from inside, murmuring. A laugh, a man's laugh.

Some scrotebag in there, laughing. Rage chased the fear away. Jade ran back to Mina's and fetched two tins of tomatoes. She unlocked her door and, with a can in each hand, kicked it wide open and launched herself into the room, screaming, 'Fuck off! Fuck off now!'

Movement. Jade hurled one of the tins towards it, missing the figure. The can bounced off the wall.

'Jade!' It was Bert. Bert, and Mina on the other side. Mina with a sweeping brush in her hand.

'Jesus.' Jade circled round, slung the other can down. 'What are you doing? I'm having a heart attack here. I could have killed you.'

'We were clearing up,' Mina said. She waved at a pile of broken glass, fragments from the TV, bits of chair.

'Jesus,' Jade said. She didn't want them there, messing with her stuff. Even her broken stuff. 'I can do that.'

'You put the kettle on,' Bert said.

'No, honest, I'll do it,' Jade said. 'You two get off.' It'd take them hours anyway, the pair of them as doddery as each other. She didn't need them fussing about. 'I'll do it.' She reached for the brush. Mina's eyebrows knitted together, her mouth pinched small. For a moment it looked like Jade would have to wrench the thing out of her hands.

But Mina let go. She nodded to the tin Jade had used as a missile. 'Is that for me?'

'Yes,' Jade said. 'I only had a chance to get a few bits. I'll go back tomorrow.'

Bert reached for the can, his legs shaking.

'I'll get it.' Jade sprinted before he could topple over.

She picked it up and handed both to Mina. 'The rest is by your door.'

Mina glanced back at the pile of crap, like she was itching to carry on.

'I can do it now,' Jade said.

'You look terrible,' Mina said. 'You should see the doctor.'

'I'm fine.' *And I'll be even better when you two fuck off home.*

Bert got his stick, which was propped in the corner, and said, 'There's bin liners there, heavy duty.'

'Right.'

'That fella,' Bert said, 'is he locked up, then?'

'What fella?' Jade said.

Bert stared at her, watery eyes like a sheep, but insistent.

'He is,' Jade said. 'And we've charged two others with the murder.'

'Clever girl,' Mina said. 'I really thought he was a fireman. He was so slick.'

Jade crossed her arms.

'Right, looks like we're not wanted,' Bert said to Mina.

'You need a good night's sleep,' Mina said to Jade, 'and proper food.'

'Yeah.' *Just go.* 'And thanks,' Jade said, as they left, sounding gruff, like she was getting a cold.

The door closed and she sank to the floor. She leant her head back against the wall. She saw Allie Kennaway, dressed up sweet, joking with her mates, mellow with weed and a few drinks, celebrating the end of sixth form. Breathless from dancing. Going out in the rain, the fine rain.

She wouldn't cry. Crying never helped. Crying made things worse. She pressed her eyes hard, summoning a galaxy of stars. They burnt. Besides, they'd caught the bastards. That was all that mattered. They'd got them, and Oliver's confession was pure gold. No need to cry.

She let her hands fall, waited for the stars to clear. She was fine, she was safe. The cuts would heal. She still had her job. She was a detective. A good one. She allowed herself a smile, which tore at the wound on her lip. A small sting.

'We did it.' That was what the boss had said as Jade left. 'We did it.' *We.*

Jade stood, hands on the small of her back. She looked round at the wreck of the room. The crap chair, broken, the remnants of the cheap TV. In the bedroom still just a mattress on the floor and a rail for her clothes, a lopsided chest of drawers with half the handles missing. She really should sort the place out properly. Fix it up a bit, buy some more stuff. She had money in the bank.

It was hard, this world, the world out there, the world in her head, but maybe it was time to make her home a bit more comfortable. Stop living as though she'd have to do a runner at any moment. After all, she had the job she wanted now. DC Bradshaw. *We did it.*

Jade took a deep breath. And another. Smiling, she tore a bin liner from the roll, fetched the dustpan from under the sink and started to clear up the mess.

CHAPTER TWENTY-THREE

Donna

Jim was home. In the living room. On what looked like Kirsten's bed. The sofa had been pushed into the bay and the television moved round. The kids were all there, draped around the place, like a pride of lions, shooting the breeze. When Donna walked in, it felt as though she was interrupting something. Conversation stopped. Kirsten and Bryony both gave her filthy looks. *Still in the doghouse, then.*

'Dad's back,' Kirsten said, as though scoring a point.

'I can see that,' Donna said. 'How come?'

'Discharged myself.'

'Oh, Jim.'

'Well, I'm better off here than stuck there,' he said.

'But your heart . . .'

'I'll be seen as an outpatient. It's just tests for now.' He was putting on a cheery front for the sake of the kids, brief smiles, a bright tone, but Donna knew him well enough to read the unhappiness in his eyes. The accident would take time to recover from physically. The trauma of knowing someone had died could take a good deal longer.

'He's got a potty.' Matt giggled, pointing to a spindly-looking chair.

'A commode,' Bryony said.

'Why?'

'That's a mistake,' Jim said. 'I can manage with the downstairs loo.'

'Can I use it then?' Matt said.

'Matthew! Gross!' Bryony curled her lip.

'It could be good. There's loads of times when I want to wee and I have to wait.'

'Use the drain,' Rob said.

Donna gave him a look.

'What's wrong with that?' he said.

'Did you get bread?' Lewis said.

'Oh, yes. Here.' She held out her car keys. 'In the boot. How long till the cast comes off?' she asked Jim.

'Three months. Maybe sooner.'

'I've been thinking,' Donna said, 'we should get some help, get someone in.'

'What for?' Jim said.

'Well, you'll be pretty much bedbound and I'm at work. We need someone to ferry this lot about, cook meals. A couple of months at least.'

'We can get takeaways,' Matt said.

'We're not living on takeaways or ready meals. Besides, there's packed lunches as well, school pick-ups, washing and cleaning.'

'If everyone had a job,' Kirsten said, 'like you said before . . .'

'I'm not doing any more jobs,' Bryony said. 'Not unless I'm paid.'

'That was just triage,' Donna said.

'What's triage?' said Matt.

'What you do in an emergency,' Donna said. 'Look, you've already got chores, all of you, and it's a miracle if they get done without regular nagging. We can get a temporary nanny—'

'A nanny?' Rob said scornfully.

'A housekeeper, then.'

'Why can't you stay home till Dad's better?' Kirsten said.

'I can't just give up work,' Donna said. 'If someone had died . . .' *Shit.* She avoided looking at Jim and went on, '. . . then I could get some leave but not for something like this. My job is paying for everything at the moment. Your dad can't work.'

Lewis came back in, a loaf in each hand.

'Let's see how next week goes,' Jim said. Why couldn't he agree with her?

'No,' Donna said. 'How are Rob and Lewis getting back from football? What about Kirsten's piano? We already have to pay for taxis to get them home.'

'If it's raining,' Matt piped up.

'It'd be simpler to sort it out now. And that's what I'm going to do,' Donna said.

Jim looked mutinous but didn't speak. Bryony rolled her eyes. The atmosphere was increasingly prickly and Donna's patience was fast running out.

'What if we don't like them?' Kirsten said.

'Cup half full,' Donna chided her. 'You don't really have to like them. And, anyway, it's only for a few weeks.'

'Where will they sleep?' Matt said.

'They won't stay here, dummy,' Kirsten said.

'You're not a dummy. But, no, they won't,' Donna said. 'Now,' she wanted to try to contain the situation, 'I bet your dad could do with a rest, eh?'

'I'm OK,' Jim said, contradicting her.

'Fine,' Donna said crisply. 'You've all eaten?'

Bryony nodded.

'What are you making?' Rob said hopefully.

'I don't know, but if you're hungry get yourself a sandwich. I've got to go out again later.'

Jim gave a shake of his head. Really not helping.

'Why?' Kirsten said, alarmed, as if Donna had announced she was emigrating.

'You only just came home,' Bryony said.

'You're always out,' Matt said. 'It's not fair.'

'Dad's back,' Kirsten said. 'We're going to watch a film. All of us together.'

'Can't you skip it?' Lewis said to Donna.

'Yes!' Matt clapped his hands.

'No,' Donna said firmly.

'You'd rather be at work than here, wouldn't you?' Bryony said. 'You can't even take us to see Dad in hospital when you promise. Because work's all that matters, isn't it?' Six pairs of eyes on Donna, accusing her.

'No, it's not all that matters,' Donna said, her temper rising. 'You matter, all of you, but so does my job. And it pays the bills. Last Friday a teenage girl was beaten to death, here in Manchester, because of who she was, because of what she was. That matters.' Donna had raised her voice. She knew shouting wouldn't help them understand but she couldn't stop. 'Tonight people who care about that, who want to stand up for that girl, who want to show support for her family and for anyone affected by this sort of hate crime, are holding a vigil. I'm going to be there. Not just because I'm the officer leading the investigation but because I'm also a mother and a woman and a human being, and that girl should still be alive.' Her voice was breaking. Kirsten looked close to tears. With supreme effort Donna spoke more calmly. 'So, I'm not staying to watch a film and that's why. We can do that another night. I'm going to the vigil.'

'We'll come too,' Lewis said.

'You don't need—'

'I want to,' he said. *Oh, Lewis. You lovely boy.*

'What's a vigil?' Matt said.

'Dad'll explain,' Donna said. 'I'm going to eat. If anyone wants to come we leave in an hour. It goes on till midnight.'

'Wow!' said Matt.

'Dad can't go,' Kirsten said.

'No, so someone might want to stay and keep him company,' Donna said, hoping Kirsten would get the hint.

Donna took the loaves from Lewis and went to the hall, then retraced her steps and said to them all, 'I'm sorry I shouted. It's just . . . it's been a very long day, and very difficult. But that wasn't fair. I'm sorry.'

Before there could be any comeback or debate she walked to the kitchen to find something to eat. Jim was home and her gut reaction hadn't been pleasure or relief but concern verging on irritation.

What was happening to her? To them? *Don't I love him any more?* The question rang in her head, unanswered. She couldn't tackle it, not now and not with him so hurt. The thought filled her with dread. She didn't even know what she wanted. But it wasn't this. It wasn't what they had.

She needed something to settle her stomach. To grab a few minutes' sanctuary so she could get her breath back and quell the shaky sensation that made her feel she was dangerously close to losing control. She couldn't afford to do that, not just because she had to be strong and keep going for her kids but because she still had so much more work to put in on the Allie Kennaway case. Weeks of building on the existing evidence, fleshing it out, joining all the dots, making it watertight. Proving herself to the team, to Steve and Teagan Kennaway. To herself as well. Making amends for her mistakes. Being the best she could be.

Steve

The first thing he saw were the umbrellas, a shield wall of rainbow-coloured umbrellas, and beads of light from joysticks and torches.

So many people.

A small stage there, an archway of multi-coloured bulbs framing it, circles of light diffused in the soft rain, a rainbow canopy on top. It looked like a large puppet booth. Steve realized the street lights around the little park had been turned off.

Music playing, a saxophone.

'"Over The Rainbow",' Teagan said, and squeezed his hand.

Yun Li escorted them through the crowd to the front. He pointed out a row of chairs set at either side of the stage, laminated reserved signs on them. 'You can sit,' he said.

'Maybe later,' Steve said. He turned to his father and spoke into his ear. 'Are you all right standing here for a bit?'

His father nodded. 'If your mum is.' He gestured to Steve's mother, who was at the far side of Teagan.

Steve bent and asked Teagan to tell Nanny they'd stand for a while.

The saxophone player, a tall woman with a blonde beehive wearing a blue gown, kept playing as she stepped up to the stage.

Looking round, Steve saw old faces and young. Couples and groups of friends, families. There were some faces he knew, friends of Allie's from sixth form, from high school, his neighbours. He caught sight of a baby – someone had brought a baby – snuggled in a sling. More people were arriving all the time.

At the front they were joined by Helena and Bets and their parents. Nods and tight smiles, teary eyes.

The music finished and a screen at the back lit up with the picture of Allie.

He was cold inside, a feeling of dread he couldn't escape.

Oh, Allie. Sarah, help me.

His father put an arm across Steve's shoulders and Teagan squeezed his hand. He wondered how they knew.

The lord mayor took to the stage. He wore his chain of office over a dark suit and a vivid pink shirt. Steve remembered the news of his appointment, the first openly gay lord mayor of Manchester. He introduced himself, Carl Austin-Behan, welcomed them all and thanked them for coming. 'Tonight's vigil is organized by the LGBT Foundation, Sparkle, the National Transgender Charity, and the City of Manchester. We are here in love and friendship to remember Allie Kennaway, who died a week ago. Our heartfelt condolences are with her family and friends. Here in this garden is the national transgender memorial, created in memory of our trans brothers and sisters. When I was appointed to office I chose to make raising awareness of transgender issues one of my special concerns, and it is with great sorrow that I find myself here tonight, knowing another person has lost their life in such tragic circumstances. To Allie's family, to her friends, I say the people of Manchester and beyond are here with you in love and unity, and we have one message to share: love not hate. Love will hold us together. We will never let hate drive us apart. We will be lighting candles and holding a minute's silence to remember Allie but, first, I'd like to invite Allie's sister Teagan to read something she has written.'

Steve was disconcerted as Teagan slipped her hand from his and walked towards the stage. His mother smiled and moved to fill the gap beside him.

'Is she OK with this?' Steve said.

'She suggested it,' his mum said.

Teagan began to read her letter aloud, tripping over the words a couple of times but picking up and carrying on like a professional. Looking so small on the stage, her voice rose high and clear.

'Dear Allie. You were six when I was born. We didn't always get on. Stuffing me in the washing basket because I was crying too much was just wrong. Like most sisters, I guess, we argued and fell out. And blamed each other. I know you dropped my Furby in the bath whatever you say. I'm so glad you were my sister. I'm proud of you for being you. You were funny, except for your impressions, which were lame. You were kind and clever. You were brave too. You knew what you wanted, who you were, and you changed your life. Even when people were horrible and bullied you, you carried on being you.'

Steve could feel himself tensing, the tears hot behind his eyes. He felt raw, too full of grief and anger, sorrow and compassion, but he didn't dare let go for fear the flood would drown him. But when he heard sighs and sniffs from the people about him, then someone sobbing, he was defeated. Tears slid down his face, his nose ran, he couldn't see.

'I wish you never had to be brave,' Teagan said, 'that people would just get on together and try and make the world a better place, not worse. Everyone should be allowed to be happy and safe and free to live how they like because we only get one chance. I miss you every minute. I want to tell everyone about how good you were at hurdles and Twister. How your favourite colour was green and your favourite food was Coco Pops and that you loved musical theatre, which you said was a total cliché, but you couldn't sing for toffee. I want to tell them you were beautiful and not just on the outside. That you couldn't roll your tongue and you were scared of pigeons and escalators. I thought you'd always be here, sometimes bossing me about but mainly being OK. Taking my side when Dad comes up with some dumb rule about bedtime or homework or chores or rationing sweets. You will always be my sister, and I will love you for ever and no one can take that away. My funny, kind, pretty, clever big sister. And maybe, one day, people won't have to be brave any more. They can just be people living their lives. Love from Teagan.'

Teagan finished and Steve clapped loudly, leading a wave of applause. She rejoined them and he hugged her close, unable to speak, then wiped his eyes.

Stewards in neon pink tabards handed out candles, all the colours of the rainbow, and soon the crowd was suffused with flickering light. There was a gentle breeze, just enough to stir the leaves in the trees that ringed the gardens.

The lord mayor said, 'We will now have a minute's silence to remember Allie Kennaway.'

Steve closed his eyes and raised his face, feeling the rain gentle on his eyelids, on his cheeks and his chin. Cool where his tears were hot.

The crowd hushed, and he felt the enormity of the moment. The overarching grief.

Oh, Allie, Allie, Allie. My lovely girl.

Allie laughing, a wheelbarrow race when she was eleven or so: the pair of them had crashed in a heap and couldn't continue for their hysteria . . . Her birth, terrifying and exhilarating . . . The shock of fatherhood . . . The habit she had of rubbing at her breastbone when she was talking, as if she'd soothe her heart. Allie crying one night after Sarah had died, sitting heavy on his knee and sobbing. The loneliest sound in the world. Till they were both covered with snot and tears. The hours spent trying to upload the first films she'd made, swearing at the software. Allie having a tantrum as a three-year-old, throwing soft toys and screaming, Steve trying so hard not to laugh at her. The first time he saw her in a dress. Allie hiccuping, 'I'm not drunk . . . I'm merry . . . Look, straight line.'

Steve was weeping. The memories crashed over him, an endless tide, and he let them rock him again and again.

'Thank you,' the lord mayor said, as the minute finished.

And a great cheer went up, bursting the silence, electrifying, making Steve's hairs stand on end. Somewhere not far away a dog gave a rapid volley of barks. Beyond that was the hum and rumble of the traffic, still moving in the city.

A group took to the stage, a choir in matching silver waistcoats. They began to sing, close harmonies, the crowd joining in as they recognized the tune. 'One Love', Bob Marley. The candles guttered in the rain. Teagan's hair was speckled with tiny drops that caught the light.